Mistaken Identity

A Detective Liv DeMarco Thriller

G.K. Parks

Copyright © 2022 G.K. Parks

A Modus Operandi imprint

All rights reserved.

ISBN:
ISBN-13: 978-1-942710-33-2

BOOKS IN THE LIV DEMARCO SERIES:

Dangerous Stakes
Operation Stakeout
Unforeseen Danger
Deadly Dealings
High Risk
Fatal Mistake
Imminent Threat
Mistaken Identity

BOOKS IN THE ALEXIS PARKER SERIES:

Likely Suspects
The Warhol Incident
Mimicry of Banshees
Suspicion of Murder
Racing Through Darkness
Camels and Corpses
Lack of Jurisdiction
Dying for a Fix
Intended Target
Muffled Echoes
Crisis of Conscience
Misplaced Trust
Whitewashed Lies
On Tilt
Purview of Flashbulbs
The Long Game
Burning Embers
Thick Fog
Warning Signs
Past Crimes
Sinister Secret

BOOKS IN THE JULIAN MERCER SERIES:

Condemned
Betrayal
Subversion
Reparation
Retaliation
Hunting Grounds

BOOKS IN THE CROSS SECURITY INVESTIGATIONS SERIES:

Fallen Angel
Calculated Risk

Mistaken Identity

For my mom and dad

ONE

The air smelled vaguely of smoke and cedar. The nights were getting longer with every passing day. Soon, there would be more dark than light. That's when evil would choose to strike.

He gripped the pen tighter. He had to warn them. The city needed to prepare for what was coming. How could they be so oblivious?

He scribbled down his dire warning. The long, slanted letters reminded him of tree branches, devoid of leaves. As if the universe had read his mind, another golden brown leaf fell from the nearest tree. Death was coming. He pulled his legs up onto the bench, using his knees to support his notepad as he continued writing.

Nearby, a family talked and laughed. He turned to see what they were doing. Instantly, he regretted that decision. One of the children had already been claimed. Evil forces were among them. It was too early. This shouldn't be happening for a few more weeks. Was he already too late?

He stared at the kid, who looked to have barely reached puberty. How could the darkness have already penetrated his soul? But the proof was as plain as day. Razor-sharp fangs had replaced the child's teeth. He made growling noises. His arms moved oddly, creating unnatural poses. But the adults did nothing but laugh. Blind. They were all blind.

Eventually, the weight of his stare caused the child to turn. The boy looked at him, smiling with those sinister teeth. He turned away, focusing on his work. There had to be a way to save the boy, to save his soul.

"Mom," the boy said, tugging on the woman's sleeve, "look."

He turned to see what the boy was pointing at, fearing the entire family had been afflicted and would come for him next. Luckily, a nearby vendor had caught his attention. *Should I warn him?* he wondered. But his fear kept him rooted in his seat. Every time he'd tried to stop things himself, he'd been chased away or arrested. The public didn't understand. Neither did the authorities. The evil had a way of manipulating the truth and making him out to be the monster, instead of the one person who could actually see the monsters for what they really were.

"Billy," the woman said, "if you want some popcorn, you have to take those silly things out."

"Can I get caramel corn?" he asked.

She smiled and reached into her purse. "Get some for everyone." She held out a twenty. "But I want those teeth first."

"Aww, Mom."

"How are you going to eat with those things in your mouth? Huh?"

"I can eat. They're just like real teeth."

"I know," the man, who must have been Billy's father, shuddered, "which is so scary." Perhaps, all was not lost. "You don't want to scare the popcorn guy, do you?"

Billy grinned. "Really? You think he'd be scared?"

"Yes, and he'd run away with his cart, and then no one could have any popcorn." The father rubbed his stomach. "And my tummy says it's time for a snack. What about yours?"

Reluctantly, Billy popped out the fangs and put them on the napkin his mother held in her hand. "Fine, but I want those back for the ride home."

The woman put the fangs in her purse. "We'll see." She pointed to the cart. "Go get a snack, but be polite."

"Yes, ma'am," Billy said before running toward the cart.

Slowly, he exhaled. The actual demons couldn't take out their teeth. This child was only pretending. No wonder no one believed him. Sometimes, he wasn't sure he believed it either.

The doctors told him the things he saw and felt were wrong. That his mind was confusing him. Tricking him. The pills he was supposed to take kept him from seeing the demons and the evil spirits. But he stopped taking them. He knew the only way to protect himself was to remain vigilant. Right now, he was the only one keeping watch over the rising darkness, and he couldn't do that and take his medication.

Returning to his work, he finished writing his note. The police would have to take him seriously. He told them everything he knew and had foreseen. He gave them examples, predictions, things to look for. He had determined a few significant events and approximately when they would occur. That would be their proof. Then they couldn't say he was crazy. They'd have to listen. The city was running out of time.

October was when the rising would happen. The underworld would breach the gates of Hell. If the police couldn't stop it, by Alholowmesse, it would be too late. He shoved the note into an envelope, peeled off the backing, and pressed the self-adhering side down. Then he addressed the envelope to Police Commissioner Cross and dropped it into the nearest mailbox.

With his help, the police would have to open their eyes to the demonic forces and the dangers ahead.

*   *   *

"You're wrong, Liv," Detective Brad Fennel said.

"How can you say that?"

"Because dinosaur movies are awesome."

I shook my head at my partner and reached for my coffee. "You know I don't like monster movies."

He rolled his eyes, reaching for the container of cookies sitting on top of the dashboard. "Dinosaurs aren't monsters. They existed thousands of years ago." He held up the grain-free sugar cookie my mom had baked. "See, even Maria thinks they're awesome."

"That's not a dinosaur. That's a bat."

He held the cookie closer to the windshield, examining it under the streetlights. "Are you sure? It looks like a pterodactyl."

"What would a pterodactyl be doing with a bunch of ghosts and pumpkins? You know my mom. She makes seasonal cookies. Dinosaurs aren't seasonal. They have nothing to do with Halloween."

"But they are delicious." He bit into the treat with a resounding crunch. "I must say, there are a lot of perks that come with being your partner, but the snacks your mom makes are at the top of the list." He washed down the rest of the cookie with a sip of coffee before reaching for another one. "Do you think you could convince her to make another batch for next shift?"

"You're just grateful you finally have a partner who doesn't ridicule your eating habits."

"Hey," he held up his palms, "I'm not as picky as you. I don't believe in putting artificial anything in my body. Meanwhile, you have this whole list of things not to eat. I know. It's all because of Emma. Blah, blah, blah." His brow furrowed. "Was she like that as a kid? I bet that's why you hate Halloween so much. Trick-or-treating must have sucked."

"Emma didn't move in with us until we were teenagers. By then, we were no longer trick-or-treating."

Brad cocked his head to the side. "What's that expression for? You look...sad."

"I don't have many fond memories of Halloween. Dad never liked the holiday. A lot of crazies are out and about. When he was a cop, he saw a lot of things, so trick-or-treating was never encouraged in my household. Then after Emma moved in and went through her wild phase—"

"You mean she's finally outgrown that?"

I laughed. "Believe it or not, she's much tamer than she

used to be. But we ended up going to a lot of parties and clubs. I don't know what it is about mixing liquor and costumes, but people go nuts. Fights, overdoses, alcohol poisonings, attempted rapes," I shook my head, "it's just a bad situation."

"So that's why you hate Halloween and monster movies by association?"

"I guess."

Brad reached for another cookie, this time picking up a pumpkin. "Halloween isn't all bad. It can be fun too."

"You're a cop, Fennel. How can you say that with a straight face?"

"Don't you remember last year when vice raided a club and busted a ton of prostitutes, except it turned out they were just women dressed in slutty costumes? That was pretty funny."

"You're proving my point."

"C'mon, Halloween isn't all bad. Why don't we do something this year so I can prove it to you?"

Before I could come up with an excuse, the radio chirped. Dispatch received reports of a possible hit and run. The address was eight blocks from our location.

"We should take that," I said.

Brad gave me a sideways look. "The call was for a patrol unit."

"The call was for any unit in the area." I reached over and picked up the radio. "That's us. Let's go."

"Fine." Reluctantly, Brad put the cookies away and hit the lights. "I'm starting to think you spend too much time with Jake Voletek. You're picking up his bad habits."

"Answering radio calls isn't a bad habit." I advised dispatch we would check it out. "We're cops. It's our job."

"We're homicide detectives. We don't patrol."

"But if it's a hit and run, they'll call us anyway. We're just saving everyone some time and paperwork by skipping a few steps."

"Dispatch said possible hit and run. Let's hope whoever reported it was mistaken. I'd really like to get through this shift without finding someone dead."

"Agreed."

We arrived at the address a few minutes later. An elderly man stood up from where he'd been sitting on his stoop and waved us over. Cautiously, Brad and I got out of the car.

"You're the police, right?" The man peered around me to get a better look at our unmarked cruiser.

"Yes, sir." I showed him my badge. "I'm Detective DeMarco. This is my partner, Fennel. What's going on?"

"Hell if I know." The man rubbed his forehead, clearly agitated. "I was taking out the trash when my neighbor pulled up. That's his car, right down there. It's the blue one." He pointed to the car parked on the corner. "I thought I was seeing things. When he drove past, I had to do a double-take."

"What did you see?" Brad glanced at the parked car.

"A guy sticking out of his windshield."

"What?" Brad hurried toward the vehicle with me at his heels.

"I didn't know what to do. I didn't want to touch him, but he doesn't look so good," the man said.

"Sir, stay back. Give us some room." I stepped off the curb and went around the other side of the car. No one was inside the vehicle. I didn't see any damage on the driver's side. No scratched paint or dents.

"Shit." Brad keyed the radio. "We need an ambulance." He gave them the location. "We're looking at a male vic, impaled through a windshield."

I came around the car, finding a bloodied man draped over the hood. His matted brown hair obscured his face from view. His clothes were tattered and bloody. But there was no blood on the car.

Removing my flashlight, I shined it at the windshield while Brad felt for the guy's pulse. "What the hell?" Brad jumped back, rubbing his fingers together.

"It's not real." I pointed to the cracked windshield. "That's a decal."

Sucking in a breath, Brad took a step back to regroup. He removed his flashlight and gave the car and body a closer look. "In broad daylight, it'd be obvious. But in the dark," he turned to the elderly gentleman who had called

9-1-1, "I can see where the confusion came in."

"You better cancel the ambulance," I said.

"Right." Brad keyed the radio while I went to speak to the man who made the report.

"Sir," I said, "what's your name?"

"Miguel Ortiz." He peered at the vehicle. "Did he kill someone? He always drives like a maniac, but I never thought he'd do something like this."

"Can you tell me precisely what you saw?"

"What about that man? Shouldn't you help him?"

"It's not real. It's just a prop. A Halloween decoration."

"Decoration? It scared the shit out of me. I thought someone was really hurt. I thought he hit that guy."

"What did you see?" I wanted to make sure Brad and I weren't missing anything. "Did you see your neighbor run into someone?"

"No, I just saw the body hanging out of the windshield. My neighbor even waved at me when he saw me staring. I thought he'd gone mad."

"Is this where he lives?" Brad pointed to the walkway which led to the nearest townhouse.

"Yes."

"Do you know his name?" I asked.

"Chris Taylor." The man moved closer to the car, giving the fake body a better look. "I don't remember decorations ever being this realistic. Who would want to put something like that on their car?"

"Your neighbor," I said.

"We'll talk to him about it." Brad pushed open the gate and went up the walk.

"May I go?" Miguel asked.

"Yes, sir. Have a good night." I stepped through the gate and moved the ten feet to Chris Taylor's door.

Several expertly carved jack-o-lanterns leered at us from the top of the stoop. Spiderwebs and bloody handprints competed for attention in each of the windows. This guy sure loved Halloween. When Brad rang the bell, witches cackled.

The door opened, and the guy on the other side said in a Lurch voice, "You rang?"

"Police." Brad moved his jacket aside, revealing his badge. "Are you Chris Taylor?"

"Yes." The man in the jersey and baggy jeans looked uneasy. "What is this about?"

"Is that blue car parked on the corner yours?"

"Yes."

"Are you aware there's a body hanging out of your windshield?"

Chris chuckled. "Is that a problem?"

"We received a call tonight about a hit and run."

Chris laughed even harder. "That's great. I thought it looked pretty hokey, but I guess someone fell for it." He leaned back. "Hey, Steve, someone called the cops because of Brando."

"Brando?" I stepped closer, peering inside through the open doorway.

"That's what we named the torso," Chris said.

"Seriously, man?" another voice called from inside the house. "That's too fucking funny. Who reported you?"

Chris turned back to us. "Who made the call?"

"That's not important," I said.

"I bet it was Mr. Ortiz," Steve said from inside the house. "Gramps doesn't know how to take a joke."

"Mr. Taylor," Brad used his commanding, authoritarian voice, "decorate however you like, but I'll tell you now, traffic cops won't take kindly to Brando. And they don't have much of a sense of humor. If you want to save yourself some trouble, I suggest you detach the torso before heading out tomorrow. If not, don't be surprised when you get pulled over. That decoration of yours may cause a distraction to other drivers. If they get in an accident, you'll be blamed. Do you understand?"

"Sure thing. I'll take care of it first thing in the morning. You have a good night now." Chris closed the door before either of us could utter another word. But hysterical laughter sounded from inside.

"This is why I hate Halloween," I said as we headed back to the car. "Do you think he'll take it down?"

"Probably not." Brad copied Chris's license plate number before returning to the cruiser. "They don't mean any harm. They're just getting into the spirit of things."

"You called for an ambulance because of it."

My partner pretended not to hear me. "Chris and his buddy aren't thinking this through or considering how distracting Brando is. But now that he had a good laugh, maybe he'll listen to what I said. If he doesn't remove it from his car by the morning, patrol will make sure he does."

"How are you going to swing that?"

"I have friends."

"Of course, you do."

Brad smiled. "Since you insisted we answer the radio call, you can write the report."

"Fine."

We were almost at the precinct when another call came in. This time, dispatch asked specifically for us. Male vic, mid-twenties, stabbed to death.

Brad whipped the car around, heading to our next location. "I was hoping we were done for the night. We can never catch a break, can we?"

"Face it. It's that time of year."

"What do you think the odds are this is another false report?" Brad asked.

"Slim to none."

"I finally get why Voletek likes to respond to other calls. Fewer bodies. Less blood. One can walk away still feeling good about the world."

"I told you, you don't have to stick with homicide."

"Nah, I'm good. Unfortunately, the people we meet on the job can't say the same."

TWO

"Hey, Fennel. DeMarco." Officer Roberts nodded at us as we approached the police tape. "Looks like you caught a weird one."

"How weird?" I asked.

Roberts lifted the tape. "You'll see. I don't want to spoil the surprise."

Beside me, Brad stiffened. "How many vics?"

"Just one." Roberts pointed to a doorway. "He's right through there."

"Is he dead?" I asked.

Roberts cocked his head at me. "For now."

"What does that mean?"

Brad put his hand on the small of my back, urging me to keep moving. Roberts had made it quite clear he didn't like me, but he saved my life once. We could be civil to one another, just as long as I ignored the quips and comments he muttered under his breath.

We strode through the house, noticing several people in costumes and makeup seated at the dining room table. An officer watched them while another one took statements in the living room. Given the looks of things, we'd have plenty of witnesses and suspects to interview.

"Hi, Brad." One of the ME's assistants spotted us as we approached the room. "Liv." She stood in the doorway, keeping us from entering.

"Carrie." I nodded to her. "I thought you mostly stayed in the office."

"Jacob asked if I'd cover for him. He's not feeling so great." She tugged on one of her gloves, oblivious to our attempts to enter the room.

"It's nice to see you. How've you been?" Brad asked.

She hitched her shoulders. "Y'know, okay. Maybe we can talk sometime."

"Sure. Whenever you want." My partner wasn't usually this clueless, but with a DB ten feet away, he wasn't at the top of his dating game. "Roberts said this is a weird one. Do we know what happened?"

"You're not gonna believe it. I barely believe it." Carrie stepped back. "He's in the casket."

"Casket?" My partner focused on the polished wood box in the center of the room. "Were they holding a wake or preparing for a funeral?"

"I don't think so," Carrie said.

"More Halloween decorations." I pointed to the twinkly, purple, spider-shaped lights strung around the room. "I'm guessing the coffin is part of it." I moved closer and peered inside. "With a dead guy to match."

The victim was dressed in a three-piece suit, complete with white gloves and tails. He wore a red vest. The jacket and pants were black. His red tie was almost the same color as the blood that soaked through the front of his shirt. Through his heart was a wooden stake. His skin was pale, nearly white. Dark, blackish-purple veins showed from beneath the surface. His eyes were open. The irises were red. I couldn't be certain, but I assumed those were colored contacts. His mouth was wide in a silent scream. A tiny stream of blood had dribbled down the side of his mouth and onto his neck.

"Did you find an ID?" I asked.

"The cops did," Carrie said.

As if on cue, the officer guarding the body moved closer. "Here you go, Detective."

Brad grabbed it with his gloved hand. "Dan Fielders. Twenty-five. He's local." He looked from the ID photo to the body in the box. "Dan's seen better days. Any idea what caused his veins to do that?"

Carrie pressed against the victim's cheek. "I'm not sure, but it looks like makeup."

"Cause of death?" I asked, figuring she'd appreciate an easy question.

"Preliminary suggests it was the stake through the heart." She glanced over her shoulder to make sure Brad remained close. "Do you want to see something interesting?"

I knew my partner. He didn't like bodies. He'd much rather examine the crime scene and question the witnesses. "What?" I asked, giving him the opportunity to step away.

Carrie diverted her focus to me, as if she'd forgotten I was in the room. "This." She leaned closer and lifted Fielders' upper lip, revealing two sharp fangs. "They aren't veneers or caps."

"You're telling me someone staked an actual vampire?"

She snorted. "Well, we know that's not true. They turn to dust when they get staked. At least, that's what the movies and TV shows would have us believe."

"So what's the deal with his teeth?" Brad went around to the other side of the coffin. "And his eyes?"

"Those appear to be contacts. As far as his teeth, we'll know more after we take some x-rays," she said. "I didn't notice any other injuries on the body. There are no defensive wounds of any kind."

"Dan Fielders must have already been in the box when he was stabbed," Brad said.

"Staked," Carrie corrected.

I gave her a look, but she didn't notice.

Brad examined the exterior of the coffin from every angle. "No scuff marks, blood trails, or drag marks on the floor. This is where Fielders was when he was killed. Since this happened in the midst of a Halloween party, we should speak to the other guests and find out exactly what they saw."

"Is this Fielders' house?" I asked.

Brad held out the ID. "The address doesn't match. He must have been a guest."

"Do you think he brought his own coffin?"

"If he did, maybe they can bury him in it," Carrie said.

I didn't find it funny, but Brad chuckled politely, even though I didn't think he found it funny either.

"We'll talk later, yeah?" Carrie asked as Brad started to walk away.

"You got it."

We searched the room but didn't find anything indicative of the murder that took place only a few feet away. No blood. No weapons. No evidence. I didn't like this.

"How do you think they got the coffin in here?" I asked.

"Carried it," Brad said. "CSU will dust everything. They might get prints or fibers, something useful."

"Let's hope." I took in the rest of the house, or as much of it as I could see from the hallway. "I keep getting *Clue* vibes."

"Me too." Brad headed for the dining room where our potential suspects were waiting. "We already figured out the room and the weapon. Now we just need the killer." He crooked his finger at the officer who'd conducted the interviews.

The cop joined us outside the dining room. "Hey, Fennel," he gave me a brief once-over, "who's this?"

"Liv DeMarco," I said.

"As in Vince DeMarco's kid?"

"Yep." I hated that question.

"Nice to meet ya." He held out his hand. "I'm Mitch Tripplehorn, but everyone calls me Tripp."

"What's going on here, Tripp?" Brad asked.

Tripp retracted his hand and reached for his notebook. "I spoke to every party guest, but they're all telling me the same thing. No one saw anything. They left the front door open. People came and went. It was a party. The more, the merrier."

I looked around the house, but I didn't sense any out of control vibes. A few beer bottles and plastic cups were scattered about, but for the most part, the mess was contained. Nothing appeared broken or out of order.

"How many people are we looking at?" I asked.

"No one knows for sure. Maybe twenty."

"I only count eight." Brad turned back to the table where the guests sat, doing a quick headcount. "What happened to the other twelve?"

"They left." Tripp consulted his notepad. "I only have a few names. Not everyone's been accounted for. The invite went out over social media, so that might give us some idea of where to start."

"What about the murder?" I asked. "Did anyone see what happened?"

"Not exactly. According to at least three guests, the vic climbed into the coffin as part of a gag. He thought he was Dracula. A woman in a red dress, corset, and cape had been talking to him most of the night. Everyone thinks she and the vic arrived together. They remember seeing her near the coffin, having some kind of argument with the vic."

"Do we know what it was about?" Brad asked.

"No, but she took off afterward. No one's seen her since." Tripp closed the notebook. "I didn't get a name or ID for her, but the host thinks it must have been the vic's girlfriend. He didn't see her, so he can't say for certain."

"Who's house is this?" It'd be best to ask the questions myself.

Tripp pointed to the man sitting at the head of the table. "Kelsey Eldridge."

"Let's see what he can tell us about the party and the vic." Brad nodded to Tripp and led the way into the dining room. After introducing ourselves, we took Eldridge into the living room. "Tell me what went on here tonight."

"I host a Halloween party every year. I invited a few friends over. We do costumes, drinks, and food. It's really chill. I just...I can't imagine...this is insane."

"How do you know Dan Fielders?" Brad asked. "Were the two of you close?"

"We..." Eldridge swallowed. "Yeah, we are." He coughed to cover his voice cracking and rubbed his eye with the side of his hand. "We share the same desk. We work for a sports network. We report the latest stories and sports scores, update the website, and write everything the sportscasters read. It's a really fun job. Dan's a blast." He sniffed, shaking his head. "Was. He was a blast." He squeezed his eyes closed and rubbed his face. "Dammit."

"I'm sorry for your loss," I said.

Eldridge nodded. "I can't believe this happened under my roof. How does something like this even happen?"

"Did you notice anyone out of the ordinary? Any uninvited guests?"

"I don't know. Everyone was in costume. I don't recognize half the people at my kitchen table in their zombie makeup and masks. I already gave the other cop the guest list."

"Did everyone show up?" Brad asked.

"I don't know. I spoke to maybe fifteen people all night. Most of them were from work."

"What about the woman in the red dress with the cape?"

"I'm not sure who that was. I barely saw her. Then again, I barely saw Dan. They might have been together. He said he wanted to bring his girlfriend. They had coordinating costumes. He was so excited. He was dressed as Dracula and she was supposed to be his bride."

"That fits with the cape," I said.

"Have you met her before?" Brad asked.

"Once or twice." Eldridge closed his eyes, searching his memory. "Vivica Smaldey. She used to be a cheerleader. Dan thought he struck gold when he convinced her to go out with him. Cheerleaders date athletes, not the news nerds who hang around the locker rooms begging for exclusives."

I wrote down her name and searched for her on my phone while Brad continued asking questions. Once I found her photo, I showed it to Eldridge.

"That's Dan's girlfriend," he confirmed.

"Since you know what she looks like, how come you aren't sure if she was the woman in the red dress?" Brad asked.

"I never saw her face. By the time I noticed her, her back was to me. I didn't really care. Everyone was welcome. I wish I'd paid more attention or said something to Dan. I didn't get a chance to talk to him tonight. I figured I'd catch him later. Now I'll never get the chance."

"Did you have something pressing to discuss?" I asked.

Eldridge shook his head, struggling against the tears.

"I'll see if anyone remembers seeing Vivica at the party." I went to speak to the other guests about what happened and what they saw while Brad finished up with Eldridge.

Two other people confirmed Vivica had been wearing the corset and cape. She, like Dan, had fangs. Another one of the guests thought they heard the two of them arguing about making out inside the coffin. Dan thought it'd be fun and kinky, but Vivica had no desire to crawl into that creepy thing. After he got inside, he refused to come out, so she left the party.

"Do you think she staked Dan?" I asked.

"No way. I remember him calling out to her to come back as she stormed off. Dan was always a lot of fun, but sometimes, he didn't know when to quit," Emmett Walters, one of the guests, said.

"Did you see anyone else approach Dan Fielders or hear him scream?"

"I don't know. Kelsey has a wicked stereo system. It was on all night, mostly playing music, but it had Halloween noises mixed in to the playlist."

"What kinds of noises?"

"Creaking floorboards, ghost sounds, screams, chainsaws. All kinds of things. It's hard to say for certain what was real and what wasn't."

I worked my way through the rest of the group, realizing Brad was doing the same thing. On the bright side, it didn't hurt that we were inadvertently double or triple checking our witnesses' stories. Unfortunately, no one knew when Dan had been stabbed. All we knew was he crawled into the coffin willingly and refused to come out.

"Hey, Liv," Brad called, "listen to this."

I excused myself to see what my partner had discovered. He was talking to Melanie Daggio, another of Dan and Kelsey's coworkers.

"Ms. Daggio recalls someone leaving a few minutes before they discovered Dan had been stabbed. What time was that?" Brad asked.

"It was just before eleven. The guy was dressed in a black leather trench coat with a matching outback hat. Like that guy. You know which guy I'm talking about."

"No, ma'am," I said.

"The hot Australian one. He had an old timey crossbow."

Brad's brow furrowed as he thought. "Are you talking about the movie version of Van Helsing?"

She grinned, pointing at him. "Yeah, exactly like that. How'd you know?"

"Lucky guess."

I gave Brad a confused look. "What am I missing?"

"Van Helsing hunted Dracula. You'd know this if you watched monster movies or read Bram Stoker."

My eyes rolled backward. "What else can you tell us about the guy dressed as a vampire hunter?"

Melanie shrugged. "That's it."

"Was Van Helsing with anyone? What time did he arrive at the party?" Brad asked.

"I don't know. I don't remember him coming in or hanging out with anyone. It's a party, y'know. People come and go. A bunch of us clustered together in the kitchen or near the stereo or on the dance floor, talking and laughing. That's just how it goes. I don't remember seeing the vampire hunter until he was on his way out, and I flitted and flirted all night. I'm quite the social butterfly." She indicated the wings strapped to her back. "Get it?"

"Yeah, we got it." I studied her eyes. "How much did you have to drink tonight?"

She blew through her lips. "Um...six or seven margaritas. They are so good. Do you want one?"

"No." Brad waved Tripp over. "Can you get Ms. Daggio some water?"

"Sure thing."

She frowned. "I'm fine."

"Did you hang out with Dan?" Brad asked.

"No. He was all wrapped up in that blonde chick. Couples are so icky sometimes. Sure, it's a party. But it isn't a make-out party. We aren't in junior high."

I didn't see how this was getting us anywhere, but Brad wasn't willing to give up yet.

Brad consulted his notepad. "You said the guy in the coat and hat left around eleven. Did you happen to see what he drove?"

"No. I just remember him going to the door. It was like ten minutes after the blonde chick stormed out."

THREE

Oh, god, he thought, *what have I done?* He sucked in the crisp, night air, relieved when it cooled the heat that had been building inside of him. His hands weren't shaking, but they should have been. He killed someone.

Carefully, he inspected the leather gloves for blood. They looked clean, but he'd get rid of them just to be on the safe side. The leather sheath prevented him from leaving prints, epithelial cells, sweat, and other things forensic scientists might use to identify him. He had no reason to panic, even though the volcano inside his stomach thought otherwise.

As of yet, he hadn't gotten sick. He didn't think he would. That was for those with weaker constitutions, who regretted their actions. Did he regret his actions? He had to stop and think about it. But the only thought that came to mind was Dan Fielders got what he deserved.

A second deep breath made him feel calmer, cooler. The sound of high heels clacking against the pavement made him smile. Whatever doubts he had vanished the moment the blonde in the blood red dress stepped into view.

Vivica was always so beautiful. She ran a hand through her golden locks, tucking them behind her left ear. "Hey, I was wondering what was taking you so long. I thought we were meeting inside." Her smile brightened. "Nice outfit."

She laughed. "That's perfect for slaying vampires."

"I thought so too." Hastily, he took off the gloves, shoved them into his pocket, and offered her his arm. "Do you want to go for a walk?"

"Maybe later. Right now, I'm in serious need of a drink." She slipped her hand around his arm and let him guide her into the crowded bar. "Thanks for doing this. Dan's so unbearable. I just had to get away from him, but I didn't know how."

"I'm always here for you. Whatever you need. You know that, right?"

"I know." She kissed his cheek and cuddled up against his side, resting her head against his shoulder as they made their way through the crowd.

With a flourish, he wiped off a barstool. "For you, milady." She giggled before sliding onto the seat. He leaned over, drumming on the counter to get the bartender's attention.

"Hey," she reached down to his belt where he had a metal cross which ended in a sharp spike, "what's this?"

"Another option."

"Okay." She arched an eyebrow. "How many options do you need?"

He pointed to an empty elastic loop. "Apparently, just the one."

She laughed. "I forgot how funny you are."

*   *   *

After we left the crime scene, we went to pay Vivica Smaldey a visit. She lived in one of the upscale apartment buildings on the west side. Professional athletes made good money. I hadn't realized the same was true of cheerleaders.

"Ms. Smaldey left earlier this evening," the doorman said. "She has yet to return."

"Then you won't mind if we knock on her door anyway." Brad pushed his way inside.

The doorman let out a grunt, but it was for show. He didn't care. We were building security's problem now. Except no one in the lobby dared to say a word to two police detectives. I pushed the button for the elevator while Brad looked around.

"Do you think she killed him?" he asked when the doors closed.

"Witnesses at the party said Fielders was alive and kicking when Vivica left."

"If that's true, one of them could be our killer. We should have taken them all in for questioning. They were at the scene."

"CSU didn't find any blood spatter on any of them. They couldn't pull prints off the stake. Right now, we have no evidence as to the killer's identity. But we know who attended the party and where they live. When we get more, we'll bring in whoever we need to. For now, we follow leads. Vivica might have been the last person who spoke to Fielders. Either she killed him, or she may have seen who did." I watched the floor number illuminate above the doors. "Do you think she asked the doorman to cover for her? He didn't strike me as the type."

"I don't think she's home, but we came all the way here. We need to make certain." Brad flexed his hand a few times.

"Are you okay?"

He looked down, shaking it out. "Yeah. I've gotten in the habit of doing that. Now it's just one of those things." He held his hand out. "See, I'm cool as a cucumber."

"I'm glad to hear it."

He smiled, bumping against my shoulder. "You know, this case would be a lot easier to crack if you'd seen a few monster movies and knew what our suspect looked like."

"I've seen the posters. I think I can figure it out."

The elevator opened, and we went down the hall to Vivica's apartment. The door was bolted shut. There were no signs of tampering or foul play. After our knocks went unanswered, we took the stairs back to the lobby. Her absence didn't bode well. Most people were usually home at two a.m.

More than likely, she killed her boyfriend and fled. That would explain the lack of defensive wounds. Given how toned cheerleaders were, she must have possessed the strength to drive a wooden stake through his chest wall and into his heart.

When we got back to the car, I called in a BOLO and had patrol keep an eye out for her vehicle. "We should check to see if her EZ Pass registered on any of the bridges or tunnels."

"My money's on the vampire hunter," Brad said.

"The only person who saw him was drunk off her ass. I wouldn't call that reliable eyewitness testimony. The DA would agree with me."

"We'll cross that bridge when we get to it. Right now, we have a dead sportswriter and a killer on the loose." He checked the rearview and side mirrors. "I don't know what to make of Fielders' teeth. Do you think he actually had fangs?"

"Carrie said they weren't veneers. Did she say they were real?"

"She never said they weren't."

"Humans don't have teeth like that."

Brad glanced at me. "Yeah."

I laughed. "Don't tell me you think our vic is an actual vampire. Carrie nixed that idea. She said he would have turned to dust."

"That depends on which mythos you follow."

"All right, Fennel, I'll bite. Do you actually believe in this stuff?"

"I've seen a lot of weird things. Tonight is no exception. But I don't think he's a vampire. However, our killer might not have been as enlightened. For argument's sake, let's say Daggio spotted the killer leaving the party."

"You mean the man dressed as a vampire hunter?"

Brad nodded. "The vampire hunter killed the vampire using the tried and true stake to the heart method. The only problem with that is a stake to the heart will kill pretty much anything."

"In this scenario, is the killer delusional?"

"Possibly, or he intended to kill Dan Fielders, knew how Fielders would be dressed, and thought he should get a costume to match."

"Which would make this premeditated murder."

"That's just one theory. But I'm guessing if you're at a costume party dressed as a vampire, and you climb into a coffin in the hopes of getting frisky with your girlfriend, you probably wouldn't take some guy coming at you with a wooden stake too seriously."

"Do you think that's why Fielders didn't defend himself?"

"Would you?"

I thought about the question the entire drive back to the precinct. "Assuming this theory of yours holds water, Fielders must have known his killer. That's how the killer would have known how Fielders would be dressed and how to coordinate appropriately." A thought came to mind. "I wonder how sharp that wooden stake was. I'd imagine it'd take brute force to push it through Fielders' chest."

"Unless he hammered it in."

"Our vic would have done something to stop that from happening. He would have screamed. Someone would have seen something." I quirked an eyebrow. "Your theory is starting to crumble."

"We're four hours past end of shift. What do you expect?" Brad took a seat at his desk. "Let's write this up and go home. I don't want Winston riding my ass over more unsanctioned overtime."

"I'll emphasize what time it was when we received the call in my report. Do the same. Hopefully, he'll catch on when he reads what happened." Halfway through, I picked up the phone and checked to see if there was any word on Vivica Smaldey's whereabouts. A patrol car was parked outside her apartment building, but she hadn't gone home yet. In a few hours, someone would check to see if she showed up at work.

Distracted, I ran her background. The retired cheerleader was now a furniture designer. The photos on her website showed her consulting with carpenters. In one photo, she wore safety goggles while she nailed together the wooden frame of a couch. Could Brad be right about the hammering, even if he wrongly identified the culprit?

"I think I just blew your theory to smithereens," I said.

"What are you talking about?"

"Check out this website." I read him the web address while he typed it into his computer. "It looks more and more like the girlfriend's responsible for Fielders' death."

"Do you know where she is?"

"No."

"Then finish your report so we can go home."

"Now you sound like Lieutenant Winston."

He scowled at me. "That's uncalled for."

I scribbled a note to dig deeper and closed the website. "CSU should be able to determine if the stake was made out of the same type of wood Vivica uses at her design studio. I might as well put in the request for a warrant." I phoned ADA Logan Winters and left a voicemail on his office phone, telling him about the case we caught and the current situation. When he got to work, he'd follow up to see if anything had changed and get the ball-rolling on getting us a court order. Until then, it'd be best to stay in our commanding officer's good graces, so I finished my report, made a few more notes, and left messages for the techs. After filing the paperwork and shutting down the computer, I followed Brad out of the building. It was time to go home.

FOUR

"Liv, it's time to get up."

"Go away."

"Where do you want me to go? It's my apartment."

I blinked a few times and stretched. My neck had cramped from sleeping weird. I rubbed it, feeling the jagged raised line of the scar that started behind my ear and ran to my shoulder. At least that didn't hurt anymore.

"I told you not to sleep on the couch." Brad moved behind me, gently rubbing his thumbs in circles until the cramp released. "Do you want coffee?"

"Please."

"Figured." He grabbed the cup from the counter and handed it to me. "Are you showering here? You can go first."

I reached for my phone. "I'll tell you in a second." After sending Emma a text, I took a sip. The smooth, rich flavor comforted and warmed me. "Damn, Fennel. That's good. No wonder Carrie wants to get back together. I can see how a girl might miss this."

"What are you talking about?"

"You're a detective. You don't need me to spell it out for you."

"She just wants to talk."

"Don't you know what that means?"

He folded his arms over his chest. "Enlighten me."

My phone chimed before I could say a word. Emma's overnight guest had cleared out. It was safe to go back to her apartment to shower and change before heading to work, which meant Brad didn't have to worry about sharing his bathroom. "Carrie misses you. I'm guessing things didn't work out with whoever she was seeing, or maybe his coffee just wasn't this good. Either way, she wants to give it another shot."

"You're insane."

"I'm just calling it like I see it." I blew across the surface of the cup and took another sip. "Do you mind if I take this to go?"

"No, but you'll have to take it like that. You've used all my travel mugs and haven't returned any of them."

"Sorry. I'll bring them back."

"When are you going to find a new place to live?"

"I'm working on it."

"Do you want to trade apartments?"

I lowered the cup, convinced I hadn't heard him right. "What?"

"Trade. I'll move into your place and you move in here. Our rents are almost the same, so it's not that big of a deal."

"No way. I wouldn't do that to you."

"It's my fault, Liv. I'm the reason you don't feel safe at home."

"I feel safe."

"Bullshit."

"Even if I don't, it's not because of you." I put the cup on the coffee table and climbed off the couch, folded the blanket, and removed the sheet. "Did it ever occur to you I'm just staying here to keep you company?"

"It has." A smile tugged at the corners of his mouth. "Are you?"

That was a factor. It had started as a joke, but there had been some truth to it that first night Brad asked me to stay. And since I hadn't wanted to stay at my place ever since a deranged killer had broken in, I had taken him up on it and continued to do so whenever I didn't feel like dealing with my parents or interrupting Emma during one of her dates.

I returned his smile. "Maybe."

"Liv, I'm okay. You see me every day. I haven't had a drink in weeks. I'm sleeping better. I feel good. You'd know if something was wrong. I can't hide anything from you, no matter how hard I try."

"I know. You need your space. Emma said I can crash with her, but she just started seeing some guy, and I haven't really wanted to deal with that." Although, it wouldn't be long before my partner was once again hot and heavy with the coroner's assistant. I'd have to move apartment hunting up on my list of priorities, but first, I'd have to find some way to get out of my lease. Maybe ADA Winters would have some ideas. "My parents will let me stay with them. They like it when I sleep at home."

"They love houseguests. They even like it when I sleep over." Brad laughed. "I still have a set of your mom's storage containers to return from when she sent me home with a week's worth of dinners. The next time you plan on heading over there, let me know so I can return them, or maybe ask her to refill them with some of those cookies." He watched as I straightened the cushions. I stopped halfway through to stretch against the back of the couch and let out a groan. "You should have taken my bed."

"It's your place. You're doing me a favor. I'm not kicking you out of your bed. You've had enough problems sleeping lately."

"Yeah, but I've finally gotten a handle on that, thanks to you." He grinned. "You know, the bed is big enough for the both of us."

"You snore."

"I do not."

"Is that what Carrie told you?" I finished the coffee and put the cup on the counter. "I'll see you at work. I didn't get any updates on our case, so I'm guessing Smaldey's still MIA."

"I'm telling you, she's not the killer. We're looking for a vampire hunter."

"You wanna bet?"

"As a matter of fact, I do. If I'm right, you and I are gonna do Halloween up right this year."

"You better find out if Carrie's working that night. She might have other things in mind."

"Liv, I'm not getting back together with Carrie. I don't want to do that again."

I searched his face, unsure what his eyes conveyed, but he was serious. "Okay."

"So Halloween? You in?"

"No, because I'm gonna win. Smaldey's involved in Fielders' murder. She might not have done it herself, but she had something to do with it."

"Ooh, it sounds like you're already doubting your convictions. This will be an easy victory for me. No wonder you want to back out of the bet."

I sighed. "Fine. But if I win, no monster movies or dinosaurs. No nothing."

"What about seasonal treats? Are they off limits too?"

"That is the only exception to the rule, and that's only because I really like the caramel apples my mom makes." I grabbed my bag off the floor and headed for the door. "I'll meet you at work."

"Don't forget to return my travel mugs."

By the time I unlocked my car, Brad had sent me a text in case I forgot. Laughing at it, I stuck the key in the ignition and drove to Emma's to shower and change. My partner was right. I needed to find somewhere to live. But that was only part of the problem.

"Morning, sunshine." Emma couldn't keep the grin off her face.

I glanced around the apartment, but I didn't see any sign of her male companion. "You're practically glowing." I narrowed my eyes. "Did you use protection?"

"Only you would ask that question before anything else."

"Well?"

"Yes. Sheesh."

I opened the cabinet and took out the collection of travel cups that I'd taken from Brad's over the course of the week, filled two of them with green smoothies from the blender, and put the rest in a tote to take to work with me. Emma watched as I took a long sip before grabbing a plate from the cupboard and helping myself to the breakfast scramble she made.

"It looks like you worked up quite the appetite, as well. Where were you all night?" she asked.

"I worked overtime. Then I crashed at Brad's."

Her eyes lit up. "That good, huh?"

"I slept on the couch."

"Sure, you did."

"Em," I shoveled breakfast into my mouth and pointed my fork at her, "don't start." But even after I put the kibosh on her teasing, she continued to smile as she slowly picked at her breakfast. "Okay, tell me about the guy that has you grinning like that."

"He's amazing." She put her fork down. "He's so sexy. He has these eyes you could drown in, and this cute little smile. It's kind of crooked and absolutely adorable. Oh my god, and his ass. Mmm. You should see him naked."

"Is he naked often?"

"Only when he's around me."

"Em, behave."

She flashed me a naughty grin. "What? It's true."

"What does he do for a living?"

"He's an x-ray tech at the hospital."

I held up my hand before she could make some kind of bone joke. "I have to get ready for work. Talk to me through the bathroom door." I put my plate in the dishwasher and went into the guest room, which used to be my bedroom, and grabbed a change of clothes. "By the way, thanks for letting me use your apartment as my closet."

"No problem." She sat outside the bathroom door. "I kinda miss having you as a roommate. So what do you want to know?"

"Nothing gory." Emma had a habit of oversharing. "How long have you been dating? Where did you go on your date? Stuff like that."

"We're not really dating. We've been flirting at the coffee cart a lot. He ordered the same organic herbal tea I did. Can you believe that? I've never seen anyone else order that. It has to be a sign."

"He sounds perfect."

"He is. Well, he was last night. We picked up takeout and came back here. You're not going to believe how many times—"

I stepped out of the shower and ran a towel over my hair, muffling most of what Emma was saying. I already knew more about Emma's sex life than anyone else on the planet. I didn't want to know anything else.

I hung the towel on the rack and got dressed. "What's his name?"

"I'm not telling you. I don't want you looking into him or making fun of him. It's still too new. We haven't even gone out on a real date yet."

"Why didn't last night count?"

"We didn't go out. We stayed in."

"So? That's how good dates end."

She let out a dramatic sigh, pushing open the door when she heard the hairdryer turn on. "Liv, I want to ask you something, but I need you to promise you won't say no."

"If I can't say no, then you aren't asking. You're telling."

"Fine. I have to tell you something." She sat on the vanity and stared at me while I dried my hair. "You remember how we made plans for your day off? Well, we have to change them."

This wasn't the first time Emma blew me off to hang out with a guy. "No problem. I'll find something else to do."

"No, we're still hanging out. I need some retail therapy and I want to see that movie, but I thought we'd go to a matinee instead."

I turned off the hairdryer and wrestled it into the cabinet. "That's cool."

"Right, and afterward, we can get dinner."

"Okay."

"And you can meet the guy I'm seeing."

"Wow. It's that serious?"

"It might be."

"In that case, I'd love to meet him." Emma rarely volunteered to introduce her dates to me. "Did you tell

Mom about him?"

"Not yet." She picked up a bottle of nail polish and shook it. "I'm glad you're so excited. The four of us are going to have a great time."

I blinked. "Four? Is Mom joining us?"

"No." Emma put the nail polish down and slid off the counter. "He's bringing a friend."

"Emma, no. You know how I feel about blind dates."

She left the bathroom and returned to the kitchen. "Too late. I already told him yes."

I followed after her. "Tell him something came up. I might have to work. I'm on call that night, remember?"

"You just said you'd love to meet him." She gave me sad, puppy dog eyes. "Don't you want me to be happy?"

The clock on the stove told me I didn't have time to argue, especially when there wasn't a chance in hell I'd win. Emma should have been a salesperson. She had a knack for guilting people into doing pretty much anything for her. The only reason I let her get away with it was because she had a heart of gold and the best intentions.

"Of course, I want you to be happy. You're my best friend." I grabbed my things, unable to shake the look she was giving me. "Fine, but I'm only agreeing to dinner. We show up. We eat. We leave."

"You have to talk to them. You have to be civil and fun. Do you think you remember how to do that?"

"I'll ask Brad for some tips."

She blocked my path to the exit. "You better not ask him to call you in the middle of dinner with a fake emergency, or I'll kill you both."

"I wouldn't dream of it." But that was a brilliant idea.

She stared at me for a full ten seconds before scooting to the side and gesturing toward the door. "Have a good day. Don't get killed. We have plans this weekend, and if you think dying will get you out of it, it won't. I will drag your corpse around with me if I have to."

"Em, don't say that. Not today."

"Why?"

"Just not today."

FIVE

When I arrived at work, Officer Roberts informed me Vivica Smaldey had been located and brought in for questioning. She was waiting in interrogation room C. Lt. Winston had spoken to her, but he didn't want to release her yet. Unfortunately, those were the only details Roberts had.

I put a smoothie down on Brad's desk before checking my messages. Brad looked up as I skimmed the sticky notes hanging from my monitor. "You were wrong," he said. "Fielders' girlfriend didn't kill him. We're still looking for the vampire hunter. At the moment, he's our prime suspect."

"Did you talk to her?"

"Not yet. I was told to wait for you." Brad worked his jaw for a moment, agitated by being given the command. He had every reason to be annoyed. He had seniority and was listed as primary on the case. Picking up the smoothie, he took a sip. "Thanks." He wasn't annoyed with me, just the situation.

I tucked the tote with his travel cups underneath my desk, pushing it across until it was beneath his. Then I picked up the phone to return ADA Winters' call. Before I dialed the fourth digit, Lt. Winston barked at me from across the bullpen.

"DeMarco, I'd like a word."

"Yes, sir." I put the phone down, noticing my partner's worried look. Now what did we do?

Winston waited for me to enter before pulling the door closed behind me. He peered out the blinds before shutting them, ensuring we had total privacy. "Why don't you take a seat?"

"What is this about?"

He dropped into his chair and stared up at me. "How's Fennel doing?"

"Sir?"

He bit his upper lip and sighed. "Your partner, DeMarco. How's he doing?"

"He's fine."

"You're sure?"

"Yes. Why are you asking? Is something going on?"

"Nope." Winston reached for a file on the edge of his desk. "Evaluations are coming up. I wanted to make sure he was on top of his game."

"He would be if you let him do his job."

Winston cocked his head up at me. "What is that supposed to mean?"

"Nothing." I still hadn't learned how to keep my thoughts to myself. "But Fennel's been at this longer than I have. He knows how to work investigations. Barring him from questioning a murder suspect makes no sense."

"He's not barred. Is that what he said?"

"No." I edged backward. "Forget I said anything, sir. I just got here. I have no idea what's going on."

"Any other complaints I should know about?"

I glanced at the stack of evaluations. "No complaints."

Winston followed my gaze, chuckling to himself. "Sit your ass down, Detective. We're not done here." Reluctantly, I sat down, feeling like a child who'd been sent to see the principal. "Look, I know things have been rocky around here. But after everything that went down in my unit, I want to make sure I know what everyone is doing and how they're feeling. I don't want to miss anything. You and Fennel just went through something pretty major, but unlike you, he hasn't spoken to the department shrink."

"He has a department-approved therapist."

"I know." Winston held up a sheet of paper. "Everything's in order. He was cleared to return to duty. But you work with him every day, so I'm asking you how he is."

"He's fine."

"And you?"

"Ready to get to work. We have a busy day ahead of us."

"I'll let you get to it, then. I just have one last question. Do you trust him?"

"Fennel?"

Winston nodded.

"Completely."

"Do you think he feels the same?"

"I'm pretty sure he does."

Winston tapped the end of his pen against the stack of files. "What about the other cops and support staff? Does he trust them too?" Winston dropped the pen. "Do you?"

I leaned back in the chair. This wasn't the discussion I thought we'd be having first thing in the morning. "The bad apples are gone. I have no reason to think anyone else was involved, unless IA or the FBI have discovered something new." I eyed the lieutenant. "Have they?"

"Not that I've heard. But I wanted to know where your heads are." He scribbled a note in the margin. "Has anyone shown any animosity toward either of you?"

"No. Everything's back to normal."

"Glad to hear it." Winston waited for me to open the door before he said, "And tell your partner I wasn't keeping him from the suspect. She asked for a lawyer."

Brad looked up when I returned to my desk. "What was that about?"

"Winston wanted to make sure the other kids are still playing nice."

"What does that mean?"

I shook away the question. "He said Smaldey asked for a lawyer before answering any other questions. Are you sure she's innocent?"

"She's asserting her rights. That doesn't make her guilty."

"Do you know where she was picked up?"

"The patrol car outside her place of business spotted her when she showed up for work this morning. As far as I know, she was alone."

While we waited for her attorney to arrive, I took care of some pressing issues with other cases and spoke to ADA Winters about our current case. He didn't see any reason why we couldn't get a warrant to search her apartment and workplace and to gain access to her phone records and internet history. After filling out the paperwork, I pulled up the guest list from Kelsey Eldridge's Halloween party and ran backgrounds on the attendees.

"Did you get the full guest list from social media?" I asked.

Brad nodded. "I've spent the morning figuring out who the party crashers were. In total, I've come up with twenty-seven names so far."

"Twenty-seven people crashed?"

"That's the total number of guests who showed up at the party. I've been looking into alibis. Everyone I've looked into has checked out, and not a single one was dressed like Van Helsing."

"Did anyone post any photos online?"

"Almost everyone did. I asked Mac to use one of her web crawlers to see if any other photos show up that aren't linked to one of these twenty-seven accounts, but so far, she hasn't found anything."

Mac was a computer genius, but things like that took time. "Do you think the killer posted a photo to commemorate his kill?"

"I don't know. I doubt it, but at least seven people crashed that party. I might not have a complete list. Plus, we can't be positive the killer didn't end up in the background of one of those photos." He stopped typing. "It's a stretch, but it's the best we can do."

"Have you spoken to the party crashers?"

"Yes. The only attendee I haven't talked to yet is waiting inside our interrogation room. But I doubt she'll have anything useful to say."

I studied the photos on her social media pages. As a former pro cheerleader, she had a large following. Some of her friends were top athletes. She didn't exactly have a household name, but she'd hob-knobbed with some swanky individuals, which made me wonder why she settled for a lowly sportswriter no one knew.

Vivica hadn't listed her relationship status. In fact, aside from a few group photos, nothing on her page indicated she was dating Dan Fielders. They looked like friends. All the photos that included both of them were group shots with captions about sports and visiting old hangouts.

"Are we sure Dan and Vivica are dating?" I asked.

"Look at his page. That should answer your question."

I clicked the link on one of the photos where Dan had been tagged. That led me to his professional page. "It looks like Kelsey got it wrong."

"Search Dan's name. It's the unverified account. It's set to friends only, but since he's dead, we've already been granted access."

I followed my partner's instructions which revealed a completely different side to Dan Fielders. His professional page made him look confident and sports minded. Everything was about teams, stats, and scores. But his private profile told another story.

Dan Fielders was obsessed with Vivica. Over the last month, he'd posted more than a hundred photos of the two of them. He'd even posted photos of the two of them getting ready for the party. In ninety percent of the shots, he was kissing her cheek. She didn't look nearly as smitten as he did, but looks could be deceiving.

"Have you gotten a look at his phone yet?" I asked.

"I went over it with the techs. His camera roll had tons of sports shots and more pictures of Vivica. Some of them were rather intimate. I'm sure she wouldn't want them getting out."

"Any videos?"

"No, just images."

"Did it look like she knew they were being taken?"

"Probably." He shrugged. "Maybe that's why she asked

for a lawyer."

"What about texts or e-mails? Did anyone make any threats?"

"No."

"What about the messages between the happy couple? Were they happy?"

"I don't know. They argued about going to the party. Vivica didn't want to go. She didn't want to risk the exposure. She preferred keeping their relationship between them."

"But Kelsey knew they were dating."

"A lot of people knew they were dating. I think she just wanted to keep photos from getting out."

"Do you know why?"

"Not a clue. But I intend to ask her about it."

"Did you notice any red flags when you looked into Fielders' records?"

"Nothing. The guy has enough friends and no obvious enemies. He wasn't Mr. Popular or Mr. Perfect. Whenever he posted sports stories, he always got a few hecklers and psychos." Brad shook his head before I could ask the obvious question. "Mac's checking, but none of them made any real threats. They mostly bitched and moaned about his predictions over draft picks or the slant he'd put on the stories he reported."

"You're a sports guy. Were they slanted?"

"Not really. The facts he reported were solid. When it came to speculating and offering his opinions, he didn't hide which teams he favored or who his favorite players were. But that's just speculation. All the sports sites do the same thing. He wasn't out of line or anything."

I brought up the sports network's website and searched for Dan's articles. A few hundred results popped up. After sorting by the most recent, I skimmed a few of them, searching for any mention of Vivica or Halloween.

I only found one brief mention. As a closing note, Dan had plugged a charity drive where several prominent sports figures would make an appearance dressed in costume. Dan talked about the haunted maze, face painting, pumpkin carving, and other events the whole family would enjoy, concluding with how he'd be there dressed as the greatest vampire of all time.

I checked the comments, but they were innocuous. However, since Dan posted his costume choice for the public to see, that could make narrowing down our suspect list even harder. I sent the article link to Mac, in the hopes that might lead her little web crawlers in the right direction. Before I could scan any more of Dan Fielders' articles, Brad's phone rang. Vivica Smaldey's lawyer just arrived.

SIX

"I don't understand why I'm here. I didn't do anything wrong." Vivica crossed her legs, doing her best not to fidget. "Why was I arrested?"

"You aren't under arrest," Brad said patiently. "We just have some questions."

"But I was told I couldn't leave. If I'm not under arrest, then I don't have to answer them."

"Ms. Smaldey," I thought I'd take a turn since this wasn't getting us anywhere, "would you mind telling me where you went last night?"

"Why?" She glanced at her attorney, who hadn't said a word.

"Did you attend a Halloween party held at Kelsey Eldridge's house?" I had photos and posts from Dan's social media account to prove it, but I hoped Vivica would stop being a hard ass and answer the question.

"Yes."

"Did you go with someone?"

"Dan. Dan Fielders. Why does that matter?"

"What's your relationship to Mr. Fielders?" I asked.

"Dan?" She arched an eyebrow. "We're dating."

"How long? Is it serious?" Brad asked.

"On and off for a few months. We were just having fun, or so I thought."

"Did Dan know that?" I asked.

She didn't say anything.

"When's the last time you saw Mr. Fielders?" Brad asked.

"Last night, at the party." She gave him a look like he was stupid. "Weren't you listening when your partner asked me that question?"

Brad ignored the dig. "What time did you last see Dan?"

"I don't know. I left around 10:45." She reached into her handbag and pulled out her phone. "Yeah, right around then. I ordered a rideshare to pick me up." She held out her phone, showing us the receipt.

"Why didn't you leave with Dan?" Brad asked. "Didn't the two of you go to the party together?"

Vivica let out a dramatic sigh and tucked her hair behind her ear. "We broke up. We went to the party together, but he's always so much. He drank too much and was acting like a total jackass, so I left."

"What condition was Dan in when you left?"

"He was a little drunk, but other than that, he was fine."

"Witnesses say you were dressed as Dracula's bride," I said.

"Yeah, and Dan was Dracula. What's your point?"

I exchanged a look with my partner. For someone who'd been told her boyfriend was dead, Vivica should have shown a bit more remorse. Instead, she seemed inconvenienced by our questions and annoyed with Dan.

"Did you have any props with your costume?" Brad asked.

"Props?" Her brows arched in genuine confusion. "You mean like a fake bat or something?"

"Teeth, bats, crosses, stakes. Anything like that."

She reached into her bag and pulled out a set of plastic fangs. "I wore these last night, and I had on a cape."

"What about Dan's teeth?" I asked.

She snorted, rolling her eyes. "Those are custom-made implants. Dan had most of his teeth knocked out during a hockey game a few months ago. Since he's obsessed with

Halloween, he thought fangs would be awesome. He's such an idiot."

"He played hockey?" Brad asked.

"No, he was getting a quote from a player who'd been sent to the penalty box when a fight broke out. He stepped right into the middle of it and took a stick to the mouth."

My partner made a note and asked for more details concerning when it happened. "Back to what happened last night. Can you run us through your evening?"

"I didn't kill him," she said. "I already told the other cops that. When I left the party, he was very much alive. In a coffin, but alive."

Brad held his pen poised to jot down notes. "Humor us, please."

"Fine." Vivica told us how Dan met her after work, got into costume, and went to Kelsey's house. She had no interest in making small talk with Dan's work friends. She remembered them from her cheerleading days and didn't want to have to answer the usual questions about why she retired or if she could still do a split. Instead, she and Dan had found a quiet place to hang out. "Kelsey turned his study into this weird funeral home scene. I don't know. He had a coffin in the room and flowers and shit. After a few drinks, Dan got really excited. He thought it'd be hilarious to pop out of the coffin like Dracula." She rolled her eyes. "He took this whole Halloween thing way too seriously."

"Then what happened?" Brad asked.

"Dan hoisted himself inside the thing and tried to get me to join him. I said no, but he just kept whining and bitching. I was so tired of that. I don't know. He was always sweet, but maybe too sweet sometimes. More like a kid than a man. He wanted a goddess or a mom, not a girlfriend. I was so sick of him whining to get his way or buying me things or trying to make me feel bad whenever I said no to his stupid ideas. He worshipped the ground I walked on and always had nice things to say." For a moment, she actually looked sad. "But it wasn't sexy. He was needy. Desperate. He was like a leach," she chuckled, "or a vampire. He knew exactly how to suck the joy out of everything. I thought he was sucking the life out of me. So I told him I didn't want to do this anymore, and I left."

"Did he follow you?" I asked.

"He called for me to come back, but he didn't follow. He was so drunk when he got inside the coffin. I doubt he could have gotten out of it without help."

"Was anyone else nearby when this happened? Can you think of anyone who can corroborate your story?" Brad asked.

"I don't know. The house was packed, but everyone was off doing their own thing. Someone probably heard Dan shouting, but I didn't look back. I don't know if anyone went to help him."

"We found Dan dead inside that coffin," Brad said. "It doesn't look like he ever made it out."

She closed her eyes and inhaled. "He could be a real jerk sometimes, but he didn't deserve that."

"Think for a minute," I said. "Are you sure you didn't see anyone else go into the room? Maybe you passed someone on your way out."

"I don't think so."

"We'd like to get your prints and DNA to rule you out." Brad waited while she consulted with her attorney.

"Yeah, okay. But we were making out most of the night. I'm sure you'll find proof of that on his body." She looked at the attorney, who nodded again. "I'd like it put on the record that I'm willingly cooperating."

While I went to tell the officer outside to send a member of CSU into the room to collect the samples, Brad asked, "Do you know anyone who would have wanted to harm Dan?"

"No. Everyone liked him. Sure, he could drive you crazy, but he had a good heart, deep down. Every time I got mad at him, I'd always feel bad about it later. He was excellent at the emotional manipulation. I'm sure he did it to everyone." Tears sprang to her eyes, and one dribbled down her cheek. She wiped it away. "Dammit."

"You're saying he didn't have any enemies," Brad asked, "even though he was a pain in the ass?"

"Not that I know of."

"Did he owe anyone money?" I asked.

She shook her head. "Honestly, are you sure this isn't some kind of joke? Halloween's his favorite holiday. He's like a big kid. He likes to play dress-up. This sounds like an elaborate ruse." She scanned the room, as if looking for a hidden camera. "This is just the kind of scam he'd pull to make me feel bad for breaking up with him."

"This isn't a joke, ma'am," Brad said. "I'm sorry. But it isn't."

"Did Dan have any wooden stakes with him last night?" I asked.

"No." Her mouth fell open. "Are you telling me someone killed him with a wooden stake?"

We hadn't divulged the details of his murder, but she'd pieced it together. "Yes," I said.

"God, I bet it was a mistake. Everyone at that party was three sheets when I left. Between Dan's bad judgment and those morons he worked with, things must have gotten out of hand." She wiped at her tears. "I should have made him leave with me to make sure he didn't do anything stupid. But I was just so fed up."

The tech came in to collect the samples. While he did, I asked Vivica a few more questions, but she'd formed a narrative in her head of what happened. And we didn't have any evidence to contradict her story. At least not yet.

"Still think she's involved?" Brad asked once we returned to our desks.

"I don't know. She made it sound like she couldn't stand the guy, but she went out with him for several months. From the things she said, it sounded like he wore her down or guilted her into it. Maybe she couldn't take it anymore and snapped."

"Except, our witness says she didn't kill him."

"Are we sure?" I asked, playing devil's advocate. "Isn't it possible our witness got a few events out of order? Vivica could have left the party, changed costumes, slipped into a trench coat and hat, returned to the party, stabbed Dan, and left."

"Does it fit the timeline?"

"It'd be close, but it's doable."

Brad grabbed the baseball off his desk and rocked back

in his chair, tossing it skyward. "Why would she kill him at the party? She could have done it somewhere far more private. They were dating. Obviously, she could have lured him somewhere else, somewhere she'd be less likely to get caught."

"But if they were alone, she'd be our only suspect. This way, she figures she has a decent shot at an alibi or a misdirect."

"It doesn't feel right." Brad tossed the ball and caught it a few more times. "After she left the party, she went to a bar. That seems like an odd thing to do if you just shoved a wooden stake through your boyfriend's chest."

"We have no way of knowing what her mindset was at the time."

Brad replaced the ball and reached for the phone. "Let me see if anyone remembers seeing her." After a few questions, he hung up. "Surprise. Surprise. A woman in a red dress, corset, and cape arrived at the bar a little after eleven and stayed until almost one. The bartender remembers seeing plenty of guys hit on her. But she didn't seem particularly interested in any of them."

"Did she leave with anyone?"

"He didn't think so, but he remembers she was talking to the guy sitting beside her for most of the night. They might have been friends."

"She didn't mention any of that to us." I turned toward the interrogation room. "Should we go back in and ask?"

Brad gestured that I remain seated. "Before we left the interrogation room, you asked Vivica where she went. She told you she stopped for a drink at her usual hangout before going home. But she kept her response vague, like she wanted us to think she had to recover from the breakup."

"The best way of getting over someone is getting under someone else."

"What?"

"It's Emma's philosophy. Rebound sex or whatever you want to call it. I assumed that's why Vivica went to the bar, to pick up a guy." I thought about the things she'd said in the interrogation room. "She lied to us. We know she didn't go home last night because we had officers watching her place. So where did she go? Or who did she go home with?"

"Stay here." Brad got up from his desk. "I'll ask."

"Why do I have to stay here?"

"I'm less threatening."

"Ha." But Brad knew how to flirt with suspects when it suited our needs. He'd lower his voice and give her that shy smile and ask if she left anything out. He'd sympathize with her plight and offer his condolences. He'd apologize for having to ask the questions and being so strict during our interview. And he'd trick her into believing it. That's why he'd been a great UC. Even I couldn't always tell where the truth ended and the lies began.

A few minutes later, he returned with a smug grin.

"Well?" I asked.

"She said she talked to a lot of people at the bar. She didn't get any names, at least none she's willing to share. After she left the bar, she went for a walk and crashed at a friend's house." He flipped open his notepad and held it up for me to read. *Asta Bleu.* "I'll give her a call and see what she has to say."

"While you do that, I'll see what I can find on her."

Asta had been arrested for indecent exposure on two separate occasions. She, like Vivica, had been a professional cheerleader. But unlike Vivica, Asta didn't retire. She'd been kicked off the team for violating her contract by posing nude for a magazine. Currently, she was working as a paralegal while she took online accounting courses and modeled on the side.

Brad hung up the phone. "Vivica showed up at Asta's place a little after two. She told Asta she broke up with Dan and was afraid if she went home she'd find him waiting there for her." He quirked his lips from side to side, which reminded me of a bunny.

"What's with the face?"

"If Dan was that clingy, wouldn't he have called Vivica a dozen times after she left the party?"

"He couldn't. He was dead."

"I know that, but supposedly, Vivica didn't."

"I told you she's involved."

"Maybe you're right."

SEVEN

Since my partner was coming around to my theory, we waited until the bar opened before paying the bartender a visit. The place didn't have any security cameras. It was a quiet neighborhood joint. But since Vivica Smaldey was a mini-celebrity dressed in a bright red dress and cape, the bartender noticed when she arrived.

"Ever since I turned the page on the calendar, we've been getting all kinds in here. Werewolves, zombies, vampires, whatever people want to be." He pointed to a corkboard plastered with polaroids. "We hold a costume contest all month. Anyone who comes in with a costume and gets her picture taken is entered to win. As you can see, we got quite a few entries, and it's only the first week of October."

Brad and I examined the board. It was easy to find Vivica in her red dress and corset. "Was she with anyone?" I asked as Brad continued to scrutinize the board.

"Like I said on the phone, plenty of guys came up to talk to her. But she blew them off, except the one guy who was sitting beside her. I didn't see either of them come in, but they just kind of sat at the bar and drank. Every once in a while, I'd see them chatting, real friendly like, but it looked pretty damn platonic. The guy might have been married or gay. I'm not sure. But the rest of the guys here were tripping over their tongues. The one beside her didn't seem to care. Maybe that's why she looked so comfortable with him. But honestly, I'd say she just wanted to be left alone to drink in peace."

"But she posed for the photo." Brad pointed to the one on the board.

"Free drinks for a month isn't a bad trade-off in exchange for a photo op, especially when a looker like her is likely to win."

"Did you get a shot of the guy sitting beside her?"

"I don't think he had on a costume." The bartender frowned. "Honestly, I wasn't paying much attention to him. I was more interested in her."

"Do you know Dan Fielders?" I asked.

"Who?"

"He's a sportswriter." Brad showed him a photo.

"I don't think so."

"Did Vivica ever come here with anyone?"

"Not that I recall. Whenever she drops in, she does so in order to meet new people, if you catch my drift."

"But last night was different," Brad said.

The bartender nodded. "She was upset. Given how she was dressed, I'm guessing her plans for the evening took a turn. I gave her space and filled her glass. That's all I know."

After we returned to the car, I said, "The bartender thought Vivica was upset."

"She told us it had to do with the breakup."

"But she broke up with Dan, not the other way around."

"Still, ending a relationship sucks." He narrowed his eyes at me. "Why do I get the feeling you've never broken up with anyone?"

"I have, but I've never felt bad about it."

"I know you, Liv. I find that very hard to believe." He continued to stare at me. "You've really never broken up with anyone, have you?"

"I've broken up with tons of guys. You've been there for

most of them. Every guy I dated while undercover, every mark, I broke it off with all of them. Remember?"

"You didn't break it off. We arrested them. And I know you felt bad about a few of those."

"Why are we talking about this? We're trying to identify Dan Fielders' killer. That has nothing to do with my dating history." I examined the bar's exterior, but it didn't provide any clues either. "Do you think Vivica came here intending to get picked up by a stranger right after killing her boyfriend?"

"If that's what she wanted to do, she would have done it. I'm guessing she came here after leaving the party to drown her sorrows. Since she didn't follow Emma's Guide to Life and jump into bed with someone the first chance she got, I'm guessing she wasn't sure if things were completely over with Dan. In the interrogation room, she told us he'd make her feel guilty. Perhaps she was already feeling guilty."

"For killing him?" I wasn't following Brad's train of thought.

"No, for breaking up with him at the party in front of his friends and coworkers."

"I thought you were reconsidering your position on this."

"I don't know what happened. We need more evidence. But given what we've been told, I find it hard to believe she killed Dan. Killing someone isn't something to be taken lightly. We see all kinds. Most killers freak out afterward. They don't stop to get a drink and crash at a friend's place. If anything, Asta would have noticed if Vivica was acting oddly, which she wasn't."

"Did you ask?"

"Of course." He had me there.

"Still, Vivica told us Dan was clingy. When he didn't call her a dozen times to apologize or beg her to come back, she should have realized something was wrong."

"Would you? Or would you have been relieved you didn't have to deal with a crazy person calling you?"

"Probably the second."

"Same here," Brad admitted. "It's also possible she

figured he was having too much fun and was too drunk to call her last night. She must have thought she'd see or hear from him today."

"Again, you're speculating."

"What do you want me to do? We don't have any lab results yet. The techs didn't pull any prints or DNA off the stake. We're waiting to see if they can match the wood to what we find in Vivica's furniture design studio, but I'm not holding my breath on that one."

I stared out the windshield. "Let's take a look at Dan Fielders' apartment and see if that tells us anything. Then we should head over to Vivica's home and work and see if something shakes loose. If all else fails, we can pay Asta Bleu a visit."

Brad pulled into traffic. "I thought I was in charge of this investigation."

"Sorry. What do you think we should do now, Detective Fennel?"

"Don't be patronizing. It's not nice." He jerked his chin at the mobile data terminal. "Pull up Fielders' address. I don't remember it off the top of my head."

"Yes, sir." I entered the information and read the address aloud. "Should I input it into the GPS?"

He gave me a sideways glance. "Sarcasm isn't nice either."

"I wasn't being sarcastic. I'd hate for you to make a wrong turn."

"Whatever you say, Liv. But I think I can figure out how to get there without the GPS telling me where to go. And no, I don't need you to tell me where to go either."

"I'd never."

"The hell you wouldn't." He kept an eye on the mirrors and traffic, making sure to switch lanes in order to make the turn with plenty of time to spare. "Y'know, Fielders lived alone. He has no next of kin. His parents are deceased. The address is in a decent neighborhood. While we're looking for clues, you should check out the kitchen appliances and closet space. If you put your name in now, the landlord might be willing to rent to you before the place even gets listed."

"Have you lost your mind?"

"What? I bet it's a nice place. It's in a nice neighborhood."

"I can't live in a dead guy's apartment."

"Why? He's not using it anymore. Someone's bound to move in."

"I can't sleep at my place because a killer stopped by to pay me a visit and because another psycho tried to kill you in my kitchen. Moving into a dead guy's apartment is not going to improve the situation."

"Hey, I'm just giving you options since you didn't like my other suggestion."

"Moving into your apartment isn't an option."

"Sure, it is. And this way, I get to move away from that damn sink that won't stop leaking no matter what I do to fix it."

"Brad, don't worry about it. I'm a big girl. I'll figure it out. Until I do, I'll stay with my parents. I won't crash on your couch anymore. I promise."

"That's not what I meant." He parked at the end of the block. The high-rise apartment building stood at the other end, but this was the best spot we'd get without double-parking or turning on the lights and making our own space. "You're welcome to stay at my place anytime. I've gotten used to you. You're not so bad to have around."

"I appreciate it, but you should have some time to yourself. I don't want to be your Dan Fielders."

"At the risk of sounding sexist, you'd be a far more convincing cheerleader than I would."

"Regardless, you get my point."

"Yeah, well, you're wrong. Yes, I want you to get your own place, but it's not because I want you gone. It's because I don't want to feel responsible for your homelessness. You loved that apartment. It took you forever to find it, and now you're back to square one."

We took the elevator up to Dan's apartment. I didn't have to look at the numbers to know which was Dan's. The door in the middle was decked out in fake spiderwebs and skulls. The welcome mat said *Beware* in creepy black print.

Out of habit, Brad reached for the knocker, which

looked like an antique with a raven's head staring at us. After our knocks went unanswered, Brad used the key we'd gotten from the building manager to unlock the door. As he pushed it open, a loud creaking sound came from within. But it wasn't the floorboards. Dan had rigged his apartment with sound effects. Vivica wasn't kidding when she said he loved Halloween. As I stood in the doorway, taking it all in, I couldn't help but think perhaps he loved it to death.

We slipped on some gloves and cautiously entered the apartment. Since Dan was murdered, we had to find out why. All we knew was this wasn't a random killing. We had plenty of suspects, but none of them had motive, except Vivica. And my partner and I couldn't even agree on that. It was time we ventured outside the box.

Halloween had vomited all over the place. Even the lights had been replaced with colored bulbs to give it an eerie, haunted house feel. Brad started in the kitchen while I checked the bedroom.

The moment I pushed open the door, a shadowy figure jumped out at me. An involuntary scream escaped my lips, and I scrambled to draw my gun. "Police. Put your hands in the air."

The guy bobbed and weaved. I stepped backward, my gun in one hand, my badge in the other.

"Liv?" Brad came up behind me, his weapon drawn. My partner aimed at the form in front of us. "Freeze. Show me your hands. Identify yourself."

The figure continued to dance back and forth, refusing to comply.

Cautiously, I stepped into the room, hitting the light switch with my badge. Dan had changed the light bulbs in his bedroom too. The glow from the red bulb illuminated the man in front of us, revealing a skeleton dressed in a cheap suit.

"I hate Halloween." I shoved the skeleton, which had been anchored to a robotic vacuum cleaner, out of my way, and cleared the rest of the room.

Brad let out a nervous laugh, leaning down to turn off the appliance. "You have to admit, this whole setup is pretty ingenious.

"Help me clear the rest of the apartment. I don't want to find any more surprises."

Brad stood in the doorway, making sure no werewolves or goblins snuck up on me while I cleared the bedroom suite and checked beneath the bed, inside the closet, and behind the shower curtain in the attached bathroom. Once I was done, I followed him into the hallway and stood watch while he made sure no one was hiding in any of the other rooms. But aside from a witch who flew in circles around the guest room, courtesy of being tethered to the ceiling fan, the place was empty.

I took a deep breath, waiting for my heart to return to its usual slow, steady rhythm. Dan Fielders had done a great job making every inch of his apartment the creepiest place on earth. He had everything from cheesy fake spiders to an animatronic mummy that grumbled awake inside a life-sized sarcophagus, where one would imagine the dining room table should have been.

"Like I said, there's not a chance in hell I'd want to live here."

"That's probably for the best. I bet Dan Fielders' spirit is hell-bent on haunting this place."

"Maybe he'll haunt his killer and force them to confess." Shaking the nervous energy off like a dog shaking off rainwater, I turned on my flashlight and returned to the bedroom. The skeleton didn't look nearly as threatening now, but I patted him down anyway.

I didn't find any weapons or wooden stakes on him. But I was pretty sure the suit he wore belonged to Dan. The size and style matched the rest of what I found in the man's closet. The one thing I didn't find were any of Vivica's things.

They'd been dating for months. Finding a sweater or bra would make sense, but they weren't here. I checked beneath the bed and in the drawers. Everything belonged to Dan.

In his side table, I found a small gun safe. Guessing that since Dan Fielders lived alone and had no reason to safeguard his weapon, I tried the most used combination, and the box opened. It contained an unloaded handgun and some ammo. As far as I could tell, the gun hadn't been fired recently and none of the bullets were missing.

I left it on top of the bed and continued searching. Dan had a stack of file boxes in the bottom of the linen closet. Scanning the contents didn't reveal any damning secrets. The boxes contained stories and articles he'd written.

Moving on, I searched the bathroom before moving to another room. I'd just made it into the guest bedroom where the witch continued to fly in circles. I knew how she felt.

"Son of a bitch," Brad cursed.

"Are you okay?" I stepped into the hallway, hand on my gun.

He exhaled loudly. "Yeah. All good."

But it didn't sound all good. I went into the living room to find my partner running a hand through his hair while he stared at the box he'd just found. Blood or some blood-like substance oozed down the sides of the cardboard.

"What is that?" I asked, unsure if I wanted to look inside.

"I'm guessing it's the *Telltale Heart*." He ran a gloved finger against the ooze and examined it under the light. Then he gave it a tentative sniff. "It smells sweet. I'm guessing it's one of those fake blood packs they make with corn syrup."

I peered into the box to find a beating heart spewing what looked like blood against the inside of the box. When enough of it built up, it oozed out the top and down the sides. Turning my flashlight to the place where the box had been, I didn't see any stains.

As if reading my mind, Brad said, "It didn't do that until I opened the box." He pointed to the lid. "The top was rigged with that wire. Opening it triggered some kind of mechanism which set it off. It's like one of those kid's toys where you pull the string and the thing jitters around. It scared the shit out of me. I thought it was a fucking bomb."

"It's a good thing Dan Fielders is dead, or I'd kill him."

"It was only a prank." Brad had more than enough experiences with bombs and IEDs. He just needed to remind himself this wasn't Kandahar. He picked up the box when the heart stopped squirting fake blood. In the center of it was a wooden stake. "However, this prank might lead us to whoever killed Dan."

EIGHT

"You found a literal stake through the heart." Carrie examined the photos we'd taken before passing the box off to CSU. "That's creepy."

"It wasn't a real heart," Brad said, seemingly oblivious to the way the coroner's assistant crept closer to him.

"But it was a real stake," I said.

Carrie glanced at me. "What did the crime lab say?"

"It's the same size, shape, and composition as the stake used to kill Dan Fielders. But the one we found in Dan's apartment didn't have any human DNA on it. We weren't able to lift any prints off of it, except Dan's."

"What about the one I pulled out of the vic?" Carrie slid her card through the reader and opened the door to the refrigerated room. "Did you get anything from that?"

"Nothing." Brad peered at the cadavers on the tables, covered in sheets. "I'm surprised Dan didn't have something like this set up in his apartment."

"He didn't have room with the mummy," I said.

"Mummy?" Carrie opened the drawer containing our vic and slid it out so we could see. They hadn't gotten around to the autopsy yet, but they'd performed the preliminary exam and a battery of tests. She picked up the clipboard and scanned it to see if anything new had been done.

"Dan had his entire apartment tricked-out like a

haunted house attraction. He had a flying witch, a vacuuming skeleton, and a sarcophagus and mummy for a dining room table," I said.

She stepped back, practically leaning against my partner's chest. "That sounds crazy. How much money did this guy have? Maybe I got into the wrong line of work."

"You and me both." Brad read the clipboard over her shoulder.

I turned my attention to Dan. The ME had already sent his clothes and personal effects to the crime lab. Aside from the gaping hole in his chest, he didn't have many marks on him. He had a faint bruise on his left shin, which looked like he'd tripped on the steps a few days ago, and a newer bruise on his right bicep.

"Personal wealth goes along with what I discovered about his fangs," Carrie said.

"They're custom-made implants," Brad said.

She looked up at him with a quirky smile. "How'd you know that? Did you read ahead?" She pressed the clipboard against her chest. "I wanted to make the dramatic reveal."

"His girlfriend told us about them when we interviewed her this morning."

"Oh." Carrie relaxed her grip on the clipboard. "Well, poo."

Poo? I raised a confused eyebrow and tried to meet my partner's gaze, but he refused to look at me.

"Anyway," Carrie put the clipboard down, "as you can see, cause of death was a puncture wound to the heart. The stake tore through a large portion of the muscle, severing several major arteries and veins. He would have bled out in less than two minutes and lost consciousness before that. It was quick. We'll know more once we cut him open."

"What about his eyes?" Brad asked.

"Colored contacts. I sent them to the crime lab with the rest of his belongings. The black veins on his face were just makeup, like I suspected. Since you already have an ID, you don't really need to worry about matching the contact prescription or pulling his dental records." She laughed at the little joke. "Seriously though, who pays thousands of dollars to have some weird looking vampire teeth screwed into his jaw?"

"Dan Fielders did." I looked down at the body and said a silent prayer. The guy might have been obsessed with the spooky stuff, but I hoped he'd rest in peace.

"So who was he? Some start-up billionaire? The heir to a dot-com empire?"

"He's a sportswriter. He lives alone. His expenses weren't exorbitant, so whatever money he saved, he put into his favorite pastime." I pointed to the bruise on his arm. "Any idea what caused that?"

Carrie gave it a closer look. "I'm guessing he banged into something. Maybe a parking meter. It doesn't look defensive. If someone had grabbed him, the bruise would have more definition. We'd be able to make out fingers. This looks like a bump, probably accidental."

"Is there anything else we should know?" Brad asked.

"The prelim didn't reveal anything else. I'm sorry, but he's going to have to wait his turn like everyone else. The COD is pretty cut and dry. I don't expect to find any surprises once we open him up."

"Thanks." Brad jerked his chin toward the exit. It was time to go.

I headed for the door. Before Brad could follow me out, Carrie asked him if they could speak in private for a moment. My partner agreed, tossing me the keys. At least I could wait in the car where it was warmer and less odorous.

While I waited for Brad, I went over everything we'd uncovered today, which wasn't much. A search of Vivica's workplace and apartment didn't reveal any wooden stakes. The wood she used in her furniture business didn't match the murder weapon. The techs had collected sawdust samples from her tools, but I didn't think they'd find a wood match there either.

The fake heart in the box had been impaled by the exact same type of stake that had been used to kill Dan. Every cell in my body said that couldn't be a coincidence. But the box had been printed. The only person who touched the outside of it was Dan. His fingerprints had also been found on the fake blood pouch which had been stuffed inside the fake heart. When Brad opened the box, the tripwire triggered a small blast which released the blood that filled up the heart, poured out the top, and oozed from the box. Whoever set that up was a sicko or a psycho. It would have served as the perfect way to send a warning to Dan, but since my partner was the first person to open the box and Dan's prints were found on the materials inside, he must have been the one to set it.

The car door opened, and Brad climbed behind the wheel. "Sorry about that. Are you ready to pay Asta a visit?"

"Sure." I waited, wondering if he'd tell me what Carrie wanted. But after two minutes of uncomfortable silence, I decided it'd be best to discuss the case instead. "Do you think Dan Fielders had money stashed somewhere to pay for his obsession? Those decorations must have cost a fortune. I hadn't thought about it much until Carrie brought it up, but large animatronics like that go for hundreds, possibly thousands, of dollars. Where did he get the money for that?"

"I reviewed his financials. I didn't notice any red flags. No daily trips to the coffee shop or excessive eating out. You saw the stuff in his apartment. He didn't have any designer labels or high-end electronics. The only thing he spent money on was the decorations. I don't think whoever killed him had economic reasons to do it."

"He wasn't robbed. All his credit cards were accounted for. His watch and phone were recovered at the scene. But it's not like we found him face-down in a dark alley. We know this wasn't a mugging," I said.

"I'm trying to figure out what it is by eliminating the things it's not."

"It wasn't a carjacking."

Brad laughed. "Fine, I see your point. But I wouldn't have been surprised if Dan's job gave him a leg up when it came to betting. This would be easier if he had a lot of debt, or we had some kind of proof he was a gambler who owed someone a lot of money. At least that would make sense. The heart in the box reads like a threat to me, given how Dan was killed, but..."

"More than likely, Dan set that up himself. Should we

assume the killer saw that and got the idea stuck in his head?"

"I don't know. According to Melanie Daggio, our witness, a guy dressed like a vampire hunter was seen in Dan's vicinity at the time of the murder. Vampire hunters carry stakes. I don't know much about wooden stakes, but maybe there's just one manufacturer. If that's the case, the stake we found in Dan's apartment might not have anything to do with his murder." Brad pulled to a stop outside Asta's apartment building. "We need to find out more about these stakes, where they were purchased, and who bought them. Once we determine that, we'll have better luck tracking down our killer." He dialed the precinct and passed along his request, adding that we also needed to know which costume shops sold vampire hunter or Van Helsing outfits that fit the description we'd gotten.

"I see only one problem with your brilliant plan."

"What's that?"

"Out of all those party guests, Daggio's the only one who remembers seeing a vampire hunter, and she was highly intoxicated."

"We don't have bad intel. What she told us fits with what happened."

"Unless she's our killer."

"She's barely five feet tall. There's no way she could have thrusted the stake through Dan's heart. She wouldn't have been at the right angle to do it. The crime techs said our killer was at least 5'8."

"Vivica's not that tall either, but with stiletto heels, I bet she is."

"We need evidence."

"No kidding. But we've scoured every bit of footage we've been able to find from last night and canvassed the neighborhood. No one else remembers seeing a guy in a leather trench coat and hat. Did he turn into a ghost and disappear?"

"Maybe." Brad shrugged. "He could have taken off the costume or changed costumes. It's tough to say. The area's residential. The few traffic cams we found were so far away, the footage is practically worthless. We didn't even get a glimpse of the rideshare that picked up Vivica, even though we saw her receipt and a couple of officers ran down the driver, just to make sure. But since we can't rely on traffic cam footage, we have to rely on what our witness said."

"We need some kind of corroboration. Based on everything we know, Vivica was one of the last people to see Dan alive. If anyone came in contact with the killer, it would have been her. But she didn't recall seeing anyone. I still think she has something to do with this."

"Which is why we're about to ask her good pal, Asta, everything she knows about last night." Brad gestured toward the front door. "Our answers await."

NINE

Asta sat across from us at her dining room table. "What do you want me to say? Viv comes over a lot. We're friends. I don't see what the big deal is."

"What can you tell us about Dan Fielders?" Brad asked.

"Not much." Asta lifted her mug to her lips and drank some tea. "He's kind of annoying. He fawns all over Viv. The jerk never knows when to quit. At first, she liked it. She's always been an attention hog. It comes with the territory, I guess."

"Territory?"

"Cheerleaders. We like the spotlight and the attention. We like the boys drooling after us. If we didn't, we sure as shit wouldn't be doing standing splits and somersaults in miniskirts." She put the cup down and eyed my partner as if he were a piece of meat. "Did you play football?"

"Baseball." Brad clicked his pen. "We weren't lucky enough to have cheerleaders."

"Oh, I bet you had plenty of girls cheering you on."

I cleared my throat, wondering if it would be too presumptuous to open a window to air out some of those pheromones. "You said Vivica enjoyed the attention Dan showed her at first. Did that change?"

Asta's gaze flicked to me. "It always does. Viv has a bad habit of hooking up with desperate losers. She throws them a bone but ends up embarrassed and irritated. What can I say? She's shallow. She wants to date A-listers, but none of them have come knocking since she retired from cheering."

"Did she and Dan fight often? Did she ever try to break up with him?" Brad asked.

"They didn't really fight. Viv would just yell at him, and he'd beg for forgiveness. He'd shower her with gifts, bring her coffee, clean her house, just whatever he could think to do to keep her happy. But she wanted out. I'm sure he knew it, but he pretended things were good between them. Dating her gave him a lot of bragging rights. He wouldn't have wanted to give that up."

"Is that why Vivica never acknowledged their relationship publicly? Was that her attempt to keep him in his place?"

"I don't think she thought of it like that. She just didn't want to be associated with someone the public at large would deem beneath her. She dated a lot of top athletes and celebrities. I'm sure she's just trying to hold on to that reputation for as long as possible."

Brad flipped to a new page in his notepad. "Did Vivica mention anything to you about what happened last night?"

"Are you talking about her breakup with Dan?"

"Yes."

"Yeah." Asta picked up the mug and held it between her palms, even though it was empty.

"Was that the first time Vivica broke up with Dan?" I asked.

"No, she tried a few times before. But he'd always come crawling back, begging for another chance."

"Would he call?" Brad asked.

"He'd call, text, make video posts, send her flowers and candy, and if none of that worked, he'd show up. I always warned her that wasn't normal. The guy's unstable. Normal people do not behave like leeches."

"Is that why she came here last night?" Brad asked.

"Yep. Viv called me around midnight and asked if she could crash here. She said she didn't want to deal with

Dan, especially when he was drunk."

"Was he ever violent?"

"Not that I know of. Viv never said anything to me. I don't think she'd put up with that, but I don't know. Why? Did he do something to her?"

We ignored the question. "What else did you and Vivica discuss last night?" I asked.

Asta narrowed her eyes, contemplating the reason for the question. "We talked about the Halloween party she and Dan went to. He's a total freak when it comes to Halloween. He picked out their costumes two months ago. Did you know he has permanent vampire fangs? The guy's just weird. I'm glad she finally told him to fuck off."

"What else did she mention about the party? Did she say anything about any of the other guests?" I asked.

"They were just a bunch of Dan's work friends. They work for a sports network, so they all know who Vivica is. That's actually how she and Dan met. He was writing a story and interviewed her. But she doesn't really like hanging around those people. They only ever talk about work. And Viv's had enough with sports."

"Why did she retire?" Brad asked, surprising me with that question. I wasn't sure how it was relevant to our investigation, but he seemed interested.

"Knee injury, but don't tell anyone I told you that."

"Since Vivica doesn't like interacting with Dan's friends, why did she agree to go to the party?" I asked.

"He was so excited to go. I know I've made her sound like a heartless bitch, but she wasn't always terrible to the guy. She went because he really wanted to."

"Did she mention anyone arguing with Dan or causing trouble at the party?" Brad asked.

"I don't think so. It sounded like the two of them made the rounds and then hung out someplace quiet." Asta got up to put her mug in the dishwasher, hoping we'd take the hint and leave. Instead, we pressed on.

"Do you know if Vivica took any photos at the party?" I asked.

"I doubt it."

"Did she mention anyone dressed as a vampire hunter

in a leather coat and outback hat? Or anyone carrying a wooden stake?"

"I don't know anything about someone in a leather coat." Asta squinted one eye and curled her lip on that same side, reminding me of a confused cartoon character. "But the stake thing rings a bell. I think she mentioned something about Dan having bought some for decoration. I don't know."

"Do you know if he had one with him last night?" Brad asked.

"How would I know?"

"Have you ever been to Dan's apartment?"

"No."

"Did Vivica spend a lot of time there?" I asked.

"I don't think so. She spent the night once, and it creeped her out. I know Viv, she prefers sleeping in her own bed, alone."

"But she slept here last night," Brad pointed out.

"It was one of those nights. It's girl code. You end up drunk or heartbroken, you crash with your friend. And you get waffles in the morning."

"Was Vivica heartbroken?" Brad asked.

"No, but she was a little tipsy. She left the party, went to a bar, drank too much, and came here."

"Was she with anyone?" I recalled what the bartender said.

"She didn't mention anyone to me. Despite what you might think about cheerleaders, we aren't all sluts. Viv wouldn't dump a guy and hook up with another one in the same night. She'd wait at least a day. Honestly, it'd probably be longer than that. She wasn't the type to cheat. She's been on the other side of that. She didn't like it very much, so I don't think she'd do it to someone else, not even Dan."

This was getting us nowhere. Brad asked a few more questions, but Asta didn't know much, or so she said.

"Can I use your bathroom?" I asked.

Asta pointed to the doorway on the left. "Help yourself."

The vanity was full of cosmetics and hair products. Hanging over the shower door were several bras and a few thongs. I peered into the trash can and checked the hamper, knowing if I found something I'd have no legal right to use it, but I had to know if Vivica had killed Dan and dumped her bloody clothes here. Unfortunately, I didn't find anything.

When I stepped out of the bathroom, Asta was standing in the hallway with Brad beside her. "Looking for this?" The red corset dress hung limply from her finger. "All you had to do was ask." She looked back at Brad with a sly grin.

I pretended not to know what she was talking about. "Sorry, I just had too much coffee today."

"Uh-huh." Asta didn't sound convinced as she dropped the dress into my hands.

Unsure what else to do, I followed Brad's lead, thanked her for her time, and went out the front door.

"I wasn't looking for the dress," I said as we headed back to the car. "I was looking for wooden stakes and blood."

"Did you find any?"

"No."

"How thoroughly did you look?"

"Let's just say we have no reason to pursue a warrant."

He sighed. "Sometimes, I worry you like to blur the lines a bit too much."

"I know where the edge is. I'm very careful not to step over it." I held the dress up, examining it. "Why did she give this to you?"

"I told her Dan was murdered and asked if she thought Vivica could have done it. I told Asta if we had Vivica's dress, we'd be able to rule her out as a suspect. And since Vivica left it at Asta's this morning, Asta was willing to hand it over."

"Smooth." I grinned at him. "It probably also helped that you played baseball, and she was giving you signals to slide into home."

His face flushed ever so slightly, and he ran the backs of his knuckles over his cheek. "She was nice."

"Uh-huh." I opened the trunk and put the dress inside an evidence bag. "Did you say you already ran a background check on her?"

"Yeah. Why?"

"Did that include looking at her nude photos?"

"We're homicide detectives. We have to be thorough."

"Do you think she's hiding something?"

He grinned. "Not in any of those photos."

"What about from the things she said?" I asked, turning serious. "Vivica's supposed to be one of her best friends, but she didn't paint her friend in a very positive light."

"She'd know better than anyone else."

"Or Asta did it intentionally to cover for her bestie. By saying negative things, we'd be more likely to assume if Vivica had something to do with Dan's murder, Asta would tell us."

"You're overanalzying this. Asta didn't know Dan was dead. Vivica never mentioned anything about that to her, which means she didn't know either. And according to Asta, Vivica turned off her cell phone."

"That would explain why she didn't think the lack of calls from Dan was odd. But that doesn't clear Vivica from suspicion."

"No, but she arrived at Asta's in that dress. She didn't have a leather coat or hat with her, and she didn't have any wooden stakes on her either. I'm telling you, Vivica didn't kill Dan."

"Maybe you're right, but Vivica didn't mention anything about the vampire hunter to Asta either, which means we're still at square one."

"Then we go back to the beginning. We have a house full of guests and a DB in a coffin. We know the coffin was something Kelsey picked up years ago. According to what the other guests told me, he sets it up at the party every year."

"That's probably why Dan went as Dracula."

"Plus, it matched his teeth," Brad said. "But everyone who's been to the party at least once before knows about the coffin, and if they knew Dan, they would know about his vampire teeth. Any one of them could have decided to dress up as a slayer and kill him."

"We already requested more information on the wooden stakes."

"In the meantime, let's double-check alibis and dig into locating security footage. If the killer had already left the party by the time the police arrived, which is what I assume must have happened, we need to figure out who he is and where he went."

"You said the traffic cam footage is useless."

"It is, which is why we have to determine which guests returned home after the party, which stayed out all night, who can corroborate that, and how they looked when they got home."

"Needle in a haystack, Fennel."

"Possibly, but without forensic evidence or a random photo showing the killer in the background of the shot, I'm out of ideas. The best thing to do is bring everyone in, one by one, and see what shakes loose. It's what I wanted to do last night. Instead, it's what we'll do today. Hopefully, we aren't too late."

TEN

He'd been glued to the morning news. He knew the local station would mention whatever horrific events happened last night. Surely, the death of a demon would be fodder for the media outlets. They loved broadcasting crazy, morbid affairs. And this morning was no different.

"A beloved local sportswriter was found dead last night. Police are still investigating the murder of twenty-five year old Dan Fielders. While they have yet to offer comment, the network where Dan worked has issued a statement. We would like to join with them in expressing our condolences to his family and friends."

A recent photo of Dan flashed on the screen. He narrowed his eyes. In the professional headshot, Dan had a nearly closed-mouth smile, but if one looked closely, the tips of his fangs showed in the parting of his lips.

"Look," he screamed, pointing at the television. "Don't you see? He's one of them."

Most of the people in the diner gave him strange looks. A few left. The server came over with a to-go cup of coffee. "Sir, your meal's on the house. But we need you to leave. You're disturbing the other diners."

"They should be disturbed. We should all be disturbed. Don't you see? The TV lady didn't even mention his teeth.

He's one of them."

"Sir," she said again, "don't make me call the cops."

"Someone should call the cops. They need to know what happened last night. They have to see the truth."

"I need the table. You have to leave. Now." She slammed the cup down, crossed her arms over her chest, and waited.

But he didn't appear to notice. His eyes remained glued to the screen. "No. Go back. Show the photo. The people need to know. They have to protect themselves."

The men at a nearby table couldn't let his ranting and pointing continue. "Hey, buddy, you don't want to cause any trouble. Do what the lady says and take a hike."

"Trouble's already here. That's why Dan had to die. But that will only slow it down. It won't stop it."

"All right, but we warned you." Three of the men got up from the table. Two of them grabbed him. One took a hold of his arm. The other held on to the back of his jacket and his other shoulder and they walked him to the door. The third man opened it, and they tossed him onto the street. "Get out of here, you freak."

His knees stung from where he landed on the concrete. They had no idea the danger they'd face. They should be begging him to help them. Instead, they thought he was crazy. Everyone did.

Brushing himself off, he decided he had to make sure the police weren't nearly as ignorant as the men inside the diner. It took him most of the day, but he finally figured out where Dan Fielders lived. Before he even approached the apartment door, he could tell dark forces had settled over the place. This was a fortress for the undead.

He tried the door, but it was locked. He knocked several times, his hand curling around the cross inside his pocket. It would protect him from the evil. At least, he hoped it would. He had never been too certain of that, but it only made sense that if these demonic creatures existed, good should also exist.

The door opened, and a woman wearing gloves and booties answered. She gave him a confused look. "May I help you?"

"Is this Dan Fielders' apartment?" he asked.

"Yes," she said, looking at him uncertainly.

"I saw the news. I heard what happened. I had to see for myself."

"Were you close?"

He peered around her, finding the room bathed in an eerie red light. Was this where the gates would open? Was he already too late? Dan had been stopped, but had others been afflicted?

"Sir?" She moved in front of him. "What's your name?"

"He lives strangely. Why is everything red?" He spotted a box on the coffee table with what looked like blood dripping from it. "Is that a human heart?"

"It sure looks like it."

"Then you know. You know all about Dan Fielders. About what he was. Who he was."

"Sir," she reached out to grab a hold of him, but he stepped back, not wanting a repeat of what happened in the diner, even though he was large enough and strong enough to overtake her, "what's your name?"

If she was helping, he wouldn't want to hurt or confuse her. He shook his head. "I didn't mean to bother you. You have much work to do."

"Stop." She chased after him, but he ran to the elevator and slipped between the closing doors.

Relieved that the cops had learned the truth about what Dan was, he relaxed. No one tried to stop him when he stepped into the lobby and headed out of the building. They knew the truth. But they might already be too late. He had to make sure Dan hadn't turned anyone else.

*　　*　　*

The parade of witnesses and potential suspects should have led to something. But it didn't. Even Melanie Daggio couldn't remember exactly who or what she saw the previous night. Regardless, my partner was determined to find a clue, some missing piece, that would lead us to the killer. So far, we had nothing.

The other guests verified the dress Asta gave us had been the one Vivica wore the previous night, but the lab didn't find a single drop of blood on it, which meant it was unlikely Vivica had stabbed her boyfriend. But the murder wasn't random. It happened at a private Halloween party. Random acts of violence required the killer and victim to be strangers, but everyone who attended the party had been acquainted, or at the very least a friend of a friend.

"What about an actual party crasher?" Brad examined the massive amounts of photos we'd collected from the guests, but not a single one captured the killer.

"We already looked into them."

"No, not the ones who heard about it from their friends who'd been invited. I mean an actual party crasher. Someone who just wandered in off the street."

"It's a residential area. How likely is that?"

"What about a neighbor or someone out for a walk? Kelsey said his front door was unlocked. Anyone could have joined in the festivities."

"True, but how many folks carry wooden stakes with them? I thought we were working under the assumption this was premeditated murder."

Brad stopped typing, focusing all of his energy on reshuffling the pieces to fit a different picture. "What if the killer's delusional?"

"Sure, why not?"

He emitted a grumbling sound from deep within his throat, letting me know he didn't enjoy the sarcasm. "Like you keep saying, this time of year brings out the crazies. What if the killer actually believes in the supernatural and paranormal? He might have watched one too many episodes of *Buffy*, figured it'd be best to always be prepared, and walks around armed with garlic, crosses, and stakes."

"I'm guessing we would have heard about it before now."

Brad reached for his notepad. "Dan Fielders had his teeth replaced roughly four months ago. Most of the photos on the sports website are prior to that, but Dan has a few recent pics of him reporting on games and interviewing athletes in the locker room." He spun the computer screen around for me to see. "I haven't seen any shots with a big, cheesy smile, but you can still see his fangs in a few of these images. Maybe one of his less stable followers spotted this, freaked out, and decided to put an end to the undead creature."

"That would mean Dan was being stalked." I didn't necessarily buy it, but each new theory brought new avenues to explore. I reached for the phone. "I'll make sure Mac's keeping an eye out, but I'm sure she would have flagged any suspicious online activity regarding Dan's personal and professional accounts."

"Probably, but it's something else to consider. And at this point, we have to consider everything."

I checked my messages, but we hadn't received any reports on the wooden stake yet. Instead, I brought up a list of Dan's recent transactions, finding several purchases at a local Halloween pop-up boutique. Picking up the phone, I dialed the store and asked if they sold wooden stakes.

"We do."

"Are they a popular item?" I asked.

"They sell okay. Most people prefer silver crosses or those big garlic bulb necklaces. It really depends on the costume. Wooden stakes aren't necessarily as flashy or obvious."

"Do you remember who you sold the stakes too?"

"There've been too many customers."

"What about records? Do you have receipts?"

"We have an old cash register. I enter the price and quantity. That's it."

"All right." I scribbled down the store's address. "How late are you open?"

"We close at six during the week. Eight on weekends."

"Thanks." Before I could suggest that we drop by the shop to ask some questions, Lieutenant Winston left his office and headed for our desks. "Heads-up," I whispered.

Brad let out a sigh and reached for a few files. He planned to escape while he could, but it was already too late.

"Any progress?" Winston hovered over us.

"Not much," I said.

"We're working on it," Brad replied.

Winston made a face like he was trying to work a popcorn kernel free from his back molar. "I just got off the phone. It looks like we caught another weird one. I'm not sure, but it could be connected to the Dan Fielders' case. I didn't get a lot of details, but it has something to do with fangs." The lieutenant placed a slip of paper on top of Brad's keyboard. "That's the address. Officers on the scene said it looks like another vampire killing. You should head over and check it out."

"Great," I mumbled.

"More fangs?" Brad pocketed the address and grabbed his jacket. "Have we looked into the dentist yet?"

"I don't think so," I said.

"I'll take care of that while you're gone." Winston spotted Detective Lisco returning from a coffee run and headed in her direction.

Not wanting to risk receiving further instructions, Brad jerked his chin toward the stairwell and hurried me away from my desk. "How many people do you think have had vampire teeth screwed into their jaws?"

"Dan Fielders makes one, which means there must be more. Hopefully, not a lot more."

"According to Carrie, caps and veneers are pretty common."

"The Halloween shop sells the cheap ones."

"Places that specialize in cosmetic dentistry and things of that nature can take a mold and have custom caps made that fit perfectly and match the rest of the wearer's teeth. Those are a lot more realistic looking."

"Is that what Carrie told you?"

"Among other things."

Now wasn't the time to pry. "I'm guessing the same guy who sold Dan Fielders the expensive implants also provides less committed patients with the cheaper options. You might be on to something."

"Only if we have a second vic who died under similar circumstances." Brad tossed me the keys. "It's your turn to drive. Do you want me to give you directions?"

"What's the address?"

He read it off the sticky note. "It's across from the park."

"I'm familiar." I headed for our destination. "A second murder changes everything."

"Why do you think Winston requested to be looped in on any odd murders? Until now, we've had no reason to think the killer would strike again."

"We had no reason to think he wouldn't," I countered.

"The LT must be psychic. Did you even consider we'd have a second vic to deal with? I sure as hell didn't."

"No, but we haven't been at this job for very long. Winston might do this for every case."

"Or he knows something we don't."

"Brad—"

"I know. The LT is not our enemy."

That reminded me of my private, morning meeting, but I didn't share any additional details with my partner. He had enough on his plate. From the way he fidgeted while keeping his eyes glued to the road ahead, I knew what he was thinking. If we'd worked harder or faster, we might have figured out what was going on in time to stop the killer from striking again.

"Hey," I drew him from his internal musings, "we don't know anything yet. This might not be connected."

"Honestly, Liv, I don't know if that would be a good thing or a bad thing."

"Me neither."

We made the rest of the drive in silence. When I pulled up, I spotted two parked patrol cars on opposite ends of the street. Police tape had already been used to rope off the area. An OCME van was parked nearby. One uniformed cop was taking a statement while another cop made sure no pedestrians contaminated the scene.

Getting out of the car, I flashed my badge at the closest uniform. "Where's the vic?"

He pointed to the bottom of a fire escape between two buildings. The alley behind it was a dead end. "I hope you got your crucifix handy. When she turns, it won't be pretty."

"What?"

"C'mon, Liv. We have actual work to do." Brad glared at

the officer. "Show more respect for the dead."

"You mean soon-to-be undead," the cop muttered.

Brad moved toward him, but I grabbed my partner's arm and tugged him toward the fire escape before he could do something we'd both regret.

"Normally, you tell me to keep my cool. Are you good?" I whispered once we were out of earshot.

"Fine."

"Hey, look at me." I grabbed Brad's wrist and forced him to turn to me. "Whatever we're about to walk into isn't your fault. It's not my fault. We do our jobs to the best of our abilities. When we have nothing to work with, the only way we can move forward is with more evidence. If this is a second victim, we'll get more evidence. And we will get this guy."

"Yeah."

"Yeah," I said emphatically. "Chill. I don't need you to hulk out on me. You're the calm, level-headed one that everybody likes. Remember that."

"They like you too."

"Roberts doesn't. Nicolo doesn't." I started to name more officers who liked to talk trash about me in the locker rooms, but Brad nudged me with his elbow.

"I thought you wanted me to chill out and be nice. You're making that rather difficult."

"Sorry."

"They should be."

Taking a breath, I approached the body. Jacob, the coroner's assistant, and Ellie, a member of CSU, were crouched over the victim. Upon hearing our approach, Ellie looked up. Her face brightened.

"Hey, Brown Eyes." She stood up and wiped her gloved hands on the legs of her coveralls.

"Hey, Ellie." Brad actually smiled. "Do I want to know?"

"Probably not. But that's why you're here. Y'know, you should pay me a visit sometime when it doesn't involve a body." She turned her attention to me. "The same goes for you, sister. They keep me locked away in the mobile lab most of the time. I miss the outside world."

"We'll do better," I promised, stepping closer. "So what

do we have here?"

"Female victim, late twenties. Her prints aren't in the system. No wallet or phone, so making an ID will take some time. As you can see, she appears to have been dressed for a costume party. I'd say she's either a saloon girl or tavern maiden."

"What's the difference?" I asked.

The victim had on a white, off the shoulder top beneath a brown vest that laced up the front. She wore a two-tiered skirt. The top layer was brown, the bottom green, which fell to her ankles over brown boots.

"About fifteen dollars." Ellie read the confused looks on our faces. "The costumes sell at different prices."

"Do you know who sells this one?" Brad asked.

Ellie shook her head. "I was just making a joke. I didn't realize it was a serious question."

"It's okay." Brad squatted down beside her. "The last twenty-four hours have been a little rough."

"I'm sorry to hear that, sugar." She gave him a one-armed hug while they stared down at the dead woman. "I'd guess she'd agree with your statement."

"What killed her?" My eyes locked on the trail of blood coating her neck and chest and pooling out around her.

Jacob pointed to the two puncture marks, approximately two inches apart. "Her jugular was perforated. She bled out here."

Ellie spun on her heels, keeping one hand on Brad's shoulder to maintain her balance while she pointed to the opposite wall. "It's weird there isn't any arterial spray."

"What about the murder weapon?" Brad slipped on a glove and asked if he could touch the body before turning the victim's head to the side and brushing the matted hair out of the way.

My stomach turned just as a bowling ball dropped onto my chest. My body flooded with heat, but cold shivers ran down my spine. *Breathe.* I forced a slow, deep breath into my lungs and turned to look in the other direction. The bright yellow police tape looked cheery compared to everything else.

"I found that at the top of her costume." Jacob pointed

to an evidence bag hanging out of Ellie's kit.

Ellie fished it out and handed it to Brad.

"What is it?" he asked. Even though my back was to him, I could feel my partner's eyes on me.

"It's a porcelain cap. Given the distance of the two punctures, this could be half of the murder weapon.

"Is it sharp enough?" I asked.

"I wouldn't think so, but the scene suggests otherwise," Jacob said.

"It is rather jagged." Ellie examined it closer. "It could have broken or the wearer filed it to a sharp edge. I'd say whoever killed this woman bit her while wearing it."

"Like a vampire?" Brad asked.

"Vampires don't exist," Jacob said matter-of-factly.

"Tavern maidens are always getting attacked by vampires. Well, the vamps go for the prostitutes first, then the tavern maidens, but you get the point." Ellie stared down at the body. "I don't know who would do something like this. But whoever this asshole is, he must have a screw loose."

"Or he's fanatical about Halloween." I exhaled slowly, feeling some of the tension drain from my body. When I turned back around, Brad was beside me.

"Are you okay?" he whispered so quietly only I could hear him. He knew neck injuries and blood loss could trigger me at inopportune times.

"Fine, now."

But he pushed his own issues aside and took the lead, so I could sit this one out, if I needed to. "Okay, so we don't know who this woman is, but you're telling me she was killed by someone wearing vampire fangs."

"It looks that way," Ellie said.

"I don't know," Jacob hedged. "That seems implausible, but who knows? If he bit her, the assailant would have been covered in blood. I'd hope someone would have noticed."

"Not if they thought it was part of his costume," Brad said.

Joining the others, I examined the torn sleeve on the victim's dress and the red marks on her arms. "She fought."

"Or she ran." Jacob turned her palms to show me the scrapes. "It looks like she fell around here. Her knees are also bruised. Given the angle of the punctures, he would have come at her from the side or possibly behind."

"When did this happen?" Brad asked.

"Around lunchtime," Ellie said. "That's when 9-1-1 received an anonymous call about a woman in the alley. The caller reported screams."

"Liv, find out if either of these apartment buildings have security cameras. Then check with the ice cream shop on the corner. More than likely, she lives in one of these buildings or knows someone who does."

ELEVEN

I watched the footage play on the screen. The victim and a man she appeared rather fond of had been rounding the bases, only a few short minutes away from sliding into home when they'd been interrupted. A cloaked figure appeared on the feed, his back to the camera. He had something in his right hand, but I couldn't quite figure out what it was. The cloaked figure stood in front of the amorous couple for a full minute without either of them acknowledging him.

Without warning, he grabbed the man by the back of his neck and yanked him off of the woman and slammed him into the brick wall. The man appeared dazed, his face flushed from the intense kissing. He brought his palms up just as the cloaked figure struck him in the stomach. The man doubled over, and the woman screamed.

She jumped off the step and launched herself at the cloaked figure. He batted her away with his free hand. She stumbled sideways and landed on all fours. That's probably when her palms got scraped and her knees bruised. I made a note of the timestamp, figuring it would save time when we started dissecting the feed at the precinct.

The woman screamed, begging the cloaked figure to

stop. He turned to her and said something, but the camera didn't record sound. Did she know the attacker?

The cloaked figure pointed to the street, urging her to leave. Instead, she scrambled over to her partner. The attacker backhanded her this time, causing her to drop to the side. She clutched her neck, but the attacker didn't even turn to look at her. He lifted his hand to strike, the two jagged spikes of the metal cross stuck out between his gloved knuckles. I paused the feed, seeing the blood where it left a wet spray against the attacker's glove and cloak. That's what killed her.

My finger twitched over the button. I didn't want to see him kill someone else, but we only found one body. I had to find out what happened to her partner.

I hit play. The man on the ground rolled to the side, getting his feet underneath him before the killer could strike again. The man ran out of the alley and back to the street. The cloaked figure didn't waste a beat before following behind.

"Make a copy of this," I said. "Do you have any cameras set up at the front of the building? I need to see that feed too."

The apartment manager changed views to another camera. "This is the only other exterior camera we have."

I kept my eyes glued to the screen as I matched the timestamp. From the way the male victim moved, I could tell he was injured. That explained why the killer didn't rush to chase him. The injured man tried to stop traffic, to get someone to help, but no one came to his aid. He stumbled in front of cars as he crossed the street. When he made it to the other side, he headed for the ice cream shop.

Five feet from the door, the killer caught up to him and shoved him into an alleyway. The camera didn't reach that far. I fast-forwarded, but no one emerged. Could the killer still be there?

"We need copies of the footage you have from this afternoon. An officer will collect it." I didn't wait for a response before I exited the lobby. "Fennel," I called, keeping one eye on the killer's last known location, "I found something."

My partner excused himself from the witnesses he had found and jogged over to meet me. "Did you watch the security footage?"

I filled him in as we crossed the street. "I don't think he has a gun, but I can't be sure. Either way, he's dangerous."

Brad drew his weapon, signaling that he'd go first. "Police." He entered, pointing to the sign *No thru-traffic.* "Come out with your hands up." He took a few more steps, but the killer was long gone.

He continued to the end of the alley, glancing up at the raised fire escapes as he passed each of them. I tugged on the side doors, but they were locked. With all the dirt, I didn't see an obvious blood trail. Ellie would have better luck finding one. I approached the next door, stopping at the macabre scene.

I knelt next to the man I recognized from the security footage as our first victim's adamant make-out buddy and pressed my fingers against his neck. Nothing. I placed my fingers close to his nose and mouth, but he wasn't breathing. Given the temperature of his skin, he'd been dead as long as his partner.

"Radio the others. We have a second crime scene."

Brad finished scouting the alley, making sure it was safe before returning to my position. "That's not a stake."

"No, it's a silver cross." I pointed to the sharp spikes which decorated the t-bar to make it look dangerous and scary. "It's what killed them both."

The jagged metal had been shoved through the man's chest, just like the wooden stake had been impaled through Dan Fielders. I tugged on a pair of gloves and gently lifted the victim's upper lip to reveal the other veneer. "He didn't bite her," I said. "From the footage I saw, they appeared rather intimate."

"And the killer?" Brad searched the victim's pockets.

"I don't know."

He pulled out the wallet and opened it. "Roger Stevens. He lives in the apartment building where we found the first vic." Brad scanned the contents of the wallet. "He has two tickets for the haunted hayride tonight."

"Haunted hayride?"

"The one the inn puts on every year. It circles the park and follows along the path of one of those ghost tours."

I gave him a bewildered look. "What inn?"

"C'mon, DeMarco, you know which inn. The one that advertises it's haunted. They do this huge Halloween bash every year. People have to book their rooms eighteen months in advance if they want to stay during the month of October." He dropped the wallet into an evidence bag. "I wonder if he had reservations?"

"What are you doing?" Ellie asked, startling us. "Don't touch that. You're going to make my job harder."

Brad held up his palms. "We're good. I have gloves."

She glanced at me before zeroing in on the body. She made the sign of the cross. "That looks painful."

"Fatal," I corrected.

Another patrol car arrived. Brad and I went to update the officers while Ellie marked the scene and prepared it for evidence collection. Jacob loaded the first victim into the back of the van before joining us at the second crime scene.

While he prepared the body for transport, I called the station to update them on the situation. By the time I got off the phone, Brad had instructed the officers to expand the search radius and start a larger canvass. I gave them a description of what the killer was last seen wearing. By now, he could be anywhere.

"His palms are cut too," Jacob said, "and his knuckles are scraped. He must have put up a fight. We might be able to pull some DNA, or maybe find a hair or other trace. Ellie, you'll want to bag his hands for transport so we don't lose anything."

"The killer caught him by surprise. He tried to escape, to go for help, but you know how people are. They didn't do a damn thing," I said.

"He's wearing a cape," Jacob pointed out. "And fangs. They probably didn't believe him or thought he was some kind of freak."

"They might have been afraid," Ellie said. "I would have been freaked out, but I still would have tried to help."

"You're trained." Jacob frowned at the victim's tattered

shirt front. "The killer stabbed him before he impaled him." Carefully, he unbuttoned the victim's shirt and moved it aside, finding the fabric stiff and uncooperative due to the dried blood. Large scratch marks had shredded the victim's abdomen. "Whoa."

"The killer held the cross in his hand with his knuckles spread so the spikes could stick out from between his fingers. He hit him like that a few times. It's how the female vic got the punctures in her neck," I said.

"I'll be damned." Jacob held the victim's shirt open while Ellie took several photographs.

"That's how they teach women to hold their keys in self-defense classes. Do you think there's something to that?" Ellie asked.

I didn't think so. "Any idea where they sell sharp, spiky crosses?"

Ellie shook her head.

"I'd guess the same place they sell wooden stakes." Brad took off his gloves and tucked them away. "Do what you can. In the meantime, Liv and I are going to see what we can learn about the killer and his victims."

I followed my partner out of the alley, glad for the warm sunshine on this crisp autumn day. The dual crime scenes left me chilled. The killer acted in broad daylight, and no one did a damn thing, just like the vampire hunter who murdered Dan Fielders in the middle of a private party.

"Do you think it's the same guy?" I asked.

"The killer?" Brad headed for the ice cream shop, but his eyes took in every single thing on the block. "It could be. The weapon's different, so I don't know for sure."

"I don't think he meant to kill the woman. He knocked her out of the way. I don't think he intended to stab her. He didn't even give her a second look after it happened."

"What are you thinking? Jealous lover?" Brad pulled open the door and held it for me. At this time of day, the ice cream parlor was empty. It was too early for dessert and too late for an afternoon treat.

"Possibly."

He flashed his badge at the teenager behind the counter. "Were you here at noon?"

"No," she looked anxious, "I start work at four."

"Was your manager here?" Brad asked.

She nodded. "Hey, Terry, there are a couple of cops out here who want to talk to you."

Terry looked like a burnt-out soccer mom. Her graying hair was pulled into a messy ponytail, and her fingertips were discolored from smoking too many cigarettes. "Is there a problem?"

"You could say that." Brad eyed the teenager. "We should speak privately."

"Bethany, go in the back and finish counting the topping containers. You know where the reorder sheet is, right?"

"Sure." The teenager walked away, glancing back at us before grabbing her phone and rapid-fire texting.

"What's going on?" Terry asked.

"Do you remember seeing Roger Stevens trying to enter your shop around lunchtime?" I described what he had been wearing.

"No, but we always have a line at that time." She patted her pockets, as if looking for a pen, took out her pack of cigarettes, remembered where she was, and tucked them into the front pocket of her apron. "I know Roger. Did something happen to him?"

"How do you know him?" Brad asked.

"He comes in here a lot. I see him and Cassie at least twice a week. He always gets a hot fudge sundae topped with strawberries, and she gets the white chocolate raspberry swirl with rainbow sprinkles."

"When's the last time you saw them?" I asked.

"Uh...Monday. They stopped by after dinner for something sweet."

"Are they a couple?" I asked.

"Engaged, I think. Or maybe they just got married. They've been coming here for years now. If they weren't so adorable, it'd be a little sickening how sweet they are on each other."

"I hate to ask, but do you know if either of them was seeing anyone else?"

Terry looked as if she'd just been slapped. "No way."

"What about enemies? Did you ever hear them mention

any problems or see anyone threaten them?"

"No."

Brad pulled up a photo he'd taken of the female victim. Narrowing in on her face, so most of the carnage was off screen, he held it out to Terry. "Do you know this woman?"

"That's Cassie."

"Do you know her last name?"

"Hang on." She went to the register and tapped on the touchscreen. After scrolling, she came up with a name. "Dunfrey. Like I said, they were last here on Monday at 7:42. She paid. They like to alternate."

"Was that the last time they came here?" I asked.

Even though Terry already answered that question, she double-checked. "As far as I know, unless they paid cash. And they never pay with cash." She peered out the window. "You're telling me that this afternoon someone killed Rog right outside my shop. Have you talked to Cassie yet? Does she know what happened to him?"

"They were together," Brad said. "Do you know if they had any plans this week? When we found them, they were dressed in Halloween costumes."

"That's right." Terry came around the counter and sat down. The conversation had made her rethink her stance on having this conversation at one of the tables. "Cassie was so excited. She had booked a room for them at the haunted inn for the entire week. They were going to do all the attractions, the hayride, maze, the walking tour, the ghost museum, all of it. It was their staycation." Her hands shook as she reached to refill the napkin holder. "I didn't know them that well. We only spoke on the slow nights, but they were nice people. Sometimes, they'd sit at that table," she pointed to the one near the window, "until I closed up. Then they'd put their chairs on top of the table, leave a tip in the jar, and go home." She shook her head. "I'm going to miss them."

"Have you ever had any problems with anyone else?" I asked. "Break-ins? Robberies? Anything like that?"

"No."

"What about fights, altercations, arguments?" Brad focused his attention on her. "Has anyone suspicious ever stepped foot inside your shop?"

"Plenty of weirdos come here, but I don't recall anyone dangerous."

"How weird?" I asked.

"How long is a piece of string?" Terry adjusted the napkin holder. "None of them ever made me want to call the cops, so I wasn't too worried."

"Did you ever notice anyone dressed as a vampire hunter or in a Van Helsing costume?" Brad showed her a mock-up of our suspect from the Dan Fielders' murder.

"No."

"What about a guy wearing black leather and carrying a silver cross?"

She shook her head.

"Carrying a wooden stake?"

Terry laughed, as if we were joking. "No. The only people who've come here dressed in costumes have been little kids, pre-teen and under. Everyone else has been dressed normally. Give it another week, and I'm sure that will change, but it's still too early in the season to get the drunks craving ice cream after leaving a party or wanting to stop by before going to one." She rubbed her mouth and stared out the window at the police tape and vehicles. "I can't believe Rog and Cassie are dead. This is a fucked up world we live in."

"Yes, ma'am." Brad copied down her information and left her his card, asking her to call if she happened to remember anything.

TWELVE

He couldn't remember exactly how he'd gotten home. Most of his day had turned into a blur. Work, he remembered that. The still wet blood clung to the black leather. It belonged to the couple.

He hadn't intended for that to happen. In fact, he'd been on his way home. But there they were. So passionate and alive. They were practically fornicating in the street.

All he wanted was for them to stop. He tried to move past, but he just couldn't. Something had forced him to stop and watch, almost like a trainwreck or ten-car pileup. Seeing them like that caused him actual physical pain, like a stabbing in his gut and sucking wound in his chest, as if his very soul was being ripped from his body.

At first, he tried to be polite. He cleared his throat, but they hadn't even noticed. No one ever noticed him. He was practically invisible, a fixture that no one listened to or saw unless they wanted something from him. And when they finally did see him, it was too late.

The outfits were more than enough, but then there was also the teeth. The man had practically been devouring her. Now he couldn't do that to anyone else. The woman should have run, gone inside, walked away, whatever. It wouldn't have mattered. He hadn't intended to harm her. But she wouldn't go. She tried to stop him. That's when he pushed her.

Shaking away the thought, he grabbed the container of bleach from under the sink and stepped into the shower fully clothed. He turned on the water and stepped under the spray, watching the rivers of red run down the drain, then he opened the bleach, poured it onto his loofah sponge and scrubbed the leather. After rinsing it again under the spray, he removed his clothes, hung them on the rack to dry, and cleaned himself. This couldn't happen again. He had to maintain control. He had to be more careful. He only hurt them because they were hurting him. It was self-defense. They had to be stopped.

*   *   *

By the time Brad and I returned to the precinct, Lt. Winston had dug deeper into the Dan Fielders' case, but nothing had surfaced. He and Detective Lisco had gone to pay the dentist a visit and did some arm-twisting to get a list of names of people who'd recently had Halloween-inspired cosmetic dentistry procedures. It was a short list.

"Only two other people had permanent vampire teeth installed," Lt. Winston said. "Lisco and I spoke to both of them. No one's made any threats or tried to kill them, but I told them to be careful since we have a vampire hunter on the loose."

"Do you think they're connected to Fielders?" I asked.

"Neither links to him or anyone else who attended Kelsey Eldridge's party."

"What about to the sports network where Dan worked?"

"Nope."

"How about ties to Vivica Smaldey or that bar she went to after leaving the party?" Brad asked.

"Lisco's still looking, but she hasn't reported any findings to me."

I turned to Brad. "The bar?"

My partner shrugged. "It could lead to something. It's the only place we know she went after leaving the party but before arriving at her friend's house."

"Do you still think Fielders' girlfriend is involved in his murder?" Winston asked.

"I don't know," I said.

Brad considered the question. "Right now, it looks like no one from Dan's life could have done this, but we're missing something. He had a wooden stake through a beating heart on his coffee table. I find it hard to believe that's a coincidence given the way he died."

"What about the crime scene you just left?" Winston asked. "Is there anything to that? Any connection I should know about?"

Brad briefed him on what we found. "I don't know, sir. It's too soon to say."

"They were in costume," I said. "The victims, Roger Stevens and his wife, Cassie. The attack occurred outside the apartment building where they lived. From the footage I watched, it appears they were heading out, got a little carried away, and headed for the fire escape for some privacy. The killer came out of nowhere, so I don't know if he was watching them or if he happened to walk up on them. But given his cloak, I'd say the attack was planned. He didn't want to be recognized."

"A cross is an odd weapon of choice," Winston muttered.

"It wasn't a real cross. It's another Halloween decoration. Given the size, it's probably a lawn ornament of some sort," Brad said. "Probably a scene setter for a cemetery."

"Are there any Halloween shops in the vicinity?" Winston asked.

"None that we noticed."

"Any idea where the killer escaped to?"

"We're still working on it," Brad said. "We searched the two crime scenes and left CSU to piece together whatever forensic evidence we might have missed. Liv and I spoke to everyone in the apartment building, but no one recalls the couple having any issues with anyone else. They were newlyweds. Cassie only moved in with Roger a few weeks ago. She hadn't even had the name on her license or credit cards changed yet. According to everyone we spoke to, they were blissfully happy. The perfect couple. The perfect neighbors. And the perfect tenants."

"Then you better figure out why someone killed them." Winston glanced at the door. "It's October. The city can't afford a bunch of whackadoos deciding it's open season on vampires. Every other person dresses up as one, and the last thing I want to deal with is more bodies dropping." He exhaled. "Find out if it's the same guy who offed Dan Fielders. One nutjob on the loose is bad enough, but two is a whole other story."

"When we figure it out, I'll let you know." Brad went to the door and held it open. "You coming, Liv?"

I watched the lieutenant for a moment, wondering if he'd make a comment that he hadn't dismissed us, but he went back to whatever he'd been doing before we entered his office. "Yeah, I'm coming."

Before I even made it back to my desk, Brad went into the conference room, grabbed one of the unused corkboards, and wheeled it over to me. "I say we focus our energy on the Stevenses' murders. They're fresh and new. It happened in broad daylight. Our chances of finding eyewitnesses and security footage are greatest right now."

"I agree."

"Great." He grabbed the stack of sticky notes from his desk and a sharpie, scribbled down the victims' names and stuck them to the board. "Let's see if we can track down our killer. Do you want to take the footage or the murder weapon?"

"Murder weapon." The last thing I wanted was to watch the happy couple get slaughtered again. Hopefully, neither of us would have to replay that footage, but I'd avoid it if I could. "I'll head to the crime lab and see if they have anything for me."

"I'll get started on parsing through the footage to determine where the killer went when he exited the alleyway."

The crime lab hadn't gotten anything done yet. Ellie had returned with the evidence she'd collected, but everything was still being catalogued. Paperwork, it was the bane of our existence.

I watched as the techs removed the various bags from the box, recorded the item, signed the form on the bag, and took custody of the evidence for further examination. When I spotted the murder weapon, I hovered closer to Ellie.

"When I told you to visit, I didn't mean this soon," she said.

"We need to find this guy. Identifying where he bought that is our first step." She'd already taken several photos of it. "I was hoping it had some kind of serial number or price tag on it."

She examined it carefully through the plastic. "I see an etching here, but it doesn't look like a serial number. Maybe a lot number. It's four digits. 2163."

I jotted that on my notepad. "Can you take some measurements? I'll start calling around to see who sells these things."

She reached for the measuring tape. "It's twelve inches by eight and a half."

The sharp spikes ran along the top and bottom of the cross bar at two inch intervals, leaving two spikes on either side of the center steel piece. The bottom of the cross was sharp and shaped like an arrowhead. The once silver metal now appeared red.

"Do you think it's a Halloween decoration?" I asked.

"What else would it be?"

"I don't know. Maybe a religious zealot doesn't care for people dressing as undead creatures or copulating in the open."

Ellie considered that for a moment. "Y'know, I heard about a series of murders that happened a few years back along the same lines, but the killings were ritualistic. The killer had tried to cleanse his victims and save their souls. They had an entire lecture dedicated to it at one of the forensic science conferences I attended." She handed me the bag, so I could get a better look at the cross. "This doesn't read like that to me, but I'm not a detective. I just analyze the evidence. You piece it together however it fits."

I put the evidence bag down. "Any idea what cloaked figure carries a cross like this and kills vampires?"

"Is that a riddle?"

"Our killer from the Halloween party the other night allegedly dressed as Van Helsing. I just wondered who this guy might be."

"You ever see the movie with the priests?"

"Is that with Meryl Streep?"

"No, it's about a group of soldiers, men of the cloth, who wage a crusade against vampires."

"Great. If it's the same killer, he's a damn movie buff."

"That might be a start." Ellie shrugged. "You should ask your partner about it. He loves all those creature movies. He dragged me to a werewolf double-feature one year. It was actually kind of fun. We loaded up on junk food and hung out all night. Of course, that was back when I had a life of my own, before the hubby and kids came into the picture."

"Brad ate junk food?"

She laughed. "Well, his version. I made the sacrifice by throwing myself between him and the popcorn, licorice twists, and candy coated chocolates. For that, he owes me his life."

"I'm sure he appreciated it."

"I know I did." She winked. "He paid."

After leaving the crime lab, I returned to my desk, searched for the murder weapon, and found the manufacturer. Only six shops sold those metal crosses. Luckily, Ellie was right. The four digits etched on the metal were a lot number. "I figured out where the killer bought the murder weapon."

"Do you think this shop keeps better records than the one that sold the wooden stake?" Brad asked.

"I'm about to find out."

THIRTEEN

Instead of a bell, a sinister laugh sounded the moment I pushed open the door. That had to be annoying for the workers. But the man behind the counter didn't even notice. He was swamped with customers. A line, seven deep, waited to checkout. Two other people were on the side, vying for his attention to ask questions. One of them held up a cat costume and pointed vehemently toward one of the aisles while he attempted to answer her question while counting out the correct change for the woman who'd just purchased a cauldron, table cover, and place setting for eighteen.

Two other employees, identifiable only by the black aprons and name tags they wore, tried to help out by fielding as many questions as they could while unpacking boxes and restocking shelves. I wandered through the crowd, scanning for security cameras. I counted four. One on the front door, another on the register, and two dark globes posted on the ceiling which probably monitored for shoplifters.

Costumes hung in rectangular pouches from pegboards on both sides of the first aisle. Coordinating accessories were tucked in the bins directly beneath them. I examined each one, hoping to find an outfit that matched the cloak our killer wore today or the leather coat and hat the killer had worn the previous night. But these costumes were too cheaply made.

"Hey," a woman grabbed my shoulder, practically forcing me to turn around, "where'd you get that?"

"What?"

She pointed to the badge hanging from a chain around my neck. "That."

"My badge?"

"Yeah. I haven't seen anything like that except these." She held up a shiny, mustard-colored star.

I unclipped it and flipped it open, showing her my photo ID. "Mine came from the city."

"That doesn't help me any. I must have gone to every shop, looking for something more realistic than this. My man was right. I'm gonna have to see what I can find at a pawn shop."

I raised an eyebrow, noticing the overflowing shopping cart beside her. Bleeding candles, bats, black cats, spiders, zombies, and clowns threatened to spill over the top if she wasn't careful. "It looks like you've scoured every inch of this place."

"And I found some damn good stuff, just not these." She tossed the cheap badges back into the bin.

"Have you seen any spiky metal crosses or wooden stakes?"

She stood on her tiptoes and craned her neck to the side. "Two aisles over. The crosses are on the endcap, near the high-end priest and nun costumes and the outdoor decorations."

"And the stakes?" I asked.

She pointed to one of the nearby bins. "They're near the bottom. You gotta dig."

"Thanks."

She gave me a confused look, probably wondering why a cop was walking around a Halloween store. Shaking it off, she joined the ever-growing line of customers waiting to pay for their purchases.

The stakes she pointed out weren't nearly as long or

sturdy as the murder weapon used to kill Dan Fielders, but I didn't expect them to be. As far as I knew, only one shop sold those particular stakes.

I headed for the display the woman had pointed out. The endcap contained dozens of different crosses, everything from pseudo-crucifixes to elaborate, ornate yard decorations. But I didn't see any that matched this afternoon's murder weapon. I scanned the shelves and pegboard again, pushing the crosses to the side to make sure the spiky one wasn't stocked behind something else.

"Are you looking for something in particular?" a guy asked as he slid a metal hook into the slot and started hanging oversized rosaries.

"I'm Detective DeMarco." I lifted the chain on my neck, not bothering to flip it open to show him everything. "I called earlier."

"Right. Right." He finished with the rosaries and used a box cutter to slice open a box labeled gravestone lights. "You wanted to know about the graveyard stakes." He led me down the next aisle, past the skeleton hands and the red zombie eyes. "What was the lot number?"

"Two-one-six-three."

He scanned the hooks with his finger before finding an empty one. "Of course they're sold out." He rolled his eyes. "We got a box of them in the back if you want to see 'em."

"Please."

I followed him through the door labeled *Do Not Enter* in giant, scary writing. The storeroom appeared to be just as large as the front-end of the shop. He didn't even have to read the labels on the rows of boxes to locate the crosses. Again, he handled the box cutter with practiced ease.

"Is this it?" He took one out and handed it to me.

I found it just as heavy and cumbersome as the one which had been removed from Stevens' chest.

"That's the one." I curled my fingers around the top, finding the grip awkward. "What are these extra spikes for?"

He fished something else out of the box. "Additional adornments. These slide right over the spikes, giving the appearance of crows or bats or spiders." He sifted through the contents. "We also got skulls and mini coffins." He held out a bag with the metal shapes. "See?"

I took a metal crow and slid it down the spike, careful not to prick my finger on the sharp edges. "These don't seem safe."

"They're probably not, but by the time we get the safety recall notice, Halloween will be over. Then it won't matter."

"I'm not sure everyone feels that way."

"Probably not, but they're selling like crazy. People are all into special effects."

"These don't seem that special."

"If you place them in front of a light source, they project a large shadow on a wall. It's actually kind of cool."

I rocked back on my heels, holding the cross in front of me. "How many of these have you sold?"

He kicked the box. "Ten per case. We got one, two," he pointed to the empty boxes piled behind the opened one, "three. So it looks like thirty, so far. Well, twenty-nine. We have one on display behind the counter. A lot of people have said how happy they are to find something they can stick in the ground and window boxes easily. Most of the other stuff is plastic. These are much sturdier."

"They aren't part of a costume?"

"No, but I guess you could use it like that if you fastened a chain around it. Why do the police care about these anyway?"

"One of these crosses was used to stab someone in the chest."

His mouth fell open. "No joke?"

"No, sir."

"Shit." He stared at the sharp edge and cringed. "That must have hurt."

"I need to know who purchased these."

"We'll do our best, but you're probably looking at thirty different people."

"Twenty-nine," I reminded him. "And maybe a few of them bought more than one."

"Possibly." He stared at the boxes piled up around us, lost in his thoughts.

"Sir," I read the name on his tag, "Bill, would you mind

pulling those records for me?"

He shook himself. "Right. Sorry."

I followed him back into the shop, where the crowd seemed to have multiplied in the last five minutes. He slid behind the counter and logged in to the second register. I positioned myself in front of him before the woman lugging around a shopping basket while struggling to keep her toddler in tow could attempt to jump the line. Unfortunately, murder trumped decency. It always did.

Bill entered the item number and waited. "It appears only twenty-four crosses were sold." He looked at the graveyard display on the table behind him. "We're missing five."

"Five what?" Glenn, the other cashier, asked.

Bill held up the cross. "Do you know where they might be?"

"Check the hold section. Someone might be coming back for a few of them."

Bill looked at me. "Just one second." He peered into the bins behind the counter before opening another door which led to a back room. From where I stood, it looked like the manager's office. Several bags were piled together in the corner with names taped to the front. Bill peered into each one, finding two more crosses.

"I don't know where the other three could have gone." He returned to the desk and hit a few keys.

"I'll take what you have," I said. "It'll help." Unless the killer stole the murder weapon. I turned my focus skyward, narrowing in on one of the cameras. "It'd really help if I could get copies of your surveillance footage too."

Bill glanced at Glenn. "Are we allowed to do that?"

Glenn looked at me. "You got cause?"

"I'm trying to identify a killer."

"That's good enough for me." Glenn jerked his head toward the manager's office. "Give her what she wants. It's the right thing to do."

Bill looked uncertain, but he did what Glenn said. Given the similar outfits they wore, I wasn't sure who was in charge. But it didn't matter. Their compliance saved me the trouble of getting a warrant.

Bill handed me the printouts as the machine spit them out. It included the purchase information, along with the date and time. Finally, something solid.

When he stepped away from the register, a collective groan sounded behind me. The customers weren't happy, which was crucial to a successful business, but not a single one of them stormed out in protest. Perhaps, they didn't want to make a scene while a member of the law enforcement community was in a position to intervene, but more than likely, it was because they desperately wanted the items they had braved the packed store to buy. And I thought Christmas was overly commercialized.

Following Bill into the manager's office, I watched as he examined the tower which housed the hard drives for the cameras. "Is something wrong?" I asked.

"Um...the footage is in there." A screen, divided into four parts, showed the current feed. "I'm not sure how to go backward or make a copy, but if you can figure it out, it's yours."

Permission was all I needed. I'd collected footage enough to know how it was done. After accessing the logs, I copied the files. "I know you're busy, but would you mind answering a few more questions?"

"As long as it keeps me from having to go back out there, I'll answer anything you want."

I cracked a smile. "Okay." I described the cloak the killer had worn. "Do you sell anything like that? I didn't see anything in the costume section."

"You weren't looking in the right place. We keep the premium costumes on the other side of the store, so we can see who's looking at them and trying them on from the register." He bit his bottom lip. "A black cloak, huh? Did he also have a top hat?"

"No."

"All right. That eliminates our Jack the Ripper costume."

"This was more like a hooded thing. Something a monk or priest might wear."

"And he carried a silver cross. That sounds like one of our Jesuit costumes or a Crusader costume. Did the cloak have any symbols or writing on the front, like a Templar Cross?"

The security cams hadn't gotten a good look at the killer's front, only his back. "I don't know."

Reluctantly, Bill led me out of the office. He selected the costumes off the rack and held them up. Unlike the others, these were on hangers, not shoved into plastic bags. But none of the costumes matched what I'd seen on the video. They weren't cut the right way. Desperate, I texted Brad, requesting a single frame from the apartment building's surveillance camera.

"Like this." I showed Bill the cloaked figure.

"That's actually part of a vampire warrior costume, but we don't sell those here. I saw them in the catalog." Before I could ask to see it, he grabbed the thick magazine from behind the desk and opened it to the proper page. "There you go."

It looked just like what the killer wore, but the item beside it also caught my eye. "What about that one? Do you sell that here?"

"No. Van Helsing's not a popular character this year."

"Do you mind if I take this too?" I studied the front of the book, making sure I had the information memorized in case Bill said no.

"I don't care, just don't tell anyone I gave that to you."

"Thanks."

With everything in hand, I headed back to work. At every red light, I'd turn and study the catalog page. Costumes from that catalog had been worn during the murder this afternoon and the one last night. That couldn't be a coincidence. But I wasn't sure what it meant. Could the same man have bought different costumes to wear to commit the crimes? Did he work at the factory or a store that sold the costumes? Had the killer been shopping at a Halloween store when he stumbled upon Halloween fanatics, like Fielders and Stevens, gotten into some kind of argument, and decided to get revenge? Road rage could be ugly. Who knew what costume rage looked like? But my guess was a stake to the heart wouldn't be much of a stretch.

FOURTEEN

"Did you get anything off the footage?" I asked.

"Besides a headache?" Brad rolled his shoulders back and hit a few keys. "I found him four blocks away from where the alley opened up. He headed east. But we lose him once he's out of camera range."

"What about other cameras?"

"I couldn't find him." He played the footage. "As far as I can tell, despite the blood on his outfit, no one gave him a second look. The canvass didn't turn up anything either."

"What about the K-9 unit?"

"They lost his trail faster than I did. Too many people. Too many scents."

I dropped into my chair. "It's a good thing I found something." I showed him the catalog and the cross. "It's not meant to be part of a costume. It's just a decoration." I told him everything I'd learned from Bill. "Take a look at this."

"Shit." Brad studied the catalog carefully. "That has to be what Dan Fielders' killer wore. Do you think they're working together?"

"Possibly, or we're looking at one guy."

"Why would he buy two costumes?"

"In case one got dirty or bloody." I swallowed. "If one guy committed these murders, let's hope he only bought two costumes." I leafed through the catalog for a phone number. "The Halloween shop that sold the killer's cross didn't have either of these for sale."

"But they had the cross. What about the stake used to kill Fielders?" Brad asked.

"It didn't come from there. Only one shop sells those particular wooden stakes."

Brad pulled up the list of Halloween shops Dan Fielders had visited. "That shop is halfway across town from this one." He called the shop to find out if they had either of the costumes in stock. When he hung up, he shook his head. "It looks like our killer or killers support several different Halloween shops."

"Let's find out which ones." I handed Brad the receipts for the cross purchases and called the number I found printed in the catalog.

"Costumes 'N More. To place a bulk order, press one. To check the status of your order, press two." I entered the url while I waited for the automated menu to give me an option that would enable me to speak to a living person. "For questions, press 8." The screen before me opened with a flash of lightning, followed by a cackling witch. That must have been the sound of the year. The website didn't offer much. It showed an array of costumes, accessories, and decorations, all of which linked to requesting a catalog for bulk sales and offered a few details on wholesale distribution. "An operator will be with you shortly." The hold music played *The Monster Mash* while I searched for a list of places to shop. No dice.

"This is Daryl. May I have your name?"

"This is Detective Liv Demarco." I gave him my badge number, in case he needed to verify my identity. "I have a few questions about the costumes in your catalog."

"Which catalog is that?"

I read the volume number to him. "Suspects in two recent homicides were seen wearing the vampire warrior costume and a Van Helsing costume from your catalog. They're on page 73. I need to know who bought them."

"We don't do direct sales to individuals. We sell to retail stores for distribution. Excess stock gets sold off to the chain bargain shops at the end of the season."

"Who sells these particular costumes?" If they'd turned into bargain basement finds, this would be another dead end.

"Let me check. Hang on one moment."

I held my breath, hoping for good news.

"All right. It looks like those are still in our current inventory. They've only been sold to two stores. Witches on East Avenue and Howls-R-Us."

"When?"

"The orders were placed six weeks ago. We fulfilled them on the twelfth."

"Almost a month ago?"

"Yes."

"Who placed the orders?"

"Aside from the store names and addresses, I don't have any other information."

Something was better than nothing. I relayed the news to Brad while I pulled up information on the two shops. Both were temporary pop-ups. One had rented a space in a shopping center for two months. The other was actually a small specialty shop inside a larger party supply store.

The specialty shop had sold only one vampire warrior costume to Michael Ortecho. I checked, but he didn't have a sheet. A quick search didn't show any link connecting him to Dan Fielders or the Stevenses. After jotting down his LKA, I moved on to the next store, figuring I'd circle back to Mr. Ortecho.

After I spoke to the manager at Howls-R-Us, she agreed to e-mail me whatever receipts she had from costume sales. But it wasn't much. The records they kept weren't nearly as itemized as the store I'd just visited.

"I'm only interested in whoever purchased the Van Helsing and vampire warrior costumes," I said.

"I really don't know. According to our records, we only had three of each costume in stock. That's one per size. Let me check something." A moment later, she returned. "I can't be sure, but a lot of those higher end costumes were sold to haunted houses and area attractions for the actors to wear. One of our bulk orders picked up three dozen costumes. For all I know, they could have scooped up the two you're interested in."

"Do you know which attraction or haunted house?"

"I'm sorry, but our records don't include that information."

"Dammit."

Brad looked up. "Let me guess. They don't keep an accurate inventory count."

"They sell every costume from that catalog at the same price and assign it the same SKU. She's sending us their records, but several different haunted attractions have wiped out most of their inventory. We're never going to find this guy."

"What about him?" Brad pointed to the name on the pad.

"He bought a vampire warrior costume from Witches on East Avenue."

"Let's check him out."

Brad brought up everything he could find on Michael Ortecho while I worked on figuring out the purchase information Howls-R-Us had e-mailed me. I pulled out every credit card holder who had made a purchase and added them to the list. Several people had paid cash, which wouldn't lead to anything. To save time, I sent an officer to pick up whatever surveillance footage the shop had. The techs would not be happy with me, but we had to identify the killer.

Not wanting to risk a slow down or being tossed to the bottom of the pile, I dialed my favorite computer whiz. "Hey, Mac, I have another favor to ask."

"This will require a lot of caffeine and sugar. Are you game?"

"You know how I feel about that," I said.

"Fine, I'll settle for a basket of your mom's homemade candies, or I'm going on strike."

"How did you hear about those?"

"Fennel already promised me he'd split his stash if I put a rush on the footage he had from the street."

"All right. You got it. Here's what I need. I already gave you the footage from that one Halloween shop. Run that against the footage of the killer and see if you spot him. More footage is on the way from a different store. I need you to do the same with that. Also, the sooner you can give me stats so I can compare them to the list of buyers, the less work I'll pass off to you and your computing wizardry."

She laughed. "I like the sound of that. Wait for it."

"What?"

"That." She laughed again. "Basics are in your inbox. Oh, and I want some of those dinosaur cookies too. Please and thank you." She hung up before I could get a word in edge-wise.

As promised, Mac had delivered. The suspect from this afternoon was approximately 5'9 to 6'1 and between 175 to 215 pounds. The thick layers of the costume and flowing cloak had made it harder to narrow down his weight. Mac believed he was light-skinned, probably white, based on the tiny cutouts on his gloves, revealing his knuckles. Given the force of the blows, he was strong. He walked with no discernible limp or impediment. She estimated his age between 21 and 40. That wasn't much, but it was better than nothing.

My first thought while processing the receipts was to pull out the women, but it was possible they had purchased the costume for a friend or relative. "Do you think the killer is married?" I asked Brad.

"Given his rage toward the happy couple, I wouldn't think so, but he could be recently divorced."

"Are you sure he wasn't one of Cassie Stevens' exes?" I asked.

"If he was, he never made any threats or caused any problems before today." Brad looked up from his screen. "Did we explore the same possibility with Vivica Smaldey? One of her former boytoys could have gotten wind of her relationship status and took out the competition."

"Officers already checked. It doesn't look like that's the case either."

Brad swiveled his chair around to look at the info hanging on our murder board. "If it's the same killer, the victims have to be connected, but I don't see how."

"They were all crazy for Halloween. That could be something. We think the costumes the killers wore came from the same manufacturer, but until we get Melanie Daggio to verify that for us, that's just another assumption under which we are operating."

"Let's take a ride." Brad palmed his keys. "I want to check out Michael Ortecho. His social media page doesn't tell me much about him. He's a mystery, but he fits the killer's stats."

"Mac gave those to you?"

"Yeah, why wouldn't she?"

"What did it cost you? She extorted me for candies and cookies." My mouth went wide. "That's what you promised her."

He shrugged. "Your mom won't mind. She likes cooking."

"You tell her that." I grabbed my jacket. "If I say it, I'll get a lecture. And a second one about volunteering her for snack duty. It'll be like elementary school all over again. I am not reliving that."

"I can't believe Maria would have a problem with helping out."

"That's because she likes you. She babies you. It's the whole Italian mama thing. She'll feed the entire neighborhood if someone asks, but if I say something, I'll get the back of her hand."

"She'd hit you?" Brad asked, incredulous.

"No, she'd show me the back of her hand." I pulled my arm back, like I was going to bitch slap him.

He laughed. "Right now, it's worth it. We need Mac to prioritize this. If not, we're stuck doing all the legwork. You're gonna have to take one for the team, Liv."

"And yet, we're still running around trying to make sense of things." I wasn't sure this was a good use of our time. We had a million things to check regarding Fielders' murder and now the Stevenses' murders.

"We'll knock everything out in this one trip. It won't take long, and it might lead to something."

FIFTEEN

We found Melanie Daggio still hungover from last night's party. Her expression said she wasn't happy to see us again. "I only left the precinct a few hours ago. Did you already find the guy who killed Dan?" she asked.

"Not yet." Brad showed her the catalog. "Was he wearing any of these costumes?"

She flipped through the pages, growing frustrated. We weren't making it easy, but we had to make sure she was clear on what she'd seen the night before. By making her look through every costume, the DA's office couldn't complain about how we obtained the positive ID.

"That's it." She stabbed at the page. "I told you that's what he was wearing."

"Are you sure?" Brad asked.

"Hat and all."

"Do you remember anything else about the way he looked?" I asked.

"No. That's about it. I didn't get a look at his face."

"Did you notice if he was covered in blood?"

Melanie looked like she might get sick. She put her hand over her mouth and swallowed a few times. "Dan's blood?" She shook her head. "No."

Despite being stabbed through the heart, the carnage had been limited to the coffin. Some transfer had probably gotten on the killer's hands or gloves, since we hadn't found any prints, but the rest had been contained by the thick, absorbent layers Dan wore.

"Did you notice if the killer had any odd mannerisms? Did he walk with a limp or have a memorable gait?" Brad asked.

She shook her head. "I barely glimpsed the guy. I didn't notice anything, except that he was wearing that."

"Thanks for your time." Brad took a step back. "We'll be in touch."

"Find him," Melanie said. "It'd make me feel better. I bet it'd make everyone else at the party feel better too."

"We'll do our best."

We returned to the car and headed to our next location. Michael Ortecho lived a few blocks from Melanie. "Do you think there's something to the proximity?" I asked.

"In a city this big? That's doubtful."

"You never know." I double-checked the address before getting out of the car.

Michael Ortecho lived in a multi-family home. The mailboxes beside the front door indicated the house had been divided into four units. Ortecho lived in C. Matching the coordinating buzzer to his apartment, I pressed the button.

The doorbell nearly fell off the wall. I pressed against it again, hoping to get the double-sided tape on the back to adhere to the brick. "I'm wondering how a guy who can't afford a real doorbell can afford to blow a hundred bucks on a Halloween costume."

"Priorities," Brad said. "Maybe he doesn't get a lot of houseguests."

"Or he gets too many deliveries."

The window on the third floor opened, and a guy stuck his head out. "What do you want?"

Brad and I exchanged a look. "Michael?" Brad asked.

"Who wants to know?"

"I'm Brad. This is Liv. We wanted to ask you about the Halloween costume you recently purchased."

"How come?"

"Brad," I hissed, but he ignored me.

"I don't think you want us to have this conversation out here where all your neighbors can hear us. Why don't you come down here or let us inside?"

Michael rested his forearms on the window frame. "Who'd you say you were?"

"Police," I said.

"You shouldn't have done that," Brad mumbled.

"Police, huh?" Michael hocked a loogie and spit in our direction. "I got nothing to say to you."

I watched the wad of saliva smack on the sidewalk beside me. "Too bad. A couple was killed this afternoon by a man wearing the vampire warrior costume you bought. If you refuse to cooperate, we'll come back with an arrest warrant. Do you want us to drag you out of your house in cuffs?"

"Bite me." Michael slammed the window closed.

"I told you not to announce," Brad said.

"We didn't have a choice." I stared up at the window for another moment, and then I rang the three other bells. The front door opened a moment later. "I'm sorry to bother you, ma'am." I showed her my badge. "Detectives DeMarco and Fennel. Would you mind answering a few questions?"

She glanced behind her, peering at the staircase. "I heard you outside. Mike's been here all day. He hasn't left. In fact, he hasn't left the apartment in the last twelve days. You have the wrong man."

"Are you sure?" Brad asked.

"Positive. Mike got into a motorcycle accident two weeks ago. He broke his leg. He's been hobbling around ever since. I offered to get someone to install one of those chairlifts until he recovers, but he wouldn't hear of it. The stubborn bastard can't get up and down the stairs without help. That's how I know he hasn't left. When he got out of the hospital, my husband, Bobby, and two of his friends had to carry Mike up there."

"Would you mind if we went upstairs and knocked on his door?" Brad asked. "We need to verify it."

"He won't answer for you, but he'll probably answer for

me."

"We'd appreciate anything you can do," Brad said.

She turned and headed up the steps. At the top, she knocked. "Mike, it's Helen. Do you mind if I come in?"

A moment later, the door inched open. "Did you get rid of them?"

"No, Mike. Just show them your leg, so they'll leave you alone. It's no big deal. They're just doing their jobs."

"What?" Mike peered around her, growing more irritated by our presence. "Nuh-uh. I didn't consent. You got no right to be here. Get out." When Brad and I didn't move fast enough, Mike lunged forward, grabbing the door before he could tumble down the stairs. His right leg bumped against the frame, and he howled. Despite the thick plaster cast which ran from the bottom of his foot to above his knee, the impact hurt. A lot.

"Mike, take it easy." Helen tried to help him, but she wasn't strong enough to stop the guy from falling forward. Brad caught him, despite the bitter curses and snarls, and got him back inside. I followed my partner, brushing past Helen.

"Easy, man," Brad said. "We just wanted to ask about the costume you bought. We didn't know you were injured. We didn't mean to inconvenience you."

Mike cursed at us in Spanish since English had no effect.

"Since we're here," I glanced around the studio apartment, spotting the costume hanging from the bar over the guy's weight bench, "would you mind answering just one question?" I pointed. "Is that the costume?"

"Yeah. Now get the hell out of my house."

"Feel better," Brad said.

Mike let out another string of expletives and spit in our direction. This time, it left a bubbly, wet spot on the carpet.

Helen waited with her back against the door, ushering us out of the apartment. "You should go. He doesn't feel well."

"Sorry for the inconvenience, ma'am." I nodded to her.

"That was...interesting," my partner mused.

"Loads of fun." Exhaling, I slammed the car door and

reached for the MDT. "We both ran Ortecho through the system and didn't come up with anything. Wouldn't his motorcycle accident have popped up?"

"I didn't check traffic reports," Brad said.

"I checked everything." I typed in Ortecho's information and waited. At the very least, a report should have been made, but the system didn't find anything.

"Maybe it didn't get added to the database yet," Brad suggested. "My gut says he's not faking the broken leg, and if he is, then damn, that man should get an Oscar."

"His costume looked too clean." I looked up at the window, seeing a pair of eyes watching us from between the slats of the blinds. "He didn't kill the Stevenses. But he's hiding something."

"Whatever it is, it's not his hatred of cops." Brad tapped on my knee to get my attention away from the screen. "Don't let him get to you. It's not worth it. People have issues. We do the best we can and hope our actions might be enough to change their minds. Worst case, next time, I'll let the jerk fall down the stairs."

"You wouldn't do that." I closed the search and rubbed a hand down my face. "You're one of the good ones."

"Cops?"

"Human beings."

SIXTEEN

After our outing, we returned to the precinct. In our absence, Lt. Winston had moved the rolling corkboard we'd been using back to the conference room and gathered every member of our unit around the table for a meeting.

"Uh-oh." Brad nodded at the room. "Do you think there's been another murder?"

"We would have heard about it over the radio." But this didn't bode well. "Let's see what's up. If we're lucky, Winston's planning a Halloween party and wants to make sure someone's bringing onion dip."

"One can only hope."

Quietly, we snuck into the back of the conference room. Our murder board was on display to the left of where Winston stood. On his right was a second board. Dozens of notes covered the corkboard behind him, indicating times, dates, and locations of reported crimes. Were they all homicides? A cold chill traveled through me, and I scooted closer to see better.

Brad leaned over and whispered to Detective Lisco, "What did we miss?"

Before she could answer, Winston cleared his throat, the full weight of his gaze resting on my partner. Lisco felt the intensity and shrank back against her chair.

"For those of you just joining us, let me catch you up to speed," Winston said. "As I'm sure you're aware, it's that time of year again. 9-1-1 has received dozens of reports which have led to more than a few fake crime scenes. However, not all of them are fake." Winston aimed his pointer at the corkboard. "These alleged crimes were nothing but Halloween pranks. Blood, body parts, decomposing corpses, these turned out to be nothing more than decorations and creepy noises. The kinds of reports we get every year, but this year is different. Several of these horrific crime scenes have turned out to be the real deal."

"Like the mutilation and dismemberment I got called to this morning," Detective Jake Voletek volunteered.

"And the double homicide Fennel and DeMarco returned from." Winston nodded to us, causing most of the room to look in our direction. "Commissioner Cross is concerned. This morning, he received a tip in the mail, warning of a coming war between humans and demons."

Lisco snorted. "Isn't that the tag line for every horror movie ever?"

Winston squinted at her. "Regardless, these Halloween-inspired crime scenes might be the work of the unknown tipster."

"Or the note's just another warning by some lunatic," Voletek muttered.

"Or a serial killer," I said.

Brad bumped his knee against mine beneath the table, letting me know it'd be okay. "Has the brass determined who sent the letter? Did the sender provide any hard details we can verify?"

"I don't know. I haven't been read in on this." Winston looked at Voletek, who appeared just as clueless as the rest of us. "We see shit like this all the time, but the murders we've seen in the last twenty-four hours have the commissioner concerned. In addition, over the last week or so, we've seen a spike in violent crimes. Gory ones. We're getting dozens of reports every single day. For the most part, the public at large remains ignorant. The news outlets haven't picked up on it, yet. But they will, which is why we need to figure out what's going on before they get wind of it and stop it if we can. Here's the kicker, people. Until a unit responds to a call, we have no way of knowing which crime scenes are real and which aren't, and to top it off, we lack credible intel on these actual Halloween-inspired murders."

"Uh, sir," a tech I didn't recognize said from the back corner, "while we were searching Dan Fielders' apartment, a man came to the door. He looked homeless and said a few odd things. Nothing threatening, but he said something about knowing who and what Dan was. He gave me odd vibes."

"Did you get a name?"

She shook her head. "He took off and hopped into the elevator before I could stop him. Building security gave me the footage, but it doesn't give us much to go on."

"See if you can find an ID. This guy might know something or be involved," Winston said.

"Yes, sir."

Winston looked from Brad to Voletek. "Right now, it looks like these murders are separate, isolated incidents, but our techs have clued me in to the possibility that might not be the case. Apparently, our victims shared a love of Halloween. We're exploring the possibility that's how or why the killer targeted them."

"Did we find anything? Mac was supposed to compare the security feeds for possible suspects." I searched the room but didn't spot Mac or any of her colleagues.

"Not yet, DeMarco. But they told me of your request. Did you and Fennel uncover anything during your outing?" Winston asked.

"Not much, except the killer last night and the one today both wore costumes manufactured by the same company."

"Is that significant?"

"It might be," Brad intervened. "We don't know yet. But in both cases, the killer attacked a couple."

"Dan Fielders was one person," Winston argued.

"True, but he and his girlfriend had a fight and she walked out minutes before he was killed. I'm thinking the killer observed the couple, didn't like what he was seeing, and decided to do something about it."

"But he didn't kill the girlfriend," Winston said.

"We don't believe the fatal wounds inflicted upon Mrs. Stevens were intentional. I saw the footage," Brad said. "The attacker wanted her out of his way so he could kill her husband. He didn't mean to stab her in the neck with the back-end of the cross."

Winston rubbed his chin. "Any idea why he targeted Roger Stevens?"

Brad shrugged.

"What about you, DeMarco? You got anything to add?"

"We're still working on it, which is why we're willing to entertain every possibility. Any similarities between the cases we've been assigned in the last twenty-four hours might be purely coincidental or the result of the same killer."

"The two male vics were both stabbed through the heart." Voletek pointed to the photos on the board. "That could be the killer's M.O."

Winston smiled. It was a creepy sight, one that I didn't particularly enjoy. Maybe that was why he normally frowned. "I'm glad to hear you say that. Given what we know and the recent string of reports we've been receiving, the commissioner believes these crimes are being committed by a single perpetrator or group of perpetrators acting together to turn this city into a real life horror film. He wants the entire department on top of this, but with bodies turning up in some very gruesome ways, most of the heavy lifting will fall on our shoulders. That's why, as of now, every call we get will be added to the list of potential new activity." He indicated the notes on the corkboard. "As soon as we have proof it is unrelated, we'll take it down and deal with it like we would any other crime. But our first assumption in any of these weird cases is that they are connected."

"That seems like a leap," Voletek said. "Why are we assuming the letter the commissioner received is a tip or warning? More than likely, it's just some nutjob blowing off steam."

Winston licked his lips, gave Voletek a hard look, and

ignored the question. "We're setting up a Halloween task force. Since DeMarco and Fennel are already working two of the main cases, they'll head this up. Voletek and Lisco, I want both of you to assist the task force. If no more bodies turn up, that should be more than enough manpower, but if more people start dropping, Jacobs, Greer, and Jennings will pitch in. We'll grow as the case load does, so I suggest we nip this thing in the bud before our entire unit is on ghost patrol. We got three weeks 'til Halloween. After that, I'm hoping life will return to normal."

"Until Black Friday," Lisco mumbled.

"Until then, we field every call we get and figure out if it's a Halloween-related crime. If so, pass it off to someone on the team. Our support staff knows this is the priority. These cases will be first in line until we stop the killer. Public safety is paramount here, and with everyone walking around like literal zombies, we gotta do what we can to make sure they're safe and none of them pose a danger to public safety."

Several detectives grumbled. It wasn't fair. But that was politics.

"You're all dedicated, hard-working, capable individuals. I applaud your efforts, but while we chase these loonies who want to recreate their favorite slasher scenes, we have other murders to solve. Even if you aren't part of the task force, you still have a job to do. Don't forget that. Dismissed." Winston grabbed a hold of Voletek's shoulder before he could leave the room.

Since we were the last to join the party, we moved closer to read the notes on the corkboard. The list on the board had been calls dispatch received, including the bogus hit and run Brad and I had responded to the previous night.

Winston crossed his arms over his chest and stared at his page of notes. "Did you know what the commissioner had planned?"

"Sir?" Voletek asked.

"Not you." Winston wrote something on the bottom of the page. "DeMarco, did you know this whole public safety initiative was in play? You and Fennel responded to a 9-1-1 call before getting rerouted to the Eldridge party."

"How could I have known?"

"Your father." Winston stared at me. "Word is he had a meeting at city hall the other night."

"Dad takes a lot of meetings. He has friends and is willing to consult with them on upcoming public works. That has nothing to do with my job or how I conduct myself."

"What about you, Voletek? Did Manny mention anything to you about this? He works directly with the commissioner."

Voletek turned his head and stared at the two murder boards. "My father and I don't talk shop that often. What did the commissioner tell you?"

"Not enough," Winston said. "That's why I'm asking you. Come on. I know you, Jake. You always have your ear to the ground. What's going on? What haven't I been told?"

"Headquarters received a tip that the gates of hell were about to open and demonic forces were going to descend upon the city. The only way to stop it was to kill the demons and those possessed." Voletek chuckled. "It's the usual nonsense. Every year, they get several letters like that. It doesn't mean anything."

"So why is the commissioner taking it so seriously this time?" Winston asked. "It's not an election year."

Voletek tapped one of the gruesome crime scene photos. "Decapitation is one of the few ways to kill evil spirits. That and burning." He pointed to the charred remnants of his victim's genitals. "The other way is a stake through the heart."

"Like with our two cases," Brad said.

Voletek pointed at him. "Bingo. I'm guessing this whole task force order," he put the words task force in air quotes, "came right around the same time the photos got logged in the system this afternoon. Am I right, Lieutenant?"

"Next time, I'd prefer some advanced warning so I don't get caught with my thumb up my ass." Winston dropped into one of the empty conference chairs, swiveling it around to look at the displayed information. "Despite the speech I just gave to the rest of the unit about catching the party responsible for these crimes, I want to know what the three of you think. Do you think one person's responsible for all of these?"

"I don't see how," Voletek said. "The killer would have to jump from murder to murder, making a quick costume change in between each one. Plus, whoever killed this poor bastard," Voletek nodded again at the photos, which made my stomach turn every time I glanced at them, "took his time. He had to cut, cauterize, burn, and hack away. He tortured his victim. These other kills were quick."

"I think I'm gonna be sick," Brad said.

"You and half the cops covering the scene," Voletek said.

"Do you have a suspect yet, Jake?" I asked.

He shook his head. "Fire got rid of a lot of evidence. It happened out near the water. No cameras. No one around. I haven't IDed the victim yet, but given the location, he's probably a homeless guy. I'm waiting for forensics to scour the area for clues. But so far, it's a black hole of nothing."

"Stick with what you're doing," Winston said. "You find any overlap with Fennel's cases, you know what to do. And if your dad or anyone else asks, just tell them you're working on the task force."

"Copy that," Voletek said.

SEVENTEEN

Brad pulled out my chair before taking a seat beside me and picking up his menu. "Do you believe that? Winston's enough of a brownnoser that he created a task force and assigned Voletek to it so he can cover for the fact that there is no actual task force."

"There is a task force," I said. "We're it."

"A task force of two? That's not a task force. That's called a Monday."

"The LT will sign off on any resources we need. Plus, it means our cases get priority. You should at least be happy about that. We don't have to keep bribing Mac for favors, which means I don't have to beg my mom to ply the department with confections."

"We already promised Mac," Brad pointed out.

"Yes, but that's a small order compared to what it could turn into if we keep catching more of these cases. Personally, I don't want to be responsible for putting the department's best tech into a sugar coma."

"Your mom doesn't use sugar."

"Refined sugars. But there are still plenty of natural sweeteners that will get the job done. Honey, maple syrup, coconut sugar, dates."

Brad grabbed my hand where I was ticking off options. "Okay, Liv. I get the point." He slumped back in his chair. "Despite everything that we've seen in the last twenty-four hours, I'm glad we didn't get called to Voletek's crime scene. Ours was bad enough, but his." He whistled.

"We're about to eat. I don't want to think about that."

As soon as Winston had left the conference room, Brad had placed post-its over the graphic crime scene photos so we didn't have to stare at them while we worked on our case. "Do you think there's anything to the warning that headquarters received?"

"About the gates of hell opening?"

"Not that part, but that this could be the work of someone who actually believes in demons and evil spirits? That would explain why Dan Fielders' killer dressed like Van Helsing, a famous vampire hunter, and why he targeted Dan." Brad bared his top teeth. "Dan's canines might have been enough to convince someone with a loose grip on reality that he really was a vampire. It sounded like whoever popped by Dan's apartment after we left thought so too."

"Do you think that's the killer?"

Brad shrugged. "We need an ID first." He sighed and rubbed his eyes.

"You look tired. You got a lot done at work before I arrived. What time did you get there?"

"Two hours before you did."

"Brad."

"What? We had an open case that needed work. I just didn't expect to end up pulling a double plus some on top of that."

"At least Winston doesn't care about overtime anymore."

"Small favors. Speaking of, the outfit and coffin didn't do Dan Fielders any favors. Frankly, if I believed in such things, I would have thought Dan was a real vampire." Brad looked around the crowded restaurant. A few people wore fun hats and headbands, already in the Halloween spirit. "Do you think the Stevenses' murders and Dan's were perpetrated by the same person?"

"I don't know."

"Me neither." Brad put the menu down. "At this point, I can't even see straight."

The server arrived to take our orders, leaving two iced teas in her wake.

I took a sip, wishing I'd gone with water instead. "I compared the receipts from the Halloween shops. A lot of people paid cash."

"That won't help us." Brad squeezed some lemon into his tea, glancing toward the bar. "Did you find any overlap?"

"Several area attractions made large bulk orders for costumes, decorations, props, accessories, basically everything under the sun. I made a list, but as far as individual names go, I didn't see any repeat buyers, at least not for the items we're interested in."

"We'll check them out tomorrow." He sipped his drink as if it were finely aged scotch. "I've had no luck finding anything connecting the Stevenses to Fielders. As far as I can tell, they have absolutely nothing in common."

"What about friends?"

"Nope. They had different careers, lived in different neighborhoods, attended different schools, hung out in different circles."

"They both liked Halloween."

"Look around, Liv. Half the city's nuts for it. That doesn't mean shit."

"It does if they shopped at the same Halloween store."

"What did their financials show?"

I let out a frustrated grunt and reached for my tea. "Nothing conclusive."

He cupped his ear. "I'm sorry. What was that?"

I gave him a shove. "Don't be a jerk. We're on the same side. I just don't know where we go from here. We have the murder weapons. We have surveillance footage. We even have one eyewitness account from Dan Fielders' murder, and yet, none of it adds up to a viable lead."

"But hey, at least we have a task force."

I laughed, even though it wasn't funny. The truth was we were scared. Two scenes, roughly twelve hours apart, did not bode well. Another victim could drop at any moment, and we didn't know enough to stop it from happening.

"Let's play what if," I suggested.

"What if we find more pleasant dinner conversation?" Brad teased.

"Do you want to?"

"Nah, what fun would that be?" The server returned with our dinner, refilled our glasses, and asked if we needed anything else. "Can I get a side salad?" Brad asked. "Lettuce, avocado, cucumbers, and carrots." He eyed the chicken on his plate. "Oh, and do you have uncured bacon?"

"I'd have to check." She stared at him as if he were insane. "Avocado is extra, so is the bacon."

"Only if it's uncured."

She scratched her head with her pen and walked away.

"Why didn't you just order the grilled chicken salad?" I asked. "Jake's right. You're worse than me."

My partner rolled his eyes. "I wanted the sides that come with the chicken. Not to mention, when you order it as a salad, half the time the chicken is cold." He sliced the chicken breast into strips and pointed at my salad with his fork. "Is it cold?"

I stabbed a piece and popped it into my mouth. "Can we get back to the topic at hand?"

"It is cold. I knew it." He speared a sauteed button mushroom and held it toward me. "Do you want some?"

"Maybe just one."

He put a few on my plate before digging into the summer squash. "All right, what if the brass is right and these crimes are connected by a group of wannabe vampire hunters? How do we find them?"

"Internet search," I said. "They'd have to interact somehow. It could be some sick game or some kind of tally sheet."

"You think they're treating this like sport?"

"Unless they have a cult. Either way, I'm guessing someone must have mentioned it on the internet."

"Do you remember when bloodplay was all the rage?

Could this be an offshoot of that?"

"Nothing in our victims' backgrounds indicates they were into that kind of thing, which is surprising given Dan Fielders' teeth."

"Vivica said he loved Halloween, but he didn't have any vampire kinks, aside from the teeth. I looked through everything I could find on him, but this was the first year he dressed up like a vampire. I'm guessing he decided on that while getting the implants."

"What about the dentist?" I asked. "Since he does novelty procedures, he could be one of these vampire freaks."

"How would we even figure that out?" Brad smiled as the server returned with a tray. She placed the salad down first, followed by a plate with sliced avocado, and another one with bacon.

"The packaging said natural." She eyed him. "Do you want it?"

"Yes, thank you." He gave her a million-watt smile and slipped her an extra tip. "I'm sorry for causing so much trouble."

She blushed a little. "Not at all. If you need anything else, let me know."

"You should have tipped her before she spit in your food," I said.

"She didn't spit in my food." He examined the plates carefully before combining the ingredients. "So do we try to get a court order to check up on the dentist?"

"Logan didn't think we had enough for a judge to sign off when this is nothing more than a whim."

"Well, the assistant district attorney would know better than two lowly detectives." Brad examined the miniature olive oil and vinegar bottles the server had brought to accompany his salad, holding the oil up to the light for closer inspection.

"You could flag down our server and ask her to run to the back to check to see if that's pure olive oil and not some kind of blend, but the label says it's 100% pure. Still, I'm sure she'd be happy to do it for you."

"Don't be jealous. People like me."

"Especially women."

He grinned, letting out that velvety laugh that always made me feel like I was wrapped in a warm blanket. "Too bad the dentist is a guy. Maybe you should work some of your charms on him, so we don't have to bother with the court order." He ate a few bites. "To be honest, I think the dentist is a waste of time. Roger Stevens' veneers didn't come from that dentist. Like I said before, the victims aren't connected."

"What if the killer or killers are targeting anyone who buys vampire teeth?"

"Then we're looking at thousands of potential victims, possibly hundreds of thousands."

The what if game was more fun when it led to something useful. Instead, Brad easily dismissed my theories with facts and figures.

Brad finished chewing and put his fork down. "What if the same man killed Fielders and the Stevenses?"

"Okay, why? What possible motive could he have? The victims aren't connected."

"Don't we have to assume his motive is based on the way his victims dressed and acted in public?"

"Again, we're looking at thousands of potential future victims. Vampire costumes are commonplace. The undead never really die."

"We could issue a release and warn the public."

"Winston won't push for that. He knows the brass wants to avoid a panic. Hence, the task force."

"Yeah, I know." Brad speared a piece of chicken with more force than necessary. "Based on what little we know, the killings appear random. We both know the statistics on those. Random murders are rarely solved. Issuing a warning's the only thing we can do."

"Only if we're looking at the same killer."

"True."

"What if this is the work of two killers? Then the motives would be different. It could have nothing to do with costumes or Halloween. It could be personal."

"Except the victims didn't have any obvious enemies. They didn't owe anyone money. They didn't have known criminal ties."

"Fielders pissed people off with his sports commentary and reporting. A fan, a sports star, anyone who met the guy might have wanted him dead. The techs are checking on some of the commenters to Fielders' online articles, but they haven't found anything yet. His profession makes him a public figure and more susceptible to random attacks and less personal motives."

"If that's the case, Fielders wouldn't have been killed at Eldridge's party, unless..." Brad put his fork down.

"Unless what?"

"A coworker killed him."

"We already checked, remember?"

"Yes, but they could have conspired together to end him. Even his girlfriend could have been in on it."

"Have you been reading Agatha Christie again?" But I wondered if Brad was correct. Unfortunately, if that were the case, we'd never be able to prove it unless we got a confession or convinced one of the accomplices to turn on the others. "We could bring everyone back in for questioning. Hold them in different interrogation rooms and bluff our asses off."

Brad reached into his pocket for a pen and wrote that in shorthand on a napkin. "It might be worth exploring."

"However, it doesn't get us any closer to figuring out the double homicide from today." I pushed my half-eaten salad away. For some reason, I didn't have much of an appetite. "I don't know. My gut says there's a pattern between these two cases. I don't think they're unrelated. Both men were stabbed through the heart with Halloween decorations."

"That could be a coincidence. Plus, the box in Dan's apartment might have been a warning."

"Except it had been sealed before you opened it and the only prints inside were Dan's. He made that himself."

"He could have shown it to someone, and that's how the killer got the idea to end him," Brad argued.

"Possibly. Which means we need to find out if Dan showed it to anyone, starting with Vivica."

Brad added that to the napkin. "Y'know, Vivica thought Dan's murder sounded like a prank. Do you think it was a bad joke gone wrong?"

"Is anyone that stupid?"

"Have you seen the kinds of videos people post on the internet?"

"Point taken."

"Dan might have been stupid or drunk enough to think a stake through the heart wouldn't kill him. Perhaps, he had tried to get it to stick out from his clothing and somehow it got driven through his chest wall. His murder could have been an accident."

"That's a lot of force for an accident."

"It would explain why he didn't have any defensive wounds and why no one heard him screaming for help when it happened."

"Wouldn't Dan's partner-in-crime have called 9-1-1?" I blinked. "Do we know who placed the call?"

"I don't know." Brad reached for his phone. "Let's find out."

EIGHTEEN

Brad put down the phone. "Kelsey Eldridge made the call. The techs will pull the recording for us to listen to, but they didn't notice anything suspicious about it. Eldridge requested an ambulance. He said his friend was in a coffin, and he'd been staked. The 9-1-1 operator thought it sounded like a party prank. EMTs arrived, expecting to find some gnarly injury. They didn't think they'd find someone dead and resting in peace."

"When did Eldridge buy the coffin?"

"A few years ago."

"That rules out the possibility he and Dan planned this stunt and it backfired."

"Not necessarily. What if Dan noticed it at last year's party and came up with the idea to rise from the dead?"

"Based on what Vivica said, Dan wanted to get frisky in the coffin. He didn't want to get dead."

"That's how the rest of the party guests remember things too."

"Unless that's not true."

"What isn't?" Jake Voletek pulled up a chair and sat down. He looked at my half-eaten salad and Brad's empty plate. "Thanks for waiting for me."

"What are you doing here?" I asked. "When we left the precinct, you said you didn't want to join us for dinner, that you'd rather get a drink."

"I changed my mind. I didn't want to sit alone at the bar." Jake eyed the salad. "Was that good? It looks good."

"Do you want some?" I pushed the plate closer to him.

Jake shook his head before waving down a server and asking for a menu. "I'm not much in the mood for rabbit food tonight. It's not been one of those days." In a split second, he scanned the menu and ordered mac and cheese and a bourbon. Brad looked uncomfortable, but Jake didn't notice. "Don't stop on my account. What were you talking about?"

"The coffin where Dan Fielders was killed." Brad finished his iced tea, so I slid my glass over to him.

"It would have been a great parlor trick if he'd come back to life, just like one of the undead," Jake said.

"That's what we were discussing. It seems the kind of thing our vic might have tried to pull off. Unfortunately, the only two options I'm aware of are alive and dead. Undead doesn't work in the real world." Before Brad could say anything else, his phone rang. "Hold on a sec. I have to take this." He answered, turning away from us. "Hey, is everything okay?"

I raised an eyebrow, wondering who he was talking to.

"No, it's fine. Tonight works," Brad said. "Liv and I are in the middle of dinner. Can you give me an hour?" He paused. "Okay. I'll see you then." He put the phone away. "Where were we?"

"Nowhere good," Jake said. "So I take it you're debating these points because you can't figure out if your two crime scenes are connected."

"You said they were," I pointed out.

"I said they could be." Jake swallowed a mouthful of bourbon and rubbed his chest. "But I don't have much basis for thinking that."

"So why'd you say it?" Brad asked.

Jake shrugged. "I got swept up in the whole pep rally thing."

"Pep rally?"

"Yeah. Winston brought out his pom-poms. He always takes the mandates that come down from on high as if they are actual gospel. The commissioner wants a task force. So Winston made one or tried to. He gets his name on the thing and checks off all the boxes. He likes to play politics. I like to egg him on."

"It's bullshit," Brad said.

"True, but it makes the LT happy, which keeps him from riding our asses." Jake took another sip. "So I'm not complaining."

"How are you doing?" I eyed the nearly empty glass which Jake had yet to put down.

"To tell you the truth, I've been better. Who's joining me for a drink? I hear it's not good to drink alone."

"How much did you drink before you came looking for us?" Brad asked.

"Not enough. Why? Do you guys want to head to the bar after I eat? I'm game."

"Actually," Brad looked at his watch, "I need to take off in a few minutes. How 'bout I drive you home after dinner?"

"Nah, I'm good." Jake reconsidered my previous offer and picked at my remaining salad. "I'll call for a ride if I get too wasted."

"I'll make sure he gets home okay," I said.

Brad eyed me. "Are you sure, Liv? I don't want to leave you hanging."

"Go." I nodded down at his phone. "Take care of whatever that is. If you need me, you know where to find me."

"Are you sure you can't stay for one drink?" Jake asked. "I'm buying."

Brad shook his head and reached for his wallet. He took out some cash and put it on the table. "Next time, Jake."

"Brad, put your money away. It's my turn to get dinner," I said.

He ignored me, flagged down the server from earlier, paid for everyone's dinner, and handed her another tip. In return, she gave him the receipt with her phone number.

"Told you," I said.

"You told me she spit in my food," Brad said.

"That's just another way to swap saliva."

"You should go for it. She's pretty." Jake watched her walk away. "I'd go for it."

"Liv, are you sure you're okay here?" Brad asked.

"Yeah. We're fine. Go."

Brad gave me a sideways hug and kissed the top of my head. "Call me when you get home, so I know you're safe."

"Brad?" I looked up at him.

"Just do it. Please."

My partner didn't usually behave this oddly. "Okay." I eyed his phone, which was in his hand. "Are you sure everything's okay?"

"Uh-huh." He nodded to Jake. "I'll see you guys tomorrow. Don't get too shitfaced, or Liv will make your life a living hell."

"Thanks for the tip." Jake waved him off, snickering as Brad left the restaurant. "For someone on his way to get laid, you'd think he'd be a bit more excited. Tough day for all of us, I guess." Jake blinked a few times. "God, what a mess. By now, you'd think I would have seen it all. But days like today still surprise me. The lengths people go to inflict pain is just sickening."

"Yeah."

He eyed Brad's empty glass. "Am I really the only one drinking?"

"Brad's on a cleanse."

"And you're joining him in solidarity?"

"Something like that."

"Brad's not here now. I won't tell if you won't." Jake shoveled a few bites into his mouth. "How about we get a bottle of wine and some dessert? Just nothing red. I don't think I can stomach that."

"I'm not hungry, but don't let me stop you."

Instead, Jake shook his head. "Nah, food's not really my preferred method of blowing off steam."

"Mine neither."

"Really? When we partnered together for a month, I don't remember us doing much else after work except getting dinner."

"A girl's gotta eat." I shrugged. "I guess I'm just boring."

"I doubt that very much." He finished his mac and cheese. "C'mon, let's get out of here. I need out of my head, and from the doodles you and Brad were making before I got here, I think you do too."

"What exactly do you have in mind?"

"You'll see. C'mon, Liv, live a little. You got to. It's in your name."

"I don't want to watch you get plastered."

"We'll do more than that."

"No."

"My, my. What do you think I have in mind?" He eyed me up and down. "Is that how you blow off steam? Because if it is, I'll let you jump my bones. All you have to do is ask."

"No, but I'm guessing that's one of your go-tos for dealing with rough shifts." Voletek had a reputation. He also had a line of waiting badge bunnies a mile long.

"Don't knock it until you try it, but I have a better idea. Something you won't object to. It'll be fun. I promise."

NINETEEN

Jake grabbed one of the plastic cups and held it under the dispenser before slipping a twenty into the machine. The tokens clinked together, filling the cup halfway. "That should be enough to get us started."

"Are you serious?" I looked at the nearly empty arcade. "This place closes in ten minutes."

"Not for us."

"What does that mean, Voletek?"

"Jake," he corrected, leading me through the rows of machines. Near the back were a few skill games. Skee-ball, basketball, whack-a-mole, and something involving a few freaky looking clowns. "C'mon, we're here to have fun. Stop looking so horrified. We spend our days analyzing horrifying things. This isn't one of them."

The overhead lights had been dimmed, encouraging the few straggling teenagers and a family of four, who couldn't decide what prize to get in exchange for their hundred tickets, that it was time to leave. However, Jake only seemed encouraged by this.

He fed a few tokens into a skee-ball machine and offered me the cup. When I failed to comply, he stuck two tokens into the neighboring machine. The starting music chimed, and the wooden balls rolled down the slot. "Don't tell me you've never played skee-ball."

"Jake, they're closing. We should go."

"One game," he insisted.

"Fine."

Halfway through, I found him staring at me. "You're absolutely terrible at this. It's like you're not even trying." He took a step toward me.

"If you try to show me how to roll the ball, I'm going to make your balls roll."

He held up his palms. "Fine, then just take a second to watch an expert."

"Expert?" I glanced at his score, realizing he must have knocked every single ball into the hundred point hole.

"That's right." He reached for another ball, pulled his arm back, and let it go. It rolled up the alley, made the jump, and landed perfectly in the upper left corner. "It's all in the amount of force. You want to arc the ball so it lands in the center, just like shooting hoops."

"Let me guess, you're an expert at that too."

He glanced at the basketball game behind me. "Do you want to find out?"

Before I could point out the arcade was closing, the man working behind the counter walked the family to the door and flipped the sign to closed. He unplugged a few of the machines near the front and turned off the neon signs in the window before making his way toward us. "My eyes must be deceiving me. Jake, is that you?"

"Shut up, Sammy," Jake said.

"Do you realize there's a woman with you?"

"I said shut up."

"Tell me that's really Bennett in drag. He's the only one crazy enough to hang out with you."

"Bennett wouldn't fit in a costume that small, and he sure as shit isn't that pretty."

"True." Sammy leaned against the side of the machine and stared at Jake, probably hoping he'd take the hint and leave.

"What?" Jake landed another hundred-pointer.

"Nothing."

"Then stop staring at me like that."

"Are you afraid I'm going to ruin your concentration and make you look bad in front of your lady friend? The least you could do is introduce us. Didn't your momma teach you any manners?"

Jake didn't even look as he rolled the last ball down the alley. Again, it landed perfectly. "Stop trying to distract me. You know that won't work."

Sammy smiled at me. "Name's Samson. My friends call me Sammy. I'm not really sure what this guy's excuse is, but he never quite takes the hint. Between you and me, I think he's a bit dense." He knocked gently against the side of Jake's head. "It's nice to meet you, Ms.?"

"Liv."

Sammy offered me his hand. "You're the first lady this knucklehead's brought here. I'm guessing he realized he's out of his league and is hoping to impress you. Don't fall for it."

"We work together," Jake said matter-of-factly, moving over to my alley to finish my game.

"Oh." Sammy dropped the teasing tone. "Rough day?"

Jake rolled another ball down the alley and missed for the first time. "Yep."

"I'll leave you to it then." Sammy unplugged a few more machines in the corner. "Lock up on your way out. I'll leave the usuals plugged in for you. Treat your partner to something nice. You know where the keys are."

"Thanks, man. I appreciate it." Jake let out a breath when Sammy clapped him on the back.

"It was nice meeting you, Liv," Sammy called.

"Same here." I watched him set the alarm and disappear out the back door. "Are we trapped?"

"No." Jake tugged the ticket ribbons from both machines and tossed them onto one of the unplugged games. "I have the alarm codes memorized." He saw the question on my face. "I've been coming to this arcade for over twenty years. I even worked here for a while when I was in high school. Don't let that grumpy old geezer fool you. He has a heart of gold. He let me hang out here as long as I wanted when I was a kid. He knew things weren't good at home after the divorce."

"It looks like he still lets you hang out here."

"That he does."

I cocked my head, wondering if Jake wanted to talk about that, but he wandered over to the basketball game.

"Don't tell me you're too old to have some clean, wholesome fun. You turned down drinking ourselves stupid, and you didn't like any of my other suggestions. This should be puritanical enough for you." Jake fed more tokens into the machine.

"Is that how you see me?"

"Not exactly, but I can't quite figure you out. We spent a lot of time together when Brad was suspended and then recovering from his appendectomy." From the look in Jake's eyes, he knew it was bullshit. "You fight mean, and you hit hard. You're also a damn good cop with a huge chip on your shoulder which looks a bit like mine." He snorted, pleased when I put a few tokens into the machine beside his and landed a few free throws. "Which is why I thought you'd play as hard as you work, but you've never shown me that side. Still, I'd think you would have something better to do than babysit me all night."

"That's not what I'm doing. Truth?" I sunk another shot.

"Always."

"I don't want to go home either."

He glanced at me from the corner of his eye. "How come?"

"Some crazy shit went down in my apartment, so that's out. Brad's busy. Emma's got a date. And if I go home, I'll spend the entire night talking to my dad about the task force. I don't want to think about any of that right now, even though the only thing I keep thinking is in the morning we're gonna get another report of another guy in a vampire costume being killed. I just don't know how to stop it. I hate feeling so useless." I tossed the ball harder than necessary, and it rebounded off the backboard and into my waiting hands.

"Tequila works wonders for things like that."

"I already told you I'm not drinking."

"Because your partner's doing a cleanse?" The timer ran

out on the basketball game. "Liv, I know Brad. He was mine before he was yours. Is he doing okay? I thought you said he had the drinking under control."

"He does." I didn't want to say much to Jake. I trusted him with my life, but this wasn't my secret to tell. "But he wants to keep it that way."

"I'm sorry. I shouldn't have said that stuff at dinner. I didn't know."

"Nothing to know."

"Right." Jake pointed to the whack-a-mole game. "Want to take out some aggression? I think that might be just what you need."

"Absolutely."

Three hours later, Jake and I had spent over a hundred dollars on arcade games. The bulk of which had been spent on a racing game that had vibrating seats and surround sound. With the pile of tickets we'd accumulated, he went to the counter and unlocked the prize cabinet. He slid the tickets inside and studied each of the options carefully before grabbing a handful of tootsie rolls and a few lollipops and sticking them in his pocket.

"Pick something. We have about a thousand tickets here."

"Jake, I'm not a kid. I don't need anything."

He studied the top shelf of the cabinet. "What about a blender?"

"I have a blender."

"Toaster?" He shook his head. "That's right. You don't eat bread."

"I eat bread."

He pointed. "Do you want the toaster?"

"No, I want to get out of here."

"I thought you'd never ask." He grabbed something off a middle shelf and closed the case. Then he led the way to the door, entered the code, and pushed it open. "Shall we go back to my place?"

"That's a given, since I said I'd drive you home."

He didn't live far from the arcade, which probably explained why he still visited so frequently. Jake was right. We'd spent a month working together and weeks hanging out when I was in the call center, and yet, I only knew what he was like at work. I pulled to a stop outside the building.

"You live here?"

"Until the end of the month." He unwrapped another piece of candy. "Lease is up, which means a rent hike." He opened his door. "Do you want to see it?"

"How much of a rent hike?" I asked.

"More than I can afford, unless I get a roommate or marry rich." Jake led me up the stairs and unlocked his apartment. "Make yourself at home. Are you sure you don't want a drink?" He went to the counter and grabbed a bottle of tequila.

"I should get going. It's late, and we have a long day ahead of us."

"Tell me about it." He brought the bottle and two glasses to the coffee table and flopped onto the couch. "Did you at least have some fun?"

"I did."

"Good." He poured tequila into both glasses, even though I said I didn't want any. "Are you sure you want to call it a night?"

TWENTY

A chill clung to the air, but it wasn't cold enough to seek shelter. With danger so close, he didn't want to be inside. He wanted to remain mobile, keeping an eye on his surroundings and the goings on in the city. By now, the police should be piecing together the truth. The evil uprising could be stopped, but only if they acted swiftly.

Nighttime always meant danger. But he wasn't as worried about the human variety. It was the supernatural that made him nervous. The subway tunnels were crawling with all sorts of otherworldly creatures. Most were humans masquerading around. Was that for their own protection? Or was it just a joke to them? The news broadcasts showed Dan Fielders for what he was. Why was everyone still so skeptical?

He bumped into a man on the train with white eyes and metallic blue spikes protruding from his skull. Cowering in fear, he threw up his hands and mumbled an apology as he headed to the other side of the car. None of the items in his pockets could protect him from whatever that thing was. He'd never seen a demon like that. How many varieties were there?

The thing with the spikes smiled at him with metal covered teeth. "No worries, mate."

For the duration of the ride, he kept an eye on the spiked beast, but it clung to the pole, talking to a woman wearing a red hood and carrying a curved walking stick. She didn't appear to be afraid.

While he tried to figure out if the spiked beast had cast some sort of spell over her, he fumbled with the wooden cross in his pocket. That wouldn't do. That would only stop the undead and possessed. Perhaps he should fill his canteen with holy water. The priests who performed exorcisms used it to cast out demons. At the very least, it should cause enough damage to slow them down.

At the next stop, the beast and the woman exited. Without thinking, he followed them. He didn't want to see the woman hurt. The metallic blue spikes stuck out among the crowd, and he followed them through the turnstile and up the stairs.

On the street, it was harder to keep up. They headed east, toward the water. The river wasn't a safe place, not for anyone. He had to save her.

In his haste, he didn't notice the bar door swinging open. The handle impacted with his stomach, forcing the air from his lungs. He stumbled backward.

The large group who just exited the bar didn't even notice him. Every member of the group had furry ears, claws, and fangs. Werewolves? Surely, they did not exist. It wasn't even a full moon. These had to be costumes.

Righting himself, he crept closer to make sure they were human. *You're losing it*, he thought. Reality and fantasy were starting to blur again. He had to focus on the things he knew were real. Werewolves were not.

"What's your problem, dude?" one of them asked when he got too close. "What the hell are you looking at? Haven't you ever seen a wolf before?"

"Stop it," he yelled at them. "Stop confusing me."

The group glanced back at him.

"Weirdo," one of them muttered.

"I'm not the weirdo. You're in danger. We're all in danger."

"Yeah, okay," another one said.

"Sleep it off, pal," a third one said.

He gawked at them as they continued down the street. By the time he turned away, the blue spiked beast and the woman in red had disappeared. Now how was he going to save her?

He was just one man. He needed help. An army. The city had thousands of police officers. But where were they? Why weren't they patrolling? Why weren't they hunting the demons and undead?

He picked a direction and set off, hoping it was the right way. The smell of the river assaulted his nostrils. The hairs on the back of his neck prickled. Evil had been done here. He remembered the smell of burning flesh and the screams. Even in his sleep, he couldn't escape the pained wails, begging for mercy.

Flashing red and blue lights attracted his attention. Spotlights illuminated the spot where the bad thing had happened. He crept closer, spotting the police tape and the uniformed officers standing guard.

"Move along, pal. There's nothing to see here," the officer said.

"What happened? Was it the woman in red?" he asked the bored patrolman.

The officer studied him closely. "Woman in red?"

"Yes, she wore a cape." He described the woman on the train. "She followed a monster." He described the man. "I don't know where they went. Is this his handiwork?"

"What do you know about monsters?" the cop asked.

Despite the crime scene tape indicating something gruesome had recently happened here, he felt relief. "They're hiding among us. They hurt the innocent. They'll hurt us all."

The officer nodded a few times. "How about you tell me your name?"

"Why? What does that matter?"

The officer gave him a tight smile. "I'm Mitch Tripplehorn. And you are?"

"Concerned." He pointed to the area which had been squared off on the ground where several people in jumpsuits appeared to be searching for something. "Did someone die?" But he already knew the answer.

"Yes."

"Was it ritualistic? A sacrifice?"

The officer waved to one of his friends. "Did you see something?"

"I see everything." He glanced in the direction of a nearby homeless encampment.

"Do you live there?" Tripplehorn asked.

"I exist everywhere."

"What about last night? And earlier today? Where were you existing then?"

He didn't answer, fearing it might be a trap.

Tripp stepped away from the tape, letting the other officer take over guarding the scene. "Is that where you're planning to spend the night?"

"I have to stay close to keep an eye out for the beast."

"How about you show me around?" Tripp asked.

"Do you think evil is hiding among us?" he asked.

"It might be. Or this beast could have hurt someone. Do you recall if he had any weapons on him?"

"Besides the metal spikes, no."

Tripp stayed close to him as they headed toward the tents and boxes. "Have you noticed anyone strange or unfamiliar in the area? Has anyone gone missing lately?"

He led the way through the tents, pointing out a few familiar faces as they made their way toward the back. "Jonah's gone."

"Jonah?"

"These are his things. He never leaves them behind. If he leaves, he takes them with him." He pointed to a sideways box covered by an old, tattered blanket. A beat-up knapsack sat underneath it.

Tripp reached for the radio clipped to the left side of his chest. "Where were you at eight a.m.?"

"I was at a diner, getting coffee."

"Which diner?"

"Marcy's."

Tripp turned his head away and whispered something in his radio while taking a headcount. "Sir, it's not safe out here tonight. Like you said, there's a monster on the loose. We're going to take everyone somewhere warm and safe."

A large transport vehicle pulled up. Several officers rounded up the encampment, causing a chorus of moans and curses.

"Get your things together," Tripp said. "You're going for a ride."

"I don't have anything, just what I'm carrying." Shoving his hands in his pockets, he took a step toward the bus before stopping and turning around. "You're the first one who's listened. You should know, I'm here to help you stop the evil forces."

"Good, we'll get you something to eat, a safe place to sleep, and a shower. The detectives will have questions in the morning. You can help them."

*   *   *

I woke up with a warm body pressed against my back. Moist breath brushed against my neck, and I buried my head under the blankets, hoping to escape. But it was too late. Gunnie's cold nose found my cheek.

"Stop that." I pushed his face away.

He barked, a high-pitched, shrill sound that would have woken the entire house, except by now my parents were already up and making breakfast. When the barking didn't work, he pawed at the blankets in an attempt to dig me out of my cocoon.

Relenting, I rolled onto my back. Gunnie wagged his tail and laid down on top of my chest, so I could pet him behind the ears. "You're getting too big for this, buddy. This is exactly why Dad doesn't want you sleeping on the bed."

But the puppy didn't seem to care.

We'd just drifted back into a nice, comfortable slumber when something clattered in the kitchen. Gunnie's ears perked up, and he lifted his head. A low growl came from his throat.

"It's okay. It's just Mom making a mess."

He listened for another thirty seconds before deciding I

was right and laid down. A minute later, he lifted his head again and stared out the window. His body went rigid for a few seconds, then he relaxed. His tail thumped against my leg, and he whined excitedly before crawling up my body and pushing the covers down with his nose.

"It's okay." I shifted, trying to ease out from underneath him while he lapped at my chin.

A moment later, the doorbell rang. Gunnie gave me one final lick and took off like a rocket, jabbing me with his front paws as he launched himself off the bed and onto the hardwood floor. He slid, scratching the wood and bunching the area rug as he struggled to gain traction before whimpering at the bedroom door.

I opened it, figuring Gunnie could deal with the intruder while I went back to sleep. But Mom's voice bellowed from below. "Liv, are you awake? Brad's here."

"Shit." I grabbed my phone, finding three waiting text messages. "I'll be right there." With lightning speed, I showered, dressed, and ran down the stairs. My partner was drinking coffee at the counter when I entered the kitchen.

"Are you okay?" he asked. "You didn't text me until early this morning."

"I texted you when I got home."

"Late night," he mused.

"What time did you get home, honey?" Dad asked. "I didn't hear you come in."

"It was after three."

"Where were you?" Mom asked.

"I gave Voletek a ride home. He had too much to drink."

"Jake Voletek?" Dad asked. "Manny's boy?" But my dad knew damn well who Jake Voletek was. He raised an eyebrow as if to say, *We'll talk about this later,* picked up Gunnie's leash, and took the dog outside.

"What were you doing all night?" Brad asked.

"Playing video games. What were you doing?"

Brad sipped his coffee and ignored the question. "Did you get Winston's message?"

"Yeah, and Mac's." I filled a mug and took a seat at the table. "It doesn't look like forensics found anything useful at either scene or in the vics' apartments. Mac said the footage from the Halloween shops is also a bust, given the costume the killer wore when he offed the Stevenses." I reached for the breakfast casserole and scooped some onto my plate, ignoring the scolding look from my mother. *Guests should get served first.* "How is it possible both of our cases have zero leads?"

"Not zero, but pretty damn close." Brad finished his coffee and helped himself to another cup. Given the circles under his eyes, he'd had a long night too.

"Brad, sit down and have some breakfast. You look like you're wasting away. Is this okay? If not, I can whip you up something else," Mom said.

"No, this looks great, Maria."

"Then sit down and eat." She pulled out the chair across from mine and took one of the clean plates off the stack, setting a place for Brad. "Mangia."

"Yes, ma'am." He sat down and filled his plate. "I'm hoping we'll get something out of Eldridge's party guests that will lead to our killer. Someone must have seen or heard something."

"You still think a coworker is responsible?" I asked. Last night, that seemed plausible, but this morning, I had my doubts. "How did they pull it off without getting covered in Dan's blood?"

"Costume change?" Brad suggested. "We know the killer wore gloves."

"But we searched every inch of Eldridge's house and didn't find anything. Evidence like that can't just walk away."

"Unless one of the guests took it with them." Brad reached into his pocket but couldn't find a pen. I handed him one from the counter, and he added that thought to the list he started the night before. "We need to nail down the timeline. We have to figure out every guest who arrived and left and when that happened."

"I thought we already tried that."

"We did, but it fell apart since so many guests seemed foggy and we didn't have much of a list. We have a better grasp now of who showed up at the party and what they wore than we did yesterday, courtesy of Mac's web crawlers and social media accounts."

"Did she find the vampire hunter wannabe?"

Brad capped the pen and picked up his fork. "He's still shrouded in mystery."

"Then why are you bothering with the rest of this when he's probably our guy?"

"Unless he isn't."

I blew out a breath. "I hate not knowing anything."

"Winston told me facial recognition still hasn't gotten any hits on the guy who stopped by Dan Fielders' apartment, but I'm hoping that might change. At the very least, I can show his photo to Eldridge's guests and see if anyone recognizes him. With any luck, it's the same guy Melanie Daggio saw in the Van Helsing costume."

"We're also supposed to follow up with the companies that purchased costumes and decorations in bulk. Between the haunted houses and escape rooms, we shouldn't have a shortage of suspects. We just need to pinpoint who had access to those specific costumes and decorations. We know the Stevenses had reservations at the inn with plans to see all the attractions. I'm sure Dan had something similar lined up. That could be our connection."

"You're back to assuming this is the work of one murderer?"

"I don't know."

Brad glanced into the foyer, wondering when my dad would return from walking the dog. "When I talked to Carrie last night, she thought the same person staked both victims."

"The metal cross through the chest counts as a staking too? Why can't we just call these fatal stabbings? That's what they are."

"With odd objects," Brad said.

"I could stab you with this fork." I held up my utensil. "You wouldn't say I staked you."

"I'd say you forked me."

"You'd like that, wouldn't you?" I crinkled my nose and narrowed my eyes before stabbing in his general direction.

"Liv," my mom placed her hand on my forearm, "you're

making a mess." She wiped up a fallen piece of scrambled egg. "Don't wave your fork around like that. You weren't this much trouble when you were a toddler."

I rolled my eyes and put the fork down.

Brad looked amused but held in his laughter. "I'm sorry, Maria. We're just overwhelmed right now."

"It sounds like it." She spooned a miniscule portion of breakfast onto her plate and took a dainty bite before reaching for an apple from the fruit bowl. "This time of year always brings out the kooks."

"Speaking of, Brad was wondering if you wouldn't mind making some more cookies."

Her face brightened. "Oh, you liked those? I wasn't sure how well they turned out. I'll get started on another batch after breakfast."

"You don't have to go through all that trouble," he said.

"It's no trouble at all. You work hard. You deserve a treat. Plus, now that you brought back my containers, it's only fair that I refill them for you."

"She says the same thing to Gunnie every time he brings her his empty bowl," I said, which earned me a slap on the leg.

For the rest of breakfast, Brad and my mom made polite conversation. I finished eating, took my plate to the sink, and peered out the window. Dad was circling the block slowly, letting Gunnie explore every fallen leaf and pinecone. Brad came up behind me, glancing back at my mom who had gone to get the ingredients from the pantry.

"Did you talk to your dad yet?" he whispered.

"No." I turned to look at him. "Is that why you came over so early?"

"That, and I couldn't sleep." He nodded out the window. "Perhaps it'd be best to have this conversation outside. Your mom doesn't like it when we talk shop."

"You read my mind."

After excusing ourselves, we headed in the direction my dad had gone. Brad kicked a pinecone into a pile of leaves. "What time did you get home last night? You texted me a little after three. I wondered what happened to you. I was getting worried."

"That's when I got home. You weren't waiting up for my text, were you?"

"No."

"Were you still with Carrie?"

He ignored the question. "What did you and Jake do all night? Were any eating utensils involved?"

I turned to look at him. "That's none of your business, but no, I didn't fork around with Jake. You ought to know me better than that."

"Right."

"We played video games. Arcade games, actually. Then we talked for a while. It turns out he's looking for a new apartment too. We ended up comparing notes and searching rental sites online."

"I bet he'd sublet your place," Brad said.

"You really think so?"

"It wouldn't hurt to ask."

"How do I explain the bloodstains in the hallway and kitchen?"

"Tell him it's tomato sauce or red wine. He won't know the difference."

"He might. He's a homicide detective and a total foodie."

Brad snorted. "He won't know. And if he's that desperate for a place, he won't care. That's just how it goes."

"I showed you mine. It's your turn to show me yours."

"I don't want to talk about it."

I stopped walking. "Is everything okay?"

"It will be."

I didn't like that answer. It's the one he always gave when things weren't okay. "You don't look like you've slept. I just...I worry."

He put his arm around my shoulders and gave me a squeeze. "Me too."

"Is that why you showed up at my parents' place unannounced? Were you afraid I spent the night with Jake?"

Again, he ignored me.

"Brad?"

"Hmm?" He kept his gaze ahead, waiting for my dad and Gunnie to circle back around and head toward us.

We promised each other no more secrets. But that didn't mean he had to tell me every detail of his private life. I just wasn't sure where the boundaries were. Truthfully, I'd never known because we never seemed to have any. "Do you think my dad knows more than we do about these murders?"

"No, but he might know something about the warning the commissioner's office received."

TWENTY-ONE

"Did you find the beast?" His leg jittered up and down.

"The one with the blue spikes?" Voletek pulled out a chair and put down a box of pastries. "Patrol searched the neighborhood, but they didn't find him or Little Red Riding Hood."

He scowled, shoving his hands into the pockets of his grey sweatshirt. "I'm not crazy."

"I never said you were. Riding Hood just happens to be what my notes say." Voletek stuck a cronut in his mouth before flipping over the notepad for the man to read. "I'm guessing that's the description we were using based on what she was wearing. You said she had on a red, hooded cape, right?"

"Yeah."

"So, what's the problem?" Voletek leaned back and chewed. He had yet to take off his sunglasses, but since the blinds were open and light was pouring into the roll-call room, which was where he was conducting the interview, at least he had an excuse.

"You didn't find either of them."

"That could be a problem, or it could mean she got away and everything's fine." Voletek nudged the pastries toward him. "Help yourself. I picked them up on my way here. They're still warm."

He shook his head, confusing Voletek who had never seen a homeless man turn down food. "The beast led her there for a reason. Evil things happen there."

"What can you tell me about that?" Voletek asked.

The man narrowed his eyes. "You know about the murder."

Flashes of burnt flesh and a bashed in skull came to mind. "What do you know about it?"

"It happened slowly. The screams were so loud. And the fire," he reached a trembling hand out to pick up the coffee cup, "only made it worse. It made it last longer. It gave the evil spirits time to escape, to inhabit others. They're among us now." He put the cup down, leaning forward. "Have you seen the news? You should pay close attention."

But Voletek was already paying attention to something else. "How did that happen?" He nodded at the man's hand. "It looks like it still hurts. Have you seen a doctor? It could be infected."

The man attempted to retract his hand, but Voletek pinned his wrist to the table. "It's fine. Leave me alone."

"That needs to be cleaned. It's a bad burn." Voletek eyed him. "How did it happen?"

He yanked his arm free, shoving it back into his pocket. In his haste, the tiny wooden cross fell out, along with a set of rosary beads. He knelt down, grabbing them off the floor.

"Were you there?" Voletek asked.

The man swallowed. "I know what happened. That is just the beginning, unless you stop it."

"Then tell me everything, starting with your name."

He started to speak, but froze as he studied his own reflection in the mirrored lenses. "Why are you wearing those?"

Voletek fingered the frame. "Sun's a bitch." He pulled them off. "Is that better?"

The man jumped backward, surprised when the detective revealed the bloody red eyes of a demon, and then he screamed.

*   *   *

"DeMarco," Lt. Winston headed for my desk, "did you speak to your father?"

"He doesn't have a clue what's going on," I said.

Winston didn't like that answer any more than I did. "All right. Maybe Voletek can use his connections to find out more about what's going on."

I glanced in the direction of Voletek's desk, but he wasn't there. Briefly, I wondered if he'd even bothered to crawl out of bed. Given how much tequila he put away the previous night, drinking double to make up for my lack of imbibing, he probably called in sick.

Brad checked his messages and read every note that had been left on his desk. "Do you want us to work out of the conference room, Lieutenant?"

"Whatever you want. You know what to do. I don't have to hold your hand." Winston retreated back to his office.

"Are you sure he likes me?" Brad asked.

"Why, because he doesn't want to hold your hand?"

"Something like that."

"We have bigger issues right now."

"No shit." Something on the edge of my desk caught his eye. Reaching over, he picked up the rectangular box. "When did you get this?"

"What?" I read the label on the side. *Desktop Skee-Ball.* Laughing, I shook my head. "Apparently, last night." That must have been the item Voletek had taken from the middle shelf.

Brad arched an eyebrow and put the box down. "Jake gave you a gift?"

"That's my prize."

"You went to an arcade?"

I stared at my partner. "I already told you that."

"I know but..." he glanced at the box again, "never mind."

"You didn't believe me?"

Before Brad could answer, his phone rang. After jotting down a few notes, he updated me on the progress from the night before. All mention of last night and more pleasant topics vanished as we got to work.

The hours ran together into one never-ending shift. Despite the parade of interviews we conducted, we still weren't any closer to identifying Dan Fielders' killer. Every single guest, including the party crashers, had alibis. Forensics backed up their stories, which meant Dan Fielders was murdered by an unknown third party.

Melanie Daggio's story remained consistent. However, no one had seen his face or recognized him from the surveillance footage taken from Dan's apartment. Luckily, after showing several other guests the costume the killer wore, two remembered seeing him. Emmett Walters recalled the man in the hat and leather coat entering through the front door a few minutes before eleven p.m. He thought the man had gone on an ice run, but it turned out that wasn't the case.

However, Vivica didn't remember seeing him at the party. She was our last interview of the day and appeared even more agitated than she had the first time we spoke to her. The reality of the situation had set in.

"I don't know who that is. I never saw anyone wearing that outfit at the party," she insisted. "I'm sure if it was someone Dan knew, he would have introduced us."

"We think this man crashed the party, intending to kill Dan," Brad said. "That's why it's really important you tell us about any problems he had with his coworkers or issues with friends."

"Was he ever stalked or threatened?" I asked.

"I don't think so."

"He owned a handgun which he kept in his bedside table. Did he own that for protection?"

"I'm not sure. He told me once that he thought a man had the right to defend his home."

"When did he get the gun?" Brad asked.

"Sometime before we met," she said.

I checked the records, but Dan had purchased it when he turned twenty-two.

"What about the decorations in Dan's house?" Brad asked. "Do you know where he bought that stuff?"

She sighed. "Going out with him was like taking a toddler to the toy store. It didn't matter where we were going or what we were doing, if he spotted a Halloween display in the drug store or at the supermarket, he had to check it out. If we walked by a boutique or party supply place, he had to go inside. That crap in his apartment came from all over the place. He even ordered stuff online when he found it clearanced, like that dumbass mummy."

"Not a fan?" I asked.

"Hell no. It's why I never spent much time at his place. It was always so creepy, like going into a joke shop. I always thought I'd be chased out by a homicidal clown."

"Did you and Dan ever visit any haunted attractions?" Brad asked.

"I feel like we did them all."

"What about the haunted hayride?"

"We did that and the haunted maze as soon as they opened. Dan wanted to make reservations for one of the haunted rooms at the inn, but they were booked solid. Thank god." She looked sad. "Crap like this excited him, but I didn't really like it. Last month, we did three different ghost tours just to get into the spirit of things." She rolled her eyes. "That's the pun he kept making. If there is an afterlife, like in *Casper*, I bet he's getting a kick out of being a ghost."

"Do you know anything about this?" Brad showed her the photos of the staked heart in the box.

"Is that a human heart?" She cringed. "That's just sick. That's not Dan's heart, is it?"

"No, ma'am," Brad said. "That's a prop. It's made to look and feel real. It has a string that makes it appear to pump. We found it inside Dan's apartment. We thought it might be a threat."

She swallowed unsteadily a few times. "I'm gonna—"

I grabbed the wastebasket and shoved it under her chin before she vomited on our conference table. My partner rubbed her back, gently pulling her hair away from her face. I grabbed a tissue box and handed her a few to wipe her mouth.

"You think whoever stabbed Dan gave him this as a

warning?" She blotted her lips. Her cheeks were red and streaked with tears. "That's so fucking sick."

"We don't know. It could be something Dan set up himself. The first time we spoke, you said his murder seemed like the kind of prank he would pull. Could this have been a practice run? Perhaps he thought he'd wear a fake heart beneath his costume that could be stabbed?"

"That would mean he was killed unintentionally," she said.

"We don't think that's the case, but we need to know everything," Brad insisted. "Is it a possibility?"

Her eyes came to rest on the open costume catalog. "That tracks, I guess. I mean if you think the killer wore a vampire hunter outfit and killed him, then this could all be a horrible misunderstanding." She sniffled, pressing a clean tissue to her eyes before blowing her nose. "That stupid son of a bitch."

"Ma'am," Brad tried to backpedal, "the heart in the box might have served as a warning. Since the killer entered the house, stabbed Dan, and left, we have to assume he meant to cause Dan harm."

"You're sure he wore this?" She stared at the catalog page.

"Yes." I waited, hoping she'd have an epiphany. Something in her eyes told me she had a thought. "What is it? Why is that important?"

"It's nothing." She tossed the tissue into the pail. "May I go? I'm not feeling well. This entire ordeal is just too upsetting. I can't do this right now. I'm sorry."

"We'll have someone drive you home," Brad said.

By the time he returned to the conference room, I'd taken out the garbage and cleaned up the mess, but the stench of vomit remained. Our questions upset her. That was far more emotion than I expected to see from the woman who had only showed annoyance and irritation the previous day.

"I guess the shock wore off," Brad said. "She's upset."

"She knows something."

"Are you back to thinking she killed him?"

"Maybe." I looked down at the catalog. "Something on

this page freaked her out. I saw it in her eyes."

"When I asked her point blank if she saw someone wearing that costume at the party, she gave us a rather convincing no."

"There's more to it, I think." I chewed on my bottom lip while Brad found a disinfectant spray and misted the room. "Can we swing by the bar before we head to the haunted houses?"

"You think the killer met her at the bar?"

"I don't know. But if she thought the costume looked familiar, we might find a photo of it on that corkboard."

Just as we were exiting the conference room, Voletek came down the hallway. He smiled, despite the insane day we were having. From his pallor and red eyes, he hadn't completely eliminated the hangover.

"Did you guys make any progress?" he asked.

"We're working on it." Brad gave him a look. "I'm not sure which reeks worse, you or the vomit. It appears you had quite the party last night. Didn't I tell you to behave?"

"Relax. Liv didn't cheat on the cleanse. Instead, I drank her share too."

"Next time, don't." Brad continued past him toward the double doors.

"What's got his panties in a twist?"

"He doesn't like bodies and unsolved murders." My nose crinkled as Voletek stepped closer. "No offense, but you stink."

"That's not me." He lifted his shirt away from his chest and sniffed it. "Okay, it is me, but it's also the dozen homeless guys I spoke to today. Yesterday's murder took place close to their encampment. It looks like the vic was taken from there, tortured, and killed in some kind of weird ritual." Voletek headed for his desk. "One of them seemed very into the concept. He cooperated for a while, but then he freaked out. He's got some kind of mental health issue. He's getting evaluated now, but we don't have enough to charge him or hold him. If he's not a danger to himself or others, they'll probably kick him."

"Run a background while you wait."

"Can't. He refused to tell me his name. He didn't have

any ID either, but he might be a suspect. He had burns on his hands, and he seems to know a lot about the murder."

"Did you run his prints?" I asked.

"They wouldn't register between the burns and scar tissue. That might make him the killer or possibly a victim who escaped. It's tough to say right now. But he knows a lot more than he should for an innocent bystander."

"That's a tough one, but I'm sure you'll figure it out. I'd help, but I gotta go. Maybe take a shower while I'm gone."

I found Brad sitting on the top step, waiting for me. "Mac just called," he said. "She hasn't had any luck with the surveillance feeds. She's tried running the stills through facial recognition, but with the angles we have, it's a crapshoot. We're flying blind on the Stevenses' murders."

"I wish we knew if this was the work of the same guy."

"Me too. But since he didn't leave a calling card behind, we can't know for sure. That's why I showed Melanie Daggio the footage from the other crime scene. But she didn't recognize the Stevenses' killer as the man from the party. Take from that what you will."

"She only paid attention to the costume."

"The same's true of Emmett Walters and the other guest who recalled seeing the vampire hunter outfit. Unfortunately, the Stevenses were killed by a vampire warrior, not a vampire hunter."

"When we get to the bar, we should check for that costume too."

"You read my mind," Brad said. "I'm curious. Do you and Voletek have the same telepathic connection?"

"Jealous?" I asked as we climbed into the car.

"A little. You guys spent the night at an arcade, drinking and playing skee-ball. I'm feeling a bit deprived. How come we never do anything like that?"

"I thought you weren't drinking. Did you break your streak last night?"

"Do you want to know what I was doing last night?" he asked, even though I could tell he wanted to get whatever it was off his chest after avoiding the question all day.

"No, that's okay. You don't have to tell me."

"Dammit, Liv. You're always such a ballbuster."

"In that case, I'll leave you alone."

He waited a full thirty seconds before saying, "Carrie's in trouble."

Only one thought came to mind. *Pregnant.* I turned to stare at Brad. Was my partner going to be a father? How could he let this happen?

"Liv, watch out."

"Shit." I hit the brake before I slammed into the double-parked car in front of me.

"Pay attention. You're driving." He exhaled. "Are you okay?"

"Are you? What are you and Carrie going to do?"

"I'm going to do what I can to get this guy to back off. She doesn't want to escalate the situation. She doesn't think he's dangerous, but I don't know. We hear about this kind of thing happening all the time. I think I'm more freaked out than she is."

"What?" I blinked, glancing from him to the road. "What guy?"

"Carrie's boyfriend, the guy she's been seeing these last few months, turned out to be a total con artist. She came home one day and found most of her stuff missing. He said someone broke in, but it turns out he stole her stuff. She didn't realize that until he tried to empty her bank account, but he didn't know her PIN. The bank notified her, and she realized what was going on."

"She needs to report him."

"She doesn't want anyone in the department to know about this. She feels stupid."

"He's a thief and a liar."

"That's what I told her. Plus, he could be dangerous."

"Did she change her locks?"

"Yes."

"What about getting a TRO?"

"She won't do it. She asked me to help her pack up his shit and supervise him when he comes to get it. She's hoping if I show up with my gun and badge, it'll scare him off. And he'll leave her alone from now on."

"Has he been harassing her?"

"Just to get his stuff back." Brad looked uneasy. "She

didn't want me to say anything to anyone, including you, but I thought maybe you could convince her to press charges against him. You've helped Emma deal with plenty of shitty men. You probably know the protocol better than I do."

"Yeah, sure. No problem."

He gave me an odd look. "Why do you seem relieved? This guy knows where she lives. If he is dangerous or vengeful, she could be in real trouble."

"That's terrible. It is. But it could be worse. He hasn't hurt her or threatened her. So he's probably just a scammer creep. Where did she meet him?"

"At spin class."

"He needs defined leg muscles and strong lungs to run away when the women he scams chase after him."

Brad laughed.

"It'll be okay," I said. "She's a lucky lady. She's got you in her corner."

"Correction, she's got us."

TWENTY-TWO

As soon as he was free, he went home to shower and clean himself up. *Disgusting*, he thought as he scrubbed his face and soaped up his body. The hot spray washed the dirt and grime down the drain, just like it had the blood. He waited for the water to turn clear before stepping out and toweling off.

Eat or sleep, he wondered, checking his reflection in the mirror. But before he could decide, someone knocked on his door.

It was an unfamiliar sound. He didn't get guests. Confused, he reached for the long-handled axe.

"Hey, it's me," Vivica Smaldey called from the other side. "Open up." She knocked again, more frantically.

He put the axe in the closet, along with his grimy sweatshirt, glanced around to make sure the place was neat enough for the woman of his dreams, and opened the door. "What are you doing here?"

She marched right past him. "You invited me back here the other night, remember? I thought it was an open invitation. Didn't you say that?"

"Oh, right." He ran a hand through his damp hair. "Do you want to sit down? I can make you something to eat."

"I'm not hungry." She looked ill.

"Viv, what's wrong?"

"We've known each other a long time. You're one of my closest friends. I always trusted you."

He smiled, moving to brush a stray strand of hair back behind her ear. "I'm always here for you. You know that." The hurt, questioning look on her face made him nervous.

"Dan's dead."

"So?"

She took a step back, as if she'd been slapped. "So? That's all you have to say?"

"What do you want me to say?"

"I called you that afternoon and told you about the party. I told you I was going with Dan."

"Viv, you don't look so good. Sit down. Let me get you a glass of water." Her questions sounded more and more like accusations. He didn't like that. He'd done this for her. He'd saved her. Didn't she realize this was for the best? She should be thanking him, not accusing him. He took her by the elbow and led her to a chair. "Stay right here. I'll be right back."

"We made plans to meet up afterward at that bar. But you were late."

"I wasn't late. I was waiting for you. We got our signals crossed, remember?"

"What were you wearing?"

His face flushed. She realized what he'd done, and she didn't sound pleased. Why didn't she understand? "Um...I don't remember."

"You had on a long leather jacket. I've never seen you wear that before."

"You hardly ever see me. You haven't made much time for us in the last few months, since you started dating Dan. He was never good enough for you. I told you that. Didn't you see what he was?"

"What was that?"

"Don't make me say it. You saw his teeth. He wasn't a good guy. It's not safe hanging around someone like that." He returned with a glass of water to find her standing in front of the open closet door. "What are you looking for?"

"The coat you wore the other night. I want to see it."

"Why?"

She spun. "Show me."

"I don't have it. I left it at work."

"I thought you quit your job," she said.

"I wish I could, but someone has to do it."

She flipped through the clothes hanging in the closet. Stopping when she got to the end and spotted the axe propped against the back. "Why do you have that?"

"I got it from work." He handed her the water and closed the closet door, blocking it by leaning against it. "What do you want, Viv?"

Despite the fear on her face, she smiled. "I want us to be together. I thought now that I'm unattached, we could finally give this a shot. What do you say?"

The corners of his mouth lifted upward. "You have no idea how long I've been waiting to hear you say that."

She smiled, but it looked pinched. "I never realized how you felt. Why didn't you tell me?"

"You always saw me as the nerdy guy who helped with your homework. I was never anything more. Cheerleaders date football players, not mathletes." As he said it, his hands balled into fists.

"That's not true. I always had a crush on you." She reached for his hand, pulling him away from the closet door. "Now that Dan's out of the way, we can finally be together. But I have to ask you one thing, and I need you to tell me the truth. Did you get rid of Dan?"

"I did what was best for you. I protected you."

She swallowed, the smile faltering as she took a step backward. She forced it back onto her face, but her voice sounded strange, tinny, when she asked, "Is that why you killed him?"

He closed his eyes. This wasn't supposed to happen this way. She wasn't supposed to look like that or ask these questions. "He'd never let you go. He'd find a way to possess you, to turn you into the thing he wanted. I didn't have a choice. I had to free you from his manipulation. You couldn't see what he was doing to you, but I could. This was the only way. Seeing the two of you together hurt me.

It would have killed me."

She turned to run, but he couldn't let her go. She was confused. She didn't understand his actions were necessary. He caught her at the door, slamming it shut before she could escape. Before the scream even left her lips, he covered her mouth with his hand. She bit his palm, and he saw red.

He hit her harder than he meant to. She crashed into one of the boxes near the door and fell into the table. Her head cracked against the edge, and she didn't move again.

"Shit." He rushed to her, fearing the worst. But she was still breathing. Unconscious, but alive.

Calmer, he picked her up and placed her on his bed. Now what was he going to do with her?

*   *   *

The bar didn't have any photos hanging on the board that matched the costumes our suspects wore. We showed the catalog and surveillance photos to the bartender, but he didn't think he'd seen anyone like that at the bar.

"I would have remembered that hat," he said. "And if some guy came in wearing a vampire warrior costume, he would have entered the costume contest."

"Maybe." But I wasn't convinced.

After leaving the bar, we scoped out the area attractions. Plenty of places remembered Dan and Vivica. It wasn't that often they had quasi-celebrities in their midst, especially ones with actual fangs. However, the Stevenses hadn't visited most of these places or hadn't made enough of an impact for anyone to remember them.

At every attraction, I inquired as to the bulk Halloween purchases. The two escape rooms hadn't even started decorating for Halloween yet. The items remained in brand new condition with the tags intact. No one had taken or worn them, and every stake and cross was accounted for.

We checked a few of the haunted houses. They'd already set everything up. One of the houses let us speak to the actors who had been assigned to wear the costumes in question. But after running names and checking alibis, that turned out to be a bust.

Several other haunted houses and area attractions refused to comply with our request for additional information. Until we handed them a court order, they refused to sacrifice their employees' and guests' rights to privacy. That seemed an extreme stance to take, but if they didn't want to cooperate, we couldn't force the issue. However, a judge could.

"Let's finish up at the inn," Brad said. "Since our victims had the haunted hayride in common, there's probably something to it."

"How do they have that in common? The Stevenses never made it to the hayride. They died before they got there."

As we approached the inn, orange, purple, and blue lights directed me around the building toward a valet parking stand. Hundreds of people were clustered around the hay bales and pumpkins. Kids chased one another, screaming and laughing. Adults drank apple cider and hot chocolate while children threw leaves at one another and climbed on top of the hay. Nearly everyone had a costume or face paint. The energy was practically infectious.

"Since when do inns have valet parking?" I asked.

"The parking isn't for the inn. It's for the maze." Brad pointed to the giant mass which had taken over the parking lot and a good portion of the grounds. Several different ticket booths were set up around the inn for the various attractions.

Flashing my badge at the parking attendant, I stepped out of the car. The smell of burning leaves and pumpkin spice assaulted my nostrils. The scent of cinnamon, nutmeg, fresh apples, and pumpkins competed for dominance. A refreshment stand stood a few yards away. The line for that rivaled the most popular food truck in the city.

"Who's in charge?" I asked.

"Um," the parking attendant glanced behind him, "I'm not really sure."

"We'll figure it out." Brad jerked his head toward the inn. "We're leaving the car here. Don't block us in."

"No, sir," the attendant said, despite the ever-growing line of vehicles behind us.

Inside, the noise was muted. A few people milled about the lobby, but they appeared to be regular guests. I didn't see anyone in costume. Two clerks remained behind the welcome desk. One wore cat ears and had painted black whiskers on her cheeks with eyeliner. The other dressed normally in a button-down shirt and black dress pants.

Brad went to the counter, offering a polite smile to the woman in the cat ears. My partner, always so predictable.

"How may I help you, sir?" she asked.

He placed his badge inconspicuously on the desk. "I have a few questions I was hoping you could answer."

"I'll do my best."

After asking about Roger Stevens' reservations and if Dan Fielders or Vivica Smaldey had made arrangements to stay at the inn, we shifted gears to the festivities outside. Since the inn ran several attractions, they had purchased costumes, decorations, and accessories from area stores and distributors. They had purchased the entire line of costumes from Howls-R-Us. When the questions became too difficult for her to answer, she called for the manager, who led us into his office.

"I can't imagine anyone we've hired would do something as heinous as that," he said. "We run background checks on every employee. As a rule, we tend to avoid hiring people with criminal records."

"What about the seasonal hires?" Brad asked.

"We screen all applications."

"I'm sure you do. But we're still going to need a list of everyone who had access to the costumes, specifically these two costumes." Brad showed him the catalog.

"Those costumes?" He chewed on his bottom lip. "We keep all the costumes and accessories in one place."

"Can you show us where?" I asked.

"Fine." He led us through the lobby and out a back door. The inn had an attached restaurant, which was no longer in service. The dining area had been converted to a dressing room. Dozens of clothing racks lined one wall while a row of tables held accessories and props. Beyond that were tables of makeup and lighted mirrors. The runway shows during Fashion Week had nothing on this place. "As you can see, it's easy access for any one of our staff."

"Then we're going to need a list of everyone who works here."

The manager shook his head. "I'm sorry, but this is our busiest time of year. I don't have time for you to harass the workers over something as ridiculous as the possibility one of them is a killer. This isn't some B-horror movie. I'm sure the costumes you're looking for are here somewhere, either on the rack or in use right now."

"Do you mind if we look around?" Brad asked.

"You can look, but that's it."

"Running such a large venture must require permits and inspections. Having this many people on the premises could be a fire hazard," I said, "particularly with all that hay and the fire pit you have. Have you spoken to the fire marshal to make sure everything is up to code?"

"We have all necessary permits," he said. "Our paperwork is in order."

"What about your insurance company? Do your premiums cover events of this magnitude? What kind of liability coverage do you have for something like this? Or do you downplay it and hope your regular coverage will handle whatever happens? Because I'd hate to see the lawsuits resulting from visitors or guests being killed on the premises."

"You can't threaten me."

I held up my hands. "That wasn't a threat, sir. I was merely voicing an observation. It'd be a shame if this had to get shut down early, particularly when there are so many people enjoying the festivities."

"Liv," Brad communicated with his eyes that I should drop it, so I did, "check over there." We scanned every rack we could find, but the vampire warrior and Van Helsing costumes were nowhere to be found. He thanked the manager for his time, and we left the vast dressing room.

"We need a warrant," I said.

"No shit. Call it in and get the ball-rolling. In the meantime, let's take a look outside. Maybe we'll spot the person we're looking for."

But as night fell and the crowd grew, our chances of locating anyone wearing either costume decreased significantly. The court order was in the works, but that would take time. Everything always took time. I just hoped we wouldn't be called to another crime scene while we waited for the ink to dry.

"The costumes were here, and now they're not." I gave my partner a pointed look as we got back into the car. "We know Dan and Vivica came here. I'm guessing Roger Stevens and Cassie probably did too. They would have had to in order to buy their tickets." I pointed to a sandwich board which announced *Get Your Tickets Here* in red and white paint. "As far as I know, they have to be purchased in person."

Brad double-checked that on his phone. "You're right." He sucked in a breath as he watched hundreds of people, mostly families with children, laugh and play. "Between the ticket sales and the missing costumes, this must be where our killer hunts. This is just like the plot of most slasher films." He scratched his cheek. "Any one of these people could be next."

TWENTY-THREE

We spent the rest of the week going over every minute detail of our victims' lives. But there was no other overlap. The only connection between our victims was the haunted hayride.

"I left Vivica another message, but she hasn't returned any of my calls," I said, hanging up the phone. "Maybe you should give it a try."

Brad picked up his desk phone and dialed. "Voicemail." He rubbed his eyes. "Have you tried Asta?"

"She said Vivica texted her a few days ago and told her she was going to get out of town for a while and go radio silent until after Dan's funeral. She didn't want to deal with the press or Dan's coworkers."

"I don't like it. We should have put a detail on her and told her not to leave town."

"Too late now." I rocked back in my chair and glanced at the conference room which had been overrun with file boxes. Officers had served warrants to every area attraction. We had over two thousand employee records to filter through, and while we'd made a substantial dent, we still weren't any closer to identifying the killer. Several officers had been assigned to parse through the information and run background checks on every viable suspect, but it would be weeks before we finished the analysis.

"Taking a break?" Voletek scooted his chair beside Brad's and flopped a file down on my partner's desk. "I could use a second set of eyes on this."

"What happened to Lisco?" Brad asked. "I thought she was helping you."

"She left an hour ago. But you guys never know when to call it a night. I appreciate that kind of dedication."

"Are you going to tell your dad that?"

"I've always said lovely things about you. I'm just not sure my dad's got that much influence over the commissioner."

Brad snapped his fingers. "Darn it."

"What do you want, Jake?" I asked.

"As you know, I've identified the victim in that gruesome homicide."

"Jonah Miller." Brad picked up the file, which contained recent surveillance photos. "It looks like you already have a suspect."

"I'm not sure. That's why I want a second opinion. Something just doesn't seem right."

"Your evidence is circumstantial. What did forensics say?"

"They didn't come up with much. The fire destroyed a lot."

"What about the murder weapon?" I asked.

"It was a knife, something with a straight edge, at least four or five inches long. The killer used it to cut and cauterize. I'm guessing he tossed it in the river when he was through."

"But you have a suspect." I took the file from Brad. "Why don't you have his name listed?"

"He wouldn't give me one," Voletek said. "He has no ID or discernible fingerprints. Tripp assumed he was homeless, but I've flashed his photo around at area shelters, clinics, and soup kitchens and no one recognizes him."

"Or they aren't talking," Brad said. "Do you think he

burned off his fingerprints on purpose?"

"My first thought was it happened when he was torturing and mutilating his victim. The wounds appear consistent with the injuries the ME found on Miller's body." He pointed to a photo in the file.

"What about DNA?" I asked. "If he's been through the system, his DNA might be on file."

Voletek shook his head. "It hasn't come back yet, but with the way things are going, I'm not holding out much hope."

"What are you doing?" Brad asked.

"I have a unit keeping an eye on him, but he's slipped them at least four times."

"That's impressive. Who is this guy? Jason Bourne?"

"I don't know. Tripp brought him in originally because he'd come up to him at the crime scene, spouting out all kinds of things about evil forces at play. I'm thinking he could be the guy who sent the warning to headquarters."

"Which would make this a task force issue," I said. "That could get your DNA analysis kicked to the front of the list."

Voletek glanced at the phone on my desk. "Well, if you think so."

"All you had to do was ask." I made the call, reading the case number off the folder. "You should have it by Monday. You know how the lab gets over the weekend."

"Thanks, princess." Voletek picked up the file and winked at me.

"Don't call me that."

"Right, sorry, your excellency." He bowed and slid his chair back to his desk.

"That does have a nice ring to it," Brad said. "Maybe you should have a nameplate made."

"I'll think about it."

Checking the time, Brad closed the files on his desk. "I'm gonna call it a night. I'm supposed to meet Carrie early tomorrow morning. Her loser ex-boyfriend's dropping by her place at 7:30, and she wants me there before that."

"Why so early?"

"He has to be at work at eight, so it makes sense to do it

before. Carrie normally works mornings, but someone's covering for her. She's a little worried this putz might try something."

"Which is why you'll be there. Do you need backup?"

"I think I can handle this, and if I can't, I'll have a patrol unit arrest the bastard."

"Good plan, just be careful. The guy's probably not dangerous, but you never know."

"What are you doing with your day off?"

"Emma and I are going to the mall. She said she needs some retail therapy. After that, we're supposed to catch a movie and get dinner."

"Have fun."

"Hey, if you need me to talk to Carrie or come with you, I can always cancel."

"This is just the pick-up. Carrie isn't even planning on seeing or speaking to him. She's going to hang out at my place until it's over. The rest will depend on if he tries anything or approaches her after he gets his stuff back. That's when I might need you to give her the talk. You could invite Emma along. She could be the example of what not to do."

"Except you're not supposed to be spreading any of this around, remember? I doubt Carrie wants to be blindsided by a third party." I narrowed my eyes. "Have you even told her you told me what's going on?"

"I mentioned it. She wasn't surprised, but she wasn't happy about it either. That's why it's probably best if you wait in the wings for now."

"Whatever you want. She's your—" I stopped myself from saying it because I didn't want Brad to berate me again. He hated it when I called her his girlfriend and he hated it even more when I called her his ex. Nothing made the man happy. "Friend."

He put on his jacket and pushed in his chair. "I'll call you Sunday and let you know how it went."

"You can call me tomorrow." Particularly during dinner, but I couldn't add that part. I didn't want him to ridicule me for agreeing to a blind date.

"Nah. Em hates it when I interrupt girl time. And with

all the overtime hours we've put in, she'll say I'm hogging you."

"The two of you don't seem to realize I have free will."

"Do you?" He tapped on my desk. "Where are you staying tonight?"

"At Emma's."

"Okay. Have fun."

TWENTY-FOUR

The sound of laughter caused him to turn. Newlyweds, as if the glowing bliss they exuded from their bleached smiles and constant exchanges of affection wasn't enough to tip off the world, they had to make an even bigger spectacle of themselves. The husband, a former triple A baseball player who dressed the part and acted like he never left the frat house, scooped his new bride off the ground and threw her over his shoulder. She squealed, brushing the long, golden locks out of her face while she pretended to beat against his back. He was just like all the athletes who'd hit on Vivica. God, how he loathed and despised them.

"Ronnie, put me down." The woman pounded on his back, giggling.

Ron heaved her a little farther over his shoulder, patting her ass. "Are you sure that's what you want, Jodie?"

She squealed again, feigning annoyance despite her delight. "Ronnie, people are staring."

"Are they?" He spun around the courtyard. "Who's staring, honey? That guy over there," he pointed, "is he staring?"

Jodie looked up, her brilliant teal eyes coming to rest upon him. She blushed, and the man watching them smiled, not because he found anything pleasant about the situation. Quite the opposite, in fact. But he knew what was expected of him. He had to act the part, even though it made him sick to his stomach. Her freckled cheeks turned a darker shade of crimson.

"Yes, he is. Ron, put me down, now." Her voice took on a sharp edge, and her husband reluctantly put her back on the ground. She wobbled for a moment on the wedge heels, using her instability as an excuse to bury her face in Ron's neck.

Ron laughed gently and kissed her forehead. "I love you, babe. You know I'm just messing around."

She said something, but he didn't quite catch it. Not that he minded. So many couples came and went. They had no idea how lucky they were and how short-lived their happiness would be. He and Viv had mere seconds together before she freaked out. Why did these people get to be happy when he wasn't?

He couldn't take it anymore. Watching them flaunt their marital bliss, day in and day out, made him want to hurl himself off the roof or worse. Didn't they realize how devastated he was? Why did they insist on torturing him?

Everywhere he turned, couples were practically copulating in public. He couldn't take it. He had to get away from them. He had to make them stop, just like those sick freaks in the alley, just like Dan Fielders. Why were unsuspecting women drawn to these creatures? Was this because of the lie Hollywood had told, making vampires out to be sexy instead of deadly?

He felt his smile cracking, so he tilted his chin down, forcing himself to concentrate on the price list taped to the table. If he waited long enough, maybe they'd go away. But Ron and Jodie weren't smart enough to wander off in their embarrassment. They had to add insult to injury.

"Excuse me," Ron stepped up to the table, his fingers dipping into the front pocket of his wife's jeans, "can you tell us about the maze?"

He looked up, doing his best to appear friendly. "It's a haunted maze."

"Is it really haunted?" Ron asked.

Jodie pinched his side, making him laugh. He turned to

look at her, causing her cheeks to flush again. "Is it scary? Like, do people in masks jump out and stuff?"

"You'll have to find out for yourselves." He pointed to the hokey *Beware* sign at the entrance.

"What time does it open?" Ron asked.

"Dusk, when the sun has set and the wind is howling," he recited in the creepy voice he'd been instructed to use. It was a miracle he didn't vomit every time he had to say it. At least these people weren't in costume. The couples who dressed up always had some kind of exhibitionist fetish, like the sports stars and cheerleaders from his past. They thought the masks would conceal their depravity, but it only drew more attention to them, making it impossible for him to ignore.

"I don't know." Jodie stared at the entrance, which had some crime scene tape draped over it. "You know I'm not really into being scared."

"That's because the babes always die first in those horror movies," Ron teased. "You know you'd be the killer's first victim."

"That's not nice. Why would you say something like that?"

"It's because you're so damn beautiful. The hot chicks always go first."

"Well, maybe I won't go at all."

"Oh, come on. It'll be fun. Right?" Ron looked at him to provide encouragement, but he appeared distracted by the register.

She looked back at the sign with the creepy scarecrow and demonic crows with their red eyes and bloody bits hanging from their plastic beaks. "Um, is there like an age range?"

The man pointed to the notice hanging from the table. *Family fun. For ages 7 and up.* In smaller print was a legal disclaimer about people with high blood pressure, epilepsy, and heart problems avoiding it, but it was the standard line one would see at any amusement park ride.

"Come on. Puh-lease." Ron rolled down his lower lip, revealing two sharp canines, and made whimpering sounds like a dog.

"Fine," she said, "but that means if we do this tonight, I get to pick what we do today."

"Anything you want, Mrs. Gesper."

She giggled, her cheeks turning a light pink. While she looked up at him from beneath her lashes, she snaked one of her hands behind his back. Ron jumped in surprise, returning her mischievous grin as he hurriedly tossed a few bills on the table.

"Here are your tickets," he said, staring at the table to avoid looking at them. Just a few more seconds, and they'd be gone. He'd never see them again, and then he could forget about the physical pain their presence caused him.

"What time do you close?" Ron hurriedly shoved the tickets into his pocket, shaking his head at the offered change.

"Midnight." He tried to keep his gaze on Ron, but he couldn't help but notice Jodie step away from her husband, her fingers trailing down his arm as she wandered across the courtyard in the direction of the inn.

"Good. We might just make that. If not, maybe tomorrow." Ron winked at the guy. "It looks like I have some husbandly duties to perform. Happy wife, happy life, right?" Ron dashed after her. At the sound of his approach, she took off running, and he chased after her.

He dropped Ron's change into the donation jar, fighting to unclench his jaw when Jodie let out another delighted shriek, which felt like a dagger piercing his heart as Ron grabbed her, kissed her, and carried her up the front steps. It was probably too late to save her.

* * *

"Stop fidgeting, Liv." Emma glared at me from across the table. "I swear, if you look at your phone one more time, I'm taking it away."

I put the phone back in the tiny handbag, which was too small to hold much of anything. Frankly, I'd been surprised to fit my badge inside, but now, it was stuck in there pretty good. It'd be a miracle if I could get it out without ripping the lining. "I told you Brad might need me to help with the

Carrie situation."

"He's a big boy. He can handle it himself." She raised an eyebrow. "Do you think they're gonna get back together?"

"I don't know." I swirled the ice around my glass. "He says no, but the reason Carrie called things off between them was because she wanted to get serious with this other guy."

"The guy who robbed her blind and tried to empty her bank account?"

"Yeah."

Emma snorted. "Been there, done that. I'm guessing that means she'll be ready for a good guy. Or, in this case, Bradley."

"Brad is a good guy."

Emma gave me that annoying look of hers, like she wanted to argue.

"He is," I said. "He just doesn't have much luck with relationships. Actually, I'm pretty sure he avoids anything serious. He has some things he has to address, but he's working on it. If he and Carrie give it another shot, it might turn out differently this time."

"I doubt that, since he's already in a long-term thing with you. Most women won't put up with that shit. Eventually, they'll get tired of always coming in second."

"Em, we're not like that. We work together. We're friends. He's like family. He's the male version of you."

She laughed into her wine. "Does that mean you want to sleep with me too?"

"I don't want to sleep with either of you." I sighed. "Let's just drop this." I looked at my watch. "The guys are already fifteen minutes late. I bet my date stood me up and your date doesn't know what to say. Why don't you text him that I had to leave, and see what happens? If he says he still wants to meet up with you, I'll go home."

"They'll be here." Emma picked up the bottle of red wine and offered it to me.

"I can't. I'm on call."

"You're always on call. You're worse than the doctors I work with. At least they know how to cut loose and have a good time. That's what Brad's looking for with these other women. Someone who doesn't mind having a good time."

I scowled at her, refusing to take the bait. "I'm having a great time hanging out with you. Didn't we have fun today? We went shopping, caught a matinee, and gave each other makeovers. Our sixteen-year-old selves would be very proud."

"That's not the kind of good time I was talking about."

"I could have a good time, if I wanted."

"I know, but you're afraid, which is why I have to make sure you remain presentable to the male half of the species, for when you finally get over your phobia and want to get busy." My best friend cracked a smile. "Someone has to make sure you don't turn into one of those yoga pants and tank top women until after you hook your man."

"But we're both yoga pants and tank top women."

"Shh." Emma pressed her finger to her lips. "We're here to meet men. They don't need to know that. At least not until we're three or four months into the relationship. By then, it won't matter."

My eyes went skyward before I could stop them. It was an involuntary reaction to her comment, but Emma saw it.

"You haven't even met the guy yet. How can you assume he's not relationship material? He could be Mr. Right, who just happened to get stuck in traffic."

"Is he stuck in traffic?"

She shrugged and drank some wine. "Possibly. He's Dino's best friend, and I really like Dino. They'll be here. I'm sure of it."

"Why do you want to date a dinosaur?"

"He's not a dinosaur." She grunted, exasperated. "What did I say about being nice?"

"Sorry, but the only Dino I know is purple with spots and a tail. Y'know, Brad also has a thing for dinosaurs. This just proves he's the male version of you."

"Liv," she warned.

I held up my palms. "Fine. I'll be nice."

"And don't interrogate them. I really like this one."

"Is that why you said it twice?"

She narrowed her eyes at me. "That tactic won't work either."

"Tactic?"

"I've got your number, DeMarco. You're staying. We'll eat. We'll talk. And you'll have fun. We used to double date all the time in college."

"That was college. Things are different now. I'm a cop. I have stricter standards. You should too."

Emma couldn't argue with me about that. "I have standards."

"How come the last guy you set me up with was a criminal? I can't date criminals, Em. I'm a homicide detective. There's a line."

"He wasn't a criminal. He was a street artist."

"You mean tagger."

"You have an excuse for everything. We haven't been out on a double date in over a year. And it's not for my lack of asking. When's the last time you even went on a real date?"

"I don't have time. Cops have bad track records when it comes to relationships. When I started working undercover, I had to put my life on hold. I was gone for months on end. You know that. It wouldn't have been safe or fair to ask some guy to wait that long, and what would have happened if I ran into him while I was pretending to be someone else? He could have blown my cover. Dating's not recommended. It just isn't."

"But you transferred. You don't work undercover anymore, which I am so thankful for." She reached across the table and grabbed my hand. "I mean it. I worried about you when you were gone. The only way I knew you were safe was by talking to Bradley, and you know how much I hate doing that."

"You and Brad are friends."

"We only tolerate one another because we love you."

I gave her a sideways look. "Bull."

"Think what you like, but he's still on my shit list after what he put you through. If it weren't for him, you wouldn't be apartment hunting again."

"That has nothing to do with Brad."

"He brought the bad juju with him when he didn't tell you what he was doing."

"He had his reasons." I turned to look for the waiter. "Maybe we should order. It's getting late, and I'm hungry. The place is going to close before our dates even arrive."

"How about we get appetizers for the table? It'd be rude if we ordered our entrees without waiting for them."

We placed our order. The restaurant had a nice ambience. It wasn't crowded or loud. In fact, it was pretty perfect for date night.

"How well do you know Dino?" I asked.

"We've gone out a couple of times."

"Is he reliable?"

She smiled devilishly. "So far."

"So he's reliable, but not punctual."

"Sometimes, it takes a little while to get there. Or has it been so long you've forgotten?"

"Emma."

"What? It's true. But I will say Dino's been pretty exceptional in that department." She grinned. "When's the last time someone made your toes curl?"

"I'm not answering that."

She made a face. "That long, huh? You're definitely overdue. Maybe Sean can help you out. He looks like he'd be good in bed. You'll have to let me know."

"What else do you know about him?"

"He and Dino are best friends. They've known each other since high school, roomed together in college, and work at the hospital."

"So you've met Sean."

"Not exactly." She took another swig of wine, gesturing for the waiter to bring another bottle. "He works in the cafeteria, and I avoid that place like the plague. The smell's enough to kill someone, and don't get me started on the nutritional deficiencies and health dangers associated with what they serve."

"Did you ever think maybe you should have been a nutritionist instead of a nurse?"

"Who says I can't do both? Anyway, I showed you his profile page. You said he was cute."

"If that's what he really looks like."

"You're so cynical. Who's the last guy you even dated?

Has there been anyone since Ryan?"

"Ryan?"

"Don't give me that. Your mom was picking out china patterns. She thought when we graduated college, the two of you would get married."

"We didn't date that long."

"True, but you were head over heels for the guy."

I didn't say anything, relieved the waiter had returned with a platter of crudité and Thai lettuce wraps. Selecting an artfully sliced carrot, I took a bite and chewed thoroughly.

"Has there even been anyone since Ryan?" she asked, unwilling to let this go.

"When would I have had time? Ryan broke up with me as soon as he realized the cop thing wasn't a phase. Not long after that, I started working undercover. I dated guys then, but not as me."

"You never talk about any of them."

"They don't count. They were part of the job."

"Like that guy who sent you the fancy gift basket when you got hurt? Axel, right?"

"Axel doesn't date."

"He sounds perfect for you."

"Except he's a car thief with a record for ag assault."

"Well, maybe not perfect, but close. Why don't you give him a call? I bet he'd like that."

"Em, I don't want to talk about this. I agreed to tonight in order to get you and my mom off my back. But I'm sure Sean will be just like everyone else. As soon as he finds out I'm a cop, he'll run for the hills. The only guys who date cops are the weird fetish guys, guys on the job, or criminals."

"Why would a criminal date a cop?"

"Special treatment."

"Oh. Well, you haven't met Sean yet. Maybe he's different. Or better yet, don't tell him you're a cop. Tell him you work for the city. That's true enough."

"What happens when he finds out?"

"By then, he'll be too enamored to care."

"That's your solution to everything." I dug into the

lettuce wraps. "At this point, I'm too hungry to care."

Emma and I had almost polished off the appetizers when my phone rang. "Don't answer that."

"I'm sorry, Em. I have to." I answered and listened to the details. "All right. I'm on my way." I hung up, dreading the disappointed look on Emma's face. "I have to go. We received reports of a possible double homicide involving a couple and Halloween costumes." I looked out the window, but I didn't see any sign of our dates. The last thing I wanted was to find out our killer had struck again. "Do you want to split the bill? I'll drop you off at home on my way."

"No, they'll be here." She checked her phone. "Can't you wait just a few more minutes?"

"This is important. If it's the same guy, the sooner we get there, the greater our chances are of IDing him."

"Fine. Go."

"Are you sure you want to hang around here by yourself? You don't want Dino to think you're desperate."

"Yes, I'm sure." She jerked her chin at the door. "We'll reschedule. I'll say you had a work emergency."

I gave her a hug. "Text me when you get home, so I know you're safe. If you don't, I'm sending officers to your apartment."

"You sound like Maria."

"I'm serious."

"I know, just like your mom."

"You should probably text her too. She'll want to know how tonight went."

"I'll put a nice spin on it, so she won't know you bailed. Next time, we're picking a day when you're not on call."

"But you said I'm always on call."

TWENTY-FIVE

Tripp smiled when I approached the crime scene tape. "Are you coming from a Halloween party?"

"Do you like my costume? I thought I'd go as a civilian."

"It's not very convincing." He pointed to my badge. "Next time, you might want to leave that at home."

"Tell me about it." Shredded crime scene tape hung from either side of the haystacks. I picked up a tattered end, but it wasn't real. It was a decoration. A solid piece of police tape had been hung across the entrance, preventing anyone from entering. At a quick glance, it was hard to tell the real stuff from the fake. "I hate Halloween."

"Given what we've been seeing, I can't say that I blame you." He stepped closer and lowered his voice. "From what witnesses have said, I'm thinking it might be the same guy from the Fielders' and Stevenses' murders. Whoever it is, he sure as shit doesn't like vampires."

"Have we gotten a description or ID yet?"

"I don't think so. We're not even sure about the number of victims." He lifted the tape, so I could duck underneath it. "We roped off the entire area and dragged everyone out. We've already taken statements from the witnesses, and we've put the employees on ice. Detective Fennel says he wants to talk to them after he examines the crime scenes."

"Crime scenes?"

"You'll see. We placed a few glow sticks which will guide you to them."

"Guide me?"

"It's a maze." He jerked his chin at the sign. "It says corn maze. But it's a hay bale maze. The bodies are in there." He pointed at the sign above my head. "Enter at your own peril." He grabbed my arm. "Just a heads-up. Your partner's on the warpath."

"That's what murders do to him."

I followed the path of glow sticks. Of all the nights to forget to bring a change of clothes. Luckily, my heels didn't snag in the dirt and hay. After making so many turns that I expected to end up back where I started, the narrow path opened into a large enclosed area.

Blood spatter covered the walls of hay on two sides. A guillotine stood in the center. A headless body slumped on the ground beside it. More blood coated the dropped blade. From where I stood, I didn't see a head. Brad stood beside it, his hands shoved into his back pockets as he stared down at something I couldn't see from where I stood.

"Fennel?"

He turned his flashlight in my direction, aiming it at the ground near my feet. "Watch where you step."

"What do we have?"

"A mess."

"I can see that." I approached the guillotine. "Is that real?"

"It looks that way." He tapped against the metal with the end of his flashlight. "The blade is, but I don't see any mechanism to get it to work."

"Where's the head?"

"We're still looking for it."

Something moved on the other side of the area, and I jumped. Brad turned his light in that direction so I could see the man in the CSU windbreaker.

"Sorry, Detective, I didn't mean to startle you." The police emblem practically glowed when he stepped into the light. "As you can see, some of the spatter is real." He moved a filter over his flashlight and shone it at the haystacks. The Luminol he sprayed glowed a purplish color under the light. "But it's not all real. Most of it is paint or food coloring."

"Dispatch told me we had a possible double homicide." I looked down. "I only see one body. Where's the other one?"

"The body's not real," Brad said. "It's a fake. Albeit, an expensive one. I'm still not sure about the others."

"Others?"

"Yeah, suffice it to say, we have plenty of options."

"Are you okay?" I asked.

"Pissed that we didn't find a way to shut this shit down when we stopped by the first time. If the manager had cooperated and let us speak to the employees, we might not be here now."

"Have you talked to him yet?" I asked.

Brad shook his head. "Voletek's questioning everyone at the inn, but so far, we have nothing that proves one of the employees or actors is to blame. All we know is someone dressed as an executioner attacked a couple. No one knows who the intended victims are or where they are." He swallowed, surveying the area. He hated bodies and crime scenes. And this was one giant crime scene or fake crime scene.

"How can that be?"

"In all the confusion, the attacker slipped away. One woman was injured and taken to the hospital, but that's all I know." He handed me the flashlight. "Take a look around and tell me what you see."

"A decapitation. Blood spatter moving outward. Additional spatter against the haystacks, but it doesn't match what would be expected from the guillotine. But since I've never known a killer in modern history to transport a guillotine to use as a murder weapon, this must have been part of the creepy maze."

"Just one part," Brad said. "They have seven different horrific death scenes spread throughout the maze."

"Is anyone actually dead?"

"That has yet to be determined."

"Why did they call us?"

"Two words. Task force."

The tech cleared his throat. "Witnesses reported they heard screaming. A man and woman were being chased by someone dressed as an executioner. The guy had a double-edged axe. At first, the witnesses thought they were actors, and it was all part of the fun. But the executioner struck another woman with his blade, demonstrating the weapon was real. That's when everyone panicked and all hell broke loose. Dispatch received so many calls, this became an all-hands situation."

Brad turned to the tech. "Do you think this could be her blood?"

"No, we already established this is too far away from where the attack happened."

"Are they sure the attack was real?" I asked. "Maybe the injured woman was another actor playing a part."

"That's a good thought, but no." The tech returned to searching the area.

"Do you know how serious it is?"

"The responding officer didn't know, but he thought he saw bone."

I swallowed, regretting eating those lettuce wraps only a few minutes ago. "What about the suspect?"

"He vanished. No one saw him or the couple he was chasing leave the maze. But 9-1-1 received several reports of screams coming from within the maze. We believe they might have gotten trapped and killed. We're checking every inch of the maze for their bodies. Given the givens, the killer might have tried to hide them amongst the fakes, especially if he's familiar with the maze or the grounds," Brad said.

"As you can see," the crime scene tech said, "we have actual blood here. The droplets and spray are consistent with an axe swing. But we don't know the source. The only victim we've identified was struck in the southeast corner of the maze. This isn't her blood." He studied the pattern. "I'll take precise measurements to get you a better approximation, but just eyeballing it, I'd say the perp was slightly taller than Fennel. He swung horizontally, like a baseball player. See how the spatter is even above and below the center line." He shone his light at the luminescent dots. "The spatter pattern wouldn't be this uniform if he'd used an up or downswing."

"Based on the amount of blood, how much damage do you think he inflicted here?" Brad asked. "Could he have killed someone in this enclosed area?"

"That's doubtful. There isn't much blood here. The spatter we see is probably from a glancing blow. He hit them, but they kept moving. I just need to find the blood trail, but with all this hay and dirt, it's damn near impossible."

"Keep working," Brad said. "DeMarco and I will see what the other techs have uncovered. Radio if you find anything else."

"Will do."

Brad led me away from the guillotine and into the narrow, winding maze. "I've already surveyed all seven potential crime scenes. Each one has at least one fake corpse, possibly more. None of the corpses match the descriptions the witnesses gave of the man and woman being chased, so I'm not sure what we're looking at. Honestly, Liv, this could be another hoax, except a lady is in the hospital."

"Do you think it was an accident? Maybe an actor grabbed a real axe instead of a prop and is too afraid to come forward."

"I'm not sure. But her injury's real. And according to CSU, at least one other person was attacked inside the maze. I've spoken to three different people who saw it happen. According to them, the assailant didn't even break stride. He continued after the couple."

"So we're looking for a maniac with an axe. That's not anything like the other homicides we investigated. Those involved stabbings. Do we think this is the same guy?"

"The location makes me think so, but I'm not sure. Then again, this scene falls under the purview of the task force, so we have to investigate. Right now, we're looking for guys carrying axes."

"How many of those can there be?"

"I already issued a BOLO. Dispatch will notify me of any

calls that come in matching our suspect's description, but we haven't found the weapon yet. And I don't think any of the bodies in the maze belong to his intended victims."

"Are you sure?"

"No, but the only bodies I didn't check were strapped to the electric chair and impaled in a pit of spikes. I'm really hoping those aren't our vics. I don't even know how he would have moved them into those positions without someone noticing."

"Yeah, a crazy guy with an axe running around and slicing people open would draw a lot of unwanted attention. He wouldn't have had the time to camouflage the bodies among the fakes." The hay was making me claustrophobic and a little itchy. "Why would anyone subject themselves to this kind of thing?"

"Most people come here to be scared. That's why it took them so long to realize something was wrong. Even the three people who helped the woman he attacked claimed they thought it was an accident. They said the executioner didn't intentionally hit her. In fact, he didn't even acknowledge her. They don't think he realized he'd nicked her with the end of the blade."

"Or he didn't care, like the man who killed Cassie Stevens."

Brad eyed me. "Everything I'm hearing and seeing reminds me of the comments we heard from Eldridge's party guests and the things we watched happen on the surveillance footage from the Stevenses' murders, but the weapon is so different. I don't know what to think. Could we be looking at three different offenders?"

"That is the one thing we've yet to answer." I stared at the walls of hay. "Why do I feel like I'm stuck in a slasher flick?"

"You and me both."

We entered a second opening. This one had a roped off area in the center where a hole had been dug and filled with sharp, bloody spikes. In the middle was the limp body of a blonde-haired woman. Two spikes had torn through her torso and neck while another had gone through her thigh.

"The witnesses said the woman being chased was blonde," I said. "Vivica's blonde, but Cassie wasn't."

Brad nodded, but he didn't look at the body. Instead, he waved his flashlight at the tech who was working in the corner of the opening. The tech looked up from his computer screen. "Anything?" Brad asked.

"No heat readings. We'll have to wait for the fire department to help us get to the body, but nothing indicates that thing was ever human. I'm guessing it's another one of the realistic corpses meant to scare visitors. Though, it'd be easier to make that determination if we could get some damn floodlights in this place instead of working off flashlights."

"What did the management say?" I asked. "Whoever's in charge of this haunted attraction should be able to tell us what's real and what isn't."

"The manager said everything's fake," Brad said. "Voletek asked if they hired an actor to dress as an executioner, but he said not this year. They had one in the past but didn't think the outfit was creepy enough. No one found it particularly scary."

"After tonight, I'm sure that will change. What about the axe?"

"The tools and weapons the actors carry are supposed to be foam or plastic. We checked them when we came here last week."

"So he brought his own axe?" I asked.

"Probably."

"I don't know," the tech said. "The spikes in that pit are metal."

"So's the guillotine blade," Brad said, "but it was blunted and dull."

I put on a glove and moved closer to the impaled body. "Brad, hold my hand."

My partner gave me a strange look but took my hand. Slowly, I leaned closer, making sure he balanced me, so I didn't fall into the pit and hurt myself. "Liv, be careful."

"I just need to get a little bit closer."

He squeezed my hand tightly as I stretched out my other arm and leaned farther over the side. The spikes weren't particularly sharp. The tips were dull. My fingers brushed against the corpse. The body had a certain amount of give, but it didn't feel like human flesh. None of the wounds were fresh or bleeding, but I felt around one of the impalements, hoping to get some blood or fluid on my hands for the tech to test.

I retracted my hand as Brad pulled me away from the pit. I held out my gloved fingers, but there was no visible blood. The tech took my glove, cut off the finger and dropped it into a tube, added a solution, and waited.

"No blood," he said. "It's another fake."

"Have you found any actual blood around here?" Brad gestured to the enclosed space.

"No."

"We have another fake body, but this time, no blood." Brad stared up at the sky. "I keep hoping someone's playing a joke on us."

The tech sighed. "I don't know, but I'm sure the injured woman doesn't find this funny."

Brad and I checked the other five macabre death scenes, but none of those bodies were real either. A few members of the K-9 unit had been called in to sniff out human remains, but they didn't find anything, so they'd scout the surrounding area. The only obvious trail of blood inside the maze came from the woman who'd been struck by the axe. Three of the staged crime scenes registered actual blood spatter, but the patterns didn't lead anywhere. Whoever left the blood must have magically transported out of the maze in order to not leave an obvious trail or even a single droplet.

We spent the rest of the night questioning every actor, worker, and witness while CSU tore apart the maze, searching for clues. Officers canvassed the area, but no one saw anything. And if they had, they hadn't realized it. No wonder I hated this time of year.

TWENTY-SIX

After leaving the haunted maze, Brad and I went to check on the woman. She was still in surgery, but the doctors were hopeful they'd be able to stop the bleeding and repair the damage. Until the anesthesia wore off, we wouldn't be able to question her.

Since that wouldn't be for a number of hours, we returned to the precinct. Officers had collected surveillance footage from the area and located the attacker on the feed as he entered the maze. But the costume he wore made identifying him impossible. His head and neck were covered by a black cloth mask. Except for the eyeholes, there were no openings. He'd secured the mask in place with a thin piece of twine tied around his neck. Beneath that, he wore a long-sleeved grey shirt, black gloves, and a black vest. His pants were black, and he had on combat boots.

"What about footprints?" I asked.

"CSU couldn't pull prints. The layers of hay made it impossible."

"Dammit."

Brad rolled his chair around our joined desks until he was seated beside me. "Any sign of the couple he allegedly terrorized?"

"I don't know. Everyone looks like they're in fear for their lives. Have you listened to the 9-1-1 calls yet?"

"Some of them. I even spoke to one of the callers. He said a guy dressed like an executioner was chasing a man and a woman. They were holding hands and running from him. He figured they must be together. He said she was blonde, and he had a cape."

"And fangs, right?"

"Probably, but I can't say for certain. The caller didn't see where they went, but he doesn't think they ever left the maze. The woman looked genuinely afraid, on the verge of hysterical. As soon as the caller got to the end of the maze, he asked the guy in charge of the attraction about it. That's when the guy said no one inside had an axe. So he called us and reported an attempted murder. In the meantime, dispatch received three other calls about the woman who'd been attacked with the axe."

"And we're sure it's not the same woman?"

"Witnesses said no. The injured woman got in the assailant's way. She wasn't running from him, and she isn't blonde."

"This is our first survivor. Let's hope she can tell us something," I said.

"I can't imagine how someone wielding an axe and dressed like an executioner eluded us and the surveillance cameras when he left." Brad rubbed his cheek. "The walls were made of hay bales. Do you think he made his own exit?"

"Wouldn't we have noticed?"

"Not if he put them back in place."

"Still, someone should have seen something."

"The lot is huge and crowded. With all the costumed actors and guests, some guy dressed as an executioner would blend right in. All he'd have to do is ditch the axe. Maybe not even that."

I'd just finished my report when Voletek entered the bullpen and dropped a few files on his desk. "That was one fucking long night." He turned to me. "Don't tell me you have court."

"It's Sunday," Brad said.

Voletek rubbed his eyes. "Right. Sunday. Jeez. It feels like we've been at this for a month." He examined my outfit. "Whatever it is, I'm definitely in favor of the dress code changes going on around here. You look fantastic, Liv."

"Thanks."

Brad glanced up from his screen. "Do you want something, Jake?"

Voletek rested his hips against the side of our joined desks, tapping the folder against his thigh. "Are you meeting with the brass later?" he asked me, ignoring Brad's question.

If I didn't explain myself, this would go on indefinitely. "I was on a date when I got called in last night."

"Oh." Voletek handed the folder to Brad. "I always knew you played hard. I'm sorry your plans got interrupted. Who's the lucky guy? Anyone I know?"

"I doubt it. He's no one I know."

Voletek raised an eyebrow but didn't inquire further. "Maybe this will make up for your ruined date. I found your alleged homicide victims. And they are very much alive."

"We figured that might be the case when no bodies turned up." Brad scanned the page. "How did you find them?"

"They found me. I put them in a conference room downstairs. They walked in a few minutes ago while I was at the intake desk. They said a man with an axe tried to kill them last night while they were at the haunted maze. The woman's pretty shaken, but her husband doesn't seem particularly worried. I figured you'd want to be the first ones to question them."

"Ron and Jodie Gesper." Brad read off their address, which was in the suburbs. "Why did they wait so long to seek help? Why didn't they call 9-1-1?"

Voletek raised his palms. "Beats me. Do you want me to ask them?"

"We'll do it." I pushed my chair beneath my desk, and Jake whistled.

Brad brushed against him, shaking his head. "Whatever you're about to say, don't. Liv doesn't want to hear another crack about the way she's dressed. Trust me, it won't be pretty."

I waited in the stairwell for my partner to join me. "How do you know Jake was going to make another quip?"

"Because it's Jake." Brad watched me from the corner of his eye as we went down the stairs.

"At least he said I looked nice."

"You mean like a princess?"

"No. And don't you dare start that either."

Brad laughed.

"What do you think of my outfit?" I asked.

"Are you fishing for compliments?"

"No. I just thought you'd have something to say."

"It's not practical for work."

I frowned. Normally, Brad was one of the first people to mention how I looked. "You're being awfully quiet. Is everything okay?" We always bantered back and forth, teasing and sniping at one another. But he'd barely said two words to me that didn't have to do with the case. "How did things go at Carrie's?"

"It's been handled."

"No problems?"

"Not yet. I hope it stays that way." He gave me a look. "I thought you were hanging out with Emma."

"I was."

"Seriously, Liv? We promised each other no more secrets but whatever. If you don't want to tell me where you were or who you were with, that's fine."

"What are you talking about?"

"Nothing." He opened the door and held it for me. "How do you want to do this? Do you want to question them together? Or do you want to talk to the wife while I talk to the husband?"

"Let's see what they have to say before we split them up."

Brad and I entered the conference room where Sgt. Rostokowski was sitting with the frazzled couple. The Gespers looked like they'd been up all night. Bits of hay had gotten caught in Jodie's hair, and mascara streaked her cheeks.

"I'll see if I can scrounge up some breakfast sandwiches. You two look famished. How about I send an officer in to refresh those coffees?" Rostokowski asked.

"That'd be great." Ron wrapped his arm around his wife's trembling shoulders. "Do you have any tissues?"

"Right here." Rostokowski snagged the box off the table in the corner and put it down in front of them. "These are Detectives Fennel and DeMarco. They'll get everything sorted out. Just tell them what you already told me."

"Thanks, Sara," Brad said.

She patted him on the shoulder as she headed out the door. I grabbed the wastepaper basket and placed it on the floor near Jodie's chair before taking a seat. Jodie stared at the table. She hadn't looked up or moved since we entered. She was dressed like a cheerleader from one of those teen movies. Even the mascot was the same. Her husband had on jeans and a black t-shirt. His hair was spiked upward and the white makeup on his skin had started to fade and flake from perspiration. He must have lost the cape somewhere.

"Hey," Ron held out his free hand, never letting go of his wife's shoulder, "I'm Ron Gesper. This is Jodie. Thanks for hearing us out. I didn't think anyone would take us seriously."

"Why don't you tell us what happened?" Brad sat down across from them and pulled out his notepad.

"It was awful." Jodie crinkled up a tissue and wiped at her cheeks. "I thought he was going to kill us. Ronnie, tell them."

Ron exchanged a look with Brad. "We've been touring all these haunted attractions. We're even staying in the honeymoon suite at the inn. It's supposed to be one of their haunted rooms, which is kind of fun."

"It's kind of ridiculous," Jodie mumbled.

Ron's cheeks flushed a little. "I've always been a sucker for the unexplainable, paranormal stuff. Anyway, the inn puts on that haunted maze every year, so we thought we'd check it out. I just...like, I know how this is gonna sound, but bear with me." Ron looked from Brad to me. "There was an actual psycho in the maze."

"He had an axe," Jodie said. "He wanted to chop us to bits."

"Can you tell us who he is?" I asked.

Ron and Jodie shook their heads.

"Can you provide us with a description? Did you see his face or notice if he had any identifying characteristics? A tattoo or anything like that?" Brad asked.

"He was dressed like one of those old-timey executioners. The kind you'd see in Robin Hood's day. Even his weapon looked ancient. It wasn't like a firefighter's axe. It was this big ass double-edged thing." Ron let go of his wife and gestured with his hands. "We never saw his face or anything like that. He was completely covered."

"How tall was he?" I asked. "How close did he get?"

"He's probably about my height, so like 6'1, maybe."

"He was fat," Jodie said.

"Babe, that might have been the suit," Ron said.

"How close did he get? Did he hurt you? Touch you?" Brad asked.

"We didn't notice him at first," Jodie said. "We were...um..."

"We were making out. We got a little lost and thought we'd take advantage of the dead end." He grinned. "We're on our honeymoon."

"Some honeymoon," Jodie said.

"He snuck up on us, grabbed Jodie's ponytail, and yanked her off of me." Ron sneered. "I thought he was one of the guys who dresses up and scares people. But I didn't like the way he touched my wife, so I got in his face to let him know. That's when he raised his axe and took a swing at me."

"Did you know the axe was real?" Brad asked.

"Not until it cut through a hay bale like butter." Ron pointed to the bandage on his arm. "The bastard nicked me with the damn thing. He could have taken off my head. That psychopath." He bit his lip, his leg jittering up and down. "I should have realized then something wasn't right.

But I just thought he was playing a part. I told him to back off and to get out of our faces or I'd report him. That's when he screamed and charged at us."

"What did he scream?" I asked.

"He just screamed." Jodie demonstrated. "And then he lunged for me. He tried to grab me. He wanted to keep me away from Ronnie. But Ron shoved him backward, grabbed my hand, and we took off running."

"He chased us." Ron rubbed his face, and Jodie hugged his arm between both of hers, resting her cheek on his shoulder. "I thought I was dreaming, that it had to be some kind of nightmare. I mean, yes, that's the point of these mazes, to get scared. But it's not supposed to be real. This dude had a real axe. He wanted to kill us."

"He sliced into some woman," Jodie said. "I heard her scream. Is she okay?"

"We don't know yet." Brad moved a legal pad and pen closer to the Gespers. "How did you escape?"

"We ended up at another dead end," Ron said.

"It was terrifying. I never felt so trapped, so claustrophobic, before." Jodie hugged her husband's arm harder, her shoulders quaking.

Ron reached over with his free hand and stroked her cheek. "I won't let anyone ever hurt you. I promise." He looked back at my partner. "I pushed over one of the walls, and we made our own exit. After that, I piled the hay back up so he couldn't follow us, and we ran back to the inn. We spoke to security. But they didn't believe us at first. No one did. But when a bunch of people started screaming outside, they left to check on things. Jodie didn't want to stay there. She was afraid he'd find us, so we got in our car and drove halfway home."

"But that didn't feel safe either," she said. "I'm not sure how it works, but since the inn puts on the haunted maze, the people who work there might have access to our information. We had to give them our names, phone number, and address when we checked in. I was afraid he might be waiting for us."

"You think the man who attacked you plans to make another attempt at your home?" I asked.

Jodie shrugged. "My life has turned into a crappy slasher flick. Isn't that what the psycho killer always does? He waits until they finally think they're safe and then bam."

"Honey, I don't think that's what's going on here." Ron tried to comfort her.

"You were the one saying I'd be the first to die. Do you already want out of our marriage?"

"First to die?" I asked.

Ron laughed, which only aggravated her further. But he smoothed it over by pulling her in for a hug and holding her against his side. "In scary movies, the hot chick always gets killed first." He kissed her cheek. "I'm not making fun of you. This is some scary shit, but I'm guessing it might be a disgruntled employee or some idiot trying to scare people." He looked at Brad. "That is what happened, right? This was just some stupid kid playing a prank or a pissed off worker trying to scare off customers. This wasn't anything more than that, right?"

"What were you wearing last night, Mr. Gesper?"

"You can call me Ron." He tugged on the front of his shirt. "I was wearing this."

"No costume?" I asked.

"Oh, I had on a cape and some plastic vampire teeth. Why? Is this because of the makeup?" He rubbed his cheek, brushing the white flakes off his fingertips.

"Someone's been attacking men dressed like Dracula. We're trying to determine if the man who attacked you last night is responsible for any of these other crimes," Brad said.

I opened my notepad and clicked my pen. "Who knew you'd be at the maze last night?"

"No one," Jodie said.

"You didn't post it on social media or mention it to any of your friends or coworkers?" Brad asked.

"No, nothing like that. I didn't even know we were going. It was Ronnie's idea. He loves this stuff."

"I didn't say a word. Hell, I even told the ticket guy that I didn't know when we'd show up, or if we'd show up. We didn't have a plan. We were just playing it by ear." Ron kissed his wife's temple. "I'm so sorry. If I had any idea, we never would have gone there."

She ran her fingers across his chest. "I know. It's not your fault."

Brad scratched his cheek, something he did when he had a thought. "How did you pay for the tickets?"

"Cash." Ron pulled the stubs from his pocket. "We got them early in the afternoon."

"Have you seen anyone suspicious following you around," I asked, "or hanging around where you've been?"

"No, I don't think so," Ron said.

"What about that groundskeeper? Y'know, the guy who was watering the bushes. That guy was weird," Jodie said.

"Does he work at the inn?" I asked.

"I think so. He had on a jumpsuit and name tag."

"We'll look into the inn employees as well as everyone who works at the maze and had access to the outfits and props." Brad pushed the paper closer to them. "I need the two of you to come up with a list of names. First, write down everyone who knows you were staying at the inn. Given how much Ron loves Halloween, someone might have assumed you'd visit the maze at some point. Also, I need a list of anyone who might want to harm you."

"Like who?" Jodie asked.

"That could be anyone. Angry coworkers, jealous exes, your neighbor who complains your parties are too loud. Anyone you can think of who might want to scare or harm you."

"What do you do for a living?" I asked.

"I work the cosmetic counter at a department store," Jodie said.

"And you, sir?"

"I used to play baseball in the minors, but when they cut me, I got a job as a personal trainer."

"At a gym?" Brad asked.

"Yeah." Ron picked up the pen. "I'm guessing you want the name and address and probably my client list too."

"It couldn't hurt."

TWENTY-SEVEN

"What do you think?" I asked.

Brad looked up from his computer screen. "I didn't find anything. Did you?"

"The Gespers gave us a lot of names to look into, but most of them are friends and family who knew they were doing the whole haunted honeymoon thing. Neither of them gave us much in terms of enemies."

"What about Jodie's ex-boyfriend? The one who keyed her car a few years ago."

"He's currently a guest of the state."

"That rules him out." Brad crossed the name off his list. "Do you think the attack was random? According to Ron, the guy interrupted their kissing, so Ron got in his face. That might have been enough to set off the lunatic. He probably swung the axe just to scare them. Given how narrow those paths are, I bet the guy missed on purpose."

"So he just wanted to scare them? Maybe he does work there or used to."

"All the actors and workers who were supposed to work last night were present and accounted for. Officers took statements from each of them when the incident occurred."

I reached for the phone. "Did you get a list of past

employees?"

"No."

"All right, let me see if the inn can help us out."

"Put the phone down. I think we already have that information around here somewhere."

"I haven't seen it."

"Give me a sec to check." He returned from the conference room a few minutes later. "It looks like we have everything. The inn hires new actors every year, so that's why we have so many file boxes."

"Anyone who worked there would know how the inn sets things up and where they keep the costumes. This could take forever."

"Let's hope Anna Moniz, his latest victim, can point us in the right direction. She should be out of surgery by now. We might as well head over and wait for her to wake up. We can swing by your apartment on the way, so you can get changed." He grabbed the keys, and we headed for the car.

"Does my outfit bother you that much?"

He gave me a sideways look before checking the rearview and putting on his signal light. "We're pursuing a violent, axe-wielding offender. I'd prefer if my partner has sensible shoes. It'll make running easier, if we have to chase him."

"Do you think the vic will be able to ID him?"

"You never know."

"Hey." I hesitated, not sure what I wanted to say.

"Hmm?"

"My Fennel-to-English dictionary is on the fritz. Do you want to tell me what I did wrong or why you've been freezing me out since last night?"

He sighed. "How was your date? Did you have fun?"

"I left before the guy showed up."

"Does he have a name? Is it anyone I know? Like Jake Voletek, perhaps?"

I laughed, but he didn't even crack a smile. "You're serious?"

"What? I tell you about my dates."

"That's because I'm there when you get those late night booty call texts."

"You're my best friend, Liv. We don't keep secrets, anymore. At least, I didn't think we did. Why didn't you mention this to me? Come to think of it, you never mention anything about your dating life. I'm starting to think there's a reason you keep it quiet."

"It's not a secret, and no, I wasn't out with Jake. Have you lost your damn mind?"

"Why didn't you tell me about your plans? You said you were hanging out with Emma."

"I was. She set this up. I didn't want to tell you because I knew you'd tease me mercilessly."

"I would not."

"Au contraire. The one night I fell asleep at Logan Winters' place, you acted like a freaking bloodhound. Remember that?"

"So? You always give me shit about my dating life. It's only fair that I do the same."

"You were my handler when I was undercover. You know every intimate detail about every single guy I've dated in the last two and a half years."

"Those don't count."

"See," I pointed enthusiastically, "that's the same thing I told Emma. Jeez. The two of you need to get together and share intel since you're both driving me crazy about my dating life or lack thereof."

He held up his palms before placing his hands back at ten and two. "I'm sorry. I'm not trying to give you grief. You deserve to be happy. I just want to make sure whoever this guy is knows that and treats you right."

"I appreciate that, but this wasn't a real date. Emma fixed me up. She likes this guy, Dino, and apparently, his friend needed someone to talk to while the two of them made googly eyes at one another. But they were running late, or so Emma says. I think they blew us off, but when she texted to tell me she got home safely, she said they had a nice time and dinner was great. So I don't know. It's Em. She doesn't always tell me the whole story."

"Does this guy have a name?"

"Sean."

"Sean what?"

"She never said, and he didn't have it on his profile page. He works at the hospital cafeteria." I cocked my head at my partner. "Why?"

"Given Emma's track record, it wouldn't hurt to run a background check."

The thought had already crossed my mind, but I didn't want to encourage him. "I'm sure he's not a killer. That was just a fluke." But Emma had a habit of dating bad boys, which probably meant Sean exhibited the same characteristics.

Brad parked in front of my building. "Any progress on the apartment hunting front?"

"Not really." We went up the stairs, and I unlocked the door. My new habit was to clear the entire place, checking every closet, behind every curtain, and beneath the bed to make sure it was safe before I let my guard down. "Aside from my furniture and a few spare outfits, Dad's moved the rest of my stuff back to my parents' house."

"What about the coffeemaker?" Brad called from the other side of the door while I changed into a pair of slacks and a button-down dress shirt.

"That's gone too."

"Dammit."

I slipped into work shoes, fastened my belt, made sure my holster, badge, and cuffs were clipped on, and grabbed a jacket. "We can pick some up on the way."

"Or we could grab some from the hospital cafeteria."

I came out of my room. "No."

"Why not? Aren't you the least bit curious about this guy?"

"Not really."

"You're not going to reschedule?"

"Not if I can help it."

"Well, I'm curious."

"Do you want to date him? I can tell you now, he's not your type. He isn't blond."

"I date more than just blondes."

"I've yet to see it. But even if that's true, he's not a she. Given your sexual preference, I thought that might have been a deal-breaker. I guess I was mistaken."

Brad and I quibbled the entire way to the hospital. It was a nice change of pace after the last twelve hours. I yawned as we made our way inside.

"Are you sure you don't want to get some coffee, DeMarco?" he teased.

"Don't start that again." I pointed to the coffee cart in the lobby. "If you want coffee, that's where we'll get it."

"Remind me on our way out." He headed for the information desk and flashed his badge and a smile at the woman behind the counter.

Her slender fingers flew over the keyboard. "Room 801. She's awake and responsive."

"Thank you." He tapped the desk and headed for the elevator.

Anna Moniz's room already had a flower arrangement and balloon bouquet. A man sat in the chair beside the bed. He looked up when Brad knocked on the door.

I held up my badge. "We're following up on last night's attack." I introduced myself. "Who are you?"

"Jason." He stood. "Jason Sagewood. I'm Anna's partner."

"Would you mind stepping into the hallway to answer a few questions, so she can rest?" Brad asked.

"Not at all." Jason looked down at Anna who had a goofy grin on her face. "I'll be right back."

"Liv," Brad jerked his chin at Anna, "maybe you can keep her company?"

"Sure." It was time to divide and conquer. While Brad questioned Jason, I moved closer to the bed. "Hi, Anna. How are you feeling?"

"Okay." Her voice came out low and sluggish. "I'm kind of sleepy."

"This won't take long." I looked at the cast on her arm. The axe had severed the bone and tore through muscles and tendons. "Do you remember what happened last night?"

"My arm almost got chopped off." A fit of giggles came over her, and I realized she was high. The morphine drip and lingering effects from the anesthesia probably had something to do with it. "Sorry." She tried to sober. "That's not funny." But she burst out laughing again.

"At least you can joke about it." I took a seat. "Can you walk me through what happened? Initial reports said you were impaled."

"That's not what happened. Well, maybe. I don't know. The blade went in and kinda got stuck. When he yanked it out, blood went everywhere."

"That sounds terrifying."

"It was." She nodded a few times. "I was turning the corner in the maze. This guy comes out of nowhere, swinging his axe. The edge caught me when he pulled it back to swing it again."

"Did he say anything?"

"No."

"Can you describe him?"

She described him the same way the Gespers had. "He didn't even look at me. He just kept walking and swinging. It was so real." She shook her head. "Surreal. That's what I meant."

"Do you have any idea who he is or why he did this?"

"Not a clue." She yawned, which made me yawn. "He kept going. He was swinging as he went. I don't know if he meant to hit me or if I got in the way. But he didn't stop. He didn't apologize. He didn't do anything. He was like a robot or those birds that dip their beaks in the water. The little ones on the desks. You flick them, and they tip over." She demonstrated with her good hand. "They're like plastic or whatever. You just set them to go and they keep going. That's the way this guy was." She settled into the pillow and closed her eyes. "I think he was a robot. That's the only thing that makes sense."

"Why do you say that?"

"A decent person would have stopped to see if I was okay or apologized. He was in a rush. He didn't notice or care."

"Did you see him chasing anyone?"

"I didn't see anything until it was too late. And after that, I just remember other people rushing toward me before I passed out." She closed her eyes. "Can I go to sleep now?"

"Sure."

I remained in the chair, glancing at her vitals on the monitor. She was lucky she survived with her arm attached. Recovery would take time, but the doctors were confident she'd have full use of her arm.

Jason stepped back into the room, and I surrendered the chair to him. Brad waited in the hallway for me. Once we were out of earshot, I told him what Anna had said.

"Jason didn't see what happened. They separated in the maze. He wanted to go left. She wanted to go right, so they figured they'd race to see who got out first. He didn't even see the guy. But he heard Anna scream. Witnesses told him what happened while they waited for the ambulance to arrive."

"And you already spoke to them," I said. "No one's given us anything to go on."

"All we know is the attacker didn't leave the maze dressed in his executioner's garb. And since there aren't any cameras covering the interior, we don't know if he took off the costume before leaving or if he made his own exit, like the Gespers did."

"When we searched the maze, we didn't find the Gespers' makeshift exit either."

"Ron must have done a great job replacing the hay," Brad said. "Maybe the killer followed their lead and made his own hole and put things back the way he found them too. That would explain a lot."

"Possibly, but what did he do with the axe? After everyone panicked, someone would have noticed a guy carrying one outside the maze."

"We searched every inch of the place. Right now, the entire maze is being disassembled. If he hid it, we'll find it. But my guess is he still has it. I'm just worried he might decide to use it again."

TWENTY-EIGHT

He rubbed his eyes and stared at the ceiling. He hadn't meant to hurt that woman. She came out of nowhere and stepped right into the path of the swinging blade. She should have been paying more attention. People who went to attractions like that ought to be on the lookout.

The executioner's costume remained in a bundle on the floor. If those damn honeymooners hadn't been taunting him, none of this would have happened. When he caught them sucking face in one of the staging areas, something inside him snapped.

With every passing day, his fuse got shorter and shorter. It didn't help matters that she was dressed like a cheerleader, which reminded him of Vivica, or that her jock husband looked like every asshole the love of his life had chosen over him. To make matters worse, the husband was one of them – a creature of the night, with his pale skin, fangs, and cape. Why women were drawn to that was beyond him.

No wonder seeing the couple together caused him physical agony. The pain wasn't in his head. It was real, a violent stabbing in his chest that only got worse as time went on. He'd done to those men what seeing them had done to him. It was only fair.

He just wanted to make them stop. He wanted the pain to go away. Why should they be happy causing him that much misery? Most acted like they didn't know what their behavior was doing. But they did. And then they'd laugh and mock him.

He tried to avoid them, knowing they would set him off and hurt him. But this last couple came looking for him. The newlyweds bought tickets to the haunted maze. Once he knew where they'd be, he hadn't been able to stop himself from checking things out. He hoped he was wrong, but when he found Ron dressed like a vampire, sucking the life from his own wife, he had to intervene.

The plan was to scare him enough to make him stop. But as with most plans, it quickly went to shit. The blushing bride reminded him of Vivica, everything from her hair to her outfit was the same. She didn't understand why he'd interfered. She didn't understand that he'd saved her.

"Viv?" He reached over and stroked her cheek. "Do you want something to drink? Maybe something to eat?"

But she didn't answer. He checked the gash on her temple, but it had stopped bleeding days ago. However, she had barely spoken to him since it happened. Whenever he tried to talk to her, she'd close her eyes and pretend to be asleep.

"I'll make you something, in case you change your mind." Her unresponsiveness made him angry, but he'd give her time. She'd come around. However, he couldn't risk letting her leave his apartment. She might go for help, so he'd taken her phone apart, pulled the landline out of the bedroom, and locked and barricaded the door from the outside every time he had to go out. He thought about gagging her, but as far as he could tell, she hadn't tried to scream for help either.

As he puttered around the kitchen, he wondered how come these other people got their happily ever afters. Everywhere he looked, couples were holding hands, kissing, and laughing. Were they laughing at him?

He couldn't take it. Maybe now, he could put this

behind him. As soon as Viv came around, the torture would stop. And he'd be able to control himself better.

But that thought provided little comfort since he had no way of knowing how long it'd take before she realized he was the hero, not the villain. "Gah." He let out a scream that surprised even him.

Everyone told him to stop dwelling and move on. Vivica was out of his league. But when she retired from cheering and faded from the limelight, he thought he'd finally have a chance. But that's when she went for Dan. He wasn't a quarterback or pitcher. He was a fucking sportswriter. A loser. A dork. Why would she pick Dan when she could have had him?

When she called him the first time to complain about Dan, he knew it was his chance. He just had to be patient, but as he watched and waited, he realized Dan had Vivica under a spell. She didn't want to be with him, but she couldn't break free.

It made no sense. Dan must have had supernatural powers, and that's when he first noticed Dan's teeth. Viv said they were implants, but no one would do something that crazy. And that's when he started noticing other men like Dan exuding the same types of powers.

He saw many like Dan congregating near the maze, just like the newlyweds last night. On the bright side, the police had shut everything down and dismantled the labyrinth. None of these creatures could use it to their advantage. And since he'd been careful, he knew the police wouldn't find the axe. He had tossed it over the side before peeling off the costume and hiding it beneath his sweatshirt.

Once he'd gotten out of the maze and slipped away amongst the panicked crowd, he found the axe and tossed it in a dumpster. By getting rid of the weapon, he hoped to eliminate the temptation to cause more harm.

He finished making her a sandwich and grabbed a bottle of water from the fridge. He didn't have much, but it was enough. Vivica was his now. He just had to convince her. He shouldn't be wasting his time on these others, but he couldn't quite help himself. Men with these fantastical powers had to be stopped before they could prey on more women and interfere with his happiness.

Now, he had to focus on damage control. The police wouldn't find anything, but even if they did, it wouldn't matter. He'd never been arrested, so they didn't have his prints or DNA on file. He'd never had any ancestry or genetic testing performed, so he figured he was in the clear. At least, that's what the internet said. Plus, the axe had been purchased by the inn to be used as decoration a few years ago, so the cops couldn't connect him to that either. And he never worked inside the maze. His job included working the ticket booth, just like every other inn employee who'd been forced to endure this seasonal torture.

He snuck away before the police arrived on scene, but his coworkers said uniformed officers asked everyone the same basic questions. They had no leads or any idea he was to blame. Considering he hadn't planned for this to happen, he had done a decent job covering his tracks.

Regardless of what he told himself, the familiar fire burned inside him. Anger and grief tore at his heart and ripped at his soul. It was a good thing he got rid of the axe. Seeing happy couples made him downright homicidal. He had to get a hold of himself, if not, things would only get worse. He'd accidentally hurt Viv and that woman who stumbled into his path. He didn't want to make another mistake and hurt any more innocents. But the ones with the fangs were fair game. Frankly, he didn't care how many of those he killed. By stopping them, he'd save others from being tortured.

*　　*　　*

Jake Voletek stood over my desk, watching me work. "While you were gone, three more calls came in. This time of year always brings out the crazies."

"Anything I should know about?" I asked.

"A man called to report a body in his neighbor's trunk. Officers went to check it out, smelled something, and radioed for a detective. By the time I got there, they realized the smell was from some nearby roadkill. The body in the trunk wasn't even a body. It was a fake arm, sold at most novelty shops."

"That's the second time that's happened. What is wrong with people?"

"You want to make a list?"

"What about the other two calls?"

"Also hoaxes."

"I guess we should be thankful."

He turned to head back to his desk, stopping to stare at my partner's empty chair. "Where's the other half of the dream team? Should I be worried Brad went AWOL again?"

"He's checking to see if nearby traffic cam footage showed anyone suspicious leaving the maze after the attack."

"What are you doing?"

"Running backgrounds on everyone involved in the haunted maze, putting together a list of potential suspects based on the descriptions we received, and looking into the inn's guest registry and employee records."

"Weren't you already doing that?"

"Yes, but we updated our description based on the reports from last night. We don't even know if this is the same guy or someone else. We could have three lunatics on our hands."

"Four. Don't forget the psycho from my case." He frowned.

"What's wrong?"

"Patrol finally located my prime suspect, but he slipped our surveillance again late yesterday afternoon. They haven't been able to find him since." He reached for the notes I'd made. "Y'know, I almost wonder..." He shook his head. "Nah. That wouldn't make any sense."

"What?"

"That my suspect could be the axe-wielder you're hunting."

"Why would you think that?"

"Timing." Voletek shrugged. "It's probably just a coincidence, but if you need an extra set of eyes, let me know."

"Thanks."

"Anything for you, princess."

"Jake," I warned.

He bowed, rolling his right hand in the air with a royal flair. "Your wish is my command."

"Bite me," I muttered under my breath.

A few minutes later, Brad's desk phone rang. Reaching over, I picked it up. "Homicide. DeMarco speaking."

"Fennel wanted us to alert him if we received any reports involving an axe. We just got a call about a live one. Officers are en route."

"Give me the address." I scribbled it down. "All right. Be advised, plain clothes detectives will be arriving on the scene." I put the phone down, grabbed a set of keys, asked Jake to take over for me, and dialed Brad's cell on my way down the steps. "Meet me in the garage. 9-1-1 just received a report of a man terrorizing a bakery with a large axe."

The engine rumbled to life as my partner jumped into the passenger seat. "Do you think it's the same guy?" he asked.

"I don't know. The report only said man with axe. The caller didn't mention anything about him being dressed as an executioner." I drove out of the garage, hit the lights and siren, and made a right. "Did traffic cams spot anyone?"

"No. Neither did surveillance. The maze was packed. These haunted attractions are big business. It looks like half the city was there when the attack happened. Whoever he is, he ditched the outfit and axe and walked away, along with a hundred other people. We'll never be able to pull him off the footage."

"Maybe we won't have to." I zoomed around traffic, yanking the wheel hard as I made another right. A blue and white raced down the street, several blocks ahead of us.

Brad checked the cross streets as I sped up. "Clear," he said as we moved through the intersection.

The blue and white double-parked at an angle outside the bakery. The officers had just gotten out of the vehicle when I pulled in behind them and killed the siren. Brad and I got out of the car.

"Shit." Brad nodded at the window inside the bakery. A large man stood with his back to us, a double-edged axe slung over his shoulder with blood dripping from the weapon's razor-sharp edge.

With the bakery door closed, I couldn't hear what the suspect was saying. But he was angry. Several customers remained at their tables, cowering in their seats. On the floor, near the door, was a guy in a business suit. I couldn't see much from here, but one of the officers pointed out the growing river of blood.

The commotion outside caused the guy with the axe to turn. He grabbed the clerk by the front of her apron and practically hauled her over the counter. He held her close, tightening his grip on the handle of the axe.

"We need a plan." Brad stopped the officers from bursting through the doors with guns blazing. "One swing, and he'll take off the clerk's head. We don't want that. So let's not piss him off. The two of you, go around back. That swinging door behind the counter connects to the kitchen. Get him in your line of sight. If things go south, shoot him."

The officers went around the building, radioing for an ambulance to our location. Brad kept his eyes on the suspect as he slowly pushed open the front door. He kept one hand near his holster, but he had yet to draw.

I pulled my piece and followed him inside, moving laterally along the back wall as I gave my partner space. If the guy with the axe made a move on my partner, I'd kill him.

"Hey, man." Brad held up his badge. "What's going on here?"

"Nothing." The guy shook his head several times. "I just want a fucking piece of cake."

"Cake's good. What kind of cake do you want?" Brad's gaze moved to the woman. He asked with his eyes if she was okay. She bit her lip, barely nodding.

"I don't know." The man with the axe nearly burst into tears. "I just don't know. I can't think. It's like there are a million ants crawling around in my brain. I just want some fucking cake. Don't ask me such hard questions."

"Okay." Brad held out his hand. "Take it easy. We'll get you some cake. But first, you gotta let the lady go. It's the only way."

I kept my eyes on the axe while I knelt on the ground to check the downed man. "Sir," I whispered, "can you hear me?" I pressed my fingers against his neck, relieved to find a strong pulse.

The back of his jacket was torn. Beneath the ripped suit was a torn shirt and undershirt. Blood continued to ooze from the wound. I turned, searching for something to staunch the bleeding. Until the situation was resolved, I had to make sure he stayed alive and didn't exsanguinate.

A woman at a nearby table offered me her scarf. I nodded, taking it and pressing it into the man's back. He jerked, letting out a groan which caused the axe-wielder to turn.

"What are you doing? Get away from him," the suspect screamed. He took a step toward me, dragging the woman with him.

"Hey," Brad sidestepped, moving to intercept, "don't worry about them. Talk to me. You wanted cake. This is a bakery. Let's get some cake."

The guy licked his bottom lip. The jitters indicated he was on something. "Stop helping him," he yelled at me. "Stop it, right now."

"If he dies, you die. Do you understand?" I aimed at his head. With the woman so close, I didn't want to risk taking the shot. The officers who'd gone around back would have a better vantage point, assuming their bullets didn't go through him and into her.

"He started it," the man said. "I told him to sit down." He looked around the bakery, filled with scared customers. "I told you all to sit down and shut up. But he," he gestured with the axe, holding it straight out in my direction, "didn't listen. He thinks he's so much more important with his stupid hair and fancy clothes. You're not better than me. You got that?"

With the axe extended toward me, the woman he was holding captive stomped down on his foot, desperate to get away. Before the suspect could retaliate, Brad charged him, pinning his weapon-wielding arm against the counter.

The woman screamed, rushing toward the door. The

bell chimed as she ran out of the bakery. Her escape caused the rest of the terrified customers to flee.

I pushed my way through the stampede, grabbing the weapon out of the man's hand while he pummeled my partner. "I got it." I tossed the axe behind the counter, out of reach.

One of the uniformed cops burst through the door, securing the weapon, while the other continued to draw down on the attacker.

Brad grunted as the guy threw another haphazard punch. Spinning, Brad released his grip on the guy's arm and elbowed him in the jaw. The attacker stumbled backward, catching himself on the counter. While he was dazed, Brad forced him face-first into the countertop and cuffed him.

While he patted him down, finding a switchblade and lighter in his pocket, I went back to render assistance to the wounded man. Officer Sanchez helped me while my partner and the other cop dragged the cuffed suspect into the back of the patrol car. A few seconds later, Brad returned.

"Are you okay?" I asked as he opened the medical kit.

"Yeah. You?"

"I'm good."

"What about him?"

By now, the guy on the ground was awake and alert, muttering curses. I wasn't sure which bothered him more, the pain or the tweaker who did this to him.

TWENTY-NINE

"Where'd you get the axe?" Brad closed the folder and stared at Lon Wirth, the man we arrested.

"I found it."

"Where?"

Wirth rubbed his tongue against the inside of his cheek, making the flesh bulge out. "The dump."

"You can do better than that."

"That's the truth."

"What were you doing at the dump?" I asked.

Wirth glanced in my direction, confused by my presence. "I was looking for shit." Brad picked up the snack cake and slowly peeled open the wrapper. The crinkling cellophane drew Wirth's attention away from me. His mouth watered, and he stared longingly at the dessert. "Can I have that?"

"That depends." Brad spread open the wrapper, placing it down on the table between them.

"On what?" Wirth hopped his chair forward, making it squeak against the floor. With his hands cuffed behind him, he couldn't grab the dessert. Instead, he leaned down, resting his chin on the table and sticking his tongue out. He reminded me of Gunnie, except Gunnie was smarter and cuter.

"You have to tell me more about the axe."

"I don't know. One of the garbage trucks dropped it off. I noticed because it was shiny. I thought it might have been a pipe or a pan, something I could sell or use. Instead, I found this really cool thing."

"Do you remember which truck dropped it off?" The waste management trucks were numbered, but Wirth hadn't paid attention to that.

"It was a garbage truck. That's all I know. They dump their loads into that one spot where stuff gets sorted before they do whatever with it. But that axe stuck out. I got to it before anyone else could."

"Where were you last night?" I asked.

Wirth peered up at me. "At the hospital. I had to get my stomach pumped. Something didn't agree with me. They kept me all night. Why?"

Brad nodded to me, and I went to check Wirth's alibi. The hospital confirmed he'd been brought in by paramedics after he passed out in a bar. They admitted him at seven p.m., hours before the attack inside the maze. Wirth wasn't our guy. I went back into the interrogation room and told Brad his story checked out.

"I just have one last question. What were you doing inside the bakery this afternoon?" Brad asked.

"I told you. I wanted cake."

"You attacked a man with an axe. You held the cashier hostage. Don't you think there are easier ways to get cake?"

"The damn bugs in my brain won't let me think straight. Not even for a second. That asshole in the suit had it coming. He's a nasty son of a bitch. Mean as fuck. Maybe now he'll think twice before cutting in line or pushing people around."

"And the woman behind the counter, what did she do to you?" Brad asked.

"Nothing." Wirth stared pitifully at the snack cake. "C'mon, I helped. Can't I have just a taste?"

"Sit up." Brad waited for Wirth to comply before he moved the treat closer. Before Brad could uncuff him, Wirth bent over and ate the cake off the wrapper.

G.K. Parks

My partner and I exchanged a look and left Wirth licking the cellophane. A robbery detective was waiting to question Wirth about this afternoon's incident. On the bright side, Wirth wasn't our problem. At least now, we had the axe. Too bad we didn't have the guy who'd dressed up like an executioner.

Brad rubbed his side as we headed back to our desks. "Forensics will analyze the blood and prints found on the axe. Maybe we'll get lucky and get an ID on the previous man who threatened people with that thing."

"Yeah." But I doubted it. I cocked my head at him. "Are you sure you're okay?"

"I'm fine." He cracked a smile. "It's nice to know you care, even if you take it to an extreme."

"That's because you have a habit of getting into trouble."

"Me?" He gave me a look. "Want to make a list? I bet you've been in more scrapes than I have."

"Do you really want to play that game?"

"Let's not and say we did." He skimmed the papers on his desk. "Did you see this?" He held up the costume catalog. "Our suspect from last night has the same taste in costumes as the other assholes we're hunting."

The executioner costume was on the same page as the vampire warrior and Van Helsing costumes, except it was in the bottom righthand corner. Given the crease and fold, I hadn't noticed it until now. "Son of a bitch."

"I'm starting to think we're looking for just one guy."

"But last night was different than the other two. No one got stabbed through the heart. His weapon of choice was much more impactful. I'm starting to think this might be some kind of widespread thing."

"Like an army of demons rising?" Brad teased. "I still don't buy it."

"Demons, no. Homicidal maniacs, maybe." I rolled my neck from side to side, hoping releasing some of the tension would focus my thoughts. "What are we missing?"

"Everything." Brad scooped up a few files and led the way to the conference room. "Common denominator. Go."

"Um...the costumes. They all came from the same supplier."

"More than likely, from the same store." He flipped the whiteboard over to the blank side and divided it in half. "Single suspect theory. The man had access to all three costumes, which means he works for the inn or was hired to cover one of the attractions." Brad pointed the end of the marker at the inn's employee records. "That means we already have everything we need on him. We just have to figure it out."

"Unless he's a guest."

"Why do you always have to make things complicated? Do you get a kick out of bursting my bubble?"

"On occasion."

"No wonder you're always such a pain in the ass." He wrote on the other half of the board, *Multiple suspects theory.* "However, if every task force crime was committed by a different suspect, it'll be harder to narrow down who they are."

"We have store receipts." I pointed to the printouts.

"Those won't lead us anywhere. We've already explored that option."

"Okay, so that leads us to the bigger question. Are these crimes even connected?"

"Every male victim wore vampire teeth."

"Not the same quality."

"No, but they were all dressed as vampires. Two of them were killed like vampires typically are on TV. Decapitation is another common form of dealing with bloodsuckers. An axe would be great for that."

"So is burning." I thought about Voletek's case.

"C'mon, that was brutal. It was slow, messy, and somewhere secluded. Our crimes are different. They happened in public or when lots of people were around. These weren't quiet crimes. The murderer wanted to show the world his handiwork. He wanted them to witness the death of a vampire. Last night's attack happened the same way. The whacko with the axe didn't care who saw him. If he did, he wouldn't have chosen the most crowded Halloween attraction to stage his attack, which brings me to my second point. Every single one of the victims had some sort of connection to the inn's haunted attractions."

"He might not be an employee. He could just use that as his hunting grounds."

Brad scribbled that onto the board. "Why sacrifice fertile grounds like that? The place is rife with men in vampire costumes. Attacking the Gespers in the maze ruined any chance he has of finding another victim. If we are looking at one suspect, then he's spiraling out of control. Something set him off."

"He went dormant for a week," I said, "at least as far as we know. Maybe that's what did it. The anticipation made him reckless."

"Could be, unless something else happened." Brad took a step back, resting his hips against the edge of the table while he studied his handiwork. "We don't know enough to build a psychological profile. We don't even know which theory is accurate. Maybe they're both wrong."

"Mac didn't find any mention online about a vendetta to kill vampires, at least nothing new or active. I checked the database, but as far as I can tell, this type of thing hasn't happened before."

"Great. Something new." Brad tapped the marker cap against his chin. "Gut theory. Go."

"We need sleep."

He turned to look at me. "That's not a theory. That's a fact. But what does your gut say about this? Which way are you leaning?"

"The inn's our connection. If we want answers, we have to dig deeper into what's going on over there and who's been paying an inordinate amount of attention to the visitors and guests. We should probably speak to the Gespers again now that they've had time to calm down and we've had time to figure some things out." I peered out the glass door. "Are they still here?"

"They aren't going anywhere. They're too freaked out." He turned to stare at the file boxes. "We spent all week on this and have nothing to show for it. We're doing this wrong. We should have gotten our shit together faster so last night wouldn't have happened."

"No one died. That has to count as a win."

"We got lucky." Brad tapped the spacebar on one of the

tech's abandoned laptops. "We might not next time." He entered a few search terms and waited. "Wirth said he got the axe from the dump."

"How does that help us?"

"The trucks dropped it off this morning, which means our suspect tossed it after the attack last night. Garbage pick-up runs on different days to different parts of the city."

"We should assume a man wielding an axe couldn't have gotten very far without someone noticing, so he probably tossed it pretty close to the scene of the crime. But no one recalls seeing anyone leaving the maze with an axe in hand. I'm not sure how that helps us."

"Again with the bubble bursting." Brad shook his head, clicking more keys. "You really need to break that bad habit."

"Then prove me wrong."

His lip twitched, and his eyes crinkled. "How about this?" He pointed to the screen. "These are the three closest streets to the haunted maze which had garbage pick-up yesterday. Let's pull surveillance footage and see what we get."

THIRTY

"Liv," Brad rested his forearm against the doorjamb to the break room, looking about ready to hit the floor, "we found something."

"Did you find the guy who attacked us?" Jodie Gesper asked.

"We hope so," Brad said. "Why don't you come take a look?"

I followed Jodie and Ron to the conference room. Brad nodded to Mac, who put the image on the big screen. I turned to see a man in a grey sweatshirt tossing the axe into a restaurant dumpster. "Is that the weapon he attacked you with?" I asked.

Ron nodded.

"Is that the guy?" Jodie asked.

"I was hoping you could tell us that," Brad said.

"I don't know." Jodie looked at her husband. "I can't tell since he isn't in costume. Can you?"

"It has to be the same guy. He has the axe. That is the axe."

"We recovered the weapon, but it doesn't tell us anything about who wielded it." I went around the table and picked up the catalog. "Did the attacker wear any of these costumes?" Even though I was certain the executioner costume was the same one on the page, it never hurt to verify such details.

"That's it." Ron pointed. "He wore it all. Right down to the gloves."

"That'll help," Brad said.

"Yeah, no problem. Like I said, if there's anything we can do, just ask."

"You don't recognize him, do you?" Brad pointed to the screen.

"Do you have any close-ups or better angles?" Ron asked.

Mac zoomed in. "That's the best I can do."

"I don't know. I don't think so," Ron said.

Jodie stepped closer to the screen. "I'm not sure. It's so hard to tell when I can't really see his face."

Unfortunately, nothing was ever simple. After the Gespers were escorted away, Lt. Winston stepped into the conference room. He hollered out the door for Voletek to join us.

"Progress report." Winston crossed his arms over his chest and waited.

"My suspect's been AWOL since yesterday afternoon," Voletek said. "I have no idea where he went. We've checked area shelters, soup kitchens, the park, the trains, everywhere we can think of. He's gone."

"Are you sure he's homeless?" Winston asked.

"Tripp found him near a homeless encampment. You saw and smelled him. It was the obvious conclusion."

"Look harder." Winston turned to us. "What about the lunatic from last night? I heard you made an arrest."

"We did. He's just not our guy," I said. "He found the axe and used it to hold up a bakery."

"The axe led us to this footage." Brad pointed to the paused feed on the screen. "We believe that's the lunatic from last night."

"Huh?" Voletek approached the screen and stared at it. "Y'know, when I brought in my suspect, he had on the same sweatshirt."

"It's a grey sweatshirt," I said. "Everyone has one. Even I own a grey sweatshirt."

"I don't know." Voletek crept across the room to where

Mac had been silently working and whispered to her while Brad updated Winston on our current working theory.

"Everything we've got is circumstantial, but the costumes and victims link back to these haunted attractions," Brad concluded. "Liv and I think this is how he's choosing his victims."

"What did management say?" Winston asked.

"The inn manager didn't want to cooperate, and since we shut down their biggest moneymaker last night and took the entire thing apart, I doubt he'll play ball," I said.

Winston sighed. "I'll make some calls and see if I can grease a few wheels. Do you have any idea who our suspect is?"

"All we have are his stats, which keep changing." I glanced back at Mac who was conferring with Voletek.

"Oh, is that my cue?" Mac blushed. "Right, well, okay. So it really just depends. We can extrapolate using the few facts we've collected from all three scenes and the footage here and from the alley where the Stevenses were killed. That gives us a white guy in his twenties to forties, around six feet tall, and a little on the higher end of the healthy BMI spectrum, possibly tipping over into overweight."

"What the hell does that mean?" Winston asked.

"A healthy BMI is—"

"Not that. I need to know pounds and build."

"Well, he could be a smidge taller, so I'd say he's in the 180-200 range, probably built, since he was swinging this giant axe around. The thing weighs a freaking ton which means he's strong. But given the photo we captured and the descriptions Liv and Brad got from witnesses, I'm guessing he's thick with a gut or beer belly. Though, I can't say for certain since I don't know if he drinks beer. In fact, do we know if he drinks at all? He crashed that one party, where everyone was drinking, but I don't think we ran the DNA on the cups, or did we? I haven't seen any reports on that."

"Mac," I gave her a look, "breathe."

She made a show of inhaling. "Right. Sorry."

"I'm starting to think we're looking for the same guy," Voletek said. "Now that your guy has broken from the object through the heart thing, I can't help but think burning and torturing might be another technique for putting down vampires."

"Did your victim have fangs?" I asked.

"It's tough to say. We found a lot of melted plastic. Some of it was polyester fibers from his clothing and plastic bags, but he could have had a cheap pair of teeth too. The guy's actual teeth had been bashed in with a hammer, so we couldn't ID him that way."

"But you IDed him. Did that yield any potential suspects?" I asked.

"Not really. The vic, Jonah Miller, was a vet, who dropped off the grid years ago. His family said the last they'd heard, he was living on the streets. They thought he died a long time ago. I haven't been able to find much else on him. I asked around at the soup kitchens and shelters. They said he mostly kept to himself. He didn't particularly like people."

"That's just fucked up." Brad exhaled. "I don't see how your case connects to this. I don't think someone like that would bother with vampire fangs. Not to mention, whoever killed him cut off his balls. That has nothing to do with putting down vampires, unless I haven't been watching the right movies."

"Maybe we're wrong about motive," I said. "We've been seeing couples getting attacked, specifically the men. Cassie's death appeared to be accidental, and based on everything the Gespers told us, it sounds like the axe man wanted to hurt Ron, not Jodie."

"You're thinking some guy's on the warpath because his woman left him for someone else?" Mac asked.

"I don't know. But it's something to consider."

Winston shook his head. "The threat HQ received had nothing to do with rejected lovers. This is about preventing the undead from unleashing their army upon us."

"If you believe such nonsense," Voletek muttered.

Winston glared at him. "I'll let that slide since you've been at this all night and day, but tomorrow, I want you back with the program. Go home. Get some sleep. And tomorrow, tackle this with fresh eyes. You have plenty of leads to explore."

"Yeah?" Voletek snorted. "Like what?"

"The inn. We go back over everything. We figure out how our victims connect to it and who they interacted with once they were there. We scrub every bit of camera footage we can find. We'll get this guy. In the meantime, Ms. Mackenzie, I want you to track this guy." He pointed to the man in the grey sweatshirt. "We know exactly when and where he dumped the axe. Figure out how he got there and where he went afterward. I want him brought in. Yesterday would be good."

"Yes, sir." Mac saluted, clicking her heels together beneath her chair before turning her attention back to the computer and reaching for a licorice twist. She ripped off the end with her teeth and chewed while analyzing the feed.

"I thought we were cleared for overtime," Brad said.

Winston clapped him on the shoulder. "You are, but you're useless if you can't keep your eyes open."

"Yes, sir."

"You don't have to tell me twice." Voletek headed for the door.

Once the lieutenant left, I reread my partner's theories. "The inn keeps its Halloween stuff in what was once the dining room. It's out of the way, so guests wouldn't have any reason to wander through there. But I don't remember the doors being locked."

"They weren't," Brad said.

"Don't they have security cameras inside?" Mac asked.

"Not in the dining room," I said.

"Still, I might be able to figure out who entered and left. After last night, I'm sure we have copies of the footage. I'll check again. It probably won't lead to a name, but if I spot this bastard," she pointed to the image frozen on the screen, "we'll know for sure we're on the right track."

"Thanks." I peered into the giant bowl of Halloween candy that Mac had been grazing on while she worked. "If you need a break, take some time to get some sleep. Winston doesn't want us to crash. That includes you."

"Actually, I'm pretty sure he thinks I'm like a weird

robot or some kind of human-computer hybrid, like the *Bionic Woman*."

"She was a computer hybrid?" Brad asked, but I pushed him toward the door before Mac could launch into a long-winded discussion on science fiction shows which would leave her breathless and me dizzy. "Now what?" Brad asked after we made it outside. "Don't get me wrong, I'm exhausted, but I'm kind of wired too."

I checked the time. "Mom's at her wino meeting, so Dad's in charge of dinner. How do you feel about steak?"

"Do you even have to ask?"

"I'll let him know to expect two more."

"I'll meet you there. I'm gonna swing by the inn and see what's what."

THIRTY-ONE

"Here." I put the container of cookies down on my partner's desk. "You forgot to take these with you when you left last night."

"Remind me to get your mom some flowers."

"You don't have to do that."

He shook the cookie container at me. "I have to repay her somehow."

I didn't bother mentioning that my mom plied him with treats as her way of thanking him for watching my back and keeping me alive. "Fine, make me look bad."

"If you want, I'll tell her they're from both of us."

"That'd be worse. Just get her something Halloween-y. A pumpkin or an autumn centerpiece. Something like that."

"Good idea."

"What is?" Lt. Winston asked.

"Fennel drove by the inn last night. Even though we shut down the maze and have everything roped off with crime scene tape, the rest of the festivities remain in full swing."

"In fact," Brad tucked the cookies into his bottom desk drawer, "the news story about a crazed killer running amok inside the maze might have made the inn even more popular."

Winston scowled. "You're joking."

"I wish I was. I didn't see nearly as many families with kids running around, so that's a plus, but a lot of teenagers and young adults were out in droves. I don't know if they didn't believe the news or if the thrill of real danger excites them."

"Fucking idiots."

"We're thinking, since the attractions haven't been shut down and even more people have come to check it out, that the killer might still be around. Liv and I thought we'd take another look and try to get the lay of the land."

"The Gespers haven't checked out of the inn yet. They gave us permission to search their room. Since Jodie's convinced the killer will make another attempt on their lives, we thought he might have tried to gain access to their room to find out more about them," I said.

"How would he know what room they were in?" Winston asked.

"They're honeymooners," Brad said. "They act like it, and Ron tells everyone they meet how they just got hitched. If they encountered the axe man prior to his attempt on their lives, Ron might have spoken directly to him or he overheard Ron speaking to someone else."

"All right. Get to it. I've beefed up patrols in the area. We have two cruisers parked outside the inn at all times. That should deter him from acting again, but if this is the work of one man, then we know he typically stalks his prey after they leave the attractions and kills them in a different location, possibly even on a different day. So keep an eye out for that."

"Will do," I said.

When we reached the inn, I was surprised to see lines at the ticket booths. Four booths were open, along with the refreshment stands. The only two attractions open this early were the haunted house and escape room. The ghost tour and hayride didn't start until dusk.

"Did you see the article on the *Journal*'s website?" Brad asked. A couple of techs were keeping an eye on the comments and messages floating around the internet, hoping our suspect might reveal himself that way. "Every single comment on the news story concerning the attack claimed it was staged to gain publicity. In fact, several people are adamant that the actors the inn hired are just real deal method actors who are getting into their roles to make it a better experience."

"Better?" I practically choked. "Anna Moniz nearly lost an arm. I'm sure she wouldn't consider that a better experience."

Brad stopped in the center of the courtyard, watching workers clear away the mess CSU had left. "As soon as we finished with the scene, the inn started rebuilding the maze. They ordered new shipments of hay and a ton more decorations. According to the article, it'll be even bigger than before."

"So our killer has more room to swing his axe?"

Brad shrugged as we weaved our way through the groups of teenagers and college kids. The smell of apple and pumpkin pies filled the air. Everywhere I looked, people were sucking on pumpkin spiced drinks, apple cider, and hot chocolate while they waited in line, chatted with friends, took photos, and texted on their phones.

"We should make sure someone's monitoring social media."

"Winston's got a team on it, but what we're able to do is just a drop in the bucket." Brad led the way through the courtyard, stopping at certain locations to get a better look at the employees working the booths. "None of them are built like our suspect."

"If he's smart, he's long gone."

When we entered the inn, the man working at the front desk looked at us. "Checking in?"

"No." Brad held up the Gespers' room key.

The front desk manager smiled, unlike the hotel manager we'd spoken to a week ago. "Very good, sir. If you or your wife need anything, please let us know."

I opened my mouth to correct him, but Brad wrapped his arm around my waist and tugged me against him. "What are you doing?" I whispered.

He communicated with his eyes for me to keep quiet and turned back to the front desk manager. "I think we're okay for now. Right, honey?"

"Yeah, I guess." What was my partner thinking?

After we were safely inside the elevator, heading up to the top floor, I opened my mouth to say something, but Brad squeezed my side and diverted his gaze to the camera in the corner. From the employee records we'd reviewed and the alibis we'd run, we had no reason to think a member of management or security was involved, but Brad seemed to have forgotten this minute detail.

When the doors opened, he headed toward the honeymoon suite, unlocked the door, and waited for me to enter. He checked the door for signs of tampering and shut it. "It doesn't look like anyone tried to gain unlawful entry."

"Housekeeping has a key." I pointed to the king-sized bed with the heart-shaped throw pillows. "They must have made the bed. They even left pillow mints." I moved closer to examine them, finding they were also heart-shaped. "Y'know, for a haunted suite, you'd think they'd lay off the romantic vibes and just stick with creepy tones."

"Perhaps that's why a psycho chased the couple through the maze." Brad pulled out an RF reader he'd gotten from Mac and scanned the room while I put on some gloves and searched for any indication the axe man had been inside. "The place is clean. No bugs."

"For what this place charges, I'd hope not."

"You know what I mean." He tucked the device away and pulled on a blue latex glove and unzipped the suitcase on top of the fold-out stand. "Even though the Gespers gave us permission to search their room and their belongings, I don't feel right about this. I just feel pervy."

"Fine. You take the bathroom. I'll look through their luggage."

"Thanks, Liv."

Jodie had packed several sexy negligees. The couple had provided us a list of every item they remembered packing. As far as I could tell, nothing had been taken. The items in the suitcase were folded neatly. The articles that had been worn were in a separate laundry bag. "I don't think he's a sexual deviant."

"Ron?" Brad asked from the bathroom.

I laughed. "I meant the guy who attacked them. If he broke in, he didn't take any of their unmentionables." I zipped the suitcase. "All of their valuables are here too."

"I don't think anyone's been inside the room except housekeeping. The mini soaps and shampoos have been replaced. The towels are fresh, and the toilet paper has that weird point to it."

"When did the Gespers check in?"

"Four days ago."

"Did Mac check the security feed from the hallway?"

"The only camera on this floor is posted at the other end. It doesn't even reach the elevator."

"That's stupid."

"I'm guessing it has to do with maintaining guest privacy."

"Still stupid."

"At least we know he hasn't been here," Brad said. "If Ron Gesper was his next target, he might have followed them back here to finish the job. You have to admit, this room is pretty secluded since it's at the end of the hallway, away from the rest of the rooms."

"That's because it's the honeymoon suite. They don't want the other guests complaining about the noise."

Brad laughed. "If these walls could talk."

I gave the bed another look. "I'd hate to see what CSU might find. But nothing indicates the attacker was here. I don't see any blood droplets on the floor. No drag marks from the axe. No footprints of any kind, thanks to the vacuum cleaner."

"Winston notified the local sheriff's department. They sent a patrol car to the Gespers' house to make sure no one's been snooping around or waiting for them to return. It doesn't look like they had any uninvited guests."

"How do you think the killer found the Stevenses? They hadn't even checked in yet. But they had tickets for the attractions. I'm sure they didn't have to provide their address."

"He probably followed Roger Stevens back to his

apartment."

"But Roger didn't buy the tickets the same day he was killed. So how long did the killer plan to strike?"

"I don't think he did. He had the outfit and the weapon, but the footage didn't look like a planned attack. It looked opportunistic."

"Isn't that what the attack on the Gespers was?" I asked. "They were making out in a dead end, away from the main path. He happens upon them, breaks up their fun, Ron returns the aggression, and the guy with the axe snaps. He chases them through the rest of the maze, swinging his axe. The blood we found in the three different areas was Ron's from where he brushed up against the hay bales or where he was struck as they tried to run away."

"Okay, so if we're looking at one guy, which is what makes the most sense at this point, then he doesn't plan his attacks. He just reacts when he sees men dressed as vampires kissing beautiful women."

"Innocent women," I said. "A barmaid and a cheerleader."

"We have different definitions of innocent."

"Going back to the horror movie genre, which I'm guessing is what is inspiring the killer's actions, the barmaids and cheerleaders are always the clueless ones. They never realize the danger. That's what I mean by innocent."

"Tavern girl." Brad thought for a moment. "Maiden."

"Whatever."

"I get your point. But Dan Fielders' murder was entirely different. That wasn't opportunistic. The killer sought Dan out. He crashed that party and killed Dan after Vivica left. Plus, her costume didn't fit the innocent vibe. She was dressed as Dracula's bride. Teeth and all."

"Maybe that's the crime that doesn't fit," I said.

"But the method of killing was closer with that one than the attempt the axe man made on the Gespers."

"Either they all fit or none of them fit," I said. But we both knew this wasn't an all or nothing situation.

"Let me see if the DNA results came back on that bloody glove the dogs found a few blocks from the maze. I'm guessing it belongs to our axe man, and if the samples match, we might be able to finally determine if we're looking at one guy for all these crimes."

"That's assuming he wore the same pair of gloves, and that's also assuming the bloody glove has anything to do with what happened at the maze."

"Bubble burster," he mumbled, checking his phone.

While he did that, I gazed out the window, finding the glass foggy. The gauzy curtain reflected in the window. Playing with the lights, I realized if it was dark in the room, the reflection made it look like an ethereal figure was standing behind me. To be on the safe side, I turned to make sure, but no one was there.

I also found a small timer hooked to the plug which connected the table lamp to the outlet. I turned the dial on the timer, and the light flickered a few times. Haunted my ass. The TV had the same timer hooked to it. Each one was set to go off at 9:23. That was early enough not to wake the guests, but late enough to creep them out.

I checked the air conditioner, but it didn't have a timer. "If this place really wanted to chill its guests to the bone, they should blast the air. After all, isn't the temperature supposed to drop when spirits are present?"

Brad eyed me while reading the message on his phone. "I thought you weren't into all that paranormal mumbo-jumbo. Don't we have a bet going, which you lost, by the way."

"We don't know if I lost. Vivica leaving town makes her look even guiltier. Or scared." I crossed my arms over my chest and studied the room. "Do you think something happened to her?"

"Asta didn't find it strange. Plus, Vivica told her friend she was getting away for a few days. Normally, killers don't let you make calls before they strike."

A knock at the door startled us. Brad pressed his finger to his lips before I could say anything. "Who is it?"

"Room service."

Brad signaled for me to cover him from the bathroom while he went to the door. He peered out the peephole, tucked his badge into his pocket, and placed his other hand behind his back underneath his jacket, prepared to pull his piece if necessary. "We didn't order any room service."

"It's complimentary, sir. We can leave it in the hallway if you prefer. We don't want to disturb you."

Brad glanced at me. "No, that's okay. I'll be right there. Just give us a second."

He tossed his jacket onto the chair, loosened his tie, leaving it hanging, and unbuttoned his shirt and belt.

"What are you doing?" I hissed.

He left his shirt tail hanging over his gun and attempted to muss his short brown hair. "Improvising."

"What the hell kind of play is this?"

"My case, my call. Stay out of sight, unless I need rescuing." He pulled the bathroom door closed, leaving it open a crack.

This entire situation reminded me of the undercover work Voletek and I had done while Brad had gone out on his own. But we didn't have any idea who our suspect was or where he was selecting his victims. This was premature. But I'd learned long ago to trust my partner. I was decent at reading people, but Brad was great at reading situations. I just hoped he wasn't wrong.

"Sorry about that." Brad opened the door. "What is this for?"

"To make up for the trouble you encountered the other night at the maze, Mr. Gesper." The front desk manager wheeled a cart into the room. "We were afraid you had no plans of returning. I'm glad you and your wife came back to the inn."

"To tell you the truth, we weren't sure what to do. We still aren't."

"I understand. If it's any consolation, your stay and meals are on us. We're so sorry this happened. If there's anything you need, just let us know. We'll take care of it."

"My wife's still freaked out. Has anyone been arrested?"

"No. Not yet. But we can assure you, security is on top of things. You won't have any more problems. I'll guarantee that."

"We'll let you know what we decide. Right now, we're still making up our minds."

The manager studied Brad's appearance. "Don't let me interrupt. Enjoy."

After Brad shut the door, I emerged from the bathroom. He pressed his fingers to his lips and searched the cart. When he didn't find any surveillance devices, he scanned everything with the RF reader.

"Brad, the inn isn't out to get the Gespers."

"I know that. But someone who works here might be."

"The front desk manager is 5'6 and probably a buck forty. He's not the guy who attacked them."

"No, but I'm betting someone on the property is." He handed me his phone, which was open to the report forensics had forwarded him. The glove the K-9 unit recovered had blood evidence on it which matched Dan Fielders, the Stevenses, and Ron Gesper. "This has to be where he picks out his targets."

THIRTY-TWO

The moment we returned to the precinct, Winston waved us into the conference room. "The glove we recovered has to belong to our killer. Did you get the report?"

"Yes, sir," Brad said. "The lab said they found two other blood types on the outside of the glove that didn't match any of the known victims. Have we received any other reports?"

Winston shook his head.

"What about Voletek's case?" I asked. "Did the lab run a comparison between those samples and the murdered vet?"

"Not a match." Winston had already updated the board. "The lab is hoping they'll be able to pull prints from inside the glove, but that doesn't look promising. The material isn't exactly the most conducive for that, which leaves us with trying to pull some epithelial cells. But it'll be months before we get anything on that."

"We could source it out to the Feds or a private lab," I said. "Turnaround time is much shorter that way."

"The brass won't approve it."

"Doesn't that go against their edict?" Brad asked. "The whole point of this task force is to stop the undead army or the guy who wants to prevent the undead army from overtaking the city, whichever the case may be." He chuckled. "That's pretty damn contradictory if you ask me."

"Either way, no dice." Winston muttered a few things under his breath. "Since it appears these murders are the result of one man, we stop the one man. This isn't a spree. At least, not yet." He studied the map. "He's finding his targets at Halloween-inspired locations. Patrol is keeping a watch at the inn, but with the constant crowd and a lot of it being indoors or out of sight, it's impossible for us to be everywhere at once. There's also a good chance he's finding his targets at Halloween shops and boutiques. His victims never crossed paths, but if the killer's another Halloween nutjob, which the change in costume for each attack indicates, then he could have stumbled upon them at a number of different places."

"The surveillance footage won't help," I said. "Mac already analyzed everything I got from the two shops where the murder weapons were most likely purchased. She couldn't make heads or tails out of who our suspect might be."

"Credit card records and receipts were also a bust, particularly when the inn made bulk purchases from every shop in the city and had plenty of items from past years stockpiled." Brad leaned his hips against the table and sat back, staring at the whiteboard where he'd written down our two possible theories. "I'm sure he's getting his costumes from the inn. We need to get surveillance inside to keep an eye out. He'll need another costume to wear for his next attack, and since he dropped one of his gloves, he'll have to replace it with something else." He leafed through the catalog. "Only a handful of costumes have gloves. The one the dogs recovered matches the Van Helsing costume. But the vampire warrior and executioner costumes have the same colored gloves." He grabbed a pen and circled four pictures. "He'll have to wear one of these."

"Biker? Traffic cop? Ninja? Gunslinger?" I gave my partner a skeptical look. "What do they have to do with hunting vampires?"

"He'd need those gloves to use as replacements."

The lieutenant took the catalog from my hands. "An executioner isn't necessarily a vampire hunter either, but he is a killer. I'd say traffic cop is out. Since he attacks using whatever weapon fits his costume, that won't work." Winston put the catalog down. "Let's hope he doesn't go with gunslinger, or we could be looking at mass casualties."

"The costume comes with a six-shooter," Brad said.

"I'll issue an alert for anyone who's purchased one lately or tries to. For once, I'd like to be one step ahead of this guy." Winston left us to debate the rest while he stepped out of the room.

"We know where he got the stakes and metal cross," I said. "But where did he get the axe?"

"The inn," Brad said. "Everything he used came from there. Regardless of what Winston says, we know that to be true."

"I agree, but that doesn't mean he's an inn employee. We ran backgrounds and checked alibis for everyone they hired to work the attractions. Even if we couldn't clear them for all three murders and the attack, everyone was cleared for at least one of them." I exhaled. "I know the glove says the guy was at all the scenes, but it could be more than one guy."

"Liv, don't. This is screwed up as it is. I don't need you looking for zebras when we have a stable full of horses in front of us."

"Wow, someone's into the whole Wild West thing."

"It must have been the mention of gunslinging, but getting back to business, we need a solid plan to stop this guy. And I've got one."

"It won't work."

He crossed his arms over his chest. "Why not?"

"For one thing, you don't look anything like Ron Gesper."

"The front desk manager didn't notice the difference." Brad stood on his tiptoes. "How about now?"

"It's not just the three inches in height you're lacking. Ron's hair is longer, and his eyes are hazel. Yours are brown."

"People don't pay that much attention. Maybe I got a

haircut and had in colored contacts. Half the time they saw Ron, he was wearing a costume. The killer attacked him when his face was painted and he had a cape. He might not know what Ron looks like either."

"Who's gonna back you up?"

"You."

"Me?" I laughed. "I don't look anything like Jodie."

"C'mon, Liv, the front desk manager already thinks you're my wife. Hell, Emma thinks so too. All you have to do is change your hair and modify your makeup. You used to do stuff like this all the time. What's the problem?"

"It's a shot in the dark. We don't know if he's hanging around the inn or if he left after what happened the other night. If he's smart, he's long gone. We have no way of knowing if he plans to finish what he started with the Gespers."

"They think so."

"They're scared. They don't know what to think. We've been through their lives with a fine-tooth comb. No one's threatened them. As far as we know, no one has any reason to want to harm them."

"It's not about them. It's about the costume. This guy wants to slay vampires. He's not done, not when Halloween's still two weeks away."

"By impersonating the Gespers, we're painting ourselves into a corner. Meanwhile, he can strike anywhere at any time. The inn might host the most attractions, but there are plenty more haunted houses and places people can go to dress up in costume. If he's smart, he'll pick another place."

"What if he doesn't?"

Brad had me there.

"Are you guessing, or are you basing this off of something?"

"Instinct. I might not know this guy, but he's hanging around the inn for a reason." Brad gestured at the slew of boxes we had yet to dissect. "Every one of those attractions has staff that gets contracted out. We're talking everything from builders to ticket-takers. The killer got his costumes from the inn, and he didn't take just any costumes. He took ones that he knew weren't being worn. He works around there in some aspect, but you're probably right. He doesn't work inside any of the attractions. But we need to be close to the action, and you heard Winston. Staking out the place from the perimeter won't cut it. There's too much going on, too many blind spots. We have to be in the middle of the action."

"We don't have to be the Gespers in order to do that. We could get teams of UCs to do that. We could have half of patrol show up in street clothes."

"But what if he wants to finish what he started? Even though we tried to keep a lid on things, I saw Ron and Jodie's name in print at least once. We have to assume he has too."

"Fine."

"Not to mention, the inn is booked solid. They won't give us a room to conduct surveillance. The hotel manager made it clear he has no interest in helping our investigation. The attack hasn't changed that. If anything, he's in CYA mode."

"No matter how much he tries to cover his ass, I doubt the media is going to let this go."

"So the inn's banking on the free publicity instead, even though it's all negative. We shut down what we can, but we're not going to get the go-ahead to shut down the entire operation, just like the city won't cancel Halloween. It just won't happen."

"I said fine. You don't have to keep trying to convince me. We'll do this. It's a good plan. It gives us a decent shot and keeps us close to the action. But we need a lot more eyes keeping watch."

"It's a good thing Winston left us in charge of the task force and gave us access to as much manpower as we need."

"From the crowds we saw this afternoon, we'll need all the help we can get. Let's just hope no one recognizes you as the detective who questioned them after the attack."

THIRTY-THREE

"Have I mentioned how much I hate Halloween?" I whispered, leaning back against his chest.

"Only thirty times in the last five minutes." Brad rested his chin on top of my head and wrapped his arms around me while we waited in line to buy tickets to the escape room. "You need to get into the spirit of things. From what the Gespers told us, they were having fun. You are not." He squeezed me tighter, leaning down and planting a loud, wet kiss on my cheek.

I giggled, flipping the blonde tendrils of my wig over my shoulder and into his face. "Behave, Ronnie. We're out in public. Contain yourself."

Brad chuckled against my ear. "I'll do my best, but you're so damn adorable." He nuzzled against my ear, tickling me and making me squirm.

I fought to keep from saying his name as I laughed, happy and giddy. I wasn't used to being undercover with him. That made this tricky. But he wasn't Brad Fennel and I wasn't Liv DeMarco. We were Ron and Jodie Gesper. Why we didn't run screaming after the guy with the axe attacked us was anyone's guess, but Brad had a plan for that too.

"Two, please," Brad said when we made it to the booth.

The girl, who looked like she belonged in high school, had dyed her hair like a rainbow, painted a white star on her cheek, and had done a rainbow pattern with her eye shadow. I wasn't sure who she was supposed to be, but that was one colorful costume. "You'll have to schedule a time. Are you going with a group?"

"No," Brad smiled at her, "it's just the two of us. It's our honeymoon."

She didn't seem to care. "The escape room is for groups of four or more. I can put you with another couple, unless you want to call someone to meet you."

"What do you want to do, babe?" I asked. "We could probably find something else to do instead, or we could go back upstairs."

He grinned, a big, cheesy smile that would have looked over the top if his expression wasn't so carefree. "What happens if we miss our time?" he asked the girl. "Does the other couple get to go by themselves?"

"No, we'd take whoever happened to be next in line." She snapped her gum. "Do you want to pick another day?"

"Nah," I shrugged away from Brad who'd been nibbling on my earlobe, "put us with another couple."

"I have an empty slot at seven."

"Seven is perfect. It's the only way to guarantee we make it to dinner. This one," I turned, squinting at him, "is liable to make us starve."

"You're the one who said we could skip this and go back upstairs." Brad reached into his pocket and pulled out some cash. "However, if we don't go to the escape room, we may never escape our room." He winked at the girl. "If you know what I mean."

"Ronnie, stop that. You're going to give everyone the wrong idea. Behave yourself."

By now, I was sure everyone within earshot was sick of us. But that was the point. We had to make a spectacle. We had to turn ourselves into targets.

"Have fun," the girl said, her tone and eyes conveyed the double meaning.

We left the ticket booth, strolling hand-in-hand toward

one of the refreshment stands. Brad twirled me, like we were dancing, which gave me the chance to look all around us. But with the limited description, I couldn't be sure the killer wasn't here.

At the refreshment stand, I wrapped my arms around Brad's middle and rested my head against his chest. He put an arm around me, looking over my head at the people on the other side of the courtyard. After collecting our hot apple ciders from a guy who could have been Santa Claus's skinny twin brother, we found a seat on the retaining wall near the inn's gardens.

Putting down his cup, Brad took out his phone and told me to smile. After snapping a few photos, he sent the images back to the team in the surveillance van half a block away and sipped his drink. "This is how the other half lives."

"I guess so."

He nodded a few times. "Getting hitched isn't so scary when it's to you." He spun the gold band around his ring finger using the pad of his thumb. "Mr. Gesper. That has a nice ring to it."

"You're such a goof, Ronnie. You were Mr. Gesper before we even met."

"You know what I mean."

"Uh-huh." I wondered who he spotted behind us that had made him fall so heavily back into character. If we announced our names any more, someone might get suspicious. Then again, from the time we had spent interviewing the Gespers, Brad's impersonation couldn't have been more rock solid. Dressing in khakis and a polo made him look more like Ron, even if he didn't have as much height or bulk.

"You look beautiful. I could just eat you up." He made a monster noise and lurched forward, but I put my hand against his chest, stopping him. His phone buzzed, and he glanced down at it briefly before glancing back at the inn, which loomed in the distance.

A crisp breeze blew hair into my face, and I smoothed it down. "Do you want to go upstairs?"

"Just as soon as I finish my cider." He reached for my

cup, finding it empty.

"Take your time." I climbed off my perch and stepped backward, swaying my body along with the breeze. "I'll be waiting." I continued moving backward, running my hand through my hair in a seductive, come-hither fashion.

Brad's face lit up, and he smiled as he watched me move blindly backward through the crowd. When I bumped into someone, I turned to apologize, and that's when he leapt from his spot on the retaining wall and rushed toward me. The grin on his face told me this was for show. I squealed and ran through the crowd.

Brad caught me at the steps, lifted me off the ground, and tossed me over his shoulder. I put my hand on my head, afraid the wig might fall off, but a million pins held it in place. Then he carried me inside, the same way the real Ron and Jodie had done.

He put me down while we waited for the elevator, rubbing the tip of his nose against the bridge of mine. My heart rate jumped, probably from all the running. I took a breath, stood on my tiptoes, and kissed him gently.

For half a second, he looked like Brad, not Ron. Then the elevator doors opened, and we stepped inside. A few other people joined us. We stood in the back, our shoulders together. Unless the killer followed us to our room, returning to the honeymoon suite was a waste of time.

By the time we reached our floor, the elevator was empty. Brad took my hand and led me to the room, probably forgetting the surveillance cameras didn't reach this far. He unlocked the door. "Should I carry you over the threshold?"

"I think we've already done that." I stepped past him and into the suite.

He hung the *Do Not Disturb* on the handle and scanned the room again for any radio frequencies. But the place hadn't been bugged since the last time we checked.

"You're paranoid." I peered out the window at the growing crowd in the courtyard. I spotted two navy blue baseball caps flanking the pie stand. "Are they making a bust?"

Brad moved beside me, wiping the window with his

palm. But the grimy, frosted look had been done intentionally, so it wouldn't rub off. "A guy matching our suspect's description kept staring at us." He dug out his phone and showed me the photo he'd taken. "I sent that to the team in the surveillance van. It looks like they want to have a word with him."

The two undercover officers wearing blue baseball caps took a seat on either side of the guy. They spoke for a while, but the man didn't run and they didn't pull out their cuffs.

Reluctantly, I stepped away from the window. One of the mirrors in the room was just as creepy as the window, so I covered it with a towel and checked my reflection in the bathroom mirror. At least the inn had been smart enough not to trick out the bathroom. They probably figured someone would get scared, slip and fall, and sue them.

"Tell me they're bringing this guy in for questioning," I said.

"It doesn't look like it. They've gone back to the surveillance van." A second later, his phone chimed. "False alarm. The guy I spotted is a reporter. They checked his credentials."

"Great, he wants to interview us."

"Not us. The Gespers." Brad poked his head into the bathroom, watching as I tried to figure out what to do with the wig. "See, I told you people would believe we're Ron and Jodie."

"They won't if my wig falls off." I blew out an exasperated breath. "I'm gonna have to dye my hair."

"It's Halloween. Everyone's wearing wigs. You could probably lose the wig and say your real hair is a wig."

"You think my real hair looks like a wig?"

He held up his palms. "Don't make me regret marrying you."

"You've had that ring for less than two hours and you already want a divorce. My mother warned me about men like you. It's the whole cow milk thing."

"How does that work when you're dairy-free?"

"I don't think it matters that I'm dairy-free. It would only matter if you are, which you aren't."

"I am when I'm with you."

"Well, then I guess the cow milk thing doesn't apply to you either."

He grinned. "I knew Maria wouldn't warn you to stay away from me."

I rolled my eyes. "Is it just me or is working together like this more complicated than it needs to be?"

"Why would it be complicated? I'm doing my job, same as you." He watched me scratch beneath my wig. "Is that really bothering you that much?"

"I'll get used to it." It was the rest I wasn't sure about.

THIRTY-FOUR

My partner rubbed a hand over his face while he stared at the closed door. From one of the other rooms, we heard a scream. I turned to look, my muscles rigid.

"Easy," he whispered. "It's part of the fun."

"This is why I don't understand Halloween. Why would anyone want to be scared?"

"It's the adrenaline rush. The fear while knowing all along there is no actual danger."

"Except for the lunatic killing people."

He chuckled, even though it wasn't funny, and pressed his lips against my temple. The other half of our party had arrived. "Don't be such a worrywart, honey. This will be a blast."

Hysterical laughter came from the same room where I'd heard the scream. Brad was right. I shouldn't be worried. Each escape room had surveillance cameras which the PD was monitoring. If the killer chose to use this as the venue for his next attack, we'd see it happen. However, since we were convinced he picked his victims from the inn's attractions, Brad thought it'd be best if we checked each one out. Hopefully, by masquerading around as the Gespers, we'd draw him out and distract him from finding another target.

"Whoa, that's some costume." The guy who said it smiled and extended his hand.

"Thanks," I said.

"Oh," he glanced at me while Brad shook his hand, "that's a cool costume too. But I meant Mr. Vlad."

"Mr. Vlad?" I glanced up at Brad.

"Vlad the Impaler." Brad nodded to the guy. "Good eye. But since we're about to be locked together in a room, you can call me Ron. This is my wife, Jodie. We just got married." He snaked his arms around my waist and nibbled on my neck. "Can you believe this is our honeymoon? It's pretty sweet, right?" He kissed along my shoulder. "Cosplay, life-sized puzzles, danger around every corner." He made spooky ghost sounds. "I get to swoop in, save the day, and rescue the fair princess."

"Ronnie, stop that." I pinched his forearm.

The guy who'd complimented him smiled even bigger and clutched his chest. "That is so romantic. Isn't that romantic, Travis?" He tugged on the sleeve of the guy beside him. "Why couldn't Brandon have been like that?"

"Get over it, Devin. He was a loser. You can do better than him. And didn't we say you weren't going to mention him at all tonight?" Travis adjusted the hood he wore, so the dog ears on his dalmatian costume hung evenly.

"Right, sorry." Devin stepped closer to us and stage whispered, "Brandon's my ex. Travis hates it when I talk about him. I think he's jealous."

Travis rolled his eyes. "For the record, we're not a couple."

"Heaven forbid," Devin muttered.

"I didn't mean it like that," Travis said.

While they bickered, I watched the room on the other end of the hallway empty out. Six people exited, laughing. One of them appeared to be drenched. I wasn't sure what happened, but that might have been what caused her to scream.

"No vampires." Brad nodded toward the group. "Maybe I'm the only one out tonight."

"One can only hope."

My partner had upped the ante, taking Ron's cape to the next level by flipping it inside out, so the red was on the outside. Everything else from his shirt to his pants to his belt was black, except for the red, silk ascot tied loosely around his neck. He had popped up the top of the cape's collar. For added effect, he'd painted his skin the same way Ron had done and added a dribble of blood down the corner of his mouth and gotten a pair of fang caps to wear.

A woman dressed like a prison guard headed for us. "Are you ready to get locked up?"

"We can't wait," Devin said.

"Let me go over the rules," she said. "Each room contains a different puzzle you have to solve. The goal for your room is to escape from the dungeon. Even if you've been here before, we switch things around, so you'll still be challenged. You'll have to find clues and solve the puzzles in order to locate the key and unlock the door. Do not damage anything in the room. If you have a question, you can ask the game-master using the intercom button on the wall. If there is some sort of emergency, notify us, and we'll get you out immediately. You have one hour to escape. Are there any questions?"

We exchanged looks with the two men who'd be partnered with us. But they shook their heads.

The woman inserted a tassled key into the lock and opened the door. "The clock starts now."

Devin and Travis dashed toward the back of the room which looked exactly like a dungeon, complete with metal bars and cages. Shackles hung from rings on the wall. Brad exhaled beside me.

"Reminds me of something else too," I muttered.

"Hey, I found some writing down here," Travis said. *"The six points to go north."*

"What does that mean?" I asked.

"We have to figure it out." Travis glanced at us. "Are you virgins?"

"What?" Brad asked.

"Is this your first escape room?"

"Oh, um, yeah."

"Okay, spread out. Start at each corner and call out

anything you find. We're looking for clues. Pretend you're detectives in one of those crime scene shows. You want to find anything that stands out or doesn't belong."

"I think we can handle that." I winked at Brad and headed for the opposite corner.

The game-master intercom was clearly labeled on the center of the back wall. The camera keeping an eye on things was hidden in the clock. But I spotted the telltale black lens above the six. This would be a terrible place for the killer to stage another attack when help was nearby. However, it would give him a bird's eye view of any vampires lurking around.

Dan and Vivica had visited these escape rooms, but we couldn't find any evidence the Stevenses had been here. Then again, we hadn't been able to find much regarding their whereabouts prior to their murders. Ron and Jodie hadn't visited yet, but it was on their list of things to do.

"I found a loose brick," Devin called. "There's a box behind it. It has a keyhole."

"No combination?" Travis asked.

"Nope. Key."

"All right, we'll look for a key," Brad said.

"I found more writing. *Four to the south*. That sounds like the points on a compass." I studied the wall, but the words had been carved near the ground.

"Are they talking about the clock?" Travis pointed to the time.

"I don't think so." Brad moved to the shelf, picking up each book as he went. "I found a key. It's in a hollowed out book."

"Bring it over here." Devin held out his hand. Once the box was opened, he pulled out a scroll. "It says *Beware of the dragon lurking in the shadows. He will light the way, but only if you pay.*"

"Dragons are all about gold and jewels," Travis said. "Look for coins or jewelry. Something of value."

"I take it we can't just hand him a twenty," I teased.

Brad laughed. "The going rate on dragons is probably higher than that."

"I wouldn't know. I've never run into any."

"Dressed like a maiden, I'd think you would have seen plenty of dragons in your day," Devin said.

"I'm a Renaissance maiden, not a medieval maiden. By the time the Renaissance came about, dragons were no more," I said.

"It's a good thing you ditched the cheerleader costume for tonight, honey," Brad smirked, "or you wouldn't know the difference between the two."

"Hey." I poked him in the side. "That wasn't nice."

He pecked my cheek, took the scroll from Devin, and held it up so I could see it. "What's this in the corner?"

"It looks like a compass." I leaned against his arm, peering at it. "Are those Roman numerals?"

"It looks like a two on what would be the eastern point." He handed it to Travis to see.

"So we have a two, a four, and a six." Travis looked around the room. "That means we might be missing an eight."

While they continued searching the room for more clues, I took a step back, studying the tiles on the floor. Something had scraped the floor near the center of the side wall, but I couldn't determine what had made the scratch marks.

Brad moved closer, keeping his distance from the shackles and chains. After giving the camera another glance, he looped his arms around my waist. I rested my head against his chest, wondering how honeymooners would act in this situation. Would they be into solving the puzzle or teasing each other?

"Are you having fun?" he asked.

"A blast." I pointed to the floor. "See that? I bet it means something."

"I found a hidden panel." Devin tugged on the chain with eight links, which caused a hidden drawer to pop out of the table. Inside was a bag with gold coins. "This must be to pay the dragon." He spun in a circle. "Does anyone see a dragon?"

"Why do dungeons have dragons?" I disentangled myself from Brad's arms as we went to check near the cot.

"It's in the name," Brad said. "That's reason enough."

Travis nearly knocked himself out by jumping up too quickly from beneath the bed. Luckily, the soft plush of his costume cushioned the blow. "I found it. I found the dragon." He rubbed his head, making the ears shake.

The wall behind the cot had a dragon drawn on it and a coin slot underneath it. Brad and Travis slid the cot out of the way while Devin reached into the pouch and removed the coins.

"How many should I use?" he asked.

"The door we want opened is on the north wall," Brad said, "so would you use six?"

"How do you know that's the north wall?" Travis looked around. "Did you see a compass? You didn't mention one."

"Only on the paper, but I pay attention. When we walked into the building, we came in from the western door, which means we moved east, and when we turned into the room, we were headed south, making that the northern door."

"Are you sure? Wouldn't that be the southern door?" Travis asked.

"It doesn't matter. This room doesn't exist in real time and space. Everything is self-contained within these walls." Devin took a coin out of the pouch. "Let's start with one and see what happens. The way the mechanism looks, it's like a vending machine. You can't put more than one coin in at a time, and if something opens or unlocks, we'll hear it as we go."

"Sounds like a plan." I strained to hear while he slid the coins into the hole.

After the fourth coin was inserted, a loud rumble came from behind the side wall, and the floor shook. "That must be the dragon." Devin pointed to the source of the sound. "He must be over there."

Travis and Brad made their way across the room. "It's solid." Travis knocked against it. "Nothing's popped open yet. Try adding a few more coins."

"Ron," I pointed to the scratches near his feet, "we're looking at a false wall."

"Or some kind of door." Brad followed the scratches to the bricks. "The mortar between the bricks is in a perfect line. If you look closely, you can see the crack where the door opens."

"You found a secret—" Before Travis could finish that thought, the rumbling grew louder, joined by an angry bellow. The wall slid open a few inches, and a guy dressed in chainmail and a helmet screamed, swinging his sword at my partner.

Brad jumped back, but the knight slashed at him again. "Die, demon." The sword crashed to the ground, adding another scratch mark to the floor.

"That thing's real." I shifted into a defensive stance, flanking the knight as he repeatedly swung at my partner. "Devin, get to the intercom. We need help."

"Take it easy." Brad held up his palms. "You don't want to do this."

"You vile, undead creature. You must be stopped once and for all." The knight swung again. As soon as the tip of the blade impacted the ground, Brad lunged at him, grabbing his sword arm and stepping down on the flat side of the blade.

I shoved the knight backward, causing him to lose his grip on the sword. Using his momentum against him, I forced his arm behind him and made him kiss the brick wall. "Who are you?"

"I am Sir Lancelot. Unhand me this minute."

"Didn't you learn it's not polite to try to chop people's heads off?"

"Jodie," Brad said, "let him go." He hefted the broken sword in his hand. "It's fake. He wasn't trying to hurt us."

"But it left scratches."

"It's chalk, lady," Lancelot said, recovering quickly by adding, "Guinevere."

"Wrong era, pal." Brad handed him the sword, apologizing. "Sorry about that. We had a close call the other night in the haunted maze. I guess we're still a little jumpy."

The knight nodded a few times. "Perfectly understandable." He bowed. "You are not a demon, but a traveler from a strange land. May I offer you this as a token of my remorse? I received this for defeating the dragon."

"That's it?" Travis stared at the key in the guy's hand. "This is the lamest escape room I've ever been to. What a rip-off."

"Sorry, Lancelot." I patted him on the shoulder. "I might have taken one too many self-defense classes, but my hubby here works at a gym. It's so hard to resist watching him work out, that I use any excuse I can." I cuddled against Brad and stared into his eyes. "My hero." He kissed me gently.

"Aww," Devin said. "That's so cute. You're just like Buffy and Angel. He's a vamp, and she kicks ass."

Unfortunately, the look on Lancelot's face told me he wasn't buying it. When we unlocked the door, Voletek and Lisco were waiting on the other side. They didn't acknowledge us, so we followed Travis and Devin out of the building. Before we made it to the door, I heard Voletek tell Lancelot he had a few questions regarding the comments he made about wanting to kill a demon.

"I thought that was a real sword," I said.

"You and me both. It looked like one, but it was foam with some kind of polish that made it look like metal. The tip was chalk, which is what made the marks on the floor look like scratches."

Devin turned around to look at us. "Wow, you guys sound like real detectives, even if you didn't exactly solve the puzzle."

"It was a stupid puzzle," Travis said. "What kind of dungeon has a knight who already vanquished the dragon? That's just lame."

"It didn't seem so lame when he swung his sword in my face," Brad said.

Devin grinned. "If I had a dime."

"I'm sorry your first escape room experience was whatever that was." Travis shook his head. "We're gonna go on one of the haunted walking tours. Hopefully, it'll be better than this. A few of our friends were supposed to join us, but they chickened out. They don't do haunted things. They're afraid a spirit will attach to them. Do you want to tag along? We have some extra tickets."

"Sure, just as long as no one else tries to stab me," Brad

said.

I put my arm around his back and leaned into him. "It's a good thing it was a sword and not a wooden stake. You're not allowed to turn to dust on our honeymoon."

Devin laughed again. "That'll be when you know it's over."

I winked at him. "Exactly."

THIRTY-FIVE

A chill hung in the air as we followed the group through the city, visiting scenes of historical murders. Minus the historical part, it was just another day on the job for us. Maybe I could have my apartment added to the list of stops.

We stopped on the spot where a bootlegger had taken his dying breath. The tour guide used that creepy, narrator voice to tell the tale while I shivered from the cold. Brad pulled me in closer, using his free hand to wrap his cape around my bare shoulders.

"You should have brought a coat."

"I wasn't counting on spending our night doing this," I said.

"Do you want my cape?"

"That's not a good idea."

"You freezing to death isn't a good idea either."

"It's not that cold out." I watched my breath turn to icy vapor.

Devin and Travis glanced back at us. Devin nudged his friend and slipped through the group to join us at the back. "Hey, you guys want to get coffee after this? You poor thing. You look like you're turning into an icicle."

"It's a good thing I've got Ron here to keep me warm." I curled both arms against my chest and tucked myself closer to him. Brad freed his other hand and enveloped me entirely in his cape.

"I vant to suck your blood," he said in a cheesy, Transylvanian accent.

"Blood?" Devin scowled. "I'll pass on that one. But I've been eyeing that pie stand all day. I'm thinking a slice of warm apple pie and a spiced pumpkin latte would be good right about now."

"Even better," Brad said, still with the accent.

"Sure, count us in." I exhaled again as Devin headed back to his spot in the center of the group as we headed for our final destination. A few steps later, we heard someone behind us. Brad stopped, turning at the noise. "I heard it too."

We stared into the shadowy alcove near the former speakeasy. "Hello?" Brad asked. But no one replied. "It must be the ghost."

"It must." But I didn't like this.

As we rounded the corner, I checked behind us, thinking I saw someone in the shadows. I whispered that to Brad and sent a text to the nearest surveillance team. The bright red of Brad's costume drew more attention than anything else. That alone should attract every vampire hunter and bull within a fifty mile radius. And in case any of them were nearsighted, the popped up collar made sure my partner wouldn't get confused with a superhero.

By the time we caught up to the group, the guide was halfway through the narrative surrounding the final ghost of the tour. But I couldn't concentrate on any of her words, and neither could Brad. He fidgeted, his body taut against mine.

A twig snapped. The sharp crack of the wood made me turn. But it was too dark to see.

"That came from across the street," Brad said.

"Are you sure?" I peered behind us before turning my focus to the other side.

"Pretty sure. I thought I saw someone moving through the shadows."

"Was he in costume?"

"I don't know. It's too dark to tell." He glanced at the nearest streetlight. "Have the van circle the block. It might make him panic. If he runs for it, we'll spot him."

I sent another text while the tour guide concluded and led us down the alley that would lead us back to the inn. A car drove past, followed by the surveillance van, which was decorated to look like a moving van.

Brad and I watched and waited, but no one darted out of the shadows. "We could try baiting him," Brad suggested.

"Do you think that's a good idea? We're not even sure anyone's over there." But we'd heard the same sounds. I didn't believe it was the wind or one of the ghosts from our tour, unless the inn hired actors to portray ghosts, which at this point I wouldn't have put past them.

"It couldn't hurt." He backed me against the wall of the alley. "Just make sure you shoot him before he turns me to dust."

"That's not funny."

Brad leaned in closer. "Good, because I wasn't joking." He brushed the blonde tendrils away from my face before moving in close enough that our lips practically touched. But in the dark from this distance, he didn't have to kiss me to make it look real. Instead, we danced around one another, teasing, but never touching. I kept glancing to the side, trying to listen over the howl of the wind and the rush of blood in my ears.

Once our faked kissing went on long enough, Brad moved down to my neck. The tip of his nose tickled my skin. I giggled, running my fingers through his hair. Still, no movement from the other side. But I could feel someone watching us.

We stayed in the alleyway, wrapped up in one another, for two more minutes. By then, the walking tour had left us behind. If the killer planned to strike, now was the perfect opportunity. But he didn't.

Another two minutes passed. "Liv," Brad whispered, "at this point, we need to kiss or you need to wrap your legs around me. Because I'm not sure how to make this look more convincing."

I ran my hands through his hair, forcing him off of me. "After what happened at the escape room, we have to be careful. If he's been watching us, he might be suspicious. Maybe we should catch up with the group. I could use some coffee, anyway."

Brad bit his lip, making his fangs stick out, before nodding. "You're probably right. That noise could have been anything." He glanced across the street one final time. "I swear I thought I saw someone in the shadows."

"Me too, but if we investigate, we risk blowing our cover. It's your call."

"Pie and coffee it is."

By the time we made it back to the inn, the tour group had disbursed. Several people had already left. A few waited in line to check out the haunted house before it closed. Devin waved to us from his seat on the bench near the fire pit. He and Travis had already gotten their coffee and dessert.

"Maybe we should keep our distance," I suggested, glancing behind us while Brad rubbed circles on my back. "We don't need civilians getting caught in the crossfire."

"Have you looked around? The attractions shut down in less than an hour, and this place is still packed. No one's even the slightest bit concerned about the construction going on around the maze or what remains of the shredded crime scene tape. We couldn't stop them from getting in the way if we tried."

"That's because they can't tell the difference between the real stuff and the fake." To be fair, I hadn't been sure either until I examined it up close. "Do you think whoever's following us will strike while there are still so many witnesses?"

"Witnesses don't seem to bother this guy much." Brad pressed his lips to my temple, smiling like a fool in love. "The problem is we haven't gotten eyes on anyone. Neither has surveillance. So we can't be sure it's the same guy. With our luck, it could be a mugger or pervert."

A second patrol car parked on the other side, closer to the inn. Since Brad and I were in the center, if the killer made a move on us or showed his face, he'd be boxed in.

The surveillance van hadn't spotted anyone, but even now, I could still feel eyes on me. And from the way my partner moved, he felt it too.

After getting two coffees, we joined Devin and Travis near the fire. At least we'd be warm while we waited for someone to try to kill us. They each had a large piece of pie and a whipped cream topped beverage. They stared at our boring cups.

"I wish we'd brought marshmallows," Devin said. "Toasted marshmallows would be great right now."

"Or smores." Travis raised an eyebrow. "You're a fitness guy, right?"

"Uh-huh." Brad took another sip, hoping to end the conversation there.

"Would you mind if I ask you a few questions? I want to train for the marathon, but I don't know where to begin."

Movement along the periphery caught my eye. I scooted closer to Brad and ran my fingers along the shell of his ear, so I could peer behind him without being obvious. Someone was hiding in the bushes near the maze, which was currently undergoing reconstruction.

I texted the surveillance van, who in turn notified the patrol units. A few undercover cops had joined us, preparing for the worst. But with so many people around, we didn't want to move on the guy yet. So we set up a net and waited.

"That depends. How active are you now?" Brad asked.

"I jog a couple of times a week and lift whenever the mood strikes."

"Or whenever he feels fat from eating too much pizza," Devin chimed in.

"You'll want to start off slow. I'm sure you can find a suggested workout routine on the internet," Brad said.

"I just wasn't sure which ones were good." Travis pulled the phone out of his pocket and tapped on the screen a few times. "I was thinking of this one. What do you think?"

Brad leaned over to take a look, and I pretended to be equally interested, while keeping a watch on what was happening a hundred feet from us.

Three plain clothes officers moved into the area from

the rear parking lot and a few nearby streets. Hopefully, whoever was keeping tabs on Brad and me wasn't paying attention to anything else. The officers spread out, taking an interest in the various stands and checking out the ticket booths for more information on when the attractions would open tomorrow.

Once the stands shut down for the night and the inn issued an announcement that all attractions were now closed, Travis and Devin looked up. "Shit, I didn't realize it had gotten so late," Travis said.

"That explains why my ass is numb." Devin kicked his leg out a few times. "We should get going. But it was really nice meeting you. You should totally friend us. Maybe we can try another escape room sometime."

"We'll do that," I said.

"I'll pick the next one," Travis said, "that way it won't suck." He offered Brad his hand. "Thanks for the workout regimen."

"Yeah, no problem." Brad removed his arm from around my shoulders and shook Travis's hand. "Be careful going home."

Devin grinned. "Night, guys. Have fun." He winked at me before tossing his cup in the trash.

Despite the conversation, Brad and I had been keeping watch the entire time. Whoever had taken cover in the brush hadn't surfaced, and if he had, I hadn't seen him do it. The wind picked up, and Brad wrapped his arms around me.

"Let's get an update." He leaned back a little, making sure I was concealed beneath his cape before I sent the text.

"Do you want them to move in?" I read the message on the screen.

He exhaled icy vapor into the air. "Most people have left by now. Only a few groundskeepers are still outside. That limits potential casualties, but he could jump out from behind the hay bales swinging an axe or firing silver bullets. It's not worth the risk. Let's wait a few more minutes for the area to clear. We have him surrounded. He can't slip away. We'll get him."

"I hope so." I relayed the message via text.

The next ten minutes dragged on for what felt like centuries. The wind picked up, and Brad moved even closer. "How about we try to provoke him? If we piss him off enough, he'll make a move and then we won't have to flush him out. Are you game?"

"Absolutely."

Brad let out a maniacal cackle, which echoed in the empty lot. Then he brushed my hair to the side, and with true Dracula flair, pushed his cape away and latched onto my neck, careful to avoid the scar.

"Oh, Ronnie." My voice came out breathy, a mix of fear and lust.

Rustling sounds came from behind the hay bales. At first, I thought it was the wind, but it was concentrated in just one spot. The killer had to be there. I shifted beneath Brad, who had yet to pull away. Whoever staked our victims probably believed they were real vampires, so Brad wanted to convince him he was also the real thing.

The rustling grew closer, moving from the hay bales to one of the stands. My phone vibrated against my thigh. Carefully, I retrieved it, hoping the light from the screen would be blocked by Brad's body.

"The team in the van spotted someone. They want us to hold position," I said.

Brad pulled his lips off my neck and wiped his mouth. "You're mine, Jodie. All mine." He moved in again, pushing me flat against the bench. He raised up, spreading his cape wide, like the wings of a bat. The red made my partner a target.

A guttural scream sounded from the distance, and Brad turned at the sound, just as floodlights blinded us. We shielded our eyes, hoping to see what was going on. Whoever had been about to charge ducked behind the retaining wall and moved into the bushes.

"Who's over there?" someone called from behind the floodlights. "What are you doing out here? Everything's closed. Come back tomorrow."

"Sorry," Brad waved back at him, "we're actually staying at the inn. We're the honeymooners. We just got a little caught up with how romantic the fire is. We didn't mean to cause any trouble."

The guy wearing an unbuttoned wool coat and gloves headed toward us. "It's okay. I didn't mean to startle you. A chaperone's the last thing you guys want, I'm sure. But that explains why no one extinguished the blaze." He turned a dial at the bottom of the fire pit, causing the dancing oranges and reds to shrink into nothing more than glowing embers. "But we're going to be working out here to get the maze rebuilt, so it's not safe for you two to be out here without hardhats and protective eyewear. If you want to enjoy the fire, you can check out the one inside. I'm sure the couches are much more comfortable than that cold bench."

"Thanks. We'll do that," Brad said. Once the construction guy left us alone, Brad texted the team. *Move in now.* "C'mon, honey, let's go inside." He flicked his eyes toward the inn before glancing back at the nearby bushes.

I took off running, as if hoping to escape with my life, and Brad ran after me. The killer broke from his hiding spot and gave chase, unable to resist the temptation to slay the demon.

THIRTY-SIX

He'd followed them most of the night, from the time they left the escape room until now. The two police detectives hadn't had a clue when they'd walked past him to question Lancelot. That had given him confidence. But he wasn't nearly as ballsy as Ronnie, who'd been sucking the life from that woman in front of the entire world. Yet, no one did a thing to stop it. In fact, that idiot with the floodlights encouraged them.

Why was Ronnie so stupid? He'd nearly killed the vampire, but he'd been spared due to the circumstances. The Gespers should have left. Jodie had been so terrified, he was sure she would have come to her senses and fled from her psycho husband. It must have been the influence the vampire exuded over her.

Seeing them together made him sick. He'd nearly doubled over with that first kiss. The way they'd gone at each other in the alley after the tour ended had brought him to his knees. The stabbing in his chest had nearly killed him. It was like daggers. He had to put an end to this. He'd die if he didn't.

So he stayed on them, hoping to recover some of his strength even as they made out on the bench. The way Ronnie sucked at her neck made the world spin. His head pounded to the point he could barely see. And what he could see was red.

They didn't look exactly as he remembered, but he might be remembering wrong. Maybe it was because she wasn't wearing a cheerleader outfit. Frankly, she would have been better off. She might have had some chance of outrunning her husband if the long skirt didn't keep getting in the way. But it was no matter, he'd put an end to this.

He broke from cover and ran after them. His focus was solely on the blood red cape. Idly, he wondered if anyone would notice bloodstains on it. He'd only made it as far as the pie stand when voices sounded behind him.

"Freeze."

He didn't stop or slow. But when two beams of light came toward him, he reconsidered.

"Police. We have you surrounded. Put your hands in the air."

Shit. The red cape stopped at the steps leading up to the inn, turning to see what the commotion was about. The beautiful maiden stood at the top, the wind blowing the skirt of her dress and her blonde hair to one side. Even now, her beauty reminded him of Vivica.

This couldn't be how it ended. He had a mission to complete. Desperately, he searched the area. The workers had turned on the floodlights in order to rebuild the maze. They'd set up near the supply truck. If he could make it there, he'd find a way to slip away.

"Let me see those hands," one of the cops ordered.

Ronnie took a step closer, perhaps to help, or to inflict more pain upon him. Steeling himself from the coming onslaught, he sucked in a deep breath and bolted to the right. He leapt over the hedges lining the parking lot. Pounding footsteps were right behind him.

Glancing back, he saw the red cape racing toward him. The strange turn of events only made him more determined to get his revenge. He took a sharp left, turned another corner, and disappeared into the back of the supply truck.

Gasping for breath, he moved to the side door, slid it

open, and hopped down. Then he rolled underneath the truck and waited. Within seconds, the police officers who'd told him to freeze ran to the back of the truck with their weapons drawn.

Cautiously, they entered, finding the side door open. "He has to be close."

Two of them went out the side door, hurrying toward the rear of the inn while the other two searched the inside of the truck.

"No one's here," one of them said. "Let's check around outside."

Before they could do that, he rolled out from beneath the truck. He'd escaped the police once by going through the maze. This time, he wasn't running away. He'd stay until his job was done. Then he'd finally be at peace.

*   *   *

Brad sat on the couch, staring out the window while he tried to play with my hair. "Why haven't they notified us he's in custody yet?" he whispered.

I'd been staring at my phone's screen, but we hadn't heard a peep. "Maybe they're waiting until he's booked, that way we can't take credit for the bust."

He glanced at me. "Did I make the right call?"

"You didn't want anyone else to get hurt. We don't even know if the man who's been following us all night is the same one who attacked the Gespers."

"It has to be." Brad ran a hand over his mouth. "It just does."

"We never had eyes on him. What were we supposed to do?"

Brad gave me a sharp look, holding his finger to his lips. "Don't talk so loud."

But the lobby was completely empty. The night manager had gone on break, possibly to check on the commotion outside. No one could overhear us, but I lowered my voice anyway. "The grounds are covered. They have him boxed in."

"So what's taking so long?" Brad got up from the couch

and went to the window. He didn't say it, but I knew he had the same thought I did. What if the cops outside needed help?

A few minutes later, Brad's phone rang. He fished it out of his pocket. "What happened?"

I waited, listening to his half of the conversation, but that didn't give me much. However, Brad's facial expressions were another story.

"Son of a bitch." He rubbed the stubble on his cheek. "How could that happen? Everyone already left." He exhaled. "Dammit." He turned to me and shook his head. *No go*, he mouthed. "Yeah, all right, we'll be here." After tucking his phone away, he offered me his hand. "Let's go to bed."

Since our covers remained active, we hadn't caught the guy. Brad and I didn't say another word until we were safely inside our room. Once there, he checked to make sure no one was spying on us while I changed into something more practical.

"You were right. Dresses aren't the best for running."

"Told ya."

Peering out the window, I watched the men with the floodlights move new bales of hay into position, slowly rebuilding the maze, while other engineers reconstructed the macabre death scenes. Instead of a pit with spikes, the pit area was filled with water and red dye. "What happened? Did we have the wrong guy?"

"Probably not." Brad moved one of the chairs a few feet in front of the door, so it wouldn't stop the door from opening, but it would slow down whoever entered. "They didn't get a good look at him, but from what they could tell, he was dressed like a gunslinger."

"You called it."

"Yeah." He joined me at the window. "He made it to the truck and went out the side door. He couldn't have had that much of a head start. The officers who pursued never got eyes on him again, but they came across a crowd of costumed people on their way to the train. He could have been in that group, or he backtracked."

"Which means he's still here."

"Possibly, or he headed in a different direction. We only had six cops on him, plus us. Except we hung back."

"We couldn't sacrifice our covers. We aren't even certain that's the right guy. For all we know, it could have been another reporter or some idiot from the tabloids."

"I know it was him. And I think you do too."

"Hanging back is the hardest part of undercover, but that's how it goes a lot of the time. And when it doesn't, when you end up announcing, those are usually even tighter situations."

"Yeah." But the storm clouds above his head only grew thicker. "Winston's been updated on the situation. He's beefing up patrols in the area, but he's pulling the blue and whites off the inn. Instead, he'll get a few unmarked vehicles to monitor things here. Assuming this guy is close, we don't want to give him any reason to rabbit again."

"Why would he remain here when he knows we're closing in on him?"

"One of the cops found a piece of paper near the bushes where he'd been hiding. It had my name, Ronnie Gesper, and our room number."

I gave the chair near the door another look. That explained it. "Great."

"Oh yeah."

"Any idea why he's so adamant to get to you?"

"He's jealous of my Halloween costume."

"That must be it." I dialed Mac. "Hey, have you made any progress on figuring out who this guy is or why he wants to harm Ron Gesper?"

"We don't have a clue. Lisco's on her way to the Gespers now. A late night visit might freak them out enough to come up with something they didn't think of before."

"Does Winston think they're hiding something?"

"I don't know. I can never tell what he's thinking, but I heard you and Brad had quite the eventful evening. Are you okay?"

"We'd be better if we'd made an arrest."

"I'll do what I can. Midnight oil is burning, baby."

"Thanks, Mac. We owe you."

Brad took a seat at the table and opened his overnight

bag. "Do you want some dinner? You always tell me I get hangry, so maybe eating will keep me from putting my fist through the wall."

"Room service doesn't run after eleven. You could try the vending machines." I just didn't think there was anything inside my partner would want to eat.

"No need. I came prepared." He pulled out a few food storage containers and several bags. "I figured you'd forget the snacks."

"I'm not hungry, just cold."

"I have some of those soup packets, if you change your mind." He pushed a container toward me. "Just add water."

"You hate these things. You always say they remind you of MREs."

"At least these are made with actual food, no chemicals or additives," he pointed to the label, "and I know you like them."

"Thanks."

He nodded.

"Hey, we're getting closer. We'll stop him."

He snorted. "We're not getting closer, Liv. He's getting closer. It's not the same thing." Sighing, he opened one of the storage containers and bit into a carrot chip. "Can you keep an eye out while I take a shower and get changed? I'll be quick."

"No problem."

Despite my words, he took his gun into the bathroom with him and left the door cracked open. "The officers said he was dressed like a gunslinger. Do you think he has a gun?"

"We haven't received any reports of anyone buying a six-shooter."

"He could already have one."

I read the instructions on the soup packet. All I had to do was pour it into a mug, fill with water, and microwave for two minutes. That didn't sound too difficult. "Why do you think he wrote down your name? Do you think we could be looking at this wrong? Did someone give him that information?"

"Possibly." The water turned on, and the rings on the shower curtain let out a scratchy squeak as Brad pulled the curtain closed. "But it was written on the label from the jacket of his costume. So it looks like he just wrote it down while he was following us."

Getting up, I grabbed one of the mugs from beside the in-room coffeemaker and filled it with bottled water. Then I stuck it in the microwave. "He didn't know who the Gespers were before he attacked them the first time."

"Possibly not. I'm not sure what I think about that."

"The Stevenses murders didn't look planned."

"He's picking his targets from here, so he must have followed them home, came back another day, and..." Brad didn't finish his sentence.

"That might be what he's doing now. He picked you. Now he's planning to follow through."

"We don't know how long he waited before he struck last time. The Gespers are supposed to check out in three days. He might not have time."

"Given that Dan Fielders was killed the night before the Stevenses, I'd say the killer didn't wait long before he made his move." The microwave beeped, and I removed my mug. "Do you want me to make you some soup?"

"I'd rather lick the bathroom tiles."

"Gotcha." I found a stirrer and swirled the dehydrated vegetables around in the hot broth, hoping they'd soften and plump up. The trick to soup packets was to let them steep.

A few minutes later, Brad stepped out of the bathroom. His skin was no longer ghostly white and the fake blood was gone. He ran the towel through his hair before taking a seat at the table. "I guess all we can do now is wait."

"I hate this part."

He smiled. "I remember. This is usually when I'd receive crazed texts from you, suggesting that you do something insane to move the investigation along."

"You'd always talk me down from the ledge."

"Yeah." He tore open a packet of tuna and scooped some out using a carrot chip.

"Y'know, if you hadn't done that, I'd suggest we search

every room in this place."

"Uh-huh." He bit into another carrot. "This is payback, huh?"

"We can't, even though we want to."

He nodded, reaching for another carrot. When he finished the tuna, he opened a container of cookies. "Do you want some?"

"Are those the ones Mom made you?"

"No." He took out a ghost and bit off its head. "This is the batch Carrie made me as a thank you."

I moved closer and stared at the cookies in the container. The cookies weren't shaped exactly the same as my mom's, and the bats were brown. "Are they grain-free?"

He held them out. "Yes, she found a recipe online. She added cocoa powder to the sugar cookie mix to make the bats. They're pretty good."

I took one and sniffed it. Carefully, I took a tiny bite. It tasted similar to the allergen-free cookies Emma baked for the pediatric ward. "Not bad." I put the cookie down on a napkin beside my mug. "You're such a cookie whore."

"I can't help it if women want to make me cookies."

"I've never had the desire."

Brad snorted, but given the late hour, we didn't have the energy to quibble over it. Instead, we stared at the door while we ate a very late dinner. It was almost two a.m. when I finally looked away.

"We should sleep in shifts," Brad said. "You can go first."

"I'm gonna take a shower first and try to warm up." I grabbed my bag and went into the bathroom, but like my partner, I didn't pull the door closed all the way. I knew he wouldn't look.

After a few minutes under the hot spray, the exhaustion set in. I dried my hair, glad to be free from that terrible wig, and changed into yoga pants and a t-shirt. After pulling down the covers on one side of the bed, I studied the sheets.

"What's wrong?" Brad sat atop the covers on the other side, aimlessly flipping channels.

"I'm hoping the maid changed the sheets since the

Gespers were here."

He laughed, that rich, velvety sound that eased my stress. "They did. Don't worry so much."

Once I got into bed, he flipped off the light. "Will the TV bother you? I can watch something on my phone. Then again, you are known to fall asleep with the TV on."

"The TV's fine. Wake me in a few hours, and we'll switch."

"Good night, Liv."

THIRTY-SEVEN

He'd been following the demon for a while now, watching as he attacked the couple with an axe and then later as he followed a different couple from the escape rooms through the streets and back to the bench near the fire pit. But with so many people dressed in costumes, he'd become confused as to which were part of the rising evil and which were humans masquerading about. So he remained hidden, unsure what to do or how to stop it. He needed a better plan. The tiny bottle of holy water wouldn't do much against the growing army.

But when the demon, dressed like an Old West gunslinger, chased the vampire who was chasing the woman, the police intervened. Despite the detective with the red eyes whom he was sure intended to sabotage his attempts to save humanity, his message had gotten through. The police had received his warning and were taking it seriously. Hope was not lost.

He snuck from one cover position to another, wanting to see how professionals dealt with a supernatural being. He'd need to know what to do in order to continue his fight to save humanity. Unfortunately, the gunslinger was too cunning for them.

As he watched in horror, the demon passed through the solid bottom of the truck and slithered beneath it, just like a snake, confusing the police. While they were distracted, the demon crawled out from beneath the truck and darted into the shadows against the building.

Unfortunately, the police searched but couldn't find him. When the two officers who remained went to search the edge of the property and behind the inn, he realized stopping the demon was up to him.

As quietly as possible, he crossed the open expanse, ignoring the workers who'd just started rebuilding the maze. When he reached the shadows where the demon had vanished, he didn't find anyone. The walls were solid. Could the creature have passed through these as well? Was he even corporeal?

He took a step back and stared up at the building. There must be a door. He followed along the side of the building, finding one marked *Employees only*. He tried the handle, but it didn't budge. It required a code, which he didn't know. Surely, the demon couldn't know it either.

Giving up, he headed in the other direction. People yelled off to his left. At first, he thought it was the construction workers, but then he realized it was the police. They wanted the work to stop. Could the maze be where the hell gates would open? That made sense, or did it?

Unsure what to do, he found a place behind the shadows to hide. This place was the center of Halloween celebrations. Therefore, the uprising should happen here. It's why the demon gunslinger was here. It's why the creature shed the blood of the innocent on the grounds. It's why, tonight, the gunslinger wanted to find more victims to sacrifice.

Finding a safe hiding place behind the dumpster, he settled in. He'd have to remain vigilant. Since the gunslinger eluded the police, he'd have to help them find him. It was the only way to end this.

*   *   *

I blinked, bleary-eyed. "Who's texting you?"

"Voletek."

I flopped onto my back. Every muscle in my body was tight and sore from being out in the cold for so long. "What does he want?"

"The police made an arrest."

"Tell me it was the asshole who slipped away."

"I'm not sure." Brad typed a reply before turning to me. "The guy they arrested is the suspect from Voletek's case."

"The homeless guy with the burns?"

"Yeah. Get this, he was lurking around in the shadows near the maze reconstruction. The officers in an unmarked spotted him hiding behind the dumpsters. When they approached, he made a run for it, shouting that they had the wrong guy and they had to stop the evil from rising."

"Are you the evil?" I asked.

"Jury's out on that one." Brad read the response Voletek sent and put the phone down. "While they were processing him, he kept spouting out nonsense about stopping a vampire uprising."

"That sounds like our killer."

"Voletek thinks he might be our guy. But the timeline's wonky since Voletek's victim had been tortured for hours before dying."

"Giving Dan Fielders' killer an alibi for the other murder." I narrowed my eyes at the digital clock on the bedside table. "Could they be working together?"

"You said we might be looking at multiple attackers. Maybe this is some kind of cult thing."

"A cult of two?"

"Okay, an accomplice thing." Brad stretched, shifting deeper into the bedding. "The only thing we can be sure of is Dan Fielders', the Stevenses' and Ron Gesper's blood were found on the glove we recovered, meaning those attacks were committed by the same guy."

I reached for my phone while Brad pulled the covers over. "I'll stay updated on the situation while you get some sleep."

"Thanks, Liv. Wake me if something happens." He gave the door one last look. "If anyone enters our room, shoot him."

"Go to sleep, Rambo." Rolling out of bed, I went to the window and pulled the drape in the corner so I could look out. The sun hadn't risen yet, but the sky had brightened.

In the last few hours, the construction workers had nearly pieced together the rest of the maze. They had another two trailers of hay to place, and then it'd be finished. By nightfall, the crowd would be larger than the previous night.

Stepping away from the window, I sent a text to Voletek, asking him to find a way to keep the inn from reopening the maze. *Until we know we have the killer in custody, it's not a risk worth taking.*

I agree, he replied. *I'll call my dad and see if he can pull some strings.*

Since I didn't have contacts with the top brass, I couldn't pull any strings of my own, and I didn't want to go to my father again. Every time I did, it undermined my position in the department and made the brass and my fellow officers question my abilities and authority. Jake could take the hit, but I still felt bad about it.

With nothing else to do, I ran through a morning yoga routine, moving as soundlessly as possible. The sun salutations and vinyasas didn't disturb my partner, who let out a few uneasy sighs in his sleep. At least the night terrors had stopped for now.

After an hour of yoga and meditation, which might have involved falling asleep for a few minutes, I took a seat at the table, propped my legs up on the other chair, and texted Emma. Then I read the news and researched vampires and crimes involving vampires.

My phone rang, which startled me, but I managed to hit answer before the first ring even finished. Brad rolled over, not fully awake yet. *Go back to sleep,* I thought as I ducked into the bathroom and closed the door halfway.

"The inn's owner agreed to give us another twenty-four hours. After the near arrest last night, they don't want to face potential lawsuits for knowingly endangering a guest," Voletek said.

"Thank you, Jake. You're a miracle worker."

"Oh yeah?"

"Yeah." I let out a breath. "Any updates on the arrest? Have you figured out who this guy is or if he's responsible for the recent stakings?"

"He won't say a word to me. He's convinced I'm a demon. He asked what happened to my red eyes."

"Did you tell him you didn't spend the night in a tequila bottle?"

"I tried, but that didn't compute. However, he admitted to sending the warning to HQ. He says the evil will walk the earth if we don't stop it. Apparently, I'm part of the first wave."

"No wonder he won't talk to you."

"Lisco and Winston are working on him. I'm sure you can imagine what it's like around here. You and Brad are lucky you're out on assignment."

"Right, lucky," I said. "What are our instructions?"

"I haven't heard Winston mention any changes yet, so I guess you stay the course. Finish checking out the attractions, if the killer picked up your trail while you were on the walking tour, he might be keeping watch over the festivities or he works at one of the booths." But I didn't see how that was possible after all the background checks we'd run.

"Did you get anything out of Lancelot last night?"

"I'd suggest you avoid him if you see him. He's on to you. Lisco and I asked a ton of questions, but he didn't know anything about the Gespers or the killer's previous victims. According to Lancelot and the woman in charge of the escape rooms, none of the victims attempted the dungeon escape, but since the police have such a large presence at the inn after the axe incident, Lancelot's fairly certain the two of you are cops or some kind of security personnel. He kept asking if he was in trouble. When pressed, he was more than willing to throw the inn's manager under the bus for suggesting he make the attack seem real. He even said the manager had ordered several metal props to add to the scare factor."

"Which props?"

"The chains in the dungeon. The metal frame for the cot,

the chainmail Lancelot wore."

"The spikes in the maze pit," I said.

"Probably that too." Voletek sighed. "Lancelot said he wouldn't put it past the manager to hire someone to pretend to attack guests to gain publicity, but he swore no one at the inn would ever put people's lives in danger by using an actual axe."

"Do you believe him?"

"I do, and given how the inn backed off when the topic of liability and lawsuits came up, I'd agree with that assessment."

"Let's hope the axe man is in custody and the rest of these Halloween buffs are safe."

"Yeah, let's."

By the time I emerged from the bathroom, Brad had turned on the coffeemaker and sprawled out in a spread eagle pose in the center of the king sized bed. He blinked open one eye and looked at me. "Was that Sean?"

I must have heard him wrong. "What?"

"You closed the door. I figured it must be your new boyfriend. How is he?"

"That was Jake. We bought ourselves one more day."

Brad stretched his arms straight over his head and twisted his hips from side to side, making his back pop. "Any progress? What about the suspect who's now in custody?"

"Winston and Lisco are working him. He thinks Jake's a demon, so he won't talk to him."

"So do most of the women he dates." Brad sat up, blinking a few times with heavy lids. "Did we miss breakfast?"

"We have another thirty minutes before they stop serving."

"Great." Brad climbed off the bed, running a hand through his hair. "Let's see what they've got downstairs. If we can't find anything edible, we're ordering room service or delivery."

"Hungry?"

"Famished."

He washed up and brushed his teeth while I pinned the

blonde wig back in place. Then we rode the elevator to the lobby, made googly eyes at one another while loading up a tray with fresh fruit and omelets from the omelet bar, and exchanged several chaste kisses and intimate touches while waiting for the elevator to return. Surprisingly, no one yakked from the over-the-top display of affection.

As the doors opened, I spotted a man seated on one of the couches. He had a cup of coffee in his hand and the paper in front of him. He wore the identifying vest that most of the vendors and ticket sellers had, but I didn't recognize him from the background checks. His cold, dark eyes stared at us from over the top of the newspaper.

"Ronnie," I ran my hand along the side of his neck while I balanced the tray using my other hand and my hip, "are you sure you want to check out the haunted house? I'm already creeped out."

Brad read the expression on my face. "That's the point. It's supposed to creep you out, but I'll protect you from the scary clowns and ghouls." He let out another one of his over-the-top cackles and reverted to the Transylvanian accent. "The real question is who's going to protect you from me? Bwahaha." He leaned in, doing his best to keep from tipping over his own tray, and kissed along my shoulder, up my neck, and to my lips. The elevator doors dinged, and reluctantly, he pulled away, leaving me stunned and breathless. "Upstairs. Now." His voice came out hoarse as he ushered me into the waiting elevator and repeatedly jammed the button.

THIRTY-EIGHT

Despite our display at breakfast, no one followed us to our room. Brad and I spent most of the day figuring out how to get someone who might not even be there to strike. Unfortunately, the rest of our unit had made little progress.

The man they'd taken into custody had finally given his first name – Ted. That was it. No last name, address, phone number, or next of kin. His DNA wasn't in the system. But the lab was comparing it to the unknown samples from the glove we found.

"Even if it matches, we can't be sure he's the killer. He could be another victim," I said. "Didn't the psychiatrists determine he wasn't dangerous when they evaluated him?"

"They never finished. He snuck out." Voletek grunted. "I'd been told he was released."

"That never made any sense since you were in the middle of questioning him," I said.

"Clerical error," Voletek replied.

"They were covering." Brad stared at the phone which sat on the table between us. "That's what everyone's been doing ever since we started investigating these crimes."

"I'm not," Voletek said.

"No shit." Brad rubbed his eyes. Lack of sleep made him

bitchy. "Are units still in place?"

"Only the surveillance team and a few unmarked cars. Surveillance tapped into the inn's security system, so we have eyes everywhere they do. The team monitoring you hasn't noticed any suspicious activity, but they caught quite the eyeful this morning. Apparently, things got pretty steamy near the elevator."

I blushed and stared at the floor. This was the last thing I needed. Rumors always flew when it came to partnerships between men and women, and given the parameters of this assignment, it'd only get worse. "Fuck."

"That steamy, huh?" Voletek teased.

"Zip it," Brad snapped. He tried to get my attention, but I wouldn't look at him. "We're supposed to be newlyweds. The last two attacks occurred when couples were getting friendly. We didn't have a choice."

"How come when I went undercover with Liv, our assignment didn't require us to get that friendly? Had I known, I would have volunteered for this one."

"Watch your mouth, Jake. Shit like that could bury Liv. You know it, so keep your thoughts to yourself, unless you want to spend several hours going through more sensitivity training." Brad flexed his fist a few times.

"Keep your ear to the ground on what's going on with the case, and let us know if our killer's in custody, that way we can go home," I said.

Brad disconnected without waiting for Voletek to say anything else. After circling the room and staring out the window, he tucked his hands into his back pockets and turned to look at me. "I'm sorry."

"Don't be. This is the job. We do whatever it takes to sell our cover. It's the only way to stop a killer."

"Are those the only conditions for Liv DeMarco to kiss anyone?"

"Brad," I looked up at him, "don't bust my chops right now. If you want to have an actual conversation, we can do that, but don't give me a hard time. And don't make a joke about that phrasing either."

"I wouldn't."

"Jake would."

"Jake's an asshole. I'm pretty sure I warned you about that when I introduced you."

"He's like a lot of the men on the force." I got up and grabbed my costume for the evening. "We do what's required of us. We don't cross lines. We don't sacrifice our integrity or our investigation. We'll have a few more snickers to deal with, but in a couple of weeks, they'll move on to something else. It won't matter. What will matter is the lives that were saved by stopping this vampire hunter from killing again. On the bright side, even if the guy they grabbed isn't the killer, at least we know the killer's fixated on you. Hopefully, that'll keep him from finding another target."

"Normally, I wouldn't be too keen on a killer fixating on me."

"I'm not either, but we survived last time. We just have to do it again." I shut the bathroom door and changed into a cheerleading outfit. At least this one had flesh colored leggings and a varsity jacket, so I wouldn't freeze.

When I stepped out of the bathroom, Brad had put the cape on over a black t-shirt and dark jeans and was adjusting his fangs. He watched me in the mirror for a moment. "Do you really think the axe man's still around?"

"I'm not sure. The man in the lobby gave me the creeps, but Ted was lurking around the inn in the middle of the night. He fits the description. Even the Gespers thought he looked like the man who attacked them. So maybe we're already done. I'm sure Lisco and Winston will get something definitive out of him soon."

"The LT could get confessions out of a priest." Brad picked up the tickets for the haunted house. "Let's get in and out. After that, we'll wander around the grounds again. Last night, he planned to strike, but he got interrupted by the construction crew and the cops. If he's still around, he won't be nearly as patient."

"Unless he learned his lesson."

"History suggests otherwise."

We held hands on our way to the haunted house. Once we got in line, Brad hugged me from behind, resting his chin on top of my head while we waited to gain admittance.

The man at the door wore a scary clown outfit. He'd been keeping tabs on us. Even as Brad handed him our tickets, he continued to size us up.

"Not very friendly for a clown, are you?" Brad asked.

The guy leered at him from beneath the white makeup. The yellow, jagged teeth made him look even more sinister. After tearing our tickets, he handed the stubs to Brad and gestured to the ominous front door. Beyond it was nothing but darkness.

Brad gave the red nose a gentle honk, hoping to illicit some kind of response, but the guy continued to stare at him. After we stepped through the door, the clown pulled it closed behind us with a thud.

"Do you think that's the guy from the lobby?" I asked.

"I don't know, but he gave me the creeps." He shuddered. "All clowns do."

"No one could tell. The honking was a nice touch."

"Face your fears, right?" He took my hand and turned sideways. "Looks like we're supposed to go single-file down the corridor. Don't let go. Keep your eyes peeled."

Our conversation might have seemed out of character, but I'd heard plenty of people in line strategizing as to how to survive the haunted house, so I didn't think anyone who overheard us would think too much about this. At least, I hoped not.

Glow paint illuminated a path on the floor, but everything else was pitch. At the end of the hallway, we heard a scream in the distance, followed by the sound of chainsaws. My heart beat faster, and Brad tightened his grip on my hand.

More screams sounded, followed by relieved laughter. False alarm.

We stopped at the only open doorway. Before we could step inside, something brushed against me. I jumped, coming face to face with a different clown. This one had a sad smile and pink hair. It moved around us, reaching into the dark room and flipping on a flickering light.

"Watch your step," he said.

Brad scrutinized him carefully before leading the way inside. "Watch where you put those hands, buddy," Brad warned. The clown chuckled and disappeared back into the dark hallway. "Why clowns?"

"Don't ask me. I don't get why they became the number one creepy thing, but they are. What is this supposed to be?"

"A bathroom." Blood covered the counters and walls. Each of the stall doors hung askew, with bloody handprints and weapons stuck through the industrial beige, plastic laminate. Brad released my hand and approached a hatchet that hung from the second door. He'd just grabbed the handle when someone in a ghost face mask burst out of the neighboring stall, her arms raised as she let out a blood-curdling scream.

Brad jumped backward, reaching for his weapon, which wasn't there. I screamed, partially from fear and partially to get the actor to back off.

"Good one. You really scared us." I latched on to Brad's hand and hugged his arm against me.

The actor remained in character, just like the ticket-taker, and continued to hover near us, attempting to herd us out of the room.

"Are those real?" Brad asked, but the woman in the mask didn't answer.

"Are they, Ronnie?" I asked. "If they are, I think we should get out of here. I've had enough realistic scares to last a lifetime."

"I'll find out." Brad checked the blade. "Plastic." He repeated that process with the barbecue forks and daggers which had been left in the other stall doors. "Even the bathroom doors are fake. I think they're cardboard." He turned back to the actor. "Are they cardboard?"

"Ronnie, we should keep moving. Remember the line outside." I turned to the girl. "No one's going to attack us with a chainsaw, right?"

But again, she didn't answer.

We continued along the designated path, encountering more of these actors who jumped out at us or snuck up behind us. Every time it happened, I fought my instincts to strike. Walking into hostile situations wasn't new to me, but under most conditions, anyone who posed a threat would be put in cuffs. However, this wasn't a hostile situation. It was only supposed to appear that way, but we had no way of knowing that for sure.

Brad yelped when someone with razor-sharp claws and teeth jumped out at us from a hidden doorway. Again, he reached for the gun on his hip, which made me glad Winston had forced us to remain unarmed. I'd hate to think how much bad press the PD would get if we pulled our guns on a bunch of actors.

"Easy, tiger." I slipped past the guy with the plastic razorblades as we entered a large room. "This is much better than the narrow hallway."

"Maybe we should find a quiet corner and hide away from these ghouls and goblins."

I laughed as Brad wrapped his arms around my waist and gave my neck a kiss. "Is that the adrenaline rush talking?"

"Mmm...maybe." He nipped my ear. "I'm not sure I can wait until we get out of here."

"We should be near the end."

"You're right," a bellowing voice said from somewhere nearby. "Your end is near." The dim lights cut out, replaced by strobe lights.

Cobwebs and paper walls weaved a path in front of us. We stumbled through it, taking a wrong turn which led us to a creepy clown. He was dressed just like the one from outside. He held a bloody sword down at his side. Beneath the flashing lights, I thought I saw blood dripping from the end, but I couldn't be sure.

We backtracked to the main path, but the clown followed slowly. I kept my eye on him and my back against Brad's. A few seconds later, the strobe lights stopped, replaced by total darkness. A chainsaw sounded in the distance, and a light illuminated a guy with a bag over his head with a knife through it. Blood dripped down the side of the bag. The guy revved the chainsaw, holding it up and lunging toward us.

I screamed, and as any good husband would, Brad wrapped his arms around me. "It's okay. I got you," he said.

The chainsaw guy didn't get any closer, and on his retreat, I noticed the saw didn't have an actual chain. It was just another fancy prop. However, I'd lost sight of the clown with the sword.

"Ronnie, where'd the clown go?" I asked.

"I'm sure he went back to his hole to hide." The room went dark again, and a few moments later, the strobe lights came back on.

We maneuvered through the rest of the maze. The entire time, I couldn't help but wonder why anyone would willingly put themselves through this type of torment. As far as I could tell, there was nothing fun about this. People must be crazy.

We made it out of that room and into the next. This one was set up like a mad doctor's lair. Intestines covered the exam tables while organs filled the glowing jars on the wall. A few cut off limbs had been scattered on the floor, and red paint, which was supposed to be blood, covered the tiles. Someone dressed in a lab coat waited near the other end of the room, pointing us to the next door.

"Maybe we should clear off one of these tables and give them a real show," Brad said in a stage whisper.

"Ronnie, behave." I slapped his arm playfully.

"It's our honeymoon. They shouldn't be the only ones who get freaky in public."

"Ronnie," I tugged on his arm, "stop that."

He pulled me toward him and gave me a big hug. "I'm sorry, honey. Forgive me." He stuck out his bottom lip, making his fangs hang over.

I stood on my tiptoes and gave him a chaste kiss. "Let's get out of here."

"I thought you'd never ask." He approached the actor in the lab coat. "Where's the nearest emergency exit?"

But the guy in the lab coat didn't answer.

Brad stared at him. "Vampires have supernatural powers of suggestion. I suggest you show us to the closest exit." He waved his hand in front of the guy's face, but the guy didn't budge.

"C'mon, Dracula, we'll find our own way out." I took his hand and led him into the next area. The door slammed behind us. I caught someone moving along the edge of the room. "Not that clown again." But I lost sight of him in the dark.

"Dude, stay the hell away from us," Brad said. "I mean it." He leaned closer to me. "Do you think that's the guy?"

"The sword looks like it might be real, but he's not in one of the costumes you picked out."

"He might have had to find something else after we spotted him last night," Brad said. "Did he have gloves on?"

"I don't think so," I whispered as we headed deeper into the vast garden room. Giant foam and plastic Venus flytraps stood in rows, like an exotic jungle. Some were partially opened with human body parts inside. One even had an entire corpse hanging from its mouth.

"We should notify backup we have a potential sighting," Brad mumbled, pulling out his phone and turning on the flashlight. He headed toward the side of the room where the clown had disappeared, keeping his light facing the ground. "Jodie, over here."

I hit send and hurried toward him. On the ground were several drops of blood. Brad knelt down, brushing his finger against one. "It's wet."

"That sword must be real." I peered at the red exit sign in the far corner. "We should go."

"I'm not letting him get away again." Movement on the other side of the room caught our attention. We turned our flashlights in that direction. "There he is."

The clown slipped through another doorway and disappeared from view. We darted across the room and followed him into the dark hallway. The only light came from our flashlights.

"He's moving fast," I whispered.

"He's running."

We felt along the walls as we went, looking for other doorways or hidden paths. The haunted house had been constructed with dozens of secret passageways so the actors could sneak up on visitors. This one led back to the maze room.

Brad jogged ahead, entering the maze, while I surveyed the room. In the dim light, it was easier to see the weaving path from the outside. Brad followed the blood drops on the ground while I made sure no one got the jump on us. Despite the nature of the attraction, every nerve ending in my body stood on end. This was hostile territory. I had to be prepared for anything.

"Ronnie, wait," I said, "where is everyone?"

Brad stopped, realizing something was off. "This is a different room."

"Are you sure?"

"No cobwebs." He pointed to the opening to the maze. "The one we left had spiderwebs hanging. This one doesn't."

"Is this part of the attraction?"

"I don't know." Brad turned around, and that's when he noticed the clown mask in the corner of the room. "Look." He crossed the room and picked it up. That's when I saw the man emerge from the shadows.

"Behind you."

THIRTY-NINE

Why did she warn him? he thought. If she'd kept her mouth shut, this could have been over quickly. Instead, she made it more difficult. Why didn't she understand he was doing this to save her? He'd even gone so far as to cut his hand to leave the blood trail to attract the vampire.

Ronnie turned around, but given the mirrored walls, he didn't look in the right direction. He'd been fooled, just like she had. They thought they were in the same room as before. But the haunted house had a mirror maze it didn't use any more. No one would interrupt him or come to the rescue. The police couldn't trap him. He'd be able to end this quietly, without consequence. Maybe now, he'd be free of the pain and torment.

She moved toward her husband while she kept her head on a swivel. For someone so alert, she should have been smarter than to fall for a man like him. If she died, it'd be her own fault, but he didn't want to kill her. He wanted to save her, just like Vivica and the other woman he tried to protect.

He crept up from behind while they circled toward his reflection. In another two steps, they'd realize their mistake. He had to act now. Save her or end him?

Against his better judgment, he shoved her through the

opening and hit the button on the wall with his elbow. The thick plastic barrier slid into place as she scrambled for the opening.

"Brad," she yelled, banging against the partition.

Why did she call him Brad? he wondered, slipping back into the shadows. But it didn't matter. By the time they found the vampire's body, Halloween would be over. She'd have moved on, and his life would finally be what he always dreamed it would be.

*   *   *

"They're mirrors," I said. "Keep your eyes peeled."

Brad pounded against the plastic, but it didn't budge. "I have to get you out of there."

"Don't worry about me. He wants you. I'll find a way out, just stay alive."

"You too." Brad pressed his palm against the clear plastic for a second before pulling away. He kept his back to the wall, keeping one hand against it as he headed back to the hidden hallway.

I didn't want to take my eyes off of him, but I couldn't stay here, not when I didn't know where here was or if that lunatic had locked himself in here with me. I didn't think he did, but I couldn't be sure. It happened so fast. By the time I turned around, the thick plastic had lowered, but with the serpentine tunnels and hidden passageways, there had to be another way out.

While I searched, I called dispatch and updated them on the situation. "We're trapped in a hidden room in the haunted house. The killer's here with us."

"All right, hang tight. We'll pull blueprints and figure out exactly where you are. Backup's on the way."

I continued to answer questions while I turned the corner, finding myself behind the mirrors. A dozen reflections of my partner from all different angles spread out before me.

Brad had gotten lost in the mirror maze. But he wasn't alone. I pounded against the partition, but he didn't hear me or didn't know where to look. "Brad," I screamed. Still, nothing. "Find us now," I said into the phone before tucking it into the pocket of my varsity jacket and throwing myself against the back of the mirror, but it wasn't glass. It was that same clear, thick plastic.

I watched in horror as a tall, meaty guy maneuvered through the mirrors toward my unsuspecting partner. Until now, the only thing I noticed was the clown mask, but with it gone, the brown leather duster and black vest stood out. They were straight from the catalog. *Gunslinger.* He hadn't changed costumes, except the gloves and mask.

He circled Brad. The gun on his belt didn't look fake. Rearing back, I kicked the barrier, making a loud thud that reverberated through the room. Brad looked around, noticing the wobbling reflections in the mirrors.

"Liv?"

The killer kept advancing on him.

Moving to the back of the narrow hallway, I took a breath and charged at the barrier, throwing my full weight against it. The plastic didn't break, but the track holding it in place did. The metal frame snapped at the top and the plastic crashed to the ground.

I stumbled through it. "Behind you," I screamed.

Brad spun just as the gunslinger raised his weapon. My partner dove for cover. The shot impacted against one of the mirrors, punching a hole through it. The spiderweb cracks left reflections in the other mirrors, making it even harder to determine location.

Brad spun, trapped in the center of the mirror maze while he searched for the shooter. I remained on the outskirts, watching him look around. Several other mirrors reflected the gunslinger getting closer. Unlike my partner, he knew exactly where to go.

I couldn't wait out here, so I headed into the maze. Following the paper walls which had initially concealed the mirrors from view. How could we be this stupid?

"Police," Brad said. "Drop your weapon."

"Do you think I'm a fucking idiot?" the killer asked.

I hurried through the maze, just as another shot rang out. It was close. Much closer than the last one. I couldn't see him, but the shooter had to be on the other side of this paper wall.

Feeling for a break in the mirror sheets, which were separated by the paper partitions, I ripped through the wall and jumped the man in the leather duster. Given his size and girth, I'd need the element of surprise. Landing on his back, I put one arm around his neck and locked out his gun arm, forcing him to aim high.

He twisted and bucked. The gun clattered to the ground before he knocked me off of him. I crashed into another one of the mirror sheets hard enough that it brought down the entire wall of paper and mirror. My vision swam and my ears rang.

The killer darted to the back of the room and hit a button with his elbow. A hidden wall panel flipped around, and he disappeared into the darkness.

"Liv?" Brad kept low to the ground as he searched the wall for the hidden switch. "Are you okay?"

I nodded, getting my feet beneath me. "The gun?"

"He grabbed it on his way out. I tried to stop him, but..." He found the switch and the panel opened again.

"Go. I'm fine."

Without wasting another second, Brad raced into the unlit corridor. I couldn't see anything in front of me, not even Brad. My partner couldn't have gotten that far ahead of me, but he was fast. Still, running unarmed into an unknown situation wasn't smart.

"Police," Brad announced off to my right. "Stop right there."

I followed the sound of his voice, narrowly avoiding banging into the wall when the hallway took a sharp turn. As I neared the end, a cold breeze nipped at my exposed skin. The air smelled of burning leaves and baked apples.

"I said stop," Brad commanded. "Put your hands on your head. You're under arrest."

I exited the house through the hidden rear door, but without any exterior lights, it was almost as dark out here as inside. Another shot echoed nearby. I pulled the phone from my pocket. The call remained connected. "We're outside the house, somewhere along the back, possibly the southeast wall, shots fired at police. All units, please respond. Repeat, shots fired at police."

I tripped on the step, landing hard on the pavement and scraping the palms of my hands and my knees. Afraid to use my cell phone flashlight to guide me for fear it'd make me an easy target, I followed the path to the opened fence door, which swayed in the breeze. Away from the house, the stars and moon provided a bit more illumination.

Ahead of me, two figures engaged in battle. But I couldn't tell which one was Brad. All I saw were shadows, wrestling and struggling for the upper hand. I ran forward as another gunshot rang out.

A millisecond later, the exterior strobe light lit up the place, temporarily blinding me before plunging us back into darkness. I tripped over a body and lost my balance. *Oh god. Brad?*

Panicked, I reached over, hoping I was wrong. "Brad?" I screamed. But he didn't answer. "Brad?"

I could hear the voices in my pocket, but I ignored them. They'd find us. But I had to find Brad. When the strobe light turned on again, I spotted the body and moved over to it, pressing my fingers against the neck. The rubbery latex feel of the skin reassured me this was nothing more than another fake corpse.

When the lights blinked back again, I realized we were in a graveyard, another staged attraction. But where was Brad?

Getting up, I pulled out my phone, updated backup on our location, and used the screen light to guide me.

"Get off of me," Brad growled. Behind the large, wooden tombstones, my partner wrestled the killer.

Before I could intervene, the killer kneed Brad in the stomach and pulled out a metal claw from his pocket. Fastening it around his fist, he slashed at my partner, trying to slice him open like he'd done to Roger Stevens, but Brad rolled to the side.

I barreled into the back of the asshole. The metal claw cut into his shoulder as he tried to stop himself from falling and I landed on top of him. Brad stomped down on his hand to hold it in place while he pulled the claw off and tossed it to the side. Then he twisted the killer's arm behind his back and pulled out his cuffs from where they'd been hidden beneath his cape.

Just as my partner fastened the second bracelet, backup arrived. Several patrol cars drove onto the property, surrounding the graveyard while their headlights lit everything up and drowned out the strobes. "Liv," Brad gasped, "are you okay?"

"Are you?"

Blood dripped down his arm to his fingertips. "He caught me with the claw, but I'll be fine."

"Let me up," the killer bellowed. "You don't understand. I didn't have a choice. You're killing me. You're killing them. You have to stop. Someone has to stop you."

"Who?" I asked as officers dragged him off the ground while Brad retrieved the gun.

"These assholes who manipulate them. Prey on them. All they do is destroy. They take whatever they want. And they taunt me by making me watch. Making me see them. It hurts. It hurts so bad. Make them stop."

"What are you talking about?" I asked.

"Liv," Brad shook his head, "don't."

"Why did you kill them?" I asked.

"Liv," my partner said sharply.

Luckily, officers had already started reading the suspect his rights. "Do you understand your rights as they've been read to you?"

The killer looked at the cop on his left, who was half a foot shorter and at least sixty pounds lighter. "I didn't do anything wrong."

"Sir, do you understand your rights?" the other officer asked.

"I understand, but you don't. I had to protect her."

"Detective DeMarco?" the first officer asked, nodding toward me.

"Not her. Vivica."

FORTY

We rushed to the killer's apartment and burst through the front door. We spread out, searching everywhere.

"I've got her," one of the officers said. "Get the paramedics up here."

As soon as we'd gotten his home address, we'd called for a bus to meet us. The paramedics pushed their way into the room and checked her vitals.

"She's unresponsive, but she's breathing. It looks like she sustained a serious head injury." They loaded her onto a stretcher and carried her out of the apartment.

For the first time in weeks, my muscles went slack. This was over. But I had no idea why any of it happened. Who was this guy? Why did he kill couples? Why did he say he did it to save Vivica?

When I stepped out of the bedroom, I found Brad surveying the living room. "This is where he lives. He doesn't look like a monster or a crazy person. He just looks like a regular guy." He pointed to the photos on the wall. "This was about her."

"Vivica." I read his mind. "You were right. We should have followed up to make sure she was safe."

"It doesn't matter. We can't change it now." But his jaw

clenched. It mattered. It mattered a lot. "Do you think she'll be okay?"

"I don't know. Head injuries are weird."

Brad pointed to the corner of the table. "It might have happened here. He might have pushed her or tried to keep her from leaving. You said she recognized him."

"The costume, not him. We didn't know a thing about him."

Brad rubbed the bandage on his arm. "We know he likes to play with sharp objects."

"Are you sure you're okay?"

"Fine." He shook his head. "Elton Mechum, a nobody. We ran a background check on him, but nothing popped."

"He didn't have a record, until now."

"We should have made the connection. We should have realized he went to high school with Vivica."

"We weren't focused on finding suspects who connected to her. We had too many other things going on. We didn't know to look since she was never attacked. He wasn't her ex. She wasn't targeted."

"It looks like we know why." Brad pointed to an open yearbook photo. In red ink, Mechum had drawn hearts around her picture. "That explains why he killed Dan Fielders."

"It doesn't explain the Stevenses or the attack on the Gespers."

He flipped through the yearbook, finding the faces of every male athlete marked out. "It might."

As soon as the warrant was signed, we tore the place apart. Most of what we found in Mechum's apartment was typical, but hidden beneath the floorboards in his bedroom were boxes of photos and journal entries.

One box had been dedicated entirely to Vivica. Every note she ever wrote him or e-mail she sent had been printed off and filed away. Mechum was obsessed with her to the point that he actively hated her boyfriends. Every time Vivica had been photographed with a man, Mechum had marked him out.

"He has a box dedicated to Dan." Brad tapped the side of the shoebox he'd been examining.

"Was he stalking him?"

"Cyberstalking, yes. But I don't see any photos or indication he knew where Dan lived."

We searched the rest of the items Mechum had concealed beneath the floor, but we didn't find anything regarding the Stevenses or the Gespers. Brad perused the yearbook again, but they hadn't been his schoolmates.

"Could he have dated the women?" I asked.

"It's possible. Let's head back to the office and sort through this mess."

Jodie Gesper had never heard of Elton Mechum, and neither had her husband. Mac searched every inch of the internet but couldn't find anything connecting the killer to the Stevenses either.

"We'll ask him," I said.

"Do you think he'll tell us?"

"I don't know. But he hasn't asked for a lawyer. He's contesting he acted in self-defense."

"We didn't attack him," Brad said. "He attacked me."

"Hang here while I talk to him."

"Liv," Brad warned.

"I'll be fine."

After being processed, we'd left Mechum inside one of our lovely interrogation rooms, hoping the wait would make him easier to crack. But when I entered the room, he looked at peace.

"You're okay," he said. "You're free from Ronnie."

"Sir, I'm not Jodie Gesper. I'm Detective DeMarco. Let's start at the beginning."

He stared blankly up at me. "Don't lie. You changed your hair and name to escape him."

I opened a folder and sat across from him. "Let's talk about Dan Fielders." I slid a photo of the sportswriter across the table. "Why did you kill him?"

He sneered at the photo, looking away. "He was suffocating Vivica. She told me. She called me."

"Did she tell you about the party at Kelsey Eldridge's house?"

He nodded.

"Did you go there to kill Dan?"

"I didn't have a choice. She couldn't get away from him. Every time she tried to break free, she couldn't. She needed me. But seeing them together hurt me. Physically, it hurt me." He tapped the center of his torso. "It felt like someone shoved a hot poker through my solar plexus."

"Did she ask you to kill Dan?"

"Viv would never ask for something like that. She didn't understand what was happening. I thought she did. I thought that's why she called, but she was confused."

She wasn't the only one. "How do you know Vivica Smaldey?"

"We went to high school together. She's my soulmate. I thought that's why it hurt when I saw them. It had to do with the deeper connection we have. I hurt when she hurts. Dan was hurting her, so I had to stop him. I had to stop it so she wouldn't hurt and I wouldn't hurt." He rubbed against the bottom of his sternum. "But that didn't stop it."

"Is that why you killed the Stevenses?" I showed him a photo of the couple in the alley.

He winced. "Stop it." He leaned back in the chair, his face contorted in physical pain.

I flipped the photo over. "Is that why you killed them?"

"They hurt me. Just their presence, their behavior, it burns." Despite how crazy it sounded, this guy was serious.

"Tell me what happened in the maze."

"I didn't want to hurt you. I just wanted to scare you away. When you and that oaf bought tickets from me, the pain returned. But seeing you doesn't hurt me, so it must be him. I think these guys are actual vampires since they have some kind of supernatural ability. As they feed off love and devotion, they grow stronger, and it sucks away part of my soul, my life-force."

I didn't know how to address that. "You came at the Gespers with an axe."

"I wanted to scare you. I didn't want to hurt you."

"I'm not Jodie Gesper. I'm Detective DeMarco."

"Fine, whatever you say." He made a face. "I didn't mean to hurt *them*. I just needed *them* to leave, to get as far away from me as possible. The pain was so intense. I couldn't think. I couldn't breathe. I had to get them to stop.

I had to kill them before they killed me."

That was it. I glanced toward the two-way mirror, where a tech was monitoring the interview. I'd gotten a confession. "You're wrong. They never did anything to you, but you killed them anyway." I got up from the table and went to the door.

Brad met me on the other side. "Do you think he's mounting an insanity defense?"

"I don't know. But we got him."

"One thing still bothers me," Brad said as we returned to our desks. "How does he connect to our task force initiative?"

"You sound like Winston."

"Bite your tongue." He made a face. "Well?"

"Ask Voletek."

"Ask me what?" Voletek swiveled around.

"What happened to the suspect you arrested?"

"Ted Brundage." Voletek slapped a notice down on our desk. "The missing persons report came in an hour ago. Ted's been missing for almost a month. No one reported it sooner because he was supposed to be on sabbatical."

"From what?" I asked.

"He's a museum curator. He's also a paranoid schizophrenic, but he's usually stable when he takes his meds. I'm still piecing things together, but I think he stumbled across a murder." Voletek flipped to a news article from a month ago. *Homeless man dies in fire.* The photo showed a Celtic symbol burned onto the victim's palm. "It's not quite the same as what happened to Jonah Miller, but I think the same person's responsible for both crimes. Ted just happened to catch him in the act while researching Celtic myths and lore. I'm reconstructing his steps, but he'd been visiting a lot of fringe groups and paganistic temples. It looks like the trauma of witnessing a murder, and probably getting burned while trying to help the victim, was enough to make him question reality. Since this happened around the time he went missing, we can only assume that's why he stopped taking his meds."

"His research, the coming holiday, and the recent trauma and murder made him send us the warning letter."

"Ted was convinced demons were amongst us and started keeping watch at the inn, where the largest group of them congregated. He was there the night the Gespers were attacked. He saw what happened to Anna Moniz and followed Mechum away from the maze and back to his house. Ever since, he's been keeping tabs on our killer because he didn't trust us to handle it ourselves."

"Whose side was he on?" Brad asked. "I mean, you are a demon."

Voletek snorted. "Anna Moniz was innocent, so he believed the man in the executioner's costume was one of the four horsemen of the apocalypse."

"It sounds like he had his myths mixed up," I said.

"That's why he needs his meds."

I thought about what Voletek had said. "So there's still a killer on the loose. We don't know who murdered Jonah Miller or the other homeless man."

Voletek grinned. "Relax, princess. We retraced Ted's steps, figured out where he was, and pulled surveillance feeds. The Wiccan community doesn't want anyone confusing some psycho with what they are about and have been bending over backward to help us. We already IDed the sicko who murdered Miller."

Brad raised a skeptical eyebrow. "You only discovered Ted's identity an hour ago. No one moves that fast."

"I've been told I'm a miracle worker." Voletek winked at me. "It's luck. The third call I made hit paydirt. Ted identified the photo as the demon behind the uprising. ESU's prepping since the arrest warrant is in the works. It looks like we both caught killers today."

Lt. Winston snuck up behind us. "Fennel and DeMarco, finish up your paperwork, and take the next few days off. Now that the threat's eliminated, the task force can be disbanded. Job well done, everybody." He nodded to Voletek. "You planning on making the arrest? Because the team's ready to roll out."

"Yep. On my way."

Winston nodded and returned to his office.

"What are you going to do with three days off?" Brad asked me.

"Sleep."

Voletek snorted as he tucked his gun into his holster and made sure he had his cuffs.

Brad turned to him. "I'm warning you now, if you open your mouth, I'm gonna knock your teeth out."

Voletek shook his head. "No reason to be violent. I wasn't going to say a word." He smiled. "But I figured you'd be the one all tuckered out."

Brad glared daggers at him, but I kicked my partner under the desk and shook my head. The more annoyed we got, the worse the teasing would become. And it wouldn't just be Jake trying to get a rise out of us.

"I'll see you in a few days, princess." Jake headed for the door.

"Don't call me that," I snapped.

He turned. "I wasn't talking to you, Liv." He blew a kiss at Brad and went through the double doors.

FORTY-ONE

Emma checked her makeup once more before tucking her compact away. "Before the boys get here, I wanted to tell you I checked on that patient you asked about."

"Vivica Smaldey?"

Emma nodded. "Surgery went well. She has a long road to recovery, but she'll live. She's already able to speak, even if she slurs a little."

"I'm glad." I reached for the bottle of white wine and poured some into my glass.

"Finally." Emma waved at the two men who entered the restaurant. "Be nice, Liv. Please."

"I'll be on my best behavior."

"You can do better than that."

A tall, athletic guy with jet black hair sat down beside her, and they kissed. Emma practically cooed at him, forgetting I was even around. A guy with medium brown hair and a crooked smile sat down beside me. He put his napkin on his lap and adjusted his silverware, looking nervous.

"Liv, this is Dino and his friend, Sean," Emma said.

"Nice to meet you." I nodded at Dino and smiled at Sean. "I'm sorry about last time."

"No problem. Emma said you had a work emergency." Sean's eyebrows furrowed.

"Yeah, it happens a lot."

"I didn't realize sanitation had so many emergencies," Dino said.

"Sanitation?" I asked, my gaze resting on Emma.

"She said you work for the city, cleaning up trash," Dino said. "I thought that meant sanitation."

"Do you work for the parks department?" Sean asked.

I couldn't believe that's what Emma had said. I waited to see if she'd correct herself, but instead, she picked up her wine glass and took a long sip. We waited each other out, causing the guys to grow uncomfortable. Emma's face said it all. It was my move. I could tell them the truth or I could lie.

"No, but I deal with a lot of wildlife." I took another sip of wine. Sean was easy on the eyes, but he didn't make my heart flutter. I wasn't sure love at first sight existed, but if it did, he wasn't the one. So scaring him away wasn't that big of a deal. "I'm a homicide detective."

Dino laughed, believing it was a joke. But Emma nudged him gently with her elbow and shook her head. "You're serious?" he asked.

"Is that a problem?"

"No, but that caught me by surprise. That must be really interesting work."

"It's mostly paperwork."

Sean's grin grew larger. "I bet you have some stories."

"None I want to share."

"I get it. I've been in my share of scrapes." Sean reached for his menu. "It's not something pleasant, but the good moments are usually pretty damn good."

"I thought you worked in the hospital cafeteria."

"I do." He opened his menu. "Before I hurt my back, I worked fire and rescue. Once I get cleared, I'll be back on the job."

"Huh. Emma didn't mention it."

"Dino didn't tell me," Emma said, nudging him again.

"Why would I?" He kissed the tip of her nose. "You have a reputation for dating EMTs and badass surgeons. If I told you Sean's a firefighter, you wouldn't have given me a second look."

"That's not true." She squinted at him. "Let's not get into your reputation."

"Oh, this is something I want to hear," I said.

Dino glanced at me. "It's not that bad."

"It better not be." I reached for my menu as the waiter came to the table.

After we ordered, the conversation became lighter, easier. The ice had been broken. Sean didn't say much, but we exchanged looks when Emma and Dino fed each other from their plates. I'd seen my best friend smitten many times, but this was different. I was glad Elton Mechum wasn't free to harm any more happy couples, or I'd fear for Emma's safety.

"Should we get another bottle of wine?" Dino looked around for the waiter.

The front door opened, and a man with short brown hair entered. He went to the bar and took a seat. I couldn't help but grin. Emma followed my gaze and kicked me under the table. *What's he doing here?* she mouthed.

I shrugged. "I'll order a bottle of wine from the bar. Would anyone like anything else?"

"Ask them to wheel the dessert tray over," Emma said. "I'm in the mood for something nice and sweet."

"Are you feeling okay? You never order dessert out."

"Yes, I do. You'd know that if you ever made time for me."

"Em."

But she waved her hand at me. "They have these baked apples that are dairy and gluten-free. They practically melt in your mouth. Dino introduced them to me last time. You and Sean should split one. They're delicious."

"I don't like apples," Sean said. "But Liv should totally check them out."

"Okay, wine and dessert it is. I'll be right back."

"You better," Emma warned. "I'll be counting the seconds."

"Do you need help?" Sean asked.

"I got this."

But the look on his face said he hoped to have an excuse to escape the happy couple too.

"Hey, did you see last night's game?" Dino asked. And with that, he and Sean were lost in conversation. Emma pointed to her eyes and then at my partner, who pretended he didn't notice.

I slid onto an empty barstool and leaned over, searching for the bartender. "What are you doing here?" I asked.

"Having dinner. You mentioned the food was good, so I thought I should try it out."

"I did no such thing."

"Didn't you?" He cocked an eyebrow at me. "It has to be good. That's why you were meeting your date here."

"And you thought I needed a chaperone?"

"It wasn't that long ago that you were my wife, so I feel I have a moral obligation to make sure whoever you date treats you right." He glanced over at the table. "Which one's Sean?"

"The one who isn't holding Emma's hand under the table."

"Are you sure that's all they're doing?"

"Brad," I snapped.

He let out a velvety smooth laugh. "Emma's pissed. I guess I should get going. You seem to have things under control here. I don't want to ruin your fun."

"Stay put." I flagged down the bartender and paid for the wine and asked for the dessert cart. Then I handed him a few folded bills. "Give this gentleman whatever he wants, on me."

"Liv, you're on a date. You're not buying me dinner."

"It's my turn. You got dinner last time."

I returned to the table with the wine and told them dessert would be coming around soon. We made small talk the rest of the night. Every few minutes, I'd glance in Brad's direction to see if he'd left, but he had a medium-well steak to keep him company.

"We should do this again, sometime." Dino extended his hand. "It was really great to meet you, Liv. Emma talks about you all the time."

"You too," I said.

"I'm gonna run to the ladies' room," Emma said.

"I'll call for a ride," Dino offered, heading outside.

Sean slipped on his coat. "Liv, I had a nice time. I hope you did too. Maybe we can do this again. I'd like to get to know you better without..."

"Watching our best friends suck face?"

He laughed. "I wasn't entirely sure how to phrase it, but yeah."

"Give me your number," I said. "I'll think about it."

"Is that the nice way of blowing me off?"

"No, it means I'll think about it. I'm careful who I date."

"On account of the job," he said. "I get that. Most people don't understand the crazy hours and all the overtime." He entered his number in my phone. "If I don't hear from you in two weeks, I'll stop holding my breath." He kissed me on the cheek. "Can I call you a cab or give you a ride home?"

"I'm okay."

"I'm sure you are." He nodded. "Good night."

He stopped outside the restaurant, said goodbye to Dino, and headed down the block. I glanced back at Brad who had finished his steak and was eyeing the bottles along the back of the bar. Deciding he'd have to fight his own battle, I stepped outside and tapped Dino on the shoulder.

"Hey, I wanted to ask you a few questions."

He looked surprised. "Uh, okay."

"Have you ever been arrested?"

"No."

"Do you use drugs or have a substance abuse problem?"

"No."

"Have you ever killed anyone?"

"Not that I know of." He looked at me like I was crazy.

"Are you married?"

"No."

"Divorced?"

He nodded. "That's been over a long time."

"Good. That's really good." I glanced back to make sure Emma wasn't going to sneak up behind me. She'd kill me if she heard what I had to say. "You seem like a nice guy. A good guy. The kind of guy worthy of Emma. Don't hurt her. Do you understand me?"

"Yeah."

I gave his cheek a pat. "Good."

I turned, just as Emma stepped out of the restaurant. She looked a little guilty, which is probably how I looked. She didn't ask what I was doing, and I didn't ask her what she was doing. Instead, she gave me a hug.

"I love you, Liv. Thanks for not ruining our night."

"You're welcome. Be safe. Call me tomorrow."

She stepped back, the feisty spark was back in her eye. "You know I will."

After they left, I went back inside to find Brad pulling on his jacket. "You're leaving?"

"Emma told me not to screw this up for you." He looked behind me, confused. "Where's your date?"

"I sent him home."

"Are you going to see him again?"

"I don't know." I made a face. "He's a firefighter."

"Oh, hell no. That's like mixing oil and water." Brad scrunched his eyes. "Does he play softball?"

"I don't know."

Shaking it off, Brad checked his phone, which let out another annoying beep.

"Who's that?"

"Carrie."

"Is she okay?"

"She wanted to see if I felt like meeting up."

"Don't let me stop you."

He turned off his phone and tucked it into his pocket. "You were right. She was hoping we could pick up where we left off. I told her I didn't think that was a good idea, but she's persistent."

"That's because you're too damn irresistible."

"That's the wine talking."

"I only had two glasses. I'm fine." I glanced behind him. "What about you?"

"Club soda and lime. I still don't think I have a problem with alcohol, but I don't want the nightmares to return either."

"What are you doing now?" I asked.

"Nothing, why?"

"Well, since I lost the bet, I thought you might want to cash in on that monster movie marathon."

"After the last few days, I figured you'd be even more opposed."

"I'm opposed to celebrating Halloween in every respect, but I can tolerate a movie."

"Even if it has dinosaurs?"

"Even if."

Brad drove us back to his place and grabbed a giant bowl of trail mix, a platter of cookies, some homemade caramels, and a few sparkling waters. "We'll start with the first one and see how far we get. I think this should be enough snacks, but we can always pause if we need more." He moved in front of the TV, blocking me from seeing what he selected. "Just remember, the monsters aren't real. They can't hurt you. This is all pretend."

"Brad, stop being an ass."

"I don't want you to freak out."

"Like you did with all the creepy clowns?"

"Hey, now, you're the one who screamed when that ghost face guy jumped out."

"You screamed too."

"I did not."

"Are we watching the *Scream* movies?" I asked.

"No," he said quickly. "No slasher flicks. I don't want to see any more scenes like that, not after we lived the real thing."

He pressed play and sat down beside me. As the credits came on, I turned to him. "Are we watching a kid's movie?"

"Shh. It's a monster movie. Look, there's the Wolfman, Frankenstein, and the Mummy."

"Brad, this is a cartoon."

"There's nothing wrong with that."

"But the monsters aren't scary. Aren't they supposed to be scary?"

"Who made that rule? This is a nice change of pace, isn't it?"

I grabbed a handful of trail mix. "You're absolutely right."

ABOUT THE AUTHOR

G.K. Parks is the author of the Alexis Parker series. The first novel, *Likely Suspects,* tells the story of Alexis' first foray into the private sector.

G.K. Parks received a Bachelor of Arts in Political Science and History. After spending some time in law school, G.K. changed paths and earned a Master of Arts in Criminology/Criminal Justice. Now all that education is being put to use creating a fictional world based upon years of study and research.

You can find additional information on G.K. Parks and the Alexis Parker series by visiting our website at
www.alexisparkerseries.com

Made in the USA
Columbia, SC
21 September 2023

23157976R00190